THE INVITATION

THE GAME AT
CAROUSEL

BOOK 2 —— THE INVITATION

ROB M. LASTREL

Podium

Cover design by Andrew Clark

ISBN: 978-1-0394-5509-2

Published in 2024 by Podium Publishing
www.podiumaudio.com

Podium

THE INVITATION

CHAPTER ONE

SCRUNCHIES

*D*id she know?

She stood at the front of the class writing on the chalkboard, her lips pursed. She spoke passionately about history, and she slapped the board with her little wooden pointer stick as if she was trying to keep everyone awake. She constantly used phrases like "This will be on the test" or "Make sure you remember this date" as she went along, but, ultimately, she was talking for no reason.

This wouldn't be on the test. It didn't matter.

Her name was Mrs. Heinz. She was one of dozens of random teachers meant to fill out this story.

I could barely hear her. She wasn't projecting loud enough because we were off-screen, and when the invisible camera returned to film the next scene, it wouldn't be pointed at her anyway, in her long-sleeve blouse and skirt down to the floor.

The camera would be pointed toward the back of the room. It would be pointed in my direction.

What I wanted to know was if she knew that, within hours, at least some of the students in this room—perhaps even she herself—would be dead?

They were all non-player characters, NPCs for short, and their purpose was to fill out the empty corners of this cursed town. They were there to be background noise. They did all the things behind the scenes: went to work, went to school, ate at restaurants, and walked the streets. But their real purpose in this game was to shuttle their blood from one room to another so it could be spilled on cue.

This was going to be a particularly bloody one.

I was already certain. No official confirmation had come my way. The veteran players were tight-lipped, and I wasn't getting any help from my Insight abilities, so I couldn't sense it that way. But the telltale signs were there, unmistakable to an experienced eye like mine.

Sunlight streamed through the windows, casting a glow over the classroom. I found myself amidst high school students, though their appearances would put them in their early to mid-twenties—a common courtesy in slashers. No one wants to see actual kids butchered. When we got to school that day and triggered the Omen that set this story in motion, the actual high-school-aged NPCs left and were replaced by this older crowd.

Bags of blood from one building to the next, moving from one room to another, all across the town of Carousel.

As I scanned the room, a thought nagged at me. Were these NPCs truly sentient beings or merely empty shells, reciting lines from a script invisible to everyone but themselves? The vets assured us they were fake, dead behind the eyes, but I'm sure they wanted to believe that. It made things easier.

My gaze settled on a feature that wasn't in the room at all: the red wallpaper. It was plastered right in front of my mind's eye. The red wallpaper was a real place somewhere out west. Players could see it anywhere they looked just by focusing their minds. There was information posted on it to help us play the game—to help us put on a show.

What I saw when I looked at Mrs. Heinz on the red wallpaper was that she was an NPC, level three. I also saw a poster for her. It featured her sprayed in sticky red blood and the character introduction, "Mrs. Heinz in *Scrunchies*."

That's how most character posters were. They said the character's name and what movie they were a part of.

The blood spray was typical of most storylines. That wasn't why I thought this one would be bloody. It was things like the sunshine. When you know something bad is going to happen, bright and colorful things become strangely foreboding.

This whole setting was so *happy*. It was set up to fall far when the knives came out.

And that word, "scrunchies." That was the name of this horror movie, a narrative set in the flamboyant 1980s or early 90s. It was obvious from the outdated room decor but also from the students' fashion choices, particularly the fabric-covered elastic bands adorning the girls' hair. Scrunchies, they're called. To be fair, they did match the leg warmers.

The movie was named after a girls' beauty product. That was ominous. Horror stories dealing with topics of women or girls are often the bloodiest. Allegedly, rampant carnage is a great metaphor for the female experience. I wouldn't know.

Mrs. Heinz was lecturing on a topic utterly foreign to me. In fact, it was foreign to everyone from the real world. She spoke of a French conqueror, a

bizarre off-brand version of Napoleon Bonaparte. This figure had seemingly con-
quered a land much like Europe, set a couple of centuries back. The details,
though skewed, painted a picture both familiar and eerily distorted—a hallmark
of Carousel.

These and a thousand other details said, "You know this place, but you've
never been here."

While Mrs. Heinz was in the middle of lecturing, my oldest friend and fellow
player, Camden Tran, turned around to me and asked if I thought that Carousel
was making a joke by naming her Mrs. Heinz, given the fact that it looked like
she's covered in ketchup on her poster.

I didn't laugh, but I did give him a smile. I could tell he was trying to make
me feel better. Things had been tense.

I responded, "Normally they use red dye and corn syrup in the movies, but I
suppose Carousel doesn't need that."

After a beat, he said, "So, my current theory for this storyline involves mind-
controlling scrunchies. What are your thoughts?"

"If that ends up being it, we're going to have to shave each other's heads," I
said jokingly.

True, Camden and I were both in need of a haircut, me more than him. It
was hard to find a barber in Carousel who you could trust not to slit your throat.

When we were young, Camden and I were the smart kids in class, but I'll
admit that he was always a much more useful type of smart kid. His interests
were always in things like science and math. Admirable pursuits, things that
resulted in certificates and awards. He had dreams of being an engineer or a doctor. I used my intellect to memorize nerdy trivia and to argue with people online.

As much as we were similar, we were different.

When we got tricked into coming to Carousel, whoever was in charge of
assigning Archetypes must have figured out our little difference because they
made him a Scholar Archetype. According to the *Carousel Survivor's Field Guide*,
a small book that the vets had made for us, the Scholar is divided into three
Aspects: Researcher, Sleuth, and Strategist.

All three useful. All three respectable. All three Camden.

It made me a Film Buff Archetype. No one knew much of anything about it
because there weren't many Film Buffs.

We continued whispering jokes back and forth with each other, just minor
things like the old days before he got popular and I got quiet.

And then the moment that we had been waiting for arrived. The little light
that was labeled "Off Screen" on the red wallpaper turned off, telling us that the
little invisible camera had returned, and we were shooting a scene.

Action!

Camden thought for a moment and then, no doubt inspired by the discussion of siege weaponry and how it was outdated by the time of whatever it was Mrs. Heinz was teaching about, said, "Remember in fourth grade when we made that giant slingshot?"

I smiled and nodded.

The whole class had been competing in pairs. We had had to make it out of stuff we had lying around the house. It just so happened that Camden's family had trampoline springs lying around in their trampoline.

"Mrs. Hoover's windshield," he said, remembering how we had accidentally sent a rock into it.

"That was a close one," I added. "If we had gotten caught, we'd still be in detention."

We had to play out parts for the movie. We had to give the camera some lines, some character, some personality. I usually left that to the others.

The thing I was interested in was figuring out how we were going to survive.

It turned out that the best cover for accidentally shooting a rock into your teacher's windshield with a giant slingshot was standing near a bunch of other little fourth graders with giant slingshots. We were good kids. No one even suspected us.

"Riley Lawrence and Camden Tran," Mrs. Heinz yelled from the front of the classroom. Her script told her to say it. "Pay attention. Since you already think you know everything about the Violet Caret Rebellion, can you tell me what year it started?"

I had no idea about the Violet Caret Rebellion. It was a fictional event as far as I knew, something made up for this scene. I wasn't even sure that she had actually been talking about that subject.

Luckily, I knew what was going on. Carousel was trying to shoot a scene designed to show that Camden and I were smart. We were its puppets. It wanted the audience to see what we brought to the story.

With butterflies in my stomach, I said, "In 1826."

Mrs. Heinz looked disappointed. "That's correct."

"And again in 1832," Camden added with a grin.

We had high Savvy stats, which meant our characters were going to be treated as intelligent. Throwing out some random date in this situation meant that we were likely to be deemed correct, as long as we said something plausible.

Stats were all about the audience's suspension of disbelief.

A high Mettle stat made them believe you could pull off feats of strength that were unlikely in real life but normal in movies, like breaking down a door or punching out an attacker.

Hustle allowed you to get away from pursuers and work quickly and accurately with your hands. Even if you weren't actually faster or more dexterous, movie magic made it happen. You ran, and as the scene went along, the enemy would fall farther behind shot after shot.

Grit dulled pain and increased endurance to levels only action stars could manage.

Moxie made your performance more convincing when you needed to pull off a ruse or manipulate another character.

Savvy made your plans work. Even dumb plans enacted by a high-Savvy character could work out. They could find information and outsmart enemies.

Camden put that to the test. Apparently, the Violet Caret Rebellion started twice.

"Reading ahead doesn't mean you're smarter, Mr. Tran," Mrs. Heinz said. "And just because you think you know everything doesn't mean you should be distracting your classmates."

Off Screen.

We let out a breath of relief.

Add up all of your stats and that was called Plot Armor. The higher your Plot Armor, the more likely you were to survive.

At that moment my Plot Armor was twenty. Camden's was fifteen.

I had gone on the Grotesque storyline and contributed, in some ways, against my will. I had set myself on fire to defeat the Big Bad and we had won.

That was my first death.

That was also why my Plot Armor was so much higher than Camden's.

I had doubled down on my strategy of high Moxie, Savvy, and Hustle.

I may have gone too far.

Mettle	1
Moxie	7
Hustle	4
Savvy	7
Grit	1

My survival strategy depended on me outsmarting and outmaneuvering opponents. I had to hope it would work because if they got their hands on me, I would tear easily.

Everything went back to how it had been before we were on-screen. Carousel got its snapshot of how clever Camden and I were. Carousel's first priority was telling a story. We were characters in that story, and we had done our part until the next scene we were in.

We sat there for thirty more minutes or so and then went back on-screen as Mrs. Heinz was passing back a test that "we" had apparently taken the week before.

Mrs. Heinz got to me and passed back my test and gave Camden his test as well.

I looked it over.

It was a multiple-choice history test. My name was written on the front, and it was a dead ringer for my handwriting. There was something I saw that was peculiar, though. All of my answers had been circled and then erased, and then a different answer was circled. It was as if I had changed all of my answers after first filling them in. It was a good thing too; I had received a 100 percent.

So had Camden. He turned around and we shared a smile for our unearned victory.

I looked around and soon locked eyes with the large NPC sitting to my right. He was looking bewilderedly at his test. He had gotten a zero—a big fat goose egg.

He was large and blonde and perpetually ticked off.

The gears started to turn in my head.

On the red wallpaper, his name was Billy Wiley. He leaned over to me and said, "You changed your answers?"

Apparently, I had.

In the events that occurred before the storyline began, my character must have noticed him cheating off of me and started giving only wrong answers until he had turned in his test, and then changed all of my answers back to the correct ones.

After the bell rang and we were dismissed from class, he looked at me and said, "You're dead, Lawrence."

Wouldn't be the first time.

CHAPTER TWO

AN UNRELIABLE SOURCE

My next class was yearbook.

It was usually hard to discern where to go between scenes unless an NPC blatantly directed you, which they were prone to do. However, in this high school scenario, I had my printed schedule from the start. It was waiting for me in the first locker I opened. The lock on that locker opened to the first combination I entered.

That's how storylines worked. They adapted to you in big ways and small ways. I was still learning exactly what that meant.

Surprisingly, I was part of the yearbook class—a choice I'd never have made in real high school, but my character seemed to differ in interests.

Upon entering the classroom, I spotted Antoine Stone. He was the one who had unwittingly invited me into Carousel's endless horror cycles. Tall, dark-skinned, and strikingly fit, Antoine epitomized the Athlete Archetype—healthy, lively, and ambitious. The sort of person you'd back in a race, vote for in an election, or that the girls would dream of dating. If not for Carousel's trap, he would probably have had a pretty great future.

Oh well.

As more students joined, it became clear that all player students were yearbook members. Camden, having shared the previous class with me, walked in right after me.

Anna Reed and Kimberly Madison entered last. Their appearance, with 1980s hairstyles and scrunchies, was so outrageous it made me guffaw. Somehow, Carousel had gotten them into wardrobe so that they fit in the aesthetic.

"Don't even say it," Anna warned, "or you'll be wearing scrunchies too."

She normally wore her hair in a headband or ponytail. The hairspray and scrunchies were a revelation.

"I didn't say anything," I replied.

Kimberly, naturally beautiful, seemed more suited to the vintage look, though her unease was evident. "I just don't understand why those girls have to be so mean," she confided.

Anna comforted her. "They're just jealous because you're beautiful."

"Why would anyone dislike me for being pretty?" Kimberly said sarcastically with a chuckle.

Antoine, quick to comfort, embraced Kimberly. He started to put his fingers through her long blonde locks but stopped when he felt the sticky hairspray.

Kimberly laughed and whispered to him.

It was hard to believe that their relationship was supposed to be a casual summer fling. Carousel had unwittingly become quite the matchmaker.

We chatted off-screen until our yearbook supervisor, Adeline, entered the room.

Unlike us college-aged players, Adeline Winter was in her early forties, though she had been college aged when she arrived. Like Anna, she typically went for practical hairstyles. Today, however, her hair was styled in a voluminous updo.

She was our teacher. She volunteered for the position. It was her way of getting back at Carousel for stealing her life away. Adeline expected the best of us.

"All right, team," she began, "have you been doing what I asked?"

We nodded in unison. The assignment had been to figure out our characters' backstories using nothing but our own investigative skills and common sense.

We had to leave our insight tropes at home, or at least the ones that might help us learn things. Tropes were what Carousel called abilities. They came on large tickets and did all sorts of things.

No insight tropes meant no Trope Master for me. Trope Master was the Film Buff's bread and butter. By looking at an enemy, I could see their tropes and meta-abilities. It was a hugely powerful ability. That's why it came with a huge downside: it took away half of my effective Plot Armor. That was about as bad as it could get. Without some serious work, that would doom me to die early and often.

I had put everything into fighting it.

In this storyline, at least, my twenty Plot Armor was not cut in half. That was good at least. It would have been better if Adeline's massive sixty-two Plot Armor wasn't raising the curve so much. I still wondered how us newbies were supposed to survive.

"Good," Adeline said. "It's not just your backgrounds you need to watch for. It's everything. To my knowledge, there is not one piece of information a trope can get you that you cannot find out through hard work and diligence." She looked at me when she said it.

She wasn't a huge fan of my insight tropes. She was unfamiliar with them, and she thought I would grow dependent on them.

She wasn't wrong.

For instance, my Casting Director trope would make short work of this "figure out your backstory" scavenger hunt we were on. It wasn't exhaustive, but it was still a really good start.

I had to leave it at the lodge.

"Tell me what you have figured out about your characters' backstories," Adeline said. "Hurry it up. We don't have much time."

Kimberly, eager to start, said, "Apparently there is a prissy redhead, Amy, who hates everything about me and would not be chill under any circumstance. She was upset because I was Prom Queen."

"You should have seen her," Anna said. "Kimberly did so well. It was like watching a scene from *Mean Girls*. She's such a good actress."

"Thank you for standing up for me, by the way," Kimberly said. "I just don't understand why she was so hostile. I tried befriending her, but she just freaked out on me. I thought high Moxie would fix that problem."

Adeline looked at her sympathetically. "Yes, high Moxie helps, but some things are set hard in stone, I'm afraid," Adeline explained. "Overcoming such scripted animosity requires significant effort that isn't really worth it in the long run. That's where tropes come in handy."

Antoine's background was somewhat similar. His character was a junior but had made the starting five on the basketball team. Apparently, some of the seniors weren't thrilled.

All the same petty high school nonsense.

I shared my story about tricking a large student into failing his history exam.

"That was kind of mean," Anna said with a grin. "I can't believe you did that."

"Ha ha ha," I said. "My character did it. Still, I don't think Billy Wiley is going to accept that excuse."

Meanwhile, Anna and Camden hadn't uncovered significant background elements like rivalries or enemies, nor found anything telling in their lockers.

"You'll find that's pretty typical of us Final Girls," Adeline said. "Carousel doesn't give us backstories like that with petty grievances unless they are just incidental. We get serial killer stalkers though, so it evens out."

Anna and Adeline were both Final Girls. They were almost always main characters, always important, and always able to kick butt despite their size.

"So, you're saying these rivalries aren't incidental?" I asked.

Adeline held up a finger, like "We'll table that," and then went back to lecturing about overreliance on tropes again.

"The key to success in Carousel," she said, "is improvisation. Molding the story to your needs. It can change the game completely."

It seemed Carousel's script targeted Kimberly for harassment, providing Anna a stage to exhibit her kindness and courage by standing up for her. And Kimberly's designation as Prom Queen fit her Eye Candy Archetype perfectly.

Eye Candy Archetypes weren't solely about attractiveness; they encompassed social finesse, privileged backgrounds, or exceptional talents, like being an author or business magnate. These traits typically rendered them famous, popular, and likable—qualities Kimberly naturally possessed. Her real-life charisma matched well with the characters she had to play.

I could understand why it would be frustrating to meet someone who was literally incapable of falling for your charms.

Time passed and we were once again on-screen.

The plot was about to thicken.

Another player joined, Todd Corrigan. Comedian Archetype. Plot Armor: 57. He was here to help out. As someone in his late twenties, he was not cast as a student. He was a lunch lady or whatever the word for a male lunch lady was. Lunch man? Lunch dude? Lunch lad?

The lunch man came bearing gifts: three large boxes of pizza.

"I bring-a the pizza," he said in a terrible Italian accent.

The pizza was from Little Hannibal's, a chain store you would only find in Carousel.

"You guys are in luck. Today's grub looks rough. We got a new supplier. Stuff smells like sulfur."

Todd glanced back at Adeline. She gave him a knowing nod and he left. He was playing a small, humorous role as a favor to us.

Meanwhile, Kimberly continued to share her background story, offering more insights into her character's complex narrative taking place here at North Carousel High.

I zoned out for a bit as we cut on and off-screen. Something was happening somewhere else.

Soon after Todd's arrival, the final player of our game, Lukas, entered the room. I was particularly interested in observing Lukas. He was a Hysteric Archetype, Plot Armor: 44. This Archetype was characterized by high energy, intense emotions, tremendous fear, and a general sense of unpredictability.

Janet Gill had been a Hysteric. I tried not to think about it.

Lukas didn't just enter, he burst into the room, his eyes wide with urgency. "I need to talk to whoever's in charge," he declared. He turned to Adeline. "Principal Winter! I need to talk to you about something deathly urgent."

Principal Winter? It looked like Adeline was both the principal and yearbook supervisor.

Trailing behind him was a short, stout man in a suit, who was red in the face. The man was clearly angry at Lukas.

On the red wallpaper, he was an NPC named Ned Tulley. School board member. Level three. Nothing to get worked up over.

"Get out of this building," Tulley said.

"Principal Winter," Lukas said. "You haven't been answering my phone calls."

"Luka—Mr. Lewandowski. You know you can't just come to school when you're suspended. We've been over this."

"Adeline," he said. "You know me. I don't get worked up over nothing."

Adeline glared at him. "I read you had a court-ordered psychiatrist. Have you spoken to him?"

"Of course," Lukas said. "We both agreed that I didn't need therapy anymore."

Again, Adeline looked at him incredulously. "Lukas . . ."

"He said I wasn't benefiting from it. Look, I know what I am doing here."

Tulley looked at Adeline. "Do you know this man?" he asked angrily.

"Yes," Adeline answered. "He's a chemistry teacher here. He *was* a chemistry teacher at least."

"This isn't about the incident," Lukas said. "I've been doing some reading. I've been doing some investigating. It's the new food supplier! There's something seriously wrong with them. The same company supplies to a women's prison out east, and now there's rioting there. It's mass hysteria, the end of the world type of stuff!"

Adeline attempted to calm him. "Lukas, let's take a step back. You can't come here when you're suspended. You know that."

"I have been writing you, writing the school board, writing everyone, and no one is listening. I think this new food supplier has something to hide. They're owned by KRSL, a chemical company. But they hide it. I had to go looking. Why would they hide that?"

"This is inappropriate, Mr. Lewandowski," Tulley said. "We've received your letters and concluded that they're nothing but the ramblings of a lunatic."

Lukas, unfazed, continued his frantic explanation. "You're not listening! This is serious. If that prison is any indication, that food could be poison!"

Adeline tried to mediate. "Let's all calm down. There might be a misunderstanding. Lukas, can you explain why you think the supplier is a problem?"

Lukas's hands shook as he spoke. "I've seen reports, data, patterns! I think they're getting really sick in there, but I couldn't get past the barricade. And now that same supplier is feeding our students. How could I not do something?'

The school board member scoffed. "Lukas, this is a reputable supplier. I use their products myself. I've even fed their food to my family."

Adeline gave Tulley a look.

The school board member's face reddened. "It was some steaks, Adeline. Just some harmless steaks. It was all really above board."

Lukas, gesturing emphatically, argued, "See. Corruption! This goes all the way to the top. I knew it. What aren't you saying?"

Adeline stepped in. "Lukas, we appreciate your concern. We'll look into it. But, right now, you need to calm down."

The school board member, trying to end the conversation, said, "This discussion is over. We trust our suppliers. Your accusations are baseless, Lukas. Our students are one of our top priorities."

Only one of them?

Lukas, not backing down, shot back, "Baseless? Wait until people start getting sick. Wait until they start growing extra body parts. What if it's radioactive? At least check if it's radioactive!"

Adeline, in a soothing tone, said, "Lukas, please just go home. You're not well."

As the school board member and Lukas continued to argue, they moved into the hallway, their voices fading. Adeline turned to us, a hint of worry in her eyes. "Mr. Lewandowski is suffering from mental illness. I don't want you to be alarmed. I'm sorry that you had to see that."

"Either way," Camden said as he raised a slice of pizza to his lips, "I'm glad we ordered out."

Lukas didn't just give an unhinged rant. He had a Hysteric trope called An Unreliable Source that was designed specifically to allow him to give us all sorts of good information disguised as rambling nonsense.

Now we had justification for our characters to be suspicious of the food.

That one scene had saved us potentially hours of investigation. We now knew that the source of conflict was the food for certain. It just so happened that the players ate pizza on the day a new, sketchy supplier came in.

Not a coincidence.

Hysterics were a tornado, but they were good allies from what I could tell.

We found ourselves off-screen again.

Adeline leaned over to us and quickly said, "All right, by this point you know what's about to happen to Lukas, right?"

We all nodded.

Lukas was going to be our First Blood. He had a trope that guaranteed it. Kimberly actually had a similar trope, but she was not so hot on using it.

Adeline said, "What I need one of you to do is to go follow behind them and see what happens. Quickly. And remember to stay off-screen."

"I'll go," I said. Normally I would be the best person to follow behind and see what happened to the First Blood player because I could usually gain huge insight into the enemy that way.

"Get a move on," Adeline said. And so I did.

Every storyline, with few exceptions, had a First Blood. The first appearance of the bad guy. It could be an injury. It could be something vague or threatening, just to get our characters scared.

Often, it was worse. It meant death.

Omen	Choice	Party	First Blood	Rebirth	Second Blood	Finale	The End

The whole Plot Cycle was lined up. It would take different forms, but almost every plot in Carousel followed something like this.

The narrative begins with the Omen, where ominous signs foreshadow impending danger. This phase sets a foreboding tone, hinting at the lurking perils ahead.

Then comes the Choice, a critical juncture where the players, despite the warning signs, decide to ignore the looming threat.

This decision propels them into the Party, a phase of exploration and immersion in the story's setting, blissfully unaware of the imminent danger.

The tension escalates with First Blood, marking the monster's initial attack, either in a literal or metaphorical sense. This event disrupts the players' sense of security and introduces real stakes.

Following this, Rebirth occurs, a transformative moment for the players. Here they experience an epiphany and shift from a reactive to a proactive stance, while uncovering the true essence of the story.

The cycle intensifies with Second Blood, where the monster strikes once more, reinforcing the gravity of the threat and escalating the conflict.

Finally, the Finale arrives. The ultimate confrontation. In this climax, no new information surfaces, and the players launch their final, decisive assault against the monster.

The cycle concludes with The End, which neatly wraps up the story, leaving the aftermath of the players' journey and their final confrontation behind.

I knew it by heart. We were just getting started. I could see the Plot Cycle on the red wallpaper like a floor indicator you might see on an old fancy hotel elevator.

The needle was almost to First Blood. It would happen soon.

I snuck out into the hall and made my way in the direction that the conversation between Lukas and the school board member had gone.

Staying off-screen wasn't so hard. I just had to stay out of earshot for the most part. Their conversation was taking them out back behind the school. After they'd left through the back door, I stayed behind and looked out through the little metal mesh window next to the door and watched as their conversation raged on.

Lukas was doing his level best to act like a true loon. But the school board member's behavior was getting even more erratic and enraged. And I could almost hear him yelling.

I watched as Lukas and Tulley continued to argue.

Lukas was facing the school, and he continued ranting when the school board member reached down and picked up a large pipe off of the ground.

Tulley wasn't an NPC anymore. He was an enemy. The change was very abrupt. It almost shocked me. He was a level forty-four enemy. Without Trope Master I couldn't see his tropes, but I watched carefully.

With a look of rage that I had never seen before in real life, the school board member beamed Lukas over the head with the pipe. And he continued to hit him over and over again until the needle on the Plot Cycle hit First Blood and then jumped forward to Rebirth.

I saw Lukas's status bar flicker and then start lighting up. It started with Incapacitated, then Unconscious. Then Dead, the final status:

Unscathed	Hobbled	Mutilated	Dead (Lit)	Written Off	Chase Scene	Planning
Unconscious	Infected	Incapacitated	Captured	Off Screen	Fight Scene	Exploring

I couldn't help him. Not only was I too weak, but his death was guaranteed. My character wasn't even supposed to be watching it happen. As far as the unseen audience was concerned, I was still back in the yearbook classroom.

You can't avoid First Blood. You can delay it, fight it, and lament it, but it will come. We had no strategic plans for helping Lukas. His death made the story move forward. It was all part of the plot.

I watched as Tulley, now an NPC again and shocked at what he had just done, started to load Lukas's body into the trunk of his red sedan.

It was time for me to go.

On the red wallpaper, I saw my Grit stat rise by one point. Lukas had a trope called Quivering Lion, which buffed his teammates when he made a brave stand, despite his fear, that got him killed. Apparently, that applied to being a whistleblower on a contaminated food storyline.

I made my way back to yearbook to report what I had seen.

CHAPTER THREE

GROUP PHOTOS

Rage virus?" Camden asked. "Like zombies?"

"No," I said. "Like angry people who attack violently. I also don't know if it's a virus."

"Huh," he said, looking over the crowds of people in the cafeteria.

"I can take 'em," Antoine said, pumping himself up. "Just stand behind me."

Camden laughed. "You don't have to tell me twice."

We were in the cafeteria helping organize group picture day, where different student groups would show up, stand on some little movable choir bleachers in front of a backdrop from a glamour shots studio, and have their picture taken by a photographer.

There was a blown-up shot of Kimberly and some NPC dressed as Prom King and Queen on the wall. Carousel did the little details well.

We didn't really have much to do other than read the next group off the list. Anna was taking care of that. Kimberly was telling everyone where to stand to make the photo better.

Us guys were standing back doing nothing. I didn't know about them, but I was just doing what my character would do.

The scene was going in and out of being on-screen.

"I suppose this scene is about showcasing the students we're about to have to fight," I said. "The future farmers of Carousel will be contenders."

I nodded toward the group in blue jeans carrying pitchforks as a jokey prop for the picture.

"Stand between me and them," Camden said to Antoine.

The football team. The science club. The debate team.

"I'll take the debate team," Camden said. "They look soft. I wonder if they'll let me join their picture."

"Probably," I said. "Of course, that might make them more likely to attack you in the big fight."

"Never mind, then," he said. "I like to stay off Carousel's radar."

"They probably wouldn't let me join," Antoine said. "And I actually was on the debate team in high school."

Antoine often lamented his highly physical Archetype. Low Savvy and low Moxie by default. He was excellent in Mettle, Hustle, and Grit, but it was clear he hated being stereotyped that way. He was a pretty smart guy. Future lawyer if he had his way.

Part of the trick of running storylines in Carousel was that you, as a player, might know important information, but your character would not.

This was a prime example. I, as a player, knew what had happened to Lukas. He had been killed by the school board member and stuffed into the trunk of a red sedan. But as a character, I wouldn't know that at all. I had followed them off-screen, and there was no indication that I should be aware of what had happened, which meant that it was difficult to come up with reasons for my character to react appropriately to the danger at hand.

There were ways to show the audience we suspected something was up, though.

On the other side of the cafeteria, Adeline was on the telephone with a worried look on her face. I suspected that she was the reason we kept going off-screen. She was calling Lukas. That way, we could all suspect some foul play had happened.

That was her contribution.

Camden had his own. He just needed a little screen time.

On-screen.

He had the bright idea of finding the local paper, which they had in the library, and using his Eureka ability to quickly find an article on the women's prison that Lukas had been talking about.

"Look at this," he said. "They've had riots for four days in a row. Everybody's tight-lipped. They're not talking about casualties or injuries or anything. But the reporter is speculating all over the place. Do you think that Lukas guy might have been telling the truth?"

"I have no idea," I said. "Honestly, when people say that school food is bad for you, I assume they're right."

"This might be serious," Camden said. "I don't know."

I didn't know what to say, so I just looked out at the crowd. There was definitely heightened agitation. Lunch period had come and gone while we ate pizza, but I couldn't tell if this energy was natural or if something was causing it. It wasn't quite extreme enough to raise alarm.

"Contaminated food and a riot at a women's prison," I said. "If it was so bad that the prisoners rioted, imagine what the high school kids are going to do."

I tried to laugh, but even as I did, I noticed that there were occasional elbows being thrown as the student groups lined up for photographs. The science club was arguing with each other. The debate team had resorted to shoving; one of them had insulted another's mother.

The football team was playing bloody knuckles, which was ominous, and the cattiness that Kimberly had been complaining about had returned with the cheerleading squad. I wasn't in earshot, but from what I could tell, Kimberly and Anna were having some plot issues with this Amy character.

It was clear to see this was all building to a fight, even without my Trope Master ability.

I started wishing I had used some of my stat tickets to beef up my physical stats. In an all-out fight, outsmarting and outrunning weren't going to be quite enough.

CHAPTER FOUR

OBLIVIOUS BYSTANDER

*E*ventually, it was time for my next class.

I pulled the schedule out of my pocket and unfolded it. I was in room B 202, which was a basement room.

Math class.

As I made my way there, I started to wonder if Carousel had its own version of math, the same way it had its own version of history and all its own consumer products.

I was off-screen, which is where I felt safest.

I found my way to the classroom and got settled into my desk, which was the only free one in the room, while a man with white hair and a sweater vest started talking about math problems. It sounded like everything was real. Maybe math was worth keeping and European dictators weren't.

I noticed immediately that the NPCs in the room were acting as if the scene had been going on for a while, which meant that there was a time skip. It was made to look as if I was in the middle of class instead of just the beginning.

I went on-screen the moment I had my book opened.

Someone knocked on the door. It was an office aide. She handed a note to the professor, whose name I didn't even have time to catch, and he said, "Riley, it looks like you're needed in the yearbook lab."

The office aide was out of the room and gone from the hallway by the time I gathered my things, stood up, and walked out of the classroom.

That was good. My memory of calculus was so-so.

I suddenly noticed how dark and long the hallway was without any people in it.

I was still on-screen.

I turned quickly toward the stairs and realized how long of a walk I had to get out. I pulled my hood over my head and put my sunglasses on the way a rebellious student might before getting yelled at by a hall monitor.

I knew what was about to happen. Enemy attacks were basically guaranteed at First and Second Blood, but they can happen any time after the Party phase.

One step after another, my ears were on high alert, listening for something that was happening around me.

And then something did happen. I noticed that on the red wallpaper, my Chase Scene indicator flicked on. Someone was behind me.

Direct confrontation while I was alone was always a bad idea. My build focused on Savvy, Hustle, and Moxie—good for manipulating situations and gaining insight but terrible for a fight. It was too late to wish I had beefed up my physicality.

I needed to survive with the tools available.

I had to be careful not to get a clear look at whoever was behind me because I had a trick up my sleeve.

Whatever enemy it was that was following me could not attack me as long as I acted like I did not notice them. The trope was called Oblivious Bystander, and it was one of the first that I had been awarded when I came to Carousel.

The hard part was I had to actually make it look like I realistically did not notice the enemy, which meant I couldn't look at them straight on, and if they were making noise, I had to come up with some excuse for why I didn't hear them.

I picked up my pace and made loud steps so that if someone was following me, perhaps I could conceivably not hear them. As I walked along the right side of the hallway, I noticed a sound. It only lasted a split second before I reacted. It was the sound of metal on metal, the sound of some type of blade scraping along locker walls.

I was prepared.

I quickly began tapping on each locker as I passed it. They would rattle with a metallic hollow sound and hopefully cover up the sound of whoever was following me.

It didn't have to be perfect. It just had to be enough to make the audience believe I was a sitting duck. My high Moxie stat gave me some extra breathing room. That stat was all about performance, after all.

Oblivious Bystander was the performance of my life.

My sunglasses came in handy pretty quickly. I had plucked them off of a mummified corpse weeks earlier for the express purpose of hiding where my eyes were looking. So far, they had worked very well for that.

As I walked, I scraped something off of the wall: an errant piece of tape that had been left up there from when someone had hung a poster. And as I did, I turned my head enough so that I could see out of the corner of my eye who was following me.

No surprise at all—it was Billy Wiley.

He was a big guy. Without my Trope Master ability, I couldn't see what tropes he had going for him, but I could see his level was equal to mine at twenty. He wasn't an NPC anymore either; like Tulley, the school board member, he was an enemy on the red wallpaper.

I didn't have more than a half second to look before I had to turn back forward and keep acting as if I hadn't noticed him, but I saw something in his right hand, something long that looked almost like a sword. That made no sense for this setting. How could he get a sword? I had to ignore it and keep walking forward.

I was almost to the end of the hallway. I just needed to go up the stairs.

Shoot, the stairs.

These stairs were the type that circled around on themselves as they wound up. They were large enough to accommodate lots of students, but the problem was, once I started to go up the stairs, I would turn around completely, and there would be no conceivable reason why I wouldn't be able to see the man stalking behind me with a blade.

I couldn't go up the stairs, but I also couldn't do something that my character wouldn't do, or Carousel would call foul and Oblivious Bystander would stop working.

What to do, what to do?

There was a hallway to my right. I tried to think about what was down that hallway. I had glanced down there, just to see, on my way to class; now, all I remembered was that there was a water fountain at the end of a dead end.

There were several classrooms that way, but I had no justification for entering one of them.

I remembered that there was something else down there, something that I could use. Quickly, I formed a plan.

My Hustle jumped up two points. That was excellent news. I had a trope called Escape Artist, which would buff my Hustle if I came up with a plan that would help me escape capture or escape in a Chase Scene. All that mattered was that my escape plan had to be plausible. When my Hustle was buffed, that told me that my plan could theoretically work.

I would just have to execute it. That was the hard part.

As soon as I came up on the hallway, I turned right immediately without looking behind me. Everything was exactly as I had remembered. I walked casually down to the end of the hallway toward the water fountain.

I had to drink from the fountain without regard for my safety. Luckily, the way the fountain was situated on the left wall, I would be turning my head away from Billy Wiley while I took a drink.

When I got to it, I lowered my head, pushed the button, and took three deep gulps of water. I felt like I was lowering my head for execution. I had to play it cool, though.

It was showtime.

I stood up and turned back down the hallway toward the stairs and straight toward Billy Wiley.

I acted shocked to see him.

"I told you," he said. "You're dead, Lawrence. I needed to pass history to be able to play football. Why couldn't you just be cool?"

I have asked myself that last question plenty of times.

Billy charged. I could scream, but that wasn't guaranteed to work. In horror movies, screams were often only good for leading someone to your lifeless body, not for staying alive.

It wasn't guaranteed that someone would hear me. It was even less guaranteed that someone would intervene if they heard me.

Screaming wasn't my plan.

I looked back over toward the water fountain. An arm's length away from it, a small red box hung on the wall, just as I remembered. It was a fire alarm. All I had to do was reach out to it and pull the lever.

But I couldn't.

My arm was frozen. My feet were frozen. A quick glance at the red wallpaper told me that I was Incapacitated. Billy Wiley must have had a trope that caused me to be Incapacitated when I noticed him attacking me.

After all, he was just a high school bully. He needed some help to be competitive. The trope ensured that any player he came up against would act shocked and would slow down before being able to react.

He destroyed the distance between us in a matter of seconds. That's when I saw the thing that he was holding in his right hand.

It wasn't a sword.

It was the blade and handle from a paper cutter. He had managed to take the entire handle off of the mechanism, leaving him with a deadly and terrifying weapon.

If he made contact with me, that would be it. I had low Grit even with the boost from Lukas. He swung his arm at me, and just before the blade struck, my Incapacitation status started to flicker, giving me just enough time to dodge.

The boosted Hustle had come in handy. I dodged that swing, then the one right after it, and then I jumped for the fire alarm and pulled the lever.

Immediately, all of the doors in the hallway opened up, with students piling out of their classrooms.

Billy Wiley kept his intense gaze on me; it was a look of hatred, but it was also feverish. I hadn't noticed when he was attacking me, but his face was flushed, and the whites of his eyes were yellow. He quickly stuffed the paper cutter handle back up into his shirt so that no one would notice he was carrying it.

"If you tell anybody about this, you're dead," he said. He turned and started walking toward the exit with the other students.

I was starting to get the idea that this guy didn't like me.

CHAPTER FIVE

WHAT'S IN THE FRIDGE?

I swear," I said. "He came at me with a blade."

"Are you okay?" Anna asked. "You need to tell Mrs. Winter. She has to expel him."

"I mean," Camden started, "you did kind of deserve it."

I punched him in the arm.

"No, I didn't."

"Don't hit me. Now I'll be coming after you too, with a stapler."

We stood outside of the school with hundreds of NPCs waiting for the fire department to declare there was no fire.

Tensions were flaring in the student body.

Teachers were running around telling football players to stop fighting each other, telling girls to stop with the yelling, and even telling other teachers to keep their cool.

It was a powder keg.

We were on-screen almost the entire time as Carousel got its shots.

Rebirth had gone by quickly given that our characters pretty much knew everything they needed for the story.

"I swear," I said. "The look in his eyes . . . it scared me. It was like he wasn't even hesitating."

We tossed a few lines back and forth here and there until Carousel had gotten what it needed.

Off Screen.

"Finally," I said. "I didn't know what Carousel was wanting me to say."

"It probably wanted you to act scared," Kimberly said.

"I did explain that I was scared."

"I mean it wanted you to show emotion," she said.

I thought I had.

We ended up waiting for twenty or so more minutes before the fire marshal let us back in. Adeline had spent time talking to various NPCs and controlling the situation. She probably would have made a good principal in the real world.

Todd had been a no-show.

We knew why. The needle on the Plot Cycle had slipped from Rebirth to Second Blood to Finale during our wait.

Todd was dead. He had come on this storyline specifically so that none of us newbies had to die for Second Blood. He died so that we could get a little more practice.

The vets were pretty selfless that way. They didn't talk about those who had died and stayed dead from failing storylines or . . . otherwise, but it was clear they would do anything to give us the best shot we had.

We headed back inside. The entrance was in the cafeteria, so, of course, that was where we ended up.

The cafeteria was filled with arguing, bickering students whose civility stood on a knife's edge.

Adeline had found her way to us and quietly gestured for us to stand near the doorway leading down the hall to the stairway so we could make a quick exit.

That's when we saw the first thing Carousel had put there for us to see.

"Mrs. Winter," I said. "I think we should leave."

"What?" Adeline said with a brave face. "The school day isn't over. We still have two periods left."

Typical adult in a horror movie. She couldn't acknowledge the problem because then we could just escape and the movie would be over—that is, if Carousel didn't decide to escalate in retaliation.

On the wall opposite us, someone had painted out Kimberly's face from her Prom Queen mural. They had written "Die, Skank, Die!" across the image.

"Amy did it," Kimberly said. "I can't stand that fake wannabe pop star."

The mural wasn't the only thing we were meant to focus on.

In the center of the cafeteria, one of the cooks was pushing a refrigerator across the room toward the exit. He looked freaked out.

His name was Marv on the red wallpaper, but that didn't matter. He was only here for a quick scene.

"Excuse me," he said as he tried to navigate his way across the room. "Excuse me!"

The students didn't move at first. They seemed distracted by their petty quarrels.

"Students, settle down," Adeline called out continuously, playing her part.

As the cook got the refrigerator to the center of the room, the cord for the unit fell down in front of it. As the cook pushed, the fridge tipped forward and the door opened.

Todd's dead body fell out onto the cafeteria floor.

He was covered in red boils as if he had been boiled alive.

The entire cafeteria went silent as the students stared.

Girls screamed all around the room.

Then the cook, Marv, took out a chef's knife from his waist belt and started staring around at the students.

"You come in here and you never appreciate how hard it is," he yelled. "Make your food, serve your food, clean up after you . . . Do I get any thanks? No!"

He started slashing his knife outward at the students. As he did, growls and angry screams sounded back to greet him.

Slowly, one by one, the students, the cook, and the teachers all started changing from NPCs to enemies on the red wallpaper.

Someone from within the crowd, a basketball player, came forward and held up a fireman's axe that he must have lifted from their truck before they left. The student quickly brought the blade down onto Marv's head, killing him instantly. Blood sprayed up into the crowd.

There was a pause.

And then all hell broke loose.

"Students, calm d—" Adeline said as she portrayed her character coming to a dark realization. She turned to us. "Run!"

As we did, the students and teachers behind us broke into an all-out brawl. Blood poured as students started bringing out improvised weapons: pitchforks from the Future Farmers of America, baseball bats—Antoine looked absolutely envious at the sight of them—fire extinguishers, forks, anything they could get their hands on.

We couldn't escape. We had a fight to win before this movie ended. It was time to regroup and make a plan.

"Not the yearbook room," Adeline said. She stopped at a phone hanging on the wall near the office and tried dialing emergency services. "Someone cut the phone line," she said.

"It's what Mr. Lewandowski was talking about, isn't it?" Anna asked.

"Maybe," Adeline said. "Quick"—she lifted a huge keyring with dozens of keys from her pocket—"there's an exit in the gymnasium."

We ran, Adeline leading the way. She acted scared, but I sensed she was just acting. She had been through much worse.

"This way!" she screamed.

We made it to the gym and halfway across before the doors to the outside opened and a horde of students came in led by a fierce but pretty redhead; Her name was on the red wallpaper—Amy.

Kimberly's nemesis was almost to us.

"She's going to kill me!" Kimberly said.

"Dammit," Adeline said, "they're after the storage room. Quick!"

She ushered us to a door near where we were. She opened it and waved us inside. We made it just in time. Adeline slammed and locked the door as people started coming toward us.

I looked around and found myself in a long, narrow room filled with boxes of old sports equipment. The place was dusty and dimly lit.

"We're supposed to believe that the preppy popular girls all ate the school lunch?" I asked. In the real world, they might be the only people not affected by a food-borne rage virus.

"Maybe they didn't eat the contaminated food and they're just taking advantage," Camden joked. We shared a nervous chuckle.

Adeline immediately started searching the room for weapons. "If you're going to make quips, do it on-screen. You're a Film Buff; that's what you're supposed to do. Right now, you need to find weapons. We don't have long."

Adeline had a trope called Mid-Fight Consensus that allowed us to have a quick discussion off-screen and get the lay of the land when we entered a new setting during a fight sequence. She didn't really need it in her normal runs with trained players, but it was great to use when schooling newbies.

"There's another way out of here," Antoine screamed. He was at the back of the room with Kimberly and Anna.

"All right. Find weapons and hold them off while I find the right key," Adeline said.

On-screen.

"It's locked," Antoine screamed.

The crowd was banging on the door we had entered.

"Buy me some time," Adeline said as she pulled out the enormous keyring and started testing each key individually. I hated that trope. She wouldn't find the right one until the last minute or until Carousel got its shot.

"Weapons," I said to Camden, but he and the others were already on it.

"A room full of sports equipment and not a single baseball bat?" Antoine yelled.

I started sifting through the cleats, helmets, jerseys, and pads.

"Bowling balls?" Kimberly cried out. "Why does the school have bowling balls?"

I looked at her and saw the racks of balls she was referring to. There were a ton of them.

"We cut the program a few years ago," Adeline improvised hastily.

Antoine reached around Kimberly and grabbed one of them. "This'll have to do," he said. He looked toward the door we had entered.

I followed his gaze. The pounding hadn't stopped. The door was clearly losing the battle. With every fist, it shook more and more.

"Give me one of those," Anna said, grabbing a ball and testing its weight in her hands.

"You realize we're not in a cartoon, right?" I asked.

In response, Anna put the ball in a mesh soccer bag and started swinging it around. She slung it into the wall, resulting in a substantial dent.

"All right, that might work," I said.

As I stared at her, I noticed something lying on the ground next to the bowling balls. Large, long springs with hooks on the sides that looked like they were designed for gymnastics equipment or something similar. There were leather weightlifting belts on a nearby shelf too.

"Camden," I said, pointing out what I had seen.

"No way," Camden said.

"It could work," I said.

Quickly and wordlessly, we got to constructing our ridiculous contraption. The pieces fit together like they were designed for that very purpose. We hooked one side of a spring to the heavy-duty shelving unit that was screwed to the wall. We hooked the other side to one of the belt holes in the weightlifting belt. Another spring went on the other side and was connected to the shelving unit on the other side.

"What are you two doing?" Anna asked as she eyed our invention.

"Might want to stand back," Camden said as he retrieved one of the bowling balls from the rack. He handed it to me. My Hustle was higher so my aim would be truer.

We had constructed a giant slingshot not so different from the one we had made as kids.

We glanced at each other as we contemplated the same realization. Carousel had put these things in this room because Camden had talked about our ill-fated slingshot from the past. The story had been changed expressly so that we could make that weapon.

This was a movie called *Scrunchies* about high school kids going savage after eating contaminated food. It was horror, I suppose, but it was also a comedy. A bowling-ball-launching slingshot fit right in.

I would never get used to Carousel responding to our actions. It made it feel like a living thing and not just some cosmic horror house.

Moments after we finished constructing our launcher, the door to the storage room burst open.

"Just a few more to go!" Adeline yelled.

Amy stood in the doorway, taking in everything before her. She had transformed. Black veins shot up her neck. The whites of her eyes were yellow and her pink scrunchie sagged as if it had gotten tugged on and some hair had been loosened.

Her bloody fists dripped onto the floor.

"Kimberly, just admit you cheated. You slept with Coach Blower, didn't you? How else would you have won? Just tell everyone you're a hussy and I'll leave you alone."

She sounded feverish and delirious, but there was a cruel and dark sound there too, as if she were possessed.

"Launch," Anna said.

I had gotten so caught up in staring at Amy that I had forgotten to launch. She had that same trope that Billy Wiley had, which incapacitated you when you first saw them.

I aimed as best I could.

Wide right. The bowling ball sailed past Amy and nailed a member of the debate team in the forehead. His feet flew up and he almost did a flip as he landed on his neck.

"Reload," I yelled. Camden grabbed another bowling ball and handed it to me.

"You have to account for the left spring being tighter," he said.

"Let's see," I said. I tried aiming to account for the difference.

I released. The ball struck Amy on the right side of her face, breaking her nose and cheekbone. The ball deflected past her and hit a cinderblock that a football player was using as a weapon. The cinderblock exploded and the football player's hand was mangled.

It wasn't just my poor aim. Carousel wasn't going to let me take her out. She was Kimberly's opponent just as I was Billy Wiley's.

Amy recovered from the blow quickly and ran screaming past me, ducking under the slingshot as I was reloading another bowling ball to launch at any other attackers who might rush in the door.

The front slowed, and I hit every single person that tried to enter squarely in the chest. They would then back away and run elsewhere into the madness outside. It wasn't time for us to get overrun yet because the focus of the current action would be on Amy and Kimberly.

Anna was ready with her bowling ball mace and managed to send it into Amy's stomach to no avail. Amy lifted right off the ground, howled, and leaked bile from her mouth, but still she tore forward.

"This was supposed to be my year!" Amy screamed. She got past Anna quickly, tearing the mesh soccer ball bag out of Anna's hands and throwing it across the room.

Antoine pushed Amy up against a wall and lifted a ball up to strike her, but before he could, he pulled away, his Incapacitation status flaring as he turned to reveal a pair of scissors sticking out of his shoulder.

Even with all of his strength, this wasn't his fight.

"You have to ruin everything!" Amy screamed as she launched at Kimberly, knocking her to the ground.

"I didn't do anything to you!" Kimberly pleaded, pushing against Amy to no avail.

Anna leaped to push her off Kimberly, but Amy's hands had a firm grasp on Kimberly's hair. Amy managed to land a kick on Anna, sending her backward.

I continued firing at anyone who dared to enter. Every shot resulted in a comedic injury for whoever I struck. They would usually lie on the ground, nursing their bruises and concussions.

Kimberly had to fight Amy, but Kimberly was spec'd for social grace and surviving, not killing. Her temperament reflected that. Kimberly was a great actress, but she froze when the time to fight came.

But like the rest of us, she could learn from her mistakes.

Amy threw Kimberly into a pile of tall boxes, still holding onto a chunk of her hair. I could hear hard, metallic objects falling out of the downed boxes. "Let me see your face. I'll be the last person who does."

She drew yet another pair of silver scissors and held them up to shine in the dim lighting of the storage room.

Kimberly stood up from the boxes. There was something in her hand: a pipe. It had come off of a pitchback stand that she had been thrown into. It was medium in length and diameter, but sturdy.

I contemplated turning the slingshot around and firing another ball at Amy, but as I did, I could almost see an idea forming in Kimberly's mind.

"You've been jealous of me since I kicked your butt in the majorettes," Kimberly said. "You just thought you deserved to win because your mom was the coach. I was better. I was always better."

Kimberly's Hustle and Mettle jumped two points.

Kimberly had activated her Convenient Backstory trope, an ability that, as the name suggests, allowed her to change her backstory in a small but significant way to adapt to the situation.

She twirled the pipe like a baton with a grace and ease that almost surprised her.

She moved forward and brought the pipe up into Amy's jaw even as Amy tried to lunge at her with the scissors. Kimberly twirled the pipe again, knocking the scissors from Amy's hand. She brought the pipe down on Amy's head.

"You know, it's really weird how you talk about me more than you talk about yourself," Kimberly said as Amy crumpled to the ground.

They continued talking but I couldn't pay any attention. The attackers stopped trying to enter one or two at a time. It would seem that the camera was back on me and Camden.

"We're almost out of ammo!" Camden called out as he handed me another ball.

I sent it flying into the chest of a future farmer of Carousel.

"I got it!" Adeline yelled, shaking the keys and opening the exit door finally.

I sent the last bowling ball flying toward the crowd, which was now swarming the storage closet.

"Lawrence!" Billy screamed out from among the crowd. I looked back to see him practically jumping over people to get at me.

"Time to go," I said, sending the slingshot back toward the door, empty. It slapped a freshman in the face but did no real damage.

Camden and I were the last ones out the door.

Antoine had gotten the scissors out and was now recovered. I could see the frustration on his face that he had gotten Incapacitated by a relatively minor wound.

He shut the door behind us and locked it. We found ourselves somewhere in the bowels of the labyrinthine high school.

Off Screen.

CHAPTER SIX

AGAIN, BUT WITH WEAPONS

I should have been able to take her," Antoine said. "She should have been out cold."

"Observe and adapt. You will run across monsters that you can kill with a punch and fully human neighbors who you can't even kill with a gun. This isn't a turkey shoot. It's a story," Adeline said as she started walking down the long hallway away from the storage room door.

"They have a trope that buffs them," I said. "Every time we attacked Amy, her level jumped up for just a second on the red wallpaper. Except for when Kimberly did it. That's why only Kimberly could take her."

Adeline laughed. "See, if you just pay attention, you can learn how to win even without your tropes."

We started on our plan for the next scene, but before we could move on, we were suddenly joined in the hallway by a large, red box. It was Silas the Mechanical Showman.

"Hehehe," he said through his worn-out voice box. "You won a ticket."

Silas was a fortune-telling machine come to life. His mechanical body moved rigidly from behind dirty glass that read, "Carousel's Own, Silas the Mechanical Showman!"

He dressed like an usher from an old movie theater, in a red vest with a round, red hat that had a chin strap. His wooden face was faded but he almost looked alive.

"It's for you," Adeline said, looking to Kimberly. Silas had appeared right next to her. Normally he appeared at the end of a storyline, but sometimes he would make an exception.

Kimberly pressed the large red button on the front of Silas's machine.

A large heavily ornamented ticket fell into Silas's dispenser slot. Kimberly smiled as she picked it up.

"Is that why we came here?" she asked Adeline.

Adeline gave Kimberly a hug. "You said you were worried about fights. I thought we might be able to do something about it."

Kimberly quickly showed Anna, who shared in Kimberly's joy.

The ticket automatically equipped to her, appearing on the red wallpaper for me to see.

Does Anyone Have a Scrunchie?
Type: Action
Archetype: Eye Candy
Aspect: Beauty
Stat Used: Moxie

The audience forms their opinion of a character by how they act, how attractive they are, and even how their hair is styled. The simple act of putting your hair up into a ponytail can signal a shift in focus and determination. Both fighters and rocket scientists usually wear their hair up and out of the way in movies.

When this trope is equipped, the player can put their hair up or in a ponytail, transferring a portion of their Moxie stat into their Savvy, Hustle, or Mettle stat depending on the task at hand.

The player can reverse this transfer by putting their hair back down properly, returning the stats to their original state in the next scene. Fails after repeated use.

"New hair, new me!"

That's why we came to this storyline? For a themed trope?

It was interesting. An action that could redistribute stats. The Eye Candy Archetype appeared to have a lot of ways to buff stats based on the situation. That could really work well with her Convenient Backstory trope.

But how could I be surprised? Everyone cared about Kimberly immediately. When she said she didn't want to use her Looks Don't Last trope to be the First Blood sacrifice, everyone jumped in to say it was okay, they understood.

How could you not love her though? She really was likable. Not just pretty, but also nice. Maybe naïve, but not stupid.

Good for her. Now she had a way of fighting back. I still didn't, but no one seemed to say anything about that. Wallflowers, Hysterics, and, apparently, Film Buffs—some Archetypes were just doomed to have a bad time more often than not.

I blinked and Silas was gone.

It was time to leave school behind. All we had to worry about were the hundred angry twenty-five-year-old teenagers in our way.

As we walked, Anna dropped back and said, "You made fun of me for swinging a bowling ball around in a bag as a weapon and then you went and made a catapult. Who's in a cartoon now?"

"I guess it's me," I said. "I think I saw little birds flying around one of their heads."

She laughed. "Do you feel blind without being able to see their tropes?"

"I feel like I lost my powers," I said. "Like Superman without being able to fly."

"Don't worry, we'll take care of you," she said.

"I'll use his corpse as a shield," Camden said.

"I have higher Plot Armor than you," I said. "So I would be a good shield."

"You still didn't get a weapon," he said, holding a small piece of the same pitchback stand Kimberly had gotten her pipe from.

"Oops," I said. He made a good point.

Adeline knew the way out. She didn't even need a trope for that; she had just run storylines in this school so often that she actually knew the layout by heart.

"If we go right, we get let out onto one of the building's lower roofs. There's a ladder there that we can climb down, but I can't help but feel we would get easily picked off," she said.

"And if we go left?" Antoine asked.

"You'll get to show off how strong you are," she said.

Antoine nodded. "I just wish I had something more than a bowling ball as a weapon."

"You'll have lots of options to choose from soon," she said. "You might have to relieve its owner of possession first."

Antoine had a look of determination. It was game time.

"Stay behind me," he said. "I've got this."

As we made our way down the hallway, we got to a double door. We went on-screen.

Adeline was able to find the key to this doorway quite easily, but as soon as we were through it, it was revealed that we had found our way back, fatefully, to the cafeteria. It was filled with fighting students.

"Back to where it all started," I joked, echoing the title of a trope I had been mysteriously awarded at the end of the Grotesque storyline.

After a few steps into the cafeteria, the room seemed to notice our arrival all at once.

Students started to make their way toward us.

Antoine was not playing around. He swung his bowling ball at the first person to get to him and hit them so hard that they spun around in a full circle before falling to the ground. He then swung it up and hit another person in the jaw. He was taking no prisoners.

And then he saw the thing he had been looking for. A young man wearing a letterman jacket was angrily swinging a wooden baseball bat at another student who could do nothing but block and try to evade.

"You!" Antoine said, pointing at the guy with the baseball bat. As the guy turned to look at him, Antoine threw his bowling ball straight at him and hit him square in the chest.

He then leaped over an unarmed assailant and grabbed the baseball bat out of the hands of its former owner, who was still reeling from the crushing weight of the ball.

Antoine felt the weight of the bat in his hands. "This is what I was after," he said.

He got buffed from using sports equipment, but now he was using sports equipment that was actually good for a fight. It was all looking up.

An assailant came at him carrying a fire extinguisher and swung it around like it was some sort of battle mace. Antoine went back and swung down hard.

Crack.

The extinguisher-wielding student was down on the ground.

"You have to be kidding me!" Antoine said as he held what was left of his baseball bat. It had broken on contact. He bent down, grabbed the fire extinguisher from the now limp assailant's hands, and went back to fighting his way across the lunch room.

Luckily, none of these students so far were actually any of our nemeses, which meant that they didn't pose an individual threat against us, and were only dangerous as a group. As long as we could pick them off one at a time, they would go down.

"Lawrence!" someone screamed from the entrance to the cafeteria. It was Billy Wiley. He had caught up with us.

Oblivious Bystander wasn't going to save me here.

Billy charged at me. Luckily, he was so incensed with rage that he didn't notice that Anna was between us. As he ran by, she tripped him.

He came falling down, and as he did, I gave him my best attempt at a field goal kick right into the face.

Well, that was easier than I expected. It's nice to have friends. Anna had learned her lesson from when she had tried to defend Kimberly. Instead of trying to take on my nemesis, she just made it easier for me.

Before his blade-wielding arm even fell to the ground, I had grabbed the blade from his hand. I felt the weight of the paper cutter. It was quite the weapon. Crazy that these things were found in schools and offices all over the place.

"Riley, you've got to work on your people skills so this won't happen as often," Camden said, trying to fit a rushed joke into all of the chaos.

Just as he finished speaking, someone ran across the room and drove a long, thin, sharpened piece of wood into Camden's stomach.

It happened so fast that I hardly even noticed her coming.

"I can hear you mocking me in class, Mr. Tran," Mrs. Heinz said. "Why can't you just sit there and be quiet if you're going to read ahead?"

It turned out that Camden did have a nemesis.

She was enraged; her hair was coming out. She had the yellow eyes and red face of every other affected person.

Camden was Incapacitated from the attack. Fortunately, his run-in with Ranger Danger had led him to beef up his Grit. It looked as though she had taken a wooden pointer, like a teacher might use on a chalkboard in class, and put it into a pencil sharpener.

Camden's wound was deep, but the pointer was so thin that he was able to power through and remove himself from Mrs. Heinz's immediate vicinity.

Camden removed the stick from his stomach and prepared himself as if he was going to attack Mrs. Heinz, but he was hesitant.

"I can't hurt an old lady," he said.

If she wasn't angry before, suddenly she was incensed.

"You little weasel!" she screamed as she launched herself at him.

He positioned the pointer stick so that, as she attacked him, it stuck into her chest. As she landed on him and he fell down backward, the pointer stick seemed to have done the job.

"I'm never getting into college now!" Camden said after a few deep, terrified breaths.

"Come on, let's go!" Anna cried out.

I stuck a hand out to help Camden up, and then we followed Anna, Adeline, Kimberly, and Antoine toward the front door of the cafeteria.

Once outside, the needle on the Plot Cycle moved to The End.

"You all did splendidly," Adeline said gleefully. "See, you didn't need all those fancy insight tropes to do a good job. You just need to pay attention. You should come back here and do this again in about five years, and then you'll all get cast as teachers and the whole storyline is much more difficult. Far less comedy and more edgy."

She walked toward the road, not quite realizing exactly how gut-wrenching what she had just said was.

"Five years?" Kimberly asked. "Do you really think we'll still be here five years from now?"

She was asking Antoine or Anna, or really anyone who would tell her, if we would all be okay.

"There's no way we're going to be stuck here that long," Antoine said softly, embracing her.

I thought he might regret that statement one day.

CHAPTER SEVEN

GRADUATION

As we walked away from the high school, Todd ran to catch up with us. He had recovered from his injuries and death.

"You guys owe me soooo much," he said. "I don't think I've ever been boiled alive."

He had a trope called Funny Bone that stopped him from feeling pain from a humorous death, so I was sure he had played up the being boiled alive part. He probably slipped and added in some physical comedy to offset the injury.

Still, he and Lukas had died to help our training. We did owe him.

As we were leaving the parking lot, a player that I had not actually shared a scene with in the storyline joined us. Her name was Valerie Choi. She was yet another Final Girl.

"How was it?" she asked as we greeted her. She had been one of the first people we had met when we came to Carousel. I had run the Grotesque storyline with her.

While we were running the plot in the school, she had been running the women's prison subplot with Lukas until he came and got himself killed for First Blood. She had made sure that her subplot would last until the Finale, then she came to see if we needed saving.

Just in case.

The vets made a habit of having a backup plan whenever they could.

They were big on planning. There was no chance we needed her help; Adeline was one of our best players, and she was a Final Girl. Even if my friends and I had died, she would have made it out.

That's all we needed. One surviving player and everyone walks away whether they died or not. This was a game of strategy. Valerie was our backup, but Adeline was our plan A.

Half a mile down the road, the school board member's red sedan was parked. As we approached, we heard a loud thumping inside the trunk.

We opened it to find Lukas having recovered from his fatal injuries.

"That's a good one," he said as he climbed out of the trunk. What a weird dude. You would almost think that he actually liked getting beat over the head with a pipe.

Before we made it much farther, we heard the familiar music and laughter from Silas the Showman. He was back to deliver all the rewards we had reaped from the *Scrunchies* storyline.

"Congratulations, you won a ticket!" he announced, but as we lined up to receive our rewards, it was clear that most of us had not won tickets.

All we had were tickets showing us which people we had killed. We hastily shoved them in our pockets. Anna got three. Antoine got six. Kimberly got one. Camden got one. I got three.

We didn't speak of them. It was one thing getting an award for killing a monster. It was different getting one for killing a person who was just deranged.

Most of us got three stars on the red wallpaper, which Adeline assured us was a good rating for a performance where we were being carried. Antoine got four, probably for the fighting display.

Every five stars we would get a new stat ticket. That was the grind.

That was enough considering we had not had to do either First or Second Blood and we had had Adeline there to help us with tropes to make the whole storyline easier. I couldn't complain.

We walked the long way back to our base, our temporary—yet dreadfully permanent—home, Dyer's Lodge. The building was at Camp Dyer, on Lake Dyer. Nothing foreboding about that.

But it was miles away. Dying and getting mutilated on a regular basis was made ten percent worse by the amount of walking we had to do. We couldn't drive, because an Omen might jump out and trigger things, thrusting us into another story.

I could see the Omens as we passed them. They could be anything. A mailman delivering letters without postage on them. An elderly woman asking you to try her special apple pie. A woman walking a large, unruly dog.

I could see them all because of my I Don't Like It Here . . . trope. It was not a Film Buff trope. It was for Hysterics, but I could use it because of my Background trope called My Grandmother Had the Gift . . . which changed my characters' backstories and allowed me to equip certain tropes. I could see the Omens and their movie posters on the red wallpaper. I could see how dangerous they were.

The mailman's storyline had a danger level of, "Get to the car now!" which was the highest difficulty I had found. He was up to no good.

I had gotten this trope when Janet was killed. It was her signature trope. I felt guilty using it even though I had done nothing wrong.

"In Carousel, we recycle," Silas said when he gave it to me. He also gave me around ten tropes I could not equip. I knew there was something off about them, but I felt like I was reading into things too much.

Finally, after an eternity of walking, we saw the sign for Camp Dyer.

Home sweet home.

In Carousel, home is the place where they don't try to kill you.

The area was heavily forested—the only places not covered with trees were the designated recreation areas and the beach. There was a little bit of everything at Camp Dyer. If I didn't know any better, I'd guess that a lot of stories took place there, so it needed to be well equipped.

But I did know better.

Camp Dyer only had one storyline that took place there. It was a storyline that was hard to trigger, one so high level that I couldn't even see what it was with my scouting trope, which was good for detecting most storylines. Usually, it even told me what action would trigger the storyline. How useful. If I didn't have to watch someone get brutally murdered to receive it, I wouldn't feel so conflicted.

Even though I didn't know much about the storyline from my trope, there sure were other hints. Creepy campers, an abandoned cabin, an odd, other-worldly feeling that I couldn't quite shake. All features of the area around Dyer's Lodge and Lake Dyer that we called home.

The lodge was so large we could see it through the trees as we approached, even though we were a ways off.

As we walked down the trail, relieved that the journey was nearing its end, four men and a woman approached us. It was a group led by an Outsider Arche-type named Travis Haley. His brother Vernon was there too, along with another Soldier player I didn't recognize—named José on the red wallpaper—Travis's girlfriend Tori, and Bobby Gill.

Bobby had arrived at Carousel on the same day as us. Janet, who I saw get killed permanently a few weeks earlier, was his wife. I felt tension coming from him. He wanted answers and no one was willing to give them.

Not even me.

"Found her," José said.

"Thank goodness," Travis said. He smiled a trickster's grin. "Adeline, we've been looking all over for you."

"What did you do now?' Adeline asked cautiously.

"Nothing. Nothing at all," Travis said. "We were just hoping to learn from your wisdom and experience."

"Uh-huh . . ." Adeline said skeptically.

"Can you kill a mummy with a rocket launcher?"

Adeline took a deep breath, relieved.

"What type of mummy and what type of rocket launcher?" Adeline asked. "Too big an explosion isn't always great for taking out an enemy because it can be anticlimactic. What you want is something incendiary, for the visual, but that won't just blow it away. Really you should be asking Arthur about this. He's the expert."

Travis backed away with his team and said, "We already asked him. He said to ask you."

Travis turned around and walked off toward the lodge.

Adeline cursed under her breath and then yelled, "That's because he thinks you're going to get yourself killed and he doesn't want to be blamed."

She turned to us. "Rocket launchers are for big enemies and big crowds. Anything else is just showing off. I've got to go talk to him before he does something stupid."

"Good luck," Anna called after her with a smile as Adeline turned and followed Travis. Valerie was hot on her heels.

"She's away for five hours and the boys are already causing trouble," Kimberly said to Anna with a giggle.

As we continued up the path toward the lodge, Camden asked, "If we find a rocket launcher, which one of us should shoot it?"

"I will," Antoine said.

I was perplexed. Mettle and Hustle affected firearm damage, but explosions were usually a Savvy thing.

"I'm sure one of the vets has blown off a few toes to figure this out," I said.

Antoine shook his head. "I'll shoot it," he said. "I'm calling shotgun."

"We know you get the shotgun," Camden said. "We're talking about rocket launchers. These are different weapons."

Antoine fake laughed.

Anna grabbed Kimberly by the hand and pulled her up the path. "You boys are all wrong. I get the rocket launcher."

"When you make the plans, you can choose your weapon," Camden said with a smirk.

Anna ignored his comment.

"I smell food," she said. "We're going to get changed."

She pulled Kimberly along. Kimberly blew a kiss at Antoine as she was whisked away. Antoine caught it and smiled a goofy smile.

"'No, I'm not trying to date Kimberly,' he says," Camden said mockingly to Antoine. "'This is my last summer to be single before graduation,' he says."

Antoine watched as Kimberly faded into the distance. "Yeah, well, things change," Antoine said. He paused. I couldn't read his face. "Anna's free, though, if you think she'd be interested. Unless, of course, she meets a handsome vampire or something."

I was new to the rapport that came so easily to them.

"She probably will meet a handsome vampire. She's a Final Girl," I said. "He won't kill her, though, because he'll love her."

"My mother said something like that to us kids every time we made a mess," Camden said. He joked, but there was a twinge of pain in his voice that I didn't think he expected. He had parents and siblings waiting for him to return. What were they thinking right at that moment?

"A luau is just what the doctor ordered for me," Antoine said. "I'm going to drink rum until the smell of high school washes off of me."

He turned and ran up the path. Instead of going inside the lodge, he ran around the outside to the beach, where the party was.

Camden and I were the only ones left after Lukas and Todd had abandoned us for their various callings—coffee and beach volleyball, respectively.

"We're doing okay, you know," Camden said. "We're going to be okay."

I nodded. Okay felt like such an accomplishment in this place. Ever since I had seen Janet get killed by an unstoppable executioner, I had felt a palpable tension every time I tried to talk with Camden or Anna, and they were my oldest friends.

Was I the only one who felt it? Camden knew I wasn't leaving him out of the loop for no reason. He had to. The vets would have clued him into our predicament. Still, it felt so easy to just wander off alone.

Camden smiled a half smile.

For half a second I thought about telling him the secret, but I immediately heard breathing in the distance. It was still doing that. Dang.

Personally, if I were designing a hellscape town where people were forced to enact horror movies, the first thing I would show them was the cloaked axe murderer who would chop them in half if they didn't play the game.

It made no sense that I was forced to keep his involvement a secret. All I could say was, "She disappeared" or "She went missing." Anything else, any attempts to clue someone in at all, would have brought the axe murderer down on me. It was maddening.

Well, in a way . . . the axe murderer was shown to all players. He was on all of the player posters on the red wallpaper, sneaking up behind us and striking a killing pose. Still. That wasn't enough.

I had thought of trying to talk about the posters, but that, too, was too far.

A voice rose up from behind me and almost made me jump out of my skin.

"Do you think they're going to tell ghost stories around the fire tonight?" an excited little NPC camper asked me. These little girls could sneak up on you without even trying.

"No," I said. "Go away."

She turned and ran, tears streaming down her face.

You had to be rude. Their sole purpose in life was to trick you into activating the Omen in the abandoned cabin that looked out on the lake a few hundred yards from the lodge. I couldn't risk encouraging them.

"You're getting really good with kids," Camden said.

"I just want to know why they only bother me," I said. I quickened my pace and went in the direction Antoine had gone, around the lodge to the beach area, where dozens of ill-fated players were blowing off a little steam by digging a roasted pig out of the ground so we could pretend we were on vacation.

Some of them had been on vacation for decades at that point.

Try not to think about it, I told myself as I found the line filled with sliced fruit and cocktails. *Try not to think about it.*

I was really good at that.

"You see," Sam, a suave Athlete Archetype with an Adventure Advanced, or AA, Archetype said, "these boars have a trope that makes it so no matter how many times you shoot them, they won't die until they're right up on top of you. They literally tackle you to the ground and die right over you, pinning you down. It happens every time."

He was explaining how he had nabbed our meal for the night.

"Never happened to me," Arthur Clayton said. He had been here so long; he had come on the same team as Adeline. "Just shoot it and it drops."

"You're lying," Sam said.

"Am I?" Arthur said playfully. He was in a better mood than usual. He was a Monster Hunter AA with a Scholar base Archetype. Basically, he was Van Helsing in a trucker hat.

He had been essential to winning the Grotesque storyline I had been stuck on. It seemed like he was built for this place, but maybe that was just twenty years of practice. He was one of the few in on the secret of the axe murderer.

"You're just messing with me," Sam said.

"Doesn't matter," Reggie said. He was a bigger guy, a Bruiser. "I had to carry the thing back to camp while being chased by that prehistoric monster. I deserve credit."

"You get credit for that," Sam said. "I'm just saying I get credit for the kill. You didn't shoot it."

Reggie grumbled and took a swig of peach tea from his hip flask.

"You boys are all wrong," Adeline said. "The only person who deserves credit is the woman who cooked it!"

She started applauding, along with others. Grace, a Detective AA with a knack for cooking, took a bow. She was a shorter woman with auburn hair.

We were all thankful to her for her culinary contributions. From what I heard she was quite the detective too.

"Thanks again, Sis," Reggie said. "The whole time I was carrying that boar, fighting off that toothed beast, I was thinking about how good you were going to make it taste."

"You didn't even kill it!" Sam exclaimed.

I got up from my seat at the tables and went to find my friends. They were kicked back in lawn chairs staring out at the lake. It was getting late, and they were ready to turn in.

"You can have my seat," Anna said as I walked up.

"Thanks," I said.

"Antoine is talking about going out on another storyline soon," she whispered to me. "Don't encourage him."

I nodded as she walked back up toward the lodge with Kimberly.

Camden had fallen asleep on his chair. He deserved a good rest after his run-in with that old lady and her pointer stick. I looked over at Antoine as he watched the waves on the lake gently bob up and down.

Something he had said was eating at me.

"What's this I hear about us getting out of here within five years?" I asked.

"Kimberly may be blonde, but she's not dumb," Antoine answered. "She knows I'm trying to make her feel better."

"Okay," I said, "but I think there's a reason that Adeline never tries to reassure us everything will be okay. She never tells us we'll be going home soon or that we will survive at all. I think that hope goes bad after a while, and then you just feel worse than you did before."

Antoine sat and thought for a moment. "Camden told me about your family. I know that losing your parents at a young age had to have been tough. Anna says that she's trying to break you out of your shell, but she doesn't seem to understand that it's not a shell. It's a shield. Every time she tries to talk to you or include you, you treat it like an attack."

I had heard this type of talk long before Carousel. When people learn something about your past, they try to use it to explain everything. It was weird to think my friends were talking about me when I wasn't around.

"I see we're getting personal," I said. "I may be a cynic, but I think that is only an advantage here. All of that has nothing to do with talking about getting out soon."

"We'll see," he said. "For what it's worth, I told her that I thought we'd be out in five years because I believe it's true. I wasn't just trying to make her feel better."

"Then you're just wrong," I said. "Look around you. There are people on this beach who have lived most of their adult lives in this town. These people wouldn't even know what to do if they ever got back to the real world."

I looked back over at the players still gathered around the bonfire.

"When my brother got here," Antoine said, "he and his team made up their minds that they were going to get out. They worked their asses off, and now, after just eight years, they're higher level than most of the players here. Even the ones that have been here longer. They did that through determination, taking risks, and believing that they could build up momentum. That tells me something about how things work here."

"They also had a mostly complete team," I said. "Lots of major Archetypes. Versatility. Enough players to tackle big storylines."

The major Archetypes were Final Girl, Scholar, Athlete, Eye Candy, and Comedian. Archetypes that could be used to play a wide variety of characters. They also had the advantage of not being extremely niche. There were always new stories they would excel at.

"Then I don't see why you're arguing, because we have everything they have," he said. "And we also have you, a Film Buff. That's something no one has. You could be our best chance at getting out of here if you weren't so obsessed with us just resigning ourselves to our fate."

"I didn't say I was resigned to our fate," I said.

Frankly, no one knew whether being a Film Buff made me anything but rare.

"Good," he said. "I hope you're not. You like it, don't you? The storylines."

I thought about how I should answer that. Obviously, I did not *like* it, but there was a part of me that took to it in a way that I was almost ashamed to say. I liked the strategy. I liked the game. I didn't like dying or watching my friends get hurt.

"It's like you said," I answered. "I'm a Film Buff."

"Most teams go out every two weeks. I think we can do better than that," he said. "I think that we can go out once, maybe twice a week and really start to stack on those levels. You just wait. Pretty soon, the veterans will be coming to us for advice."

He kept looking out over the water. I followed his gaze. There was something out in the darkness, peeking up out of the water, watching us. A chill went up my spine. Nothing was normal here.

"We are going to do incredible things here," he said. It almost felt like he was talking more to himself than he was to me. He needed to believe it.

He stood up from his seat and walked to the lodge.

On the off chance that the power of positive thinking wasn't Carousel's weakness, we were going to have to grind our way out of here. If he wanted to play the optimist, that was okay.

I just wanted to get my friends out of here.

I sat there on the beach until I started to feel eyes on me, and not eyes from one of the lake monsters.

A woman in her mid-thirties was watching me from near the bonfire. She had dark hair, a tan leather jacket, and ripped jeans. Dina Cano. The fifth person I had ever seen die. The first one I had seen die in Carousel.

She was an Outsider Archetype. In *The Final Straw II*, she had intentionally taken a pumpkin and smashed it. When that attracted Benny the Haunted Scarecrow, she taunted him until he killed her.

Adeline told me some people react weirdly to Carousel, that maybe her actions had been an extreme form of denial. Maybe if she taunted Benny, the cast and crew of the prank show would come out and reveal that everything was fake.

Still, I didn't know what to think of her.

After a while, I shook Camden awake and led him back to our room.

Dina was still watching, though she tried to pretend she wasn't.

What did she want?

CHAPTER EIGHT

THE DETOUR

I couldn't sleep that night. My body yearned for rest, but my mind was relentless. I kept looking out across the lake at the mountain, where the purple lights would sometimes cast onto the clouds above. I really wished it had been overcast so I could see the light just then. Some sign of a way out of here would have made me feel sane.

I was still numb from death. It was strange; I kept having these miniature moments of panic where I would forget that I wasn't dying. Right as I was about to sleep, I would suddenly jolt awake and pat my body down looking for the gashes and cuts that I remembered receiving.

They were never there, of course.

Still, injuries didn't leave the deepest mental scars. Maybe it was because they usually disappeared while you were still supercharged on adrenaline and going through shock. Maybe it was because death was something even Carousel couldn't wipe away completely.

When I had taken a shower, the hot water running over my skin had been uncomfortable. That skin had been burned weeks earlier. It's like my mind hadn't really gone back to normal.

As I lay there, I considered saying all of this to Camden. I could only imagine that he was going through the same thing after having been stabbed to death by Ranger Danger. But I'd never been good at talking about things like this, and after having been inducted into the small group of people keeping Carousel's enforcer a secret, it almost felt hypocritical to try and be open about my feelings. Like I didn't deserve to.

I contemplated exactly how much I could tell my friends about the axe murderer. The truth was, I suspected that I wasn't even allowed to acknowledge that I knew what happened to Janet. There were no ways to cheat around that. Arthur,

Roxy, Reggie, Valerie—they acted completely dumbfounded by what happened to the people who disappeared. They didn't hint much at all. They didn't try to get clever about it.

All of the other players had been able to connect the dots over time. You had to play the game. They knew *why* players disappeared more or less. They just didn't know *how*.

A further question: did I need to tell them? Most players followed the rules pretty closely without being told there was a literal axe hanging over their heads.

They knew there were consequences.

Why risk it if there was nothing to gain? What was the difference between an axe murderer and spontaneous combustion as far as the other players were concerned? Missing is missing. Dead is dead.

A final question: how long would I wait before *I* tried to get clever and ended up saying too much? The problem solver in me wanted to outsmart this restriction. I only hoped that desire would fade with time. I thought about how I might hint things to them, how I might test the boundaries.

When was I going to stop staying up all night asking myself these questions? When was I going to know why I had to keep the secret in the first place?

I never fell asleep that night. I just remember it eventually started to get lighter outside and the birds started to chirp, and the little campers came out and started chasing each other around playing tag and daring each other to go into the abandoned cabin.

Morning at Camp Dyer, as always, came without my permission.

The next morning was breakfast as usual. The veteran players treated me normally. The ones that I didn't know that well still glanced at me for an extra few seconds, but they seemed more curious than unwelcoming.

Grace had planned for us to eat tacos that morning. Some of the senior players had just done a run to Eternal Savers Club, Carousel's version of Costco, where you could get huge savings on bulk items. Of course, I was pretty sure they'd just cleared a storyline there and then looted it for everything that was on our shopping list, but either way, we saved a lot of money.

Every time someone made a run to ESC, it was like Christmas came to Camp Dyer. They would bring back bags full of candy, microwave snacks, and whatever other goodies were on sale.

I sat with my friends, and we ate and laughed like we hadn't just taken turns slaughtering a high school full of rage zombies.

Antoine was still talking about how we were going to go out on another storyline so that we didn't lose momentum.

Chris, Antoine's older brother, was happy to make some suggestions.

"You're about to the level where you could really appreciate this," he said. "It's basically a bunch of games. As close as you would get in Carousel, anyway. It's not a normal storyline. It's an anthology. Everyone cuts their teeth on it."

What a salesman. Chris was a lot like Antoine, or should I say Antoine was a lot like Chris. Antoine had clearly modeled his look and behavior after his older brother. The major difference was that Chris's eyes didn't shine as bright. His smile was never as genuine.

Chris had been in Carousel for eight years. So much had been stolen from him—a contract in the NFL, his family, his twenties. Yet he smiled and acted tough to impress Antoine. He told stories about fights with vampires and mud monsters trapped in industrial-sized freezers.

"It's basically a brain teaser more than anything," Chris said. "And there is a chance, a small chance, you can find the treasure storyline. I don't want to spoil it for you, but ghostly bootleggers are worth the hassle."

"We aren't looking for a storyline right now," Anna said. "We just got back from one."

"A training storyline," Chris said. "I thought Antoine was saying you all wanted to be real players."

"Can I ask a favor if you're going into town?" someone asked from behind us.

I turned to look, and, to my surprise, it was Dina, the Outsider who had arrived at Carousel at the same time we had. She had latched on to a few different teams since we had gotten there so they could train her to be an Outsider, which was a difficult Archetype to do well.

I couldn't see her Plot Armor level or any of her tropes because she had an Outsider ability that made it hard to get any insight into her. Guarded Personality, I think it was called.

"Sure," Anna said.

"I've been talking with Lara. You know Lara?"

We all did. She was the most helpful Psychic Archetype at Camp Dyer.

"Well, she told me I needed to go see this palm reader woman in town. I can't travel alone. I was hoping that maybe you would go with me. You've got a scout now. I asked Janet before, but she said no. It would just be a quick detour from your storyline. I promise."

It was like she was asking me personally, not the group.

I was taken aback. I didn't know what to say. The trope that I had gotten from Janet—I Don't Like It Here . . . —was a good scouting trope, but it wasn't the best one. The information it gave was based on a vague feeling of unease and fear, but it would probably keep us alive.

"You mean like a real psychic?" Kimberly asked. Truthfully, she sounded like she was excited. I think Kimberly had been into astrology back before Carousel. Astrology probably didn't have the same appeal anymore. After all, Carousel had different stars.

Dina nodded.

"Are you sure it's safe?" Anna asked.

Dina shrugged. "I don't think that Lara would have told me about her if it wasn't safe."

"Do you mean Madam Celia?" I asked.

Dina looked surprised. "Yeah, you heard of her?"

"I met her on the Grotesque storyline," I said and coughed. I didn't want to invite questions about that.

"We can take you," Anna said with a smile. "It's no trouble. And if we don't manage to make it to this new storyline on time, I'll be fine with that."

Before we could ask any more questions—like, "Why do you need to go see a psychic?"—Dina was up and gone.

"Meet you out front in an hour?" she asked as she left.

And that was that.

"Wonder whose turn it is to die now," Camden said as she walked away.

Kimberly gave him an exasperated look. "Don't say that!"

To be fair, it was a good question. Storylines meant death.

Honestly, I felt really cool guiding the team through Carousel. Arthur had always looked cool when he was telling us what to do to prevent triggering Omens. I had likened it to traversing a war zone. Everyone was really afraid of storylines, so they listened to every word that came out of my mouth.

"Switch to the other side of the street."

"Wait for this NPC to pass."

"Don't stare into that shop's windows."

"Don't walk too close to the sewer grate."

Stuff like that. I would have looked a whole lot less badass if they knew that the reason we were avoiding all those things was because I saw phrases on the red wallpaper like, "This place gives me the creeps," "I'm getting goosebumps," "Something doesn't feel right," and, of course, "Honey, I'm scared."

If we could have walked in a straight line, we would have been there in an hour, maybe an hour and a half. It took us nearly three.

"Ethereal Emporium: Antiques and Spiritual Readings" was a standalone shop in an outlet strip mall next to a restaurant that served baby back ribs and another store called "Johansen's Fine Furs."

Once we were in the parking lot, we were home free.

As we approached the emporium, the others waited for me to give the all-clear before they entered. I gave them a curt nod.

Dina was in first.

Say what you will about Madam Celia Dane, but her store smelled amazing. I could almost feel my aura cleansing itself with every breath I took.

When we entered, a bell on the door rang. No one was out front when we got there. The place was filled with antique furniture and stacked curios: crystal balls, a rabbit's foot, various tarot card decks, and other occult items.

"Watch out," I said. "Some of the things in here are Omens. But . . . you have to buy them to trigger them."

"Put your credit cards away, ladies," Camden said.

How convenient. Omens for sale. It was *such* a hassle to have to go find one on your own.

Perhaps the most interesting item in the store was a red mechanical box in the corner.

It was Silas the Showman.

The only difference was that this model was not powered on. The mechanical fortune teller stayed silent. His lights stayed off. I wasn't going to risk pressing his button to see if anything happened. I took a moment to examine him up close. I half-expected him to wake up and start jabbering but he never did.

"Hello?" Dina called out.

We listened intently toward the back of the store. The door had been open, so surely an employee was there.

As we were listening, a loud roar like a lion or bear sounded from across the parking lot.

"It's fine," I said as we stared out the window to see what had made the noise.

"Greetings!" a voice called from the back.

A doorway at the back of the store was covered in a colorful beaded curtain that you had to walk through as you passed from room to room. As I turned to look, Madam Celia—the tall, serious woman I had met weeks earlier during the Grotesque storyline—entered the room through a shower of beads.

Madam Celia Dane, Proprietor of Ethereal Emporium: Antiques and Spiritual Readings. NPC. Plot Armor: 50.

"You have come for guidance," she said. It wasn't a question. She said it like it was a fact. It was a good guess; most people who go to psychic shops probably were looking for guidance. Or lost wills.

Dina stepped forward. "Yes. I heard you might be able to help me."

Madam Celia gave her a look over. "I may not be able to help you directly, but I can certainly set you on your path. Come. Sit."

Celia gestured toward a room near the back that was closed off. We walked in the direction she pointed and entered a small, enclosed room with a giant table in the middle surrounded by seats with overstuffed cushions. The room was dark, and the air was thick with incense.

"I've never done this before," Dina said.

Madam Celia gave her a smile. "Don't worry, dear. I have enough experience for the both of us."

We crowded into the room, each taking a seat. We allowed Dina to sit in the chair opposite Madam Celia.

Madam Celia took one of Dina's hands and held it. She closed her eyes.

"You are on a quest," she said.

Dina nodded, but then, realizing that Celia couldn't see her, said, "Yes, I am." Her voice came out weak and vulnerable in a way that I hadn't expected.

Madam Celia didn't say anything for a while. It was like she was somewhere else mentally. Even in the dimly lit room, I could see her eyes moving behind her eyelids.

"You poor thing," she said. "Dealt an unfair hand."

Dina didn't say anything. But she looked very uneasy, sad maybe.

Who in the room hadn't been dealt an unfair hand?

"And you came here hoping that I would give you the answers. But that isn't my role here. We all have a role here, in Carousel. You'll learn that soon enough. You came seeking that which you treasure, but will you leave with your prize? I cannot tell you the way, but a darker power might be able to."

"A . . . darker power?" Dina asked. She sounded hesitant.

"I think it would be very strange for you to turn your nose up at this point," Celia said with the ghost of a smirk.

Dina looked down.

"I don't know what it will take for you to get to the end of your story. But I do know the next step."

She reached a hand into her pocket and pulled out a ticket. She handed it to Dina.

"You will need your friends' help for this," she said. "To get to the end and back again you will need many things to accomplish many feats. Don't worry. There is a path that will lead you there. You need . . . a guide who knows the way."

"Where?"

"One step after another," Madam Celia said. She pointed to the ticket that she had just handed Dina. "This is your next step. If only you have the bravery to take it. Now go. Never make the mistake of thinking you have time to waste."

Madam Celia herded us out of the store and back out into the parking lot. There were still animal noises coming from somewhere in the strip mall.

"Are you going to tell us about that?" Antoine asked.

Dina didn't say anything. She took out the ticket and showed it to us. We examined it. It was different than the tickets we'd seen before, slightly smaller than a trope ticket. It had only stylish art nouveau imagery on it and read:

> Private Showing
> Feast your eyes on the one and only darkly
> delicious show from a world of the highest stakes.
> Win in a game of skill and chance.
> Get your answers if you win, or if you lose, play:
> Antemortem

Beneath that were directions to a place called Berryman's Dive. It ended with, "A Private Showing just for you! Storylines guaranteed to be your level or your money back."

"What is this?" Kimberly asked.

I'd been trying to figure that out myself. It presented itself like an actual movie ticket, but the address was to what I assumed was a dive bar. And then it hit me.

"Madam Celia is a quest-giver," I said. Most of the others looked at me, puzzled.

"That makes sense," Camden said. He would know.

"A quest-giver?" Anna asked.

"In a video game, a quest-giver is an NPC whose job is to give you a quest to do. A mission. I think that's what Madam Celia is. You go talk to her, and she gives you directions to a storyline."

The others took turns staring at the ticket. They all seemed interested. Up until that point, we had only gone on storylines that the more senior players had vetted. We had never actually tried to let Carousel guide us, but it clearly had the ability to. After all, Roxy had said that there was a tutorial. There **had** to be quest-givers.

"You don't think that what she said was true?" Dina asked. I think from the look on her face she really didn't want me to be right. I think that she wanted Madam Celia's words to be real and not just an NPC playing a part.

I shrugged my shoulders. "Has anything actually been real here? Everything's just a performance stacked on another performance."

Dina didn't say anything. She almost looked sad, but within a few seconds, she had wiped away any trace of emotion.

CHAPTER NINE

HAPPENED A-PAWN

Back to camp?" Anna asked.

"That sounds right to me," Kimberly said.

Antoine shook his head. "We're going to run a storyline, remember."

"A storyline?" Camden asked. "I don't recall."

We all looked at each other.

I ignored their talking and looked at Dina. She was still examining the "Private Showing" ticket she had just received.

"Maybe you should run that thing by the vets before you actually use it," I said.

Anna nodded and added, "Just in case."

"Do you think . . . if you're already . . ." Dina started. She thought for a moment. "Never mind. I'll talk to the vets."

Antoine had a strange look on his face. "If you want, you can come the direction we're going. We could use an Outsider on the squad."

"I'm sorry to bother you," Dina said. "You've done enough for me."

"Come on," Antoine said. "You have to do a run soon. Might as well come with us. It couldn't hurt."

"Maybe," Dina said.

"Whatever you decide," I said, "I'm going to the pawn shop near town square. Arthur told me it has some interesting stuff."

Antoine's face lit up. "Chris said something similar. He said you can find items related to your last storyline sometimes."

"I don't know. I just want to check it out, and since we're close, I want to go now. Might have to put off the whole storyline thing," I said.

Anna smiled. She didn't want to go. Actually, I suspected Kimberly didn't want to go but she didn't want to seem like a wuss to Antoine, so Anna pretended it was her that was reluctant. Just a guess.

"And we're off," I said.

Navigating through town was more difficult than going through the outskirts. There were more Omens packed closely together. Luckily, I was able to get us through. All it took was a ton of stress and an extra helping of caution.

We couldn't go directly through town square. That place was filled to the brim with Omens. We could only go there in between scenes like the last time. Luckily, there was a way to get to the pawn shop without going through town square.

There was a back alley.

That sounded like a bad idea at first; the back alley must be filled with Omens. But it wasn't. There were only three.

One was inside a dumpster. I didn't know what it was, but I could hear it growling. Another involved a man wearing a tinfoil hat and talking to himself. Those were easy to avoid.

The third was a little bit trickier. There was a green ooze rising up out of a sewer grate. The sewers of Carousel had to be filled with storylines because this was the third Omen I had seen related to them.

"Don't step in the ooze," I said.

"Let me get this straight. You want us to *avoid* the glowing sludge?" Camden asked with a grin.

"Yes. You'll just have to trust me," I answered.

Everyone made it past with little trouble.

Once we were through the alleyway, we had made it.

We gazed up at Happened A-Pawn Pawn Shop, our destination.

Walking into the pawn shop, I immediately noticed that something was different about this place. Nearly every object in the entire store displayed information on the red wallpaper. Not just the Omens, though there were those too. Everything.

The guns hung up on the wall behind the counter told me how much ammunition they could hold and how powerful they were. I hadn't really considered the idea that some weapons might be more powerful than others. Obviously, I knew a handgun wasn't as deadly as a shotgun or a rifle, but comparing rifles to each other felt ambiguous and pointless when it was the user's Mettle that actually mattered.

This was a movie world. Guns didn't have specifications in most movies. They performed as the plot demanded.

There weren't just guns; there were knives, swords, and weapons of all sorts. A mall ninja would go crazy in this shop. If there were ever a citywide zombie apocalypse, this would be the first place I would go.

But the supplies didn't end there. There were things that might not seem useful at first glance. The shop was filled with all types of props, outfits, and tools.

There were hunting supplies, hiking supplies, and an entire section devoted to used arts and crafts supplies. There were canvases—one of which was an Omen—paint, and a portable easel. There was a typewriter that you could carry around in its own little case. There were musical instruments, cameras, and a variety of other electronics.

The selection of Omens was even greater than that at the psychic's shop.

"Do not touch anything," I said to my friends as we walked in.

"Riley," Anna said, "I think . . . I think we can see them too."

"The Omens?"

She nodded her head. Normally, players without scouting tropes could only see Omens when they were right on them and in danger of activating them—or right after they had activated them.

This place really was special.

As I looked around at everything the shop offered, my eyes eventually rested on a familiar sight. In the corner of the shop, broken down and inoperable, was Silas the Showman again. He didn't move; he didn't speak. His lights were off. And yet I could never really feel like he wasn't watching.

In addition to seeing information about the objects in the shop, I could see their cost. I could also see whether any of them required special tropes to be able to be used in a storyline. Some said that tropes were required, and others said they were merely recommended.

After looking around the shop for a while, I saw under the glass of the counter a collection of tickets. Tropes of all kinds. I took twenty minutes just to read them all. Unlike the other objects in the pawn shop, these did not have prices on them. I suspected I would have to haggle.

While looking through the tropes on the red wallpaper, I noticed that the cards listed their Aspects. Normally, a player couldn't see Aspect-related things until they had their own Aspect. None of us had gotten to that point yet.

Aspects modify the base Archetype. If this were a video game, an Aspect appeared to be a subclass or something like that.

Name	Archetype	Aspect	Type	Stat	Effect
A Rare Find	Antiquarian	N/A	Perk	Savvy	The player will be presented with valuable artifacts that, if recovered and kept undamaged, will increase the loot won at the end of the storyline.

Align-ment Reveal	Outsider	Stranger	Action	Moxie	A player who has kept their involvement with the main cast ambiguous until the Finale can then reveal they are an ally, boosting all of their stats. Keeping a distance from the main storyline is more difficult than it seems.
Amateur Para-normal Investiga-tor	N/A	N/A	Back-ground	N/A	The player has always been interested in the paranormal and likes to spend their nights and weekends hunting ghosts, goblins, and cryptids. Grants access to the following tropes: Trail Cam (Adventurer), Accidentally Captured on Film (Artist), EVP (Psychic), Sleuth's Starter Kit (Detective), Legacy Hunter's Journal (Monster Hunter), and Ouija Is Just a Boardgame (Psychic). LEVEL I.
Are Their Feelings Real?	Femme Fatale	N/A	Buff	Moxie	If the player strikes up a budding romance with an ally, they will both get higher Grit for the remainder of the storyline or until the question of the player's true feelings is answered.

Call in the Military	Soldier	Com- mando	Rule	N/A	Changes the win con- dition to waiting it out until after the military arrives. The player must contact them first. The player will see a countdown until victory. Enemies will be more aggressive and better at finding play- ers. Be cautious when equipping this trope, as storylines will scale to a level justifying military intervention.
Charlatan	Psychic	Occultist	Action	Moxie	Revealing oneself (or being revealed) to be a fraudulent psychic invalidates all predic- tions (good or bad) and psychic abilities. If performed at the Rebirth midpoint, it also rids the story of its supernatural qualities and morphs the story into a more realistic scenario that only appears supernatural (when plausible).
Clue Magnifier	Detective	N/A	Insight	Savvy	When examining a scene, the player will receive applicable clues on the red wallpaper. A magnifying glass or similar can be used as a prop to great effect.

Don't Dead Open Inside	Any	N/A	Insight	Plot Armor	Increases the frequency of on-scene, explicit information related to the plot or enemy.
Eagle Scout	N/A	N/A	Back-ground	N/A	The player was in the Scouts growing up. The following tropes can be equipped: Know Your Knots (Adventurer), Prepared for the Outdoors (Adventurer), I Need Duct Tape and Towels (Doctor), Follow the Leader (Wallflower), A Keen Sense of Direction (Adventurer), Monsters Fear Fire (Monster Hunter), and The Benefits of an Active Lifestyle (Athlete).
Fight Magic with Magic	Monster Hunter	N/A	Rule	Plot Armor	Allows the player to bring occult objects into the story that are usable for hunting monsters, creatures, or supernatural entities. As player Plot Armor increases, they can bring more items and more useful items.
Flickering Lights	Departed	N/A	Action	Savvy	The player can cause lights or other electronics to flicker as a means to communicate with living allies. The higher the Savvy, the higher the control over the flickering.

Fresh Meat	Outsider	New-comer	Rule	Moxie	Revealing oneself to be a new student, employee, etc. during the Party phase will cause ornery or pugnacious NPCs to gravitate toward you, increasing the odds of the player finding useful information, endearing the player to protective NPCs, and letting allies go off-screen.
Give Him the Hook!	Comedian	Joker	Action	Moxie	Telling a bad joke on purpose lowers Plot Armor.
Golden Rule	Wallflower	Under-dog	Insight	Moxie	Being kind to NPCs can result in them striking up a useful friendship, which can be used to obtain information off-screen.
Hang a Lamp-shade	Film Buff/ Comedian	N/A	Buff	Savvy	Pointing out a cliché or unrealistic plan buffs the planner's Savvy and increases the likelihood of success.
Human Shield	Guardian	N/A	Buff	Grit	When protecting an ally from damage, the ally will, to the extent plausible, not take damage. The player will take it instead.
I Had a Troubled Child-hood	Outsider	Criminal	Rule	Moxie	The player gains proficiency with lockpicking, hotwiring cars, and other criminal skills if they convincingly portray themselves as having a criminal history.

Intimida-tion Is Charisma	Bruiser	Bully	Rule	Mettle	In situations that involve persuasion where intimidation is a plausible means to persuade, the player's Moxie is equal to their Mettle.
It's All in Your Head	Doctor	Psychia-trist	Action	Moxie	Allows the player to prescribe medication to temporarily dampen or eliminate mental trauma—even if that trauma is caused by real supernatural beings. This can protect them from otherworldly tormentors and even suppress possession, if only for a while.
Kick the Dog	Outsider	Criminal	Action	Moxie	Doing an evil or revolting act in the Party phase lowers the player's Plot Armor but ensures they will have a cinematic death at Second Blood.
Limber	Athlete	Fitness Expert	Buff	N/A	Allows the player extra Hustle when doing a task that requires flexibility.
New in Town	Outsider	New-comer	Insight	Moxie	Introducing yourself in a friendly manner will increase the odds of NPCs reciprocating, giving directions or general advice.

Not Important Enough	Wallflower	Extra	Rule	N/A	As long as the player does not engage in the plot, they will not be targeted by an intelligent enemy with no specific motive to do so. Prevents being targeted for both First and Second Blood. After the midpoint, they will be considered Written Off and will not be permitted back on-screen except through the effect of another trope.
Not Just a Pretty Face	Eye Candy	Beauty	Buff	N/A	The Eye Candy's Moxie is used in place of Savvy when the highest-Savvy ally is dead, unavailable, or has a plan fail.
Peek over the Shoulder	Wallflower	Stand-In	Insight	Moxie	The player can get a peek at an NPC's current scripted action by getting physically close to them.
Photographic Memory	Scholar	Sleuth	Perk	Savvy	The player can store limited visual information on the red wallpaper.
Pointing Out the Obvious	Hysteric	Defiant	Buff	Moxie	Reiterating obvious problems ad nauseam will buff allies' Grit and Savvy.

Preg-nancy Reveal	Any Female Character	N/A	Buff	Moxie	Revealing pregnancy on-screen buffs the player's Grit and increases the lover's Mettle upon death.
Prepared for the Outdoors	Adventurer	N/A	Rule	N/A	Allows the player to bring standard outdoor equipment, such as climbing gear, hiking equipment, etc.
Save the Cheer-leader, Save the World	Damsel	N/A	Rule	N/A	Changes the win condition to rescuing the player, assuming they are successful in being kidnapped or put in prolonged risk of harm.
Shared Experi-ence	Final Girl	Team Leader	Rule	Moxie	The Final Girl's exploits will slightly increase the loot of all players, regardless of involvement in the storyline.
Sitting by the Phone	Wallflower	Under-dog	Rule	Moxie	After establishing friendships with allies early in the story, the player can sit out much of what follows until they are called in (through a plausible method) for help in the Finale. Engaging in the plot will invalidate this trope. The player is considered Written Off until they are called back in.

The Bul-letproof Table	Soldier	GI	Rule	Moxie	In a fight scene, anything the character hides behind will be imbued with the movie magic required to stop projectiles, claws, acid, or similar attacks. Must be at least plausible and the portrayal must be convincing.
The One That Got Away	Hysteric	Craven	Rule	N/A	Upon the death of the rest of the party, the win condition changes to escape. Player will be able to perceive a safe zone. However, in any sequel storyline, you will be targeted first.
Third Eye Cam	Psychic	Seer	Insight	Savvy	The player will be able to see the deaths of other players and NPCs in real time. Whether they can reveal that information on-screen depends on the nature of the story.
Trail Cam	Adventurer	N/A	Insight	Savvy	Allows the player to place video cameras around the setting in an attempt to capture proof or information.
Uncon-scious Revelation	Artist	N/A	Insight	Savvy	The player will subcon-sciously include hints of supernatural phe-nomena in their artistic work, be it a book, painting, or the like.

I had money. Two hundred and thirty Carousel dollars. I wanted to split it with my friends. Maybe I was trying to make up for the whole axe murderer thing, but I wasn't sure.

"If you see anything you could use," I said. "I might be able to help you buy it. I mean, I just got a lot of money. I don't think there's anything better to spend it on."

"Thanks," Antoine said. "Just need a little."

He was holding a wooden baseball bat that cost sixty dollars. His tropes would give him a bonus for using that and allow him to carry it into most storylines. Seemed like a good buy.

He laughed. I laughed. He finally had a baseball bat. I wondered how long it would take for him to lose it.

"You think Dina might know something we don't?" he asked casually and quietly.

I shrugged my shoulders. "She was acting weird," I said. "But she has never exactly been normal."

"We should invite her again to come along with us," he said. "Maybe befriend her. Figure something out."

"She'll want to go on that storyline she got a ticket for," I said.

"Maybe once she trusts us . . . Maybe we go with her," he said. "I'll talk to Chris about it. If there's something up about Private Showings, he would know."

I nodded. Antoine backed away as Kimberly approached us.

"I don't know what I want," Kimberly said in frustration. I couldn't blame her. There was no obvious prop that Eye Candy might need. A purse, maybe? But she brought one with her and never used it in storylines, so that was probably not right.

"I could get you this Pregnancy Reveal trope," I suggested, pointing to the trope in the case.

She looked at me like I had slapped her.

"Just because . . . it would be useful. It's a buff," I said. "Or not. It's probably too expensive anyway."

At first, I thought I might have offended her, but then she started laughing. She was teasing me.

"I'll take it," Kimberly said. "But I don't want any jokes."

"I wasn't going to . . ."

She shrugged her shoulders. "Good."

Camden was easy. He wanted Photographic Memory, a trope for keeping information stored perfectly on the red wallpaper.

"It would have made *The Astralist* a breeze," he said. "I mean, more than it already was."

Easy for him to say. He didn't get kidnapped.

That was three friends down.

"Anna?" I asked.

She looked through the selection. She didn't seem to find anything that appealed to her, though I think she was just being polite.

"You're already giving me that other Final Girl trope," she said. "You don't need to get me anything else. Unless that one ends up being affordable."

She pointed to Shared Experience.

I could see that being useful. It wouldn't have much in-story use, but ensuring every player got decent rewards was a good effect.

I started thinking about what I would want for myself. There were a couple of tropes available that I liked. Hang a Lamp Shade and Don't Dead Open Inside would both work for me and seemed useful. But something else caught my eye.

A portable tape player. Yellow plastic. Thin metal headphones with yellow earpads. The kind that sat on your ears, not covered them. The kind you might have seen back in the early 90s. They were bright and visible. They were perfect for someone who wanted to pretend that they couldn't hear you.

The Oblivious Bystander strategy just got even more viable.

They cost eighty dollars. They didn't require a trope to bring them into a storyline unless you were trying to listen for ghosts, in which case you would need a trope for that. The record function would not work without the associated trope for that either. It didn't matter. I just needed them as a prop.

There was a tape inside of it that read, "90s Instant Classics." I imagine they were made-up 90s songs like every other made-up thing in Carousel, but they would do the trick. I probably wouldn't even have the volume up.

Sunglasses + Headphones = Truly Oblivious.

Combine that with a newspaper or similar and I would be nearly untouchable when using Oblivious Bystander. At least, that was the theory.

Now where was that shopkeeper? I found a little bell on the counter and rang it.

From the back of the shop, someone with a deep voice yelled, "I'm coming, I'm coming."

Moments later, a door near Silas the Showman opened up and a large man walked through it. He was six and a half feet tall and built like a truck. His hair was cropped short. He wore an unbuttoned short-sleeved collared shirt with a white undershirt and cargo shorts.

Taron "Tar" Bellows. Owner, Happened A-Pawn Pawn Shop. Plot Armor: 50. He had tropes on the red wallpaper that I couldn't see, just like Celia Dane.

"I see you've already raided the place," he said. He came behind the counter and pulled out a small pair of reading glasses. He stretched them over his face and looked down at me through them. "Now, what do you need me for?"

I cleared my throat.

"We were hoping to buy some of these tickets," I said.

"And a baseball bat," Antoine added.

"And a baseball bat," I said. "And maybe that Walkman."

Tar looked over where I had pointed. "Walkman?"

"The tape player," I said. Walkman wasn't a Carousel brand.

"Bat and tape player is one forty. What tickets you looking for?"

I pointed out Photographic Memory, Pregnancy Reveal, and Shared Experience.

He gingerly grabbed them from behind the counter. His large fingers made the tickets look small.

"This one is fifty," he said, placing Photographic Memory on the counter.

I quickly realized I wouldn't have enough money.

"These are two hundred and two ten," he said about Pregnancy Reveal and Shared Experience, respectively.

I went over budget quickly.

"Before I forget," I said. I pulled out the ten tickets I had gotten from Silas after the Grotesque storyline and laid them on the counter. "I was wondering if you could tell me anything about these."

"Let's take a look," he said.

He began shuffling through them and rearranging them. I didn't know if he was sorting them by rarity or what.

"You've got some good stuff here," he said. "Friends in High Places, now that is a useful ticket. Why would you want to part ways with that?"

"I can't use it."

He shrugged.

"Watching Over You . . . " he said. "Not as rare, still useful."

He put Watching Over You . . . down right next to Friends in High Places. Friends in High Places. Watching Over You.

I paused. Friends in high places watching over you. Was that just a coincidence? I knew the titles didn't seem random, but I had dismissed them after talking to Arthur. Strange.

Anna leaned over and said, "We also have some money, if that's not enough." She put 110 dollars on the counter. All of their combined earnings.

"Just in case," she said.

Tar ignored her and continued with my tropes.

"A Glitch in the Matrix. Did that one confuse you, or are you just not interested?" he asked. I was puzzled. Did he not realize that not everyone could use every ticket? He placed A Glitch in the Matrix down on the counter.

"Accidentally Captured on Film. Now that is a run saver," he said. "You ever thought about becoming an Artist?"

I shook my head.

"All right," he said.

He placed Accidentally Captured on Film next to A Glitch in the Matrix.

A Glitch in the Matrix. Accidentally Captured on Film.

"Lot of good stuff you have here. Almost hate to take it off you. I mean, players get certain tropes for specific reasons."

"Wait a second," I said. I grabbed the tickets I had received from Silas after the Grotesque storyline.

A Glitch in the Matrix.

A Story Within a Story.

Watching Over You . . .

Who You Truly Are . . .

Friends in High Places.

This Is Going to Sting a Bit . . .

Accidentally Captured on Film.

Back to Where It All Started . . .

The Intrepid Guide Who Knows the Way.

"Are you saying that there *is* a code?" I asked. Was I not crazy?

"You know, kid," Tar said, "I got my favorite show on in the back. I'm really not looking to haggle and trade. Tell you what. Since the boss isn't looking, how about I just take the cash? Easier that way."

I looked him in the eyes. They were dark. He met my gaze.

"What do you say? Just the cash? You keep those tropes. Just in case. They might grow on you. I'll take the cash. You get these new tickets and your goods, and we'll call it even."

I nodded.

"Good. Now get out of here. I'm closing up shop."

I gathered the tickets and the Walkman. Antoine got his bat. We handed Tar the money. We turned to leave. I never even got to discuss the going price on the enemy tickets we had been collecting every time we killed an enemy.

"Come back soon, you hear. We have a rotating stock. Never know what we'll have."

"Thanks," Anna said as we left.

"What's going on?" Antoine asked.

"Was there something wrong with your tickets?" Camden asked.

There was almost certainly something wrong. The titles of the tickets I had received from Silas . . . I always thought they were strange. I thought they had a message. I had dismissed it before after Roxy and Arthur had told me it was normal, but the way the NPC had laid them out in front of me like that . . .

What was it that Roxy said happened to old Film Buffs? That they started thinking Carousel was talking to them?

Maybe they were right.

CHAPTER TEN

EVEN MORE STORIES FROM THE CAMPFIRE: FATAL FOLKTALES

Anna got her way. Or should I say, Anna got Kimberly's way. We didn't end up running the new storyline that day.

We ran it two days later. Antoine was practically chomping at the bit by then.

Dina decided to join us. She wasn't exactly our friend, but she did seem like she wanted to be there.

"I'm guessing that's the Omen," Antoine said.

Ahead of us was a busted gate leading to private property. Where normally a gate like this might say something like, "Trespassers Will Be Shot" or something similar, this one went in a different direction.

"Say no to the Carousel Turnpike!"
"Beware! Enter at your Own Risk!"
"They join you as you go!"
"You will think they belong!"
"No Camping."
"No Hiking."
"The Turnpike Will Doom Us All."
"Keep count of your group."

The signs were put around the gate in no particular order. They were hastily painted on chunks of old plywood.

On the red wallpaper, my scouting trope called this storyline *Even More Stories from the Campfire: Fatal Folktales*. Its difficulty level was "Something Isn't Right Here," which I assumed was not the highest difficulty. I was still figuring out how the scale worked.

"We trigger it by agreeing to join the teenagers behind the bush," I said. All I knew was how to trigger it. I hadn't seen the teenagers yet.

Everyone turned to look. There was a bush about fifteen yards onto the property. If you squinted, you could see that two figures had hidden in the bush and were staring out onto the property.

"Wait," Anna said. "Before we go, we should really be able to see your tropes, Dina. Just in case we need to know."

Dina considered this. We had been told that Outsider's information on the red wallpaper was hidden, even from allies. It was because of a trope they got early on.

"Okay," Dina said.

Suddenly, Dina appeared on the red wallpaper. I hadn't seen her there since the corn maze.

Here's how all of our stats and tropes appeared before we tackled the storyline:

Player Stats	Plot Armor	Mettle	Moxie	Hustle	Savvy	Grit
Riley	20/2	1	7	4	7	1
Antoine	16	4	2	5	1	4
Anna	18	4	4	3	2	5
Kimberly	14	1	5	3	1	4
Camden	15	2	2	2	6	3
Dina	16	2	2	3	2	7

Anna Reed is the Final Girl.

As the **Last One Alive**, she cannot die until the rest of the party is killed. Her **Who's with Me?** trope allows her to buff allies in the Finale, and **Let's Not Fight** buffs allies when she defuses infighting.

A Kind Face makes NPCs more likely to reveal important plot information, and **Shared Experience** allows players to gain loot based on her efforts. Borrowed from me, she also has the **Stick to the Plan** trope, which allows her to get doomed plans back on track by rallying allies as if victory is still possible.

Antoine Stone is the Athlete.

It's Part of the Uniform gives him higher Mettle when attacking with sports equipment.

Gym Rat buffs Mettle and Hustle by revealing athletic backstory.

Just Walk It Off heals the Hobbled status by walking.

The Playbook allows him to see the phases of a coordinated plan.

Camden Tran is the Scholar.

Eureka! helps him find important information within text.
Right Tool for the Job buffs Savvy and Mettle when fighting an enemy with their weakness.
Zippos Are Cheap boosts Savvy for plans that expend a Zippo lighter.
Hide and Seek allows him to outsmart an enemy during a chase instead of outrunning them.
Photographic Memory allows him to display visual information committed to memory on the red wallpaper.

Dina Cano is the Outsider.

Guarded Personality resists all Insight abilities.
An Outsider's Perspective alerts her to new, out-of-place, or unusual information.
Better Late than Never buffs Mettle and Hustle if she waits until the Finale to assist allies on-screen against the enemy.
A Haunted Past allows her to equip various tickets related to past trauma.
Encouragement from Beyond soothes her when stressed, scared, or in pain and may provide useful information.

Kimberly Madison is the Eye Candy.

Convenient Backstory allows her to change her backstory to assist with the current task, buffing the relevant stat.
Social Awareness allows her to see the Moxie stat of all enemies and NPCs and get a sense of their relationships with each other.
Get a Room! boosts the odds of important discoveries when exploring with a love interest during the Party.
A Hopeless Plea forces the captor to explicitly deny her release when she asks to be released.
Pregnancy Reveal buffs her Grit when she announces she is pregnant and buffs the father if she is killed.
Does Anyone Have a Scrunchie? allows her to transfer Moxie to Savvy, Hustle, or Grit by putting her hair up.
She left **Looks Don't Last** at home again.

Riley Lawrence is the Film Buff.

Trope Master grants me the ability to perceive enemy tropes, but at the cost of sacrificing half of my Plot Armor.

With the power of **Cinema Seer**, I enhance the Savvy and Grit of my allies by accurately predicting cinematic and impactful plot elements (but must save it for good predictions).

As an **Oblivious Bystander**, I remain untargeted by enemies while I convincingly act oblivious to their presence.

Escape Artist boosts my Hustle in order to execute plausible escape plans.

Through **Casting Director**, I gain insights into the roles players assume within storylines. Drawing on my upbringing, **Raised by Television** enhances relevant stats when I take larger-than-life or cinematic action inspired by TV or movies, though it often attracts a downturn in fortune soon afterward.

With **My Grandmother Had the Gift . . .** I can equip various tickets related to intuitive or supernatural abilities "inherited" from my grandmother.

I Don't Like It Here . . . provides me with insight into the location of Omens and how to avoid triggering them.

With that, we headed off into the field.

CHAPTER ELEVEN

THE STRAGGLER

As we started walking toward the teens hiding in the bush, I leaned in toward the group and said, "Just from that title I can tell you that this is probably a horror anthology."

Even More Stories from the Campfire: Fatal Folktales had all the generic hallmarks that you would come to expect from a movie that was really just multiple short stories put together. More than that, it sounded like it was a sequel to an anthology series.

"How does that change things?" Antoine asked.

"I have no idea," I admitted. "I don't know if this is just one of the stories or all of them. Just be ready."

"Maybe after we finish one story, we unlock the next one," Anna suggested. "Maybe we get a ticket or something."

I shrugged. That sounded a little generous.

Usually, in a horror anthology, there was a frame narrative or outer story. Often, someone inside that story tells the other stories in the anthology, sometimes simply reading them from a book. Other times a horror anthology could be several interwoven stories happening all at once.

I really hoped it wasn't the second option.

We walked along the path until we reached the bush where the two teens were crouched down looking out into the field. The needle on the Plot Cycle was pointed to Omen still. We hadn't triggered the story yet.

The realization that I was about to be back in a storyline suddenly hit me. "Don't forget to stay in character on-screen," I said.

Most of them looked my way and nodded in a way that signaled, "We know."

They had never done anything to make me think that they would intentionally break character, but still, I worried.

As we approached, the two teens noticed us and stood up.

One of them, a short young man with a backward baseball cap on his head and an oversized jacket, said, "I thought you were going to chicken out."

My friends and I exchanged glances.

"Nope, not us," Antoine said. "We're not afraid of anything."

"Good," the second teen said. He wore a T-shirt and jeans that had really wide legs, like you might have seen twenty years ago. He finished the look off with gelled hair and a seashell necklace. "You'll get to prove it. Old Man Akers shot the last kids who snuck onto his property."

Their names were Rudy and Jake, respectively. NPCs, Plot Armor: 3. They might have been fourteen or fifteen.

"Well, come on," Rudy said, turning his cap around. "Let's go."

They turned to leave.

"Is this a kids' story?" Camden asked.

I wasn't sure. "Maybe."

"If it's for kids, that means it's less scary, right?" Kimberly asked.

You *would* think that, wouldn't you?

As we followed them, the Plot Cycle switched from Omen to Choice to Party. We were officially in the storyline.

Looking at my friends, I noticed that nothing appeared on the red wallpaper to tell me what their roles in the story would be. I didn't know if that was because we didn't have specific roles, or because of the fact that this was an anthology.

The pasture was bordered on both sides by forest. The sun was setting, and it would be nighttime soon. It was setting fast enough that I was pretty sure it would be dark by the time we got to where we were going. We were off-screen as we walked, with occasional exceptions. By the time we saw the truck, the sun was already gone from the sky.

"Shh," Rudy said. "He could be anywhere near here."

There were hay bales placed sporadically around the pasture. The bales were large and appeared to circle around the location where the truck was. We could see an orange glow coming from the other side of the truck. There was a campfire.

Jake and Rudy hid behind one of the larger hay bales and waved us over to come hide with them.

On-screen.

Jake turned to us and said, "I dare you to sneak around to the other side of the truck."

I wasn't sure who he was talking to. The others must not have been either because they didn't respond.

After a moment, he added, "I thought you guys were so brave."

"Why don't you do it if you're not afraid," Antoine said. "You just want us to do it because you don't have the nerve."

Rudy started to laugh. "He's right. You do it."

Jake looked flustered, maybe a little scared. "Then you come with me!" he said to Rudy.

"Fine," Rudy said. "Let's go."

The two of them departed from behind the hay bale and slowly crept toward the truck. With every step, they got slower and less sure of themselves. As they got to the truck, they didn't quite know what to do next, so they waited for a bit before taking one last look back at us and sneaking around the other side.

Off Screen.

Then we waited.

And waited.

"I think they're dead," Kimberly said.

"Better them than us," joked Antoine.

We waited some more.

"It's possible we're going to have to go over there to make this thing go forward," I said.

"You do it," Antoine said.

"You have higher Grit than me. What are you afraid of?"

Antoine started to respond but then stopped when Anna started to speak.

"You two are as bad as they are," she said. "We should all go over there."

On-screen.

I guess it was decided. We all stood up and slowly made our way to the truck. One by one we peeked our heads around and slid to the other side.

Rudy and Jake were sitting on logs around the campfire roasting hot dogs on the end of sticks. As we approached, they started to laugh.

"Want some?" Rudy asked. "The old man has a bunch."

"What are you doing?" Anna asked. "Don't eat his food."

"Well, he's not eating it. Don't want it to go bad," Jake said.

Dumb little kids in movies are worse than creepy little kids in movies. That's my official opinion.

"What are you doing on my property?" a voice asked from behind us.

Great.

There were several audible gasps as we all turned around to see an old man with a cowboy hat and long graying hair. He wore work clothes and boots. Folded over his left arm was a double-barrel shotgun. He walked slowly, his years informing his every movement.

All I could see from him on the red wallpaper was his name. Weird.

"Stealing my food?"

"We were just borrowing it," Jake said. "We'll pay you back. Please don't hurt us."

Old Man Akers didn't seem as angry as I might have expected. Instead, he looked worried.

"You kids shouldn't be out here. Don't you know about this place?" he asked. "Don't you know that this property is haunted by all manner of foul things?"

"We just wanted to see," Rudy said.

Akers simply took in a deep breath and let it out slowly.

"Well, go ahead and sit down. There's no use running away now. You'd never make it out. Best stay here around the fire."

We gathered around and found logs to sit on. Old Man Akers pulled a chair out of the back of his truck and sat down next to a blue cooler, presumably the one that held the hot dogs.

"You have no idea what sort of predicament you're in," he said. "This land is cursed five times over. Maybe six. You'll be lucky to make it out alive."

Rudy and Jake looked at each other and then at the rest of us.

"You're just saying that to scare us," Rudy said.

"I said it because it's a fact. Haven't you ever heard any stories about this plot of land? If you had, you would never have come here."

"We just thought they were rumors," Jake said.

"Yeah, well, that's just because whoever told you didn't tell the story right. They left out the important parts. The parts that chill you to the bone and make certain that you will never make the same mistake as the people in the story.

"Well, gather around. We might have just enough time for me to tell you how much trouble you're in. I've lived on this land my whole life. I know every-thing there is to know about the things that go bump in the night around here."

Here we go. Looks like we got option one: a frame story where someone tells other stories. It might have been too early to say, but I thought we lucked out. Then again, we still didn't know how things worked.

"Well, the first story happened almost a year ago tonight. Out in the woods to the west. Another group of kids, a few years older than you, decided to come out and see if the rumors were true. It just so happened that they weren't the only ones visiting me that night."

Suddenly, the campfire was gone. It was replaced by a metal barrel with burning scraps of wood inside along with a few smoldering, crumpled balls of newspaper.

We weren't in the pasture anymore.

Anna, Kimberly, and I were huddled around the burn barrel next to a for-ested path. Antoine, Dina, and Camden weren't there.

We were off-screen.

The sensation of instantly being somewhere else was strange and disorient-ing. It tickled my brain. We looked at each other with strange smiles on our faces.

I looked around us. The others were nowhere to be found. Something else had changed: my Casting Director trope had activated. We finally had roles on the red wallpaper.

"We're student journalists for the University of Carousel," I said. "We're out here investigating some disappearances. We think that the police missed something after a couple of hikers and a woman whose car broke down went missing."

"That explains this," Anna said, lifting a 90s model instant-print camera and a notebook into view.

I dug into my pocket. I also had a camera like that.

Kimberly produced one just like it.

"Anna, you're the editor. Kimberly and I are just reporters."

They nodded.

We heard yelling in the distance, not far up the path.

On-screen.

"Let's check that out," Anna said. "Cameras out."

Kimberly and I nodded.

The stars in the sky were just bright enough to guide our path. We crept in the direction of the sound. The forest was thick; if we left the path, we probably wouldn't find it again.

"It looks like there's a house up there," Anna said.

We found a tree to hide behind as we peered up toward the house. There was a light up there like the kind that might come from a lantern. People were arguing.

Off Screen.

"That's Camden and Antoine," Kimberly said. "Who's that lady with them?" She answered her own question as she got a better look. "Roberta? An NPC?"

I peeked over at them and looked at the red wallpaper.

"They're lawyers for the city trying to convince Old Man Akers to sell his property so they can build a turnpike," I said. Antoine and Camden had gotten completely different roles than we had. That explained why they had an NPC with them—someone to tell them what they were doing there because they didn't have me.

"Look, we're talking about a lot of money here," Antoine said. "Don't you want to live the high life, doing whatever you want?"

"I already do!" Akers said. "You don't understand how much trouble you're in. These woods do not like outsiders."

I whispered to Anna and Kimberly, "Carousel's really got Antoine's number, doesn't it?"

I think practicing law was among the things that Antoine wanted to do with his life. Politics was another.

"Hush," Anna said.

Old Man Akers started yelling again. "I'm telling you, you have to go right now. It isn't safe to be here!"

"Is that a threat?" Roberta, the NPC, said.

"Lady, the things that walk in these woods do not threaten. You need to march out of here now. The three of you. Either stay together or walk alone. Never just walk with only one other person. You won't know they are among you until it's too late."

"This guy's a joker," Roberta said in a whisper yell that was clearly meant to be heard by everyone. She looked back at Akers. "If you ever want to get serious, we can make it worth your while. The city doesn't have to get your consent, you know. They can exercise eminent domain and snatch this place up at the market rate. If you play ball, we can skip all the court costs."

Akers wasn't having it. "Get off my property. Now. Together. Remember this: the number that entered will always be the number that leaves. Whether all three of you will be among those leaving is another question."

On-screen.

"What is he talking about?" Kimberly asked. "Do you think that has something to do with the missing people?"

"Who knows," I said. "I've heard of stranger things."

"Hmm," Tony muttered. It was almost like he had just woken up. His clothes were filthy like he'd been wearing them for days. His face was gaunt, his hair was hastily tied back behind his head.

"We need to make a plan. Get closer to the house. And we can't let those lawyers see us," Anna said. "Where's your camera?"

She was looking at Tony.

He held out his hands slowly. They were empty.

"Anyway," Anna said, "get documentation."

At the last moment, she said, "Let's stick together. No groups of two. No harm at least humoring him, right?"

Off Screen.

"We need to get a message to Antoine and Camden," Anna said.

"Wait," I interjected.

I looked around at the four of us. Our statuses on the red wallpaper had changed. I could still see all of the usual information, but there was something extra. It was the same for all four of us. It was all bad news. We were all labeled as monsters.

STRAGGLER	
Tropes	
UNDETECTABLE	This creature warps the minds of its victims so that they will not notice that it does not belong, despite all the evidence.

BY THE BOOK	This villain can be defeated by properly understanding its lore and following its rules.
FATE WORSE THAN DEATH	This creature does not want to kill its victims, though in the end they will wish it had. Victims are Written Off instead of killed.
NON-COMBATANT	This villain cannot be attacked on-screen until it attacks the player or is otherwise identified as hostile. Attacking it will not be effective, nor will it change the story. It will cause the player to go off-screen for a time.
WHICH ONE DO I SHOOT?	Players will not be able to differentiate this creature from other players through the mere use of observation, insight tropes, or common sense. However, these combined with clever plans and an understanding of lore may suffice.
MARKED EXITS ONLY	The players will not be able to escape the setting except by following the rules.
BLOODLESS	First and Second Blood need not involve injury or death in this storyline.
IT'S ALL RIDING ON THIS!	The players will win or lose at the Finale. They cannot be completely defeated until then.

We were in big trouble. These rules meant that any of us could be a monster. I had counted four of us. I had the memory of doing it.

Didn't I?

CHAPTER TWELVE

THE RULES OF THE FOREST

W hat is happening?" Kimberly asked. "Why does the red wallpaper say that I'm a monster?"

She started to back away from us.

"It says that we all are," Anna said. She looked at me. "Do you know what's going on?"

I looked from Anna to Tony to Kimberly. "Yeah. It messes with our minds so that it blends in."

I explained all of the tropes to them as best I could. Truthfully, the entire experience was incredibly difficult to describe. I had known Anna since we were kids, and yet, looking at her . . . I didn't know for sure if she was an ally. Somehow, my mind just couldn't process simple logic.

Kimberly and Tony I hadn't known for as long. Either of them could be a Straggler, whatever that was, and I would have no idea.

It was like I was adding all of the evidence up, but when it came time to make a conclusion, nothing appeared on the other side of the equation.

On-screen.

"We should leave," Tony said. His voice cracked and he coughed hard.

Anna shook her head. "We can't leave until we find evidence of what happened to these people. We're reporters first and foremost. We have a duty to find the truth."

"I don't know," Kimberly said. "With what that guy was saying about there being something dangerous about the forest, I agree with Tony. We should just go."

"We came here to do a job. We should at least investigate before giving up, right?" Anna said.

We had to move forward. We couldn't just leave, but we also had to play our characters and had no idea what was going on.

"Let's just make it quick," I said. "We're going to feel like real idiots if someone else cracks this story because we got afraid of some ghost story."

Kimberly and Anna nodded their heads. Tony seemed more hesitant.

"Hide," Anna said.

The lawyers were walking back down the path straight toward us. Our characters wouldn't want to be seen. Arguably, we might want to interview the lawyers, but that didn't fit the scene as well. We would have to let Antoine and Camden take care of themselves until we could get a chance to talk to them off-screen.

We ducked down behind some bushes to let them pass. As they went by, Tony stood up and went right after them. He walked with a slight limp, but he was moving as fast as he could, trying to catch up.

"Tony, get back here," I hissed as he left. He didn't listen to me.

"What is he doing?" Kimberly asked.

"I have no idea. He's an idiot," I said.

"I guess he's going that way," Anna said as the lawyers and Tony disappeared in the distance. They didn't seem to react much at all to his arrival; perhaps that was a viable choice for his character to make.

"Now we have to stick together, the three of us. We need to look around this house and see if we can find evidence of the missing hikers or the woman. On the off chance that there's not a supernatural entity involved," she said with hefty sarcasm, "we're going to have to actually find out what happened to these people."

We got closer to the house. As we did, we saw Old Man Akers standing at the back of his pickup truck. There was a dirt road that led out of the forest in a different direction than the one we had come from. He was fiddling with something in the back of his truck. As we got closer, I was able to tell that he had shovels, a pickaxe, and similar tools tucked into a storage compartment in the bed of his truck. He was closing it up as we arrived.

"This way," Anna said.

She directed us around to the left in the opposite direction than Akers was facing. As we circled the property, we crept past a woodshed filled with firewood, a propane tank, and a small generator under a tarp. Nothing useful.

As we moved closer to the actual house—a small log cabin that looked like it could have been built a hundred years ago—we noticed something.

Leaning up against the side of the cabin were two hiking backpacks.

"Look," Anna said.

"Should we take a picture?" Kimberly asked. "For evidence?"

Anna nodded. That was what our characters would do. Why else would we have cameras?

Kimberly held up her camera and snapped a photo. The camera let loose a flash and a loud mechanical noise as a photograph began poking out of the front of the device.

"Shoot," Kimberly said under her breath. "Do you think he heard that?"

Anna waved for us to get closer to the backpacks. "If he did, then we only have a few seconds."

We ran up to the side of the house. Anna grabbed one of the hiking packs and I grabbed the other.

"Go," she said. We ran back out into the forest, just out of view of any prying eyes.

Unfortunately, none of our characters had thought to bring a flashlight. We started rifling through the backpacks looking for some clue as to who they might have belonged to. As I sunk my hand into one, I found a small square leather object. A wallet.

"What were the names of the hikers?" I asked.

Anna pulled out the notebook that she had started the storyline with. She flipped through the pages, trying to read them by a ray of moonlight.

"Here it is," she said. "Edgar and Norman Barns. Brothers."

"Edgar Barns," I said, holding up a Carousel driver's license.

"Maybe it wasn't monsters after all," Anna said with a smile.

Of course, it probably was monsters. But this would be a great clue to help move the story forward.

Footsteps. A crunching twig.

Someone was walking toward us from the direction of the house.

"Hello," Old Man Akers said loudly. "I know you're out there. You had better not be those damn lawyers. If you are among the living and you would like to stay that way, show yourself."

"Dammit," I said.

"Leave the packs," Anna said quietly.

She stood up and raised her hands. "Don't shoot," she said. "We're just student reporters from U of C. Don't shoot."

"Come out here," Akers said. "I'm not going to shoot you."

"We're coming out," she answered.

We stood up and slowly walked out from behind the bush.

"What are a bunch of kids doing out here this time of night? Don't you know what this place is?"

"We're here looking for some missing people. That's all."

Akers rolled his eyes and took a deep breath. It was much the same as he had done around the campfire for the frame story.

"Well, come on out here and I'll talk to you, but don't be sneaking around my property," he said.

We did as he asked.

"You kids are in way more trouble than you realize being out here. Just had to run off a few lawyers for the same thing. But with the lawyers, I'm not so concerned. Come on around front."

We followed him around the side of the house to where the large lantern on the back of his tailgate was set up.

"So, ask your questions," Akers said.

Anna took out her notebook. "We're here investigating three missing people. We think the police missed something."

Akers nodded in understanding. "Police chief doesn't send anybody into the forest. He understands. Might be the only person around here who does."

"Understands?" Anna asked.

Akers nodded. "Understands that these woods are not to be entered by settlers."

Anna took a moment to think about what he had said. "We're just looking for three people. Have you seen anyone around here? Two hikers, Edgar and Norman Barns"—she took out her notebook and started flipping through the pages again until she found what she was looking for; she looked at it for a moment, almost as if she thought she had read it wrong—"and one woman who was in a traffic accident nearby, Dina Cano. She's been missing about a week."

Dina was in an accident near here? No wonder we hadn't seen her yet. We needed to find her and explain things. She must have been confused, having arrived alone.

"Never heard of them," Akers said, "though I suppose you saw those hiking packs that I found in the forest. You can look through those to see if they give you any clues. Truth be told I think you're too late. The Stragglers have got them by now."

"The Stragglers?" Anna asked.

"The Stragglers. They wander through the woods looking for newcomers to pass on their curse. Same creatures that you need to be worried about if you would ever like to make it out of here."

Anna, Kimberly, and I exchanged glances.

"Is that what you were talking about with those people earlier?" Kimberly asked.

Akers smirked. "Heard that, did you? Thought I would try to warn them. I ought to try to warn you too."

"Are we in danger?" Anna asked. She was entertaining his story to see what he would say. She was playing her character as not being superstitious.

Akers nodded his head. "May even be too late."

"Can you tell us about them?" Anna asked.

"Sure can," he said.

"Do you mind if I write this down?" Anna asked.

"Do whatever you like, just pay attention. If you want to survive, you've got to learn the rules. No one wants to learn the rules, not until it's too late. I suppose the best way to tell you about the Stragglers is to start from the beginning.

"It started here hundreds of years ago, back before the town even existed. The people that lived here first, the originals, they understood this forest and this land. They respected it. They knew that it was different, that it was charmed. They never took anything from it, not timber, not flora, not fauna—not without asking for permission first.

"They lived that way for many generations. But then the settlers came. The locals tried to warn them, to tell them to respect the forest. At first, it seemed like the settlers would listen. The original inhabitants even taught them how to ask for permission to enter the forest. The forest granted them permission, only allowing five or fewer to enter at a time and only to take what they could carry, to be responsible and respectful.

"It lasted that way for a year or two, but then the settlement grew. The settlers got greedy. What they saw in the forest were vast resources. One year, in the spring, they sent in twenty workers to gather timber. With them, they sent in a team of oxen that could haul entire trees out of the forest. In doing this they broke their promise to the forest. So, after they'd worked a day, they went to leave. Only five made it out. The rest were stuck to wait in the forest until they could find someone to replace them.

"And so it goes that that curse has become the law of the land. There is no peace between the settlers and the forest anymore. Any who enter will be beset by the Stragglers, those that did not make it out of the forest. They look to find someone to take their place, to take their curse. Over the centuries most of them have succeeded. However many enter will leave, though the Stragglers may be among them."

Anna chewed on her bottom lip. "Are you saying that's what happened to the missing people? That they got lost in the forest and became Stragglers?"

Old Man Akers shook his head. "There are a lot of things that could happen to them around here. But that's a likely choice. You never know—months from now, a year, a decade, your missing people might just come wandering out of the woods one day having found someone to replace them. In fact, you may be the very ones to replace them yourselves."

He smirked.

"Well, I hope not," Anna said. "So, if someone comes out of the forest and wants to join our group, we shouldn't allow them to, right?"

Akers laughed. "Won't be that easy. You won't know a Straggler when you see one. Everyone I tell this to doesn't believe me, but I hope you will. To you, it will just seem like a person who's a part of your group. You won't be able to tell them from anyone else. The forest alters your mind. In fact, wouldn't be surprised if someone in your group right now is already one of them."

Who? Anna? Kimberly? According to their tropes, you wouldn't even be able to tell them apart through common sense. What other way could there be?

"So that's the rule, huh? If they attack us, how do we kill them? Monsters have to have weaknesses, right? How do we keep ourselves safe?" I asked. I may have laid on the mocking tone a little too thick. Akers didn't seem to notice.

"Weapons won't offer them an escape from their curse, I'm afraid. I understand your temptation to think of them as monsters, but I would encourage you to think bigger than that. Whatever they are, they're trapped here, bound by ancient magic. It's hardly fair to judge them by it. They are what they were when they entered. These Stragglers were people once. They may well be people again one day.

"I've seen it happen many a time. In fact, nearly sixty years ago one of the original settlers made it out of the forest after centuries of wandering. His mind was mostly gone but you could see the relief on his face, finally being free.

"He ran from the forest, ran until his feet bled. Didn't take long. He had been walking for so many years that even being free of the curse wasn't enough to return him to perfect health. Of course, the man that replaced him is still there. I see him from time to time. When they first get there, you can tell they have a hesitance to pass their curse on to someone else, but as time goes by, they get over that."

Anna was writing this down diligently in her notebook. "If you don't mind me asking, why do you think you haven't been cursed?"

Old Man Akers chuckled. "I have permission to be here. The entities that roam this forest and the land around it leave me alone. Those that don't, I know how to take care of."

"You're saying we're screwed?" I asked with a smirk.

Old Man Akers chuckled again.

I continued.

"You say they have to wait for someone to come as a replacement. Haven't we already replaced them?" I asked, trying to poke holes and fill out my understanding. "Couldn't they just leave as soon as we showed up?"

He shook his head. "Not quite. Shaking the curse isn't that easy."

He grabbed his lantern off the bed of his truck and started walking back toward his cabin.

"They've only got two ways of getting out of here. They either need to pass their curse onto you directly after separating you from your group and getting you alone, or they need you to lead them out while leaving their replacement behind. Otherwise, they can wander in circles until kingdom come and they won't so much as find the tree line."

So, they had to interact with us to get out. If one of them managed to worm their way into our group, they could head out of the forest with Tony, Anna, and Kimberly, leaving me behind to wander.

"What if the lawyers show them the way out?" Anna asked. "Are we trapped?"

"You just worry about you. Let the lawyers worry about the lawyers. They can only leave with the amount they entered with, same as you."

That meant that even though we were in the forest at the same time as the lawyers, we didn't count as being in the same group.

"Shit," I said. "Tony."

Anna looked at me curiously, but then I could see that she got it.

"We need to go now," she said.

Tony was a part of our group. If he left the forest, he could bring three Stragglers with him, leaving us as replacements.

We thanked Akers and then left.

We had to hurry.

I looked at the Plot Cycle. First Blood had just been struck. In this story, it didn't mean literal death or injury, but something bad must have happened. Hopefully, it hadn't happened to us.

CHAPTER THIRTEEN

THE CONTRADICTIONS

We weren't a mile down the trail before we ran into the lawyers. It's not that they had been taking their sweet time—no, it's that they were walking back toward the cabin.

Antoine and Camden gave us a flash of acknowledgment when they saw us. They were quick to drop it, though. They couldn't be sure if we were really their friends.

The other seven lawyers didn't acknowledge us.

Even Tony didn't seem happy to see us.

"Was this the way to the exit?" Antoine asked. "We got turned around somewhere. Somehow."

That didn't seem possible. It was a pretty straightforward trail back to the parking lot. Literally, it was a straight trail—how had they managed to get turned around?

Unless . . .

Unless they had a Straggler with them. They could only leave with the amount that they had come in with. If they had a Straggler, they would have too many people and they would never find the exit. But which one didn't belong?

The lawyers had the strangest looks on their faces. Like they were angry or sad. One of them, a man wearing a plaid shirt and a yellow construction vest, was silently crying. These lawyers certainly were acting funny. They didn't seem to like each other much either. They refused to stand close to each other.

I noticed that one was missing.

"Didn't you have another lawyer with you?" I asked. "A woman?"

Antoine nodded. "We had two. Dina and Roberta. They got mad and left together after we got lost."

They had found Dina . . . I hoped that she was okay.

It was strange. He had just called Dina a lawyer. Wasn't Dina one of the missing people from Anna's notes? How could that be possible . . . Unless—

"Did you all hear what that guy in the cabin was talking about?" Camden asked. "Crazy stuff. Did you talk to him?"

We didn't say anything at first. Was Camden a Straggler looking for information? Did Stragglers even need information?

"We talked to him," Anna said. "Learned a few things."

She took her notebook out of her pocket. "I wrote it all down here."

They made eye contact for a moment. Neither fully trusted the other. Slowly, Anna held the notebook out for Camden.

He was just as slow to grab for it. He flipped through it for ten or fifteen seconds before handing it back.

"Interesting stuff," he said. "Very interesting."

If Camden was who I thought he was, then he now knew everything. Anna had taken notes from Old Man Akers's story. Between Camden's Eureka and Photographic Memory tropes, he would know almost everything we did.

Or was he just playing the part in hopes of tricking one of us into taking his place in the forest?

Who knew?

There were other things we didn't know. Things like how to tell Stragglers from non-Stragglers. Akers made it out like it was possible, but as I gazed around the group in the moonlight, I was lost. Truly lost.

This was a mind teaser. There had to be some way that we could use clever planning and lore knowledge to tell everyone apart. We needed to figure it out quickly too. There were around fifteen Stragglers out there in the forest—enough to replace every single one of us.

"Tony missed the whole conversation," Anna said. "Ran off before we even met the guy."

"Sorry," Tony said. "I just really wanted to leave."

"Wait," Antoine said. "How do you know Tony?"

"He goes to school with us," Kimberly answered.

Camden and Antoine looked at each other. Camden started to back away from Tony.

"Tony is a member of our law firm. He came here with us," Camden said.

"No," Tony said. "Wait."

Camden's look of confusion turned to one of horror. At first, I was confused too but then I managed to follow the same logical trail that he had.

The scales fell from my eyes.

"No, that can't be," Anna said.

She must have figured it out too.

Tony had to be a Straggler. I couldn't believe it. I thought back to everything we had been through. We both worked on the school paper. Didn't we? Did I?

Was it possible Camden and Antoine were lying? It was like half my brain was missing. I was all questions and no answers.

What I knew was that Tony was my friend from school. Yet he was apparently a lawyer who was hired by the city. Both could not be true.

The forest tricks you into thinking that Stragglers belong. Tony had attempted to join two different groups, so he had two different backstories. The contradiction was enough to wake us up to his true nature.

He was cursed.

He was a Straggler.

This must have been how we were supposed to figure out who the Stragglers were. You learn a piece of their lore—in this case, the fact that the forest tricks you into thinking you know them—and then you find contradictions. You had to find some indirect way of figuring out who they were.

"No, please let me explain," Tony said. He was trying to think. He closed his eyes and breathed rapidly, willing his addled mind to come up with an explanation. "Just a second."

He began to cry.

As I looked at him, I suddenly realized how ragged and ghoulish he looked. He had been out here for a long time from the look of it. I had noticed and yet . . . I had never really *seen* him.

"Please. Please," he said. "I can't stay here any longer. Please."

Everyone started to back away from him. The group of lawyers looked particularly upset. He dropped to his knees.

"Just let me go. I promise I'll bring someone back for you. I won't be long. Please."

"How is that possible?" Kimberly asked. "How can he . . ."

She was having the same problem that I was. Now it was obvious that Tony was a Straggler, a cursed being forced to walk endlessly for the sin of having entered this forest. And yet, Tony was my friend. I knew him. We had come here together.

Or so I thought.

"We need to split up," one of the lawyers said. "We should all just run out of the forest. There could be more of them."

I was waiting for someone to suggest that. Akers had made it seem like splitting up was a viable option, but truthfully, it was just a good way to leave someone behind.

"No!" Camden said. "We don't want to leave the forest. Not yet. Not until we're sure that there are no Stragglers with us. They can only leave with us if we stay together. We need to head back to the cabin. That's the only landmark we have all been to. As long as we stay together and don't try to get out of the forest, they can't take our place."

"That makes no sense," one of the lawyers said through chapped lips. "We were just there. You're just trying to get us to go deeper into the forest."

He was a tall man named Nicholas. He wore a threadbare long-sleeve shirt and a climbing harness. As he spoke, he moved his fingers through his mess of hair.

"Please!" Tony yelled. "This isn't fair!"

He jumped to his feet and approached Kimberly, who screamed as he got close.

"Please," he said. "We can figure something out. Don't scream."

She backed away.

Antoine started to move to protect her, but at the last moment, it looked like the fear that she might be a Straggler left him staring at her in confusion.

"Let's not resort to violence here," Anna said, looking at me and Antoine expectantly.

I paused, confused at what she was looking at me for.

Then I realized: Let's Not Fight was one of her tropes. If she broke up a dispute between two players, all involved would get a buff.

That meant she could tell who the players were simply by trying to activate her trope. If the people she was talking to were players, it would work. If not, at least one of them was a Straggler. It would probably also prove she was a player.

I imagine it would have worked too. If we'd had time to test it out.

Tony had finished crying. He got up from his knees and walked toward me. Of course he picked me. I had the lowest Plot Armor. He grabbed onto my arm and started pulling me away from the group.

"Let's go," he said. "Let's get out of here."

I struggled against him as he pulled me. I had to assume that our Mettle scores were tied because I was making no progress.

I started pulling against him.

The lawyer, Nicholas, came to my aid. He grabbed onto my arm and pulled me away from Tony.

"Get out of here," he said to Tony. "Get back."

I backed away into the darkness. I needed to find my way back to my friends. I looked over in their direction. Most of the lawyers had split as soon as Tony started getting aggressive. Those idiots were doomed. To my left and right, figures began coming into view. It was the lawyers, or maybe it was someone new. Other students from U of C?

"Riley, come here," Anna called.

"Yeah, Riley," a voice called out from the darkness. "Come this way. We'll go together."

All attention was on me. Many of them were saying my name—Anna, Camden, Nicholas, the other lawyers, and even Tony.

But who could I trust?

What group had I come in with? Anna, Kimberly, Tony, Austin, Pietro, and Jaime, right? No, that wasn't right. Tony was a Straggler. But if he was a Straggler, maybe Jaime or Kimberly was too. How could I tell? If I joined a group and walked out with them, could I be leaving my friends behind?

I had to make a decision quickly. They were all drawing in toward me.

"This is a prank, isn't it?" I said loudly, putting my hood up. "Well, you guys have had your last laugh at my expense. I'm going back to the cabin. If any of you wants to stop playing this game, come with me."

I put on my headphones and said loudly, "Whenever you want to stop being jerks, I'll talk to you."

I tried to sound like I was over it, like I was not willing to play along anymore, like I thought everyone was my friend and that Stragglers were just make-believe. A prank.

That was what I needed for my plan. I couldn't just run away for it to work—I had to pretend I didn't think I was in danger. I left the group and walked briskly into the woods. When I was a few hundred feet away, the Plot Cycle closed in on Second Blood.

I knew splitting up was a bad idea. I just had to trust that my friends, whoever my real friends were, would be able to figure things out without me for a while.

I needed to use Oblivious Bystander.

Unfortunately, no matter how high my Moxie was, Oblivious Bystander would not work in a Chase Scene that my character was aware of.

My character had to be, well, oblivious.

When using the bystander trope, my own perception was unimportant. All that mattered was the audience. If the audience knew who the Stragglers were, then watching one sneak up on me would create tension.

So, theoretically, if someone approached me and Oblivious Bystander activated, I could safely assume that they were a Straggler. The opposite might have also been true. If someone could approach me without activating the trope, then they must not be a Straggler. That was how I could beat the curse.

I had to design a test. The question was, how did I convincingly pretend to be oblivious? I had just been accosted by at least one Straggler. I had my new pair of headphones and the Walkman. How realistic was it for me to use that right now?

I would play the skeptic. Horror movies loved to indulge the skeptic, if only so they could be brought kicking and screaming into reality. I would play into the Stragglers' schtick and pretend I didn't know anything was wrong, pretend I thought it was all a prank. If my character thought the Stragglers were just his friends messing with him, Oblivious Bystander would activate.

That plan was borderline at best, but I had prepared for this. I had been stacking points into Moxie for edge cases just like this. I had to hope that it would be enough.

I was freaked out, so my character was too. I had to hope I had portrayed his skepticism well enough, even with everything I had already done before. I couldn't even remember which scenes had been on-screen or off-screen. I had to hope I hadn't messed things up too bad.

I went off-screen for thirty seconds or so. Then I was back on-screen. It was time.

I bent over, breathed in deeply, and pushed play on the Walkman. The volume was down next to nothing. I took deep breaths and let myself calm down. I even hummed to the music.

That would have to be enough. My Moxie was high. I had invested heavily in it. That should be enough to make up for the *slightly* unrealistic timing of my moonlight serenade.

I had to hope I didn't get approached while I was getting things working. I started walking through the forest in the direction of the cabin.

Within a few minutes, a shadowy figure was trailing me. I didn't pay them any mind. I became aware that I was on-screen and in a Chase Scene. I continued to walk like I hadn't noticed anything at all. The figure followed but never came close.

This was so much easier than humming to myself to try to drown out noise.

I got a good enough look at him in my peripheral vision that I could see his name was Thadeus. He was dressed in a ripped old cotton shirt. He was barefoot.

The more time went on, the surer I was that Thadeus was a Straggler. He had clearly activated Oblivious Bystander.

He followed me for a time. When I went off-screen, he left, off to find someone else. That was unusual. He should have continued following me because of my low Plot Armor. I wasn't going to question it. Success was success. I actually smiled to myself like an idiot.

Of course, then I was back on-screen.

Another figure appeared behind me. It was Pietro, my friend from school. Except he must not have been—Oblivious Bystander had activated. He followed me but only got close enough to let the camera see. He too faded into the distance with time.

Then there was another.

And another.

And another.

How many of those lawyers had been Stragglers?

How many fellow students were, for that matter?

I soldiered on.

"Dina?" a voice cried in the distance. "Where did you go?"

It was Roberta, one of the NPC lawyers. I zigzagged to keep her out of my eyeline.

"Dina, why would you do this? We were friends. Please, I'm scared. I want to go home."

My character didn't react. I was listening to music, after all.

"Din—" she cried out. She appeared to notice me. She grew quiet.

It was like I could see Roberta slowly realize what was happening as soon as she saw me. She started to follow. Of course, as I suspected, she was cursed. If I had to guess, she had been cursed by none other than Dina.

Dina had been a car crash survivor in the woods for a week. That was her role. Somehow, she had convinced some of the others that she was a lawyer. The only way that could happen was if she was a Straggler.

Dina had started the storyline as cursed but was probably already out of the forest now. Cutthroat, even if Roberta was just an NPC.

Roberta, like all of the other Stragglers, eventually gave up. There was really no point in chasing me once I knew. It wouldn't be cinematic. I would just run from a Straggler. They needed someone who they could prey upon.

I smiled to myself as I stepped out of the thick part of the woods and into the space where the cabin sat.

I froze.

I had come face to face with Kimberly. I hadn't seen her at first because the forest was so thick. She was standing next to Old Man Akers's truck, her slender arm reaching through the tiniest crack in his driver's side window, attempting to grab onto the lock.

She looked at me. I looked at her.

Was she a Straggler?

I had no idea. I thought I knew her, but I couldn't trust my memory. After all, I thought I knew Tony.

I turned and ran.

CHAPTER FOURTEEN

THE LAST TRUCK OUT

I circled back around to the backside of the cabin. I took a long path. There was no sign of anyone, player or Straggler. The cabin lights were off, and the windows were shuttered. Old Man Akers was probably inside waiting out the horror that was going on in his backyard.

I heard voices on the other side of the cabin.

I slowly made my way around, making sure to keep away from clearings where I could be easily seen.

"Let's just leave," a man's voice said.

"It would be faster if we drove," a woman said. It was Kimberly. She was still there.

"We don't have the keys. Let's just walk down the road. We'll be out of here in thirty minutes. It'll all be over," another man said.

"No, it'll be fine," Kimberly said. "I had to write an article on car thefts on campus. I learned how to hotwire a truck just like this one. Won't take more than a second."

She had just used Convenient Backstory.

I heard the sound of the pickup truck's door opening and quickly shutting, followed by the clunky *thunk* of an old-fashioned manual car door lock.

I moved around until I could get a view of what was happening.

Kimberly sat in the cab of the truck. She was fiddling with something under the dash. Even from a distance, I could see that she was nervous, scared. I truly wanted to believe that she was my friend, that she had actually entered the forest with me, but my mind wouldn't help me find that conclusion.

I was a distance behind the truck, looking at her through the back window. I remembered seeing shovels and other tools in a compartment in the back of the truck. If I could only get over there, I could grab one.

But could I even use it? Stragglers couldn't be attacked until they attacked you. Not a bad way to test for a Straggler, if a little risky.

Two men were with her. Had they been there before?

I didn't get a good look.

I recognized one of them; I had seen his face on his driver's license. It was Edgar Barns, one of the missing hikers. I suspected that meant the other man was his brother. I looked at their names on the red wallpaper to confirm my suspicions.

The Barns brothers stood outside the truck. Edgar was by the driver's side door and Norman was by the passenger side. It was crazy to think that they had managed to survive in the forest for so long without their packs.

Did they know about the Stragglers?

"What's taking so long?" Edgar asked.

Kimberly cleared her throat and said, "I'm just trying to loosen this panel so I can start the truck. It'll only take a minute."

Edgar moved his hand to the door handle. "Just let me in. Let me try."

Kimberly responded with a note of fear in her voice, "I got it. It'll be done soon."

"We don't have to take the truck," Norman said. "We can just walk. If we follow this dirt road, it can't be more than a couple of miles until we're free and clear."

Kimberly stopped fiddling with the panel under the dash. "You know what? I think I want to go find Anna."

"We don't need Anna," Edgar said. "We need to get out of here just the three of us."

They started to pull the handles on the doors, trying to force their way into the truck.

"We really just need to leave," Norman said. "Please."

I couldn't see Kimberly's face, but she sounded like she was . . . I couldn't put my finger on it; the magic of the forest prevented me. If I had to guess, she might have sounded confused, maybe even scared, but with my addled mind, I was having difficulty putting that together.

Was one of them a Straggler? Were they all Stragglers? In my mind, it felt possible that none of them were and they were just all so afraid that they were acting strange.

"I would just really like to go," Kimberly said. "Will you . . . will you let me go?"

There was a brief silence.

As if it was against their will, the brothers said one after the other, "No."

Suddenly, it was like a shroud had been lifted. I saw before me two Stragglers attempting to persuade Kimberly to leave the forest with them.

They had unwillingly revealed themselves.

Kimberly had a trope called A Hopeless Plea. It forced captors into revealing whether they would release her. She'd gotten it during the Astralist storyline. Truthfully, I couldn't think of a good use case for such a trope; it seemed mostly like it was designed to mock her.

But she had found a way to make it useful. How much of this had been her plan? Putting herself in a position where the two men would trap her so that she could get them to reveal themselves. Logically, the trope would only work on the Stragglers. By revealing that they would not release her, they had outed themselves and simultaneously exonerated Kimberly.

I could see all three of them clearly now. Kimberly was my friend. The Barns brothers were Stragglers.

Kimberly moved her hands under the dash. The truck roared to life.

From the other side of the clearing, three figures emerged: Anna, Camden, and Nicholas.

Anna was holding one of the shovels from the back of the truck. The three of them jumped into the back, pushing the Barns brothers as they went. The brothers tried to get in with them, but they were pushed away.

Had this all been a trap to weed out some Stragglers?

I looked at the Plot Cycle. Not only was this likely a trap, but it was also the final battle. I had missed it dodging Stragglers in the forest.

Kimberly put the truck into gear and backed up, away from the Stragglers. She was moving toward me, backing the truck in a circle so that she could turn around. The others hunkered down in the bed of the truck.

Any second, they were about to drive down that dirt road and leave me behind.

I ran after them. I yelled, but the roar of the truck must have masked my scream. I was in trouble. I needed some way of signaling them. I considered throwing my Walkman at them. I reached into my pocket and found the camera.

In a last-ditch effort to get their attention, I started firing off flashes. The camera was doing its best to keep up.

Flash.

Flash.

Flash.

Kimberly slammed the brakes.

I ran up to the back of the truck and grabbed onto the tailgate. No sooner were my feet off the ground than the truck took off again.

I pulled myself into the back.

"You had better be real," Anna said.

We drove until we were out of the forest. The Plot Cycle switched to The End. Suddenly, we were back in front of a campfire. Anna, Kimberly, Camden, Dina, and I had all made it.

Antoine was gone.

I tried to figure out how that had happened. My mind was clear now that we were out of the forest. Anna, Kimberly, and I had escaped together. We all made it.

Dina had been a Straggler and had been replaced by Roberta the NPC lawyer. She made it.

But Camden and Antoine had a group of three as well with Roberta. Roberta was replaced by Dina. Antoine must have been replaced by that man in the climbing gear who, surprisingly, was not actually a lawyer.

Dammit.

I looked around at my friends. They were all coming to the same realization. We had left him behind. Kimberly was crying.

"That doesn't sound that scary," one of the teenage NPCs said after Old Man Akers finished his story.

"You don't think so?" Akers said. "Well, if you want scary, I think we have time for another story. This one takes place nearly ten years ago," Old Man Akers said. "Back when a local investment firm funded a huge operation to reopen the mine on the southeast side of the property. They would soon figure out why it had been closed in the first place."

I was staring at the place Antoine had been sitting. His baseball bat was still there. The realization dawned on me that we would have to play through each story minus the players we lost along the way. This one might end up being more complicated than I originally thought.

Suddenly, I was in the very back seat of an SUV. These were back-to-back.

I looked around.

Anna and Camden were in the middle seat. Kimberly was up front. Driving was a man in his early thirties. He had well-groomed brown hair and a cocky smile. He was wearing a brand-new thick button-up shirt, the kind you might see on a blue-collar worker, but this guy didn't come across as blue-collar; his hands were well manicured.

I could tell because his left hand was on the steering wheel and his right hand, on the center console, was intertwined with Kimberly's.

She looked shocked to find herself holding hands with him, but she didn't say anything. She looked back at us, trying to maintain her composure. She had been crying around the campfire. Now, she had a bright face full of makeup.

The thing is, I recognized the guy driving.

It was Nicholas.

I had only seen him twice and only for a brief moment each time. Nicholas was the Straggler that had replaced Antoine in the forest, leaving him trapped there. This story was set eight or nine years before that story, though.

"You guys feeling lucky?" Nicholas asked.

We all said yes, though we weren't quite sure what getting lucky would mean for us that day.

I looked around at each of my friends to see what our roles were in that story. Kimberly was Nicholas's fiancée and the daughter of the main investor and partner in Nicholas's mining operation. Camden was his lead geologist and mine engineer, whose research had led the firm to pursue the endeavor. Anna and I were Nicholas's employees.

Except we weren't. We were really working for a group called STP, or "Stop the Poison," an environmentalist organization protesting the dig site on Akers's property. We were undercover, trying to get proof that Nicholas's company was using dangerous and polluting extraction methods in their mining operations.

There were some layers to this one.

"I can almost taste it. Gold, amethyst, sapphire. The find of a lifetime," Nicholas said.

Camden, who was flipping through a thick folder filled with scientific graphs and walls of text, said, "I'll remind you that a find of this . . . abundance is one that should be taken with a grain of salt."

Nicholas shook his head. "You told me that, but I just can't imagine that Ehbert Mining would fabricate all of their reports."

Camden looked like he had more to say but held his tongue.

"You can confirm their readings when we get there. There is no way they would lie about the property. Not when they are dealing with someone as notoriously litigious as my father."

"Will do," Camden said. He looked back at me and gave me an exasperated look.

"Look, honey," Nicholas said. "The local baristas got here before we did."

At first I wasn't sure what he was talking about. However, as we pulled up onto Akers's property, we passed a dozen or so protesters holding signs. They said things like "There Is No Safe Mining" and "Save the Animal Refuge."

The protesters had blocked off the entrance to the property.

"You capitalist pigs are going to poison the drinking water of dozens of protected species. Find it in your heart to change," a woman yelled.

I recognized the voice. I shifted so that I could get a better look at who it was that was screaming at us.

It was Dina. She wore a button on her shirt with the letters STP. She was part of the same organization that Anna and I were, though she was obviously not undercover.

An egg hit the windshield of Nicholas's SUV.

"Those motherfuckers," he said.

"Here, let me wash it off for you," one of the protesters, an older man with long hair, said. He splashed a bucketful of dirty, scummy water onto the windshield. "This was taken from near your mine down in Clearlake. You expect to do the same thing to an animal sanctuary?"

"A sanctuary?" Kimberly asked.

Camden flipped through his folder. "There's a designated animal refuge to the east. That's what all these environmentalists are concerned about."

"Pfft," Nicholas muttered.

An animal refuge to the east, a haunted forest full of Stragglers to the west. This mine was right in the middle of all the action.

Eventually, we were able to make it through the gate and onto the property. The mine was at the back, far past where we had sat around the campfire and to the right of the forest where Old Man Akers's cabin was.

When we got there, there were already a dozen or so work trucks and a multitude of people running around getting things ready. There were lots of workers ready to get into the mines as soon as they were opened up.

As we drove closer, we headed downhill further and further until, eventually, we got to the place where the mine's entrance had been carved out of the earth. There was no mountain above it as I had always pictured mines to have. It was just dug down into the earth. The rocks that the cavern entrance was carved into were solemn and gray. Old support beams were being replaced with newer struts of both metal and wood around the entrance.

As we got out of the SUV, Nicholas yelled, "Why am I standing in mud?"

A worker with a white hard hat, one of the higher men on the totem pole, I assumed, approached and said, "Just got the draining system online. Things got a little wet. It rained a lot last week."

"Is the mine flooded?" Nicholas asked. He had clearly not thought far enough ahead to consider this possibility.

"The mine is sealed," Camden said. "Unless groundwater seeped in at a higher rate than usual, the inside of the mine should be dry, mostly. This assumes the maps you gave me are accurate. If not, we can drain it, though the budget and schedule will take a big hit. There are more details in the report."

Nicholas looked annoyed at this comment.

As we approached the mine, we stopped off at a truck and put on hard hats and bright neon vests. I could see how excited Nicholas was to get into the mine.

He would have to wait. Old Man Akers walked over to us and approached Nicholas.

"Please reconsider," Akers said. "You do not know what you're getting yourself into. What lies beneath the surface on this land ought to stay there."

Nicholas was having none of it. "Well, it's not going to. I own it."

He pulled out a folded stack of papers. They were longer than ordinary paper and far more ornate.

"I've told you this a hundred times. I have the mineral rights to this land for the next"—he unfolded the paper and read through it—"ninety-three years out of a 150-year leasehold. What's in this mine is not yours to keep."

Old Man Akers shook his head in disappointment. "The mine was sealed for a reason."

"Yes," Nicholas said. "And it's being opened for a better one."

"I cannot help you," Akers said.

That wasn't strictly true. He could tell us what was in the mine, but that didn't seem to be his modus operandi.

Akers turned tail to leave, but before he did, he looked at me, Anna, and Camden. "How much is he paying you to follow him to your doom?"

He didn't stick around for a response.

Off Screen.

Nicholas walked around ordering people to do this and that. He didn't seem entirely too knowledgeable about the process or the operation, but you could tell that he really liked being in charge.

My friends gathered around to get some information. I explained to them all of their roles.

"That explains this," Anna said, retrieving a small, discreet film camera from her pocket. "I was wondering why I needed it."

I checked my pocket. I had one too. They were small cameras—nothing but a button and a flash bulb, half the ordinary size.

"Any tropes?" Camden asked.

"Not that I can find," I said. "Whatever the monster is here, it must be inside the mines."

"My report says that this mine makes no sense," Camden said. "It says that this whole thing is impossible. Dozens of different types of jewels were reported along different seams inside the mine. My official recommendation was that they shouldn't pursue this operation. Nicholas and his father were the ones that pushed it through. I have some documentation on that."

He held up the folder containing all of his character's scientific information. "I think there's something more going on with them. Keep your eyes peeled."

"Where is his father?" Anna asked.

We all shrugged.

"Well, maybe that's something that his fiancée should ask him," I suggested, looking over at Kimberly.

Kimberly rolled her eyes. "I don't even know if my tropes will work on him," she said. "Get a Room and Pregnancy Reveal both require me to have a romantic interest. Can I use an NPC for that? If I do, do I have to pick that one?"

Truthfully, I wasn't sure whether they would work. I had always pictured her using those on fellow players. "It's worth trying," I said. "The audience shouldn't know the difference."

Kimberly got quiet for a moment. "He's the one who . . . left Antoine in the forest, right?"

Anna nodded her head.

"I didn't even realize," Camden said.

"Just try to find out what you can," Anna said. "I understand if you don't feel comfortable."

Kimberly nodded.

"It looks like things are about to start," Camden said.

The workers were gathering around the entrance to the mine. A large yellow crane had been constructed above the entrance. Huge cables were wrapped around something near the opening of the mine.

On-screen.

We moved closer for a better look. The entrance to the mine had been sealed shut by what looked like concrete, rebar, and huge pieces of timber. Thick metal cables were attached to the seal. Men with drills had been chipping away at it, breaking it down until it could be hauled away. They were almost through.

"Here we go!" Nicholas yelled.

Kimberly walked up beside him. He put his arm around her. "Almost there," he said.

There was a large earth mover with a jackhammer attachment up near where the concrete seal was. It was working on breaking the concrete while the crane up above drew its cables tight. I could hear the physical strain in the metal. The jackhammering echoed all over the property.

Crack!

Something had burst. Suddenly, the concrete seal came flying out of the entrance of the cave, hauled up into the sky by the crane. As it did, a large chunk of the concrete swung over and crushed the earth mover from the side, almost injuring its operator.

As the seal was being lifted away, a burst of wind blasted forth from inside the mine. It was one of the strongest gales I had ever felt. But the wind itself wasn't what shocked me the most.

What shocked me was that the burst of air sounded almost like a scream.

CHAPTER FIFTEEN

A SEARCH IN VAIN

No time like the present," Nicholas said loudly to all of those nearby. His voice cracked. I don't know if it was because of the strange screaming sound or because he was just nervous. "The investors will be here tomorrow. We've got to get things ready."

The workers began running around trying to bring loads of trucks toward the mouth of the mine. They all looked like they were worried about getting yelled at by Nicholas. I couldn't blame them.

"Tomorrow?" I asked.

Nicholas nodded.

"Why are they coming so soon?" Anna asked. It might have been better to let her ask the questions. I had a high Moxie, but she had a trope that specifically helped her get information from NPCs. Until I understood how the game worked behind the scenes, I was probably better off letting her take care of it.

Nicholas ran his fingers through his hair, a nervous affectation. "We promised a lot of things to get this project funded. Investors want to see where their money went."

He put his arm around Kimberly and began walking toward the mouth of the mine, yelling inane commands to the workers nearby.

Off Screen.

"Something's definitely up," Camden said. "I've been looking through this file some more. They really cherry-picked my report to try to get this mine project going. My character has no idea why they're so confident there will be paydirt down there."

I didn't understand it either. In fact, if I were to guess, I'm not sure that Nicholas knew everything. Despite his blue-blooded upbringing and his projected confidence, he seemed nervous. Maybe it was just because they'd taken a gamble on this mine. Maybe it was something else.

"We're going to find out what's going on sooner or later. Something tells me we're not going to be happy when we do," I said.

Progress moved slowly in between scenes. There was an elevator right at the entrance to the mine. It was in a state of disrepair. NPCs were working around the clock to try to fix it so that it could be used by the investors the next day. I wondered how this kind of thing would work off-screen. I thought maybe the elevator would be magically fixed, but no. They were actually working on it, swapping out parts and messing with the electrical systems.

Being an NPC must have been a really thankless job.

On-screen.

Nicholas and Kimberly eventually made their way back to us.

"Get suited up," he said. "We're not going to wait around, getting nothing done. I intend to see gold by sundown."

He pointed us over toward a table that had been set up next to a truck. The table had climbing equipment on it. We walked over to it and started putting on harnesses. Luckily, the table also had flashlights that we could use.

Nicholas took off his vest and jacket and handed them to Kimberly. He started to put on his harness. As he did, I noticed that Kimberly had subtly started to pull the deed he had waved at Akers from his jacket pocket.

"Are you coming down, hon?" he asked her.

Kimberly paused. I think she was legitimately having a hard time deciding. I couldn't blame her. If I had a choice not to go into the clearly haunted mines, I would have a tough time too. Part of the trouble was guessing what her character would do. It was unlikely that her character would want to climb down the side of a shaft into a mine.

"I think I'll stay up here," she said. She wrapped his jacket and vest around her arms, concealing the deed.

"You can wait for the elevator," he offered. "Might be a little dangerous climbing down there, but I have to do it. It's my job."

Kimberly smiled. "Be careful, won't you?"

He smiled back at her. "I'll be fine."

I had no idea how to rappel down the side of a mine shaft. To my left, the elevator was still being repaired. Workers were strapped to the metal scaffolding that held the elevator in place. They were busy grinding and welding.

We were climbing down a small wall right next to the elevator. A long, thick rope was tied off at the mouth of the mine and dropped down the hole that we would be climbing into. I had no idea how to do it. Nicholas did, but he was sparing with the instructions.

"Put this around the rope, pull it tight, and slowly let yourself down," he said.

Anna did seem to understand what he was trying to say, so I was able to watch her do it first. I was told to go next. Camden would be after me. Nicholas stayed at the top with Kimberly. Ironically, Kimberly was the only member of our team who could teach herself how to do this in an instant with her Convenient Backstory trope, and she didn't have to do it at all.

Have I mentioned that I'm afraid of heights?

At every step, I thought I was going to fall to my death. The rope went through a large carabiner. We had to control our own descent. I was in no hurry to get to the bottom.

After Anna had called up that she was down, I started my climb. I probably took five minutes longer than she did. By the time I got to the bottom I was exhausted and my heart was racing.

There was a burst of static, like a radio tuned to a channel without a signal. I didn't know where it was coming from, but it sounded like it was coming from where Anna was. Anna started patting her clothes down, searching for the source of the sound, until, eventually, she found it in a small pocket of her jacket. She had a small square device attached to ten feet of thin wire. She pulled it out of her pocket along with all of the wire.

We had been switching back and forth between on-screen and off-screen as we descended. Now we were on-screen.

I held my flashlight up to the device that she was holding. It was a small radio.

"Anna, do you copy?" a broken-up voice sounded from the device.

We looked at each other. We had to stay in character, but this development surprised both of us.

She brought the device to her mouth, pushed the small button on the side, and said, "I hear you. We're in the mine. We don't have a great signal."

There was silence for a moment.

"We found an air shaft," the voice said. "We might be able to shimmy down. Is it safe?"

Anna looked up at me hoping that I would have the answer. I shrugged.

"It looks safe, but the boss is coming down soon."

"Be sure to get pictures of anything we can use. We'll stand by."

Off Screen.

"STP?" Anna asked me once we had a moment of privacy.

"That would make sense," I answered.

Our characters were secretly part of the environmental organization called STP and were sent here to get evidence against the mining company. I hadn't known where that plot thread was going to take us; now I was starting to get an idea.

We could hear Camden coming down from above. Anna quickly wrapped up the little radio and put it back in her pocket.

I took my flashlight and started shining it around the room where we had found ourselves. There was nothing that stood out as an immediate threat. The ceiling for most of the room was only six feet high. It was supported with old beams of wood that were wider than I was.

There were two tracks leading off down the main paths. They must have been for minecarts, though I didn't see any carts there. A main path went off to the left and another went straight forward. To the right was the bottom of the elevator.

The entire space was claustrophobic and utterly quiet. I couldn't see the source of the screaming sound. I began to hope that it was just the wind rushing through the tunnels.

After Camden made it down to the ground, Nicholas was right after him. He didn't walk step by step like we did. Instead, he let himself fall quickly, slowing his descent by pulling on the rope. He was clearly experienced at this.

"Here we are," Nicholas said. He started looking around the room like he was expecting to see stacks of gold right in front of him. "Where is the nearest vein?"

Camden pulled his file folder out from under his shirt, where he had stored it for the climb down. He grabbed a map and started familiarizing himself with it.

"Right this way," he said. "There's supposed to be an untouched vein right through there. They estimated it as being worth millions of dollars, and *if* their measurements are correct, it probably is," Camden said. He pointed toward a small crevice off of the main path we had taken.

We shined our flashlights over in that direction. It would be a tight squeeze for all of us. I could see Nicholas's smile growing wide as we walked closer. The two of us had to crouch down because the ceiling was so low. Now, trying to squeeze into place through a gap that had not yet been widened was going to make things even more difficult.

Nicholas sent Anna in first. He followed afterward.

It took him a minute to squeeze through the gap. While I stood there, I noticed how humid it was down in the mine. I'd expected it to be drier. I swore that I could hear drips in the distance, but I couldn't say where they were coming from or if they were just in my mind.

Camden squeezed into the area we were headed and then I followed behind him. When we got there, Nicholas's smile had disappeared.

"Is the gold deeper in the rock?" he asked. "We need it to be something very visible and obvious so that the investors feel confident and don't end up pulling the plug on this."

Camden consulted his notes again. I held the flashlight for him so that he could see.

"According to their reports, there should be visible veins of gold right where we're standing. That was the claim at least," he said.

"If it says that they're here, then they're here," Nicholas said.

Except they weren't.

I've seen pictures of gold mines before. Glittering metallic veins creeping through stone walls. Old-fashioned miners giving toothless smiles to the camera as they present a promising vein.

There was nothing here. It was just plain brown and gray rock.

"This must be a mistake," Nicholas said. "You must have misread the map."

Camden humored him. He retraced our steps along the map, but they led straight to where we were now.

We spent at least an hour on- and off-screen looking around, hoping to find some crag filled with gold. Nicholas swore that the map must have been written incorrectly and that the real vein was nearby, so we scoured the area looking for any sign.

All we found were more minecart tracks and more brown and gray rock.

That's not quite true. We also found water leaking down the walls, forming little streams that eroded their own miniature canyons in the rock beneath our feet.

"I thought you said it would be dry down here," Nicholas said.

"This is dry for a mine like this," Camden responded.

We went off-screen, yet the story continued.

Nicholas was about to say something heated, but before he could, we heard yelling in the distance. Back the way we came, someone was yelling Nicholas's name.

"Oh, what now?" he asked.

A worker with a white hard hat, the same one who had explained the drainage system, was yelling for Nicholas.

"What? Don't you know we're doing something?"

The worker held up his hands in a supplicating gesture. "I just thought you ought to know that your father is almost here," he said.

This news must have surprised Nicholas because a flash of fear appeared on his face.

"He's not supposed to be here today."

The worker shrugged.

We followed him back to the entrance. In the hours that we had spent down in the mines, the NPCs had managed to fix the elevator. We took it back up to the surface. Personally, I was very glad to be out of the mines.

But something was strange. We had been off-screen ever since the NPC with the white hard hat, Gary, had come to get us. We didn't come back on-screen for a long while.

As we left the mine, Nicholas took off his hard hat and started running his fingers through his hair. He was clearly not prepared to see his father.

He turned around and looked at us. "Don't say that we didn't find the gold. Say we didn't get to it yet."

We all agreed.

Outside the mouth of the mine, Kimberly was waiting for us. Nicholas gave her a distracted side hug and then continued walking forward.

As soon as Nicholas was gone, Kimberly practically threw the deed to Camden.

"See if that tells you anything," she said. "I thought it might."

Camden opened it and flipped through it quickly. A look of surprise grew on his face.

"That's interesting," he said.

"What?" Anna asked.

He turned the deed around so that we could look at it. Specifically, he was focused on the last page where the signatures were.

The agreement was a leasehold for mineral rights—a temporary transaction. It was signed by the land owner, a Douglas Akers, and by Gerald Hesper, the owner of Ehbert Mining, the company that had opened the mine.

"So?" I asked.

Camden grabbed a piece of paper from his folder and held it out.

"Hesper is Nicholas's last name," he said. "Gerald is his father."

"Wait," Kimberly said. "What does that mean?"

What it meant was that there was a mystery. Gerald Hesper had been the one to open this mine. His company had probably been the one to seal it. Why were they now trying to reopen it? And why had they lied about there being gold?

"It means we've been lied to," Anna said.

Overhead, I heard a helicopter. I turned to see a sleek black chopper heading directly for us. It landed in the flat pasture beyond where the earth started to descend down to the mouth of the mine.

As the doors opened, three ex-military types in black suits exited and then turned to assist an elderly man, who needed a wheelchair once he was on the ground.

Gerald Hesper. NPC. Plot Armor: 35.

His three bodyguards were each called "Guard" on the red wallpaper. They also had thirty-five Plot Armor.

As Nicholas ran out to greet his father, my friends and I looked around at each other and wondered where this story was going and how these high-level NPCs played into it.

Even as Nicholas, Hesper, and his guards came down into the recessed area to greet us, we didn't come back on-screen. Surely this would be something the audience would need to see.

What was going on?

CHAPTER SIXTEEN

THE WATERS BELOW

The older Mr. Hesper was a tight-lipped and introspective man. When he saw his son coming, he nodded in greeting. He sat in his wheelchair like he was a king on his throne. His guards slowly pushed him down the steep incline to the mine opening.

Nicholas went for something that might have been a hug, but it wasn't reciprocated, so it ended up just being a shoulder touch.

Hesper wore expensive work clothes that he must have purchased when he was a much younger man because they were now several sizes too large for him. He must have been seventy or eighty years old.

"I didn't know you were getting in this early," Nicholas said.

Gerald Hesper largely ignored his son's comment, responding only with a polite smile.

"Have you been down into the mines yet? Is the elevator in working order?" he asked.

Nicholas cleared his throat. "We took a short journey into the mines. Had to climb down myself, but we were just about to go search for the gold veins when we got word that you had arrived. The elevator is repaired now. I told them we had to have it done as soon as possible. We couldn't wait for tomorrow."

Hesper nodded.

Nicholas gestured toward Kimberly. "You remember my fiancée, Kimberly Madison, from the holidays?"

"Yes, of course."

Kimberly glanced over at us for just a moment before walking forward and putting her arm around the man in the wheelchair.

She had her hand placed gently on her stomach. I thought she was about to do her Pregnancy Reveal, but as the old man looked up at her with his stern, piercing gaze, she lowered her hand and backed away from him.

"It's nice seeing you again," she said.

I thought that it was strange she didn't attempt to use her Pregnancy Reveal trope there, but maybe she simply thought better of it.

Then I realized why.

We were still off-screen. If the audience didn't see her reveal, it wouldn't work. Glad she was paying attention.

I still didn't know why we weren't on camera. An important-seeming character had just been introduced. The only thing I could think of was that Dina was doing something even more important. Even then, we had been off-screen for so long . . .

"I do hope that you will be joining us in the mines," Hesper said.

Kimberly was hesitant.

"Don't you think she ought to stay up here?" Nicholas interjected. "After all, there are safety concerns. We wouldn't want to endanger her."

"I would think someone who wants to be part of the family would want to see what the family does," Hesper responded.

Nicholas looked to Kimberly, pleading with her to understand, as he said, "I suppose she should be all right. I fixed the elevator, after all."

"Wonderful," Hesper said. "Now, shall we go find the treasure?"

I thought it was strange that a man in a wheelchair would want to go into a mine that had been abandoned for decades, but the plot was clearly leading us there. I knew Hesper was up to something nefarious. If I had to guess, I'd say he was hoping to leave the mine without the wheelchair. Maybe even without us.

But my character wouldn't know that, not quite. The script clearly had us trudging back into the mines.

I was nervous in a way I had yet to be in a storyline. I had never been able to get a glance at any enemy. Hesper was technically an NPC, so I couldn't read him; reading enemy tropes was my main method of getting a grasp on a storyline. Without that, I felt like any terrible thing could happen. The mine itself didn't reveal any tropes like the cornfield in *The Final Straw II* or the castle in *The Astralist*.

I had no idea what I was walking into. This must be what it felt like to not be a Film Buff. It was scarier.

With the elevator fixed, getting back down into the mine was as easy as pushing a button. As we descended into the darkness, my heart rate started to rise.

A glance at the Plot Cycle told me that First Blood had passed. Maybe something was going on elsewhere after all. Dina might have an explanation, assuming we found her.

Only time would tell.

Last time, moving through the passages of the mine had taken a long time because we were unfamiliar with the area. This time it took a long time because we were led by a man being pushed in a wheelchair on the uneven ground. Every time we came to a tight hallway his guards would have to pick his chair up and force it through.

We went down the same path we had originally. I was eager to get to the same area that we had found before and see if Hesper would explain why there was no visible gold there despite the map saying that there was.

It wasn't meant to be.

Ten minutes into our journey, we were led off the path that we had traveled on before, deviating far to the left down a narrow corridor that we had all but ignored on our first trip through.

"This area isn't marked on the map," Camden said.

"Oh, really?" Hesper replied. "Strange."

He wasn't even keeping up the pretense of having never been to this place before. He was leading us around by memory. Maybe that was just because he was an NPC off-screen and didn't need to explain, because the audience wasn't watching, but it seemed off.

After we had walked for ten minutes, I saw light up ahead of us. It flickered and moved like a flashlight. After a few moments, it shut off.

I could hear scuffling up ahead.

Two of Hesper's guards moved forward, a flashlight in one hand, a pistol in the other.

"We can hear you there," one of the guards said.

There was silence for a moment.

The guards ran forward, and we could hear more movement.

"Get on the ground," one of the guards said. His voice echoed back to us from ahead.

As we rounded a corner, we were able to see the people involved.

It was Dina and the long-haired activist who had thrown an egg at Nicholas's car. Dina was on her knees. Maybe she could have run for it, but one look at the guard's Plot Armor would probably prevent that. He would have high enough stats to catch her or kill her if he wanted to.

All that was left to do was comply, so she did.

The long-haired activist, however, stood still.

His name was Corey on the red wallpaper. He was an ordinary NPC with three Plot Armor.

He stood still as the guards held their guns on him and Dina. He didn't even really seem to be paying them any attention.

"Looks like we have some uninvited guests," Hesper said. I could see him smiling. "They can come too, then."

And then he just kept going.

The guard pushing him wheeled him around Dina and Corey. No more dialogue. No confrontation. No explanation. That didn't make sense. Finding activists in his mine should at least bring about more than a simple line.

And why were we still off-screen? Everyone was here now. What was the camera looking at? Was the camera even on?

Something was very wrong here.

Two guards behind us. One in front of us pushing Hesper. Dina and Corey walked directly in front of me, Anna, Camden, and Kimberly. The other players and I looked at each other nervously. We all knew something was wrong.

All of that was very concerning, but it wasn't the most unsettling thing going on.

Soon after we began walking through the tunnels, Corey, the NPC activist, started to talk. No one asked him a question. No one spoke back to him. To top it off, we were still off-screen, so this dialogue was certainly not scripted, at least not for this scene.

Yet he talked.

And talked.

I could only conclude that he was broken. It was like he hadn't broken character—he was just in the wrong scene.

Was the storyline itself broken?

Hesper, Nicholas, and the guards didn't even so much as acknowledge him as he spoke despite the fact that he was talking about Hesper. As he spoke, tears formed in his eyes.

"The first thing you got to understand is that this is not about mining gold. This is about keeping the gold they have. The evidence inside this mine will be enough to keep them tied up in the courts for years and possibly even put them in prison.

"It all started thirty years ago. What you got to understand is that this place wasn't always this type of mine. It was a gravel pit originally. That's why the entire area around here is dug out.

"Then they found the cavern and started mining. That would have been about thirty-two years ago. A couple of years later, they start reporting findings of gold and jewels. But something strange started happening on the outside.

"The animals in the refuge next to the mine, they start going crazy. They become aggressive; they stopped eating. They started fighting with each other. Ecologists, biologists, zoologists, they didn't know what was going on. Entire ecosystems in that forest just disappeared within a matter of weeks.

"Something they were doing in this mine was making that happen. I don't know if they were using chemicals or some weird type of sonic vibrations, but it was making all the animals around here go cuckoo. It was so bad, even the government started looking into it. Next thing you know, Hesper pulls out of the mine and seals it shut. They come up with some excuse. They say it's a business decision. Or they say that the owner's wife just died and he's too bereaved to move forward.

"I say that's bullshit. They were trying to dodge fines and lawsuits. They ended up greasing the right palms and getting out of the whole thing. We didn't have any evidence of what they were using in the mine, so they just walked away scot-free.

"Now that it's being opened back up by the same guy, we know we only have a limited amount of time to come in here and find evidence of what they've done before they destroy it all. Have you seen any chemicals or strange machinery that you don't recognize?"

No one responded. Finally, Corey stopped talking. No one acknowledged it, but it was very strange and out of place.

We went through several different forks and tunnels before we found our destination.

The place they brought us to looked a lot like any other pathway in the mine except for one thing—there was a large crack in the wall.

It was big enough for a person to fit through and it was dripping wet. A slow trickle of groundwater leaked down from the top of the crack all the way to the bottom.

For the first time in a long time, we were finally on-screen.

Kind of.

The Off Screen light flickered. We were mostly on-screen, though.

"What is this?" Anna asked.

"A miracle," the old man answered. "My miracle."

He turned from Anna to Nicholas.

"You know I love you," Hesper said. "Ever since the day you were born you were my favorite person. Even more than your mother."

Nicholas looked confused. "Thanks . . . Dad."

"I could never tell you my plan for this place. I always wondered if you would still go along with it if I did. If you would understand. But that would be asking too much of you."

"What are you saying?" Nicholas asked.

"You had to come on to this land. You had to come into this mine. You had to do it of your own volition. I truly believe that there is power in consent, in choice. You chose to enter this land despite all warnings. Maybe you'll make another choice, just one more, for me."

Nicholas looked around at all of us. He was speechless.

"It was thirty years ago that I found the water. You can hear it down there if you listen. It's almost like it's talking to you." His voice was almost dreamy.

He was right—I could hear subtle splashing from the hole in the wall, echoing up through the crack.

"Jump into the water," Hesper said, "of your own free will. It will be so much more powerful that way. I know that's the mistake I made last time."

"Wait, what are you talking about?" Nicholas asked.

"Jump into the water. I always imagined what it would be like down there, but I was never brave enough to look. Please be braver than I was."

"Dad, you're scaring me."

Hesper looked to the ground, resigned.

"I should have known it was too much to hope for, but your gift will be wonderful either way."

The guards, whose guns had been aimed at Dina and Corey, aimed their guns at Nicholas instead.

"Go into the water."

Hesper looked exhausted.

"Dad, what are you saying?"

"Turn me around. I can't look," Gerald said. He actually sounded sad.

One of his bodyguards turned him around and the other two began training their weapons on Nicholas.

"Go in."

Nicholas didn't make a move. He seemed to have just realized how serious this was.

One of the bodyguards grabbed hold of Nicholas and started shoving him into the crack in the wall. Another trained his weapon on Nicholas in case he managed to get away and the third had his weapon on . . . us.

Running would be useless. If they wanted to shoot us, they wouldn't miss. Their stats were high enough to ensure that. If they wanted to chase us and catch us, they would succeed at catching at least some of us.

Nicholas pleaded with his father. He tried fighting back but that was futile. The bodyguard was too strong, and the threat of the bullet was scarier than the threat of the unknown.

After a struggle, he dropped into the hole to the sound of a splash a few seconds later.

"Why?" Nicholas called up through the hole. He had survived.

Hesper's bodyguard turned him back around. He didn't mind seeing what was about to happen. Not to us.

"Unfortunately, you won't be of much use to me, but still, I can't have you talking. Into the hole. It's where you're going alive or dead."

That was fairly persuasive.

The Off Screen light was flickering faster and faster.

We were led to the hole one at a time to drop down into whatever water lay beneath. Even though I knew it was futile, my mind worked in a million directions looking for alternatives. The problem was that when you don't know the script, you don't know if the alternatives are worse.

The next part of the story was down that hole. Hopefully, at least down there we would stay on-screen.

"Wait," Kimberly said, attempting to summon every ounce of emotion she could. "Please don't do this. I'm pregnant."

If her Pregnancy Reveal trope was going to work, it would have to be that moment. The trope was all about eliciting sympathy from the audience, after all. We were technically on-screen too, even if the light was flickering.

It certainly didn't elicit sympathy from Hesper himself.

Hesper laughed. "I don't know if you're telling the truth. I'm afraid it doesn't matter. I made this decision a long time ago."

A cartoonishly evil horror anthology villain. I was wondering if we would get one of those.

I had a feeling that this interaction was why they were NPCs instead of enemies. Although they were antagonists, they were only here to get us into the water below. That was their purpose. We weren't meant to fight them. We would lose if we tried.

Anna was the first of us, then Camden, Dina, Kimberly, and Corey, who spent the entire time cussing out Hesper as if he knew him personally. Gerald Hesper paid him no mind.

When it was my turn, I lowered myself in. As soon as I got close, I could feel a strange, tangible force on my skin. There was something down there. I could try for a thousand years and I would never be able to describe the sensation.

With one look back at the guns and Gerald Hesper, I dropped through the hole in the wall.

CHAPTER SEVENTEEN

THE UNKNOWABLE

As I dropped into the crack in the wall, I immediately found myself sliding down a steep incline. The rock was slick and wet. My feet scrambled against the stone, seeking to stop my fall or at least slow my descent, but years of erosion had rendered the surface smooth.

I reached out my hands as I fell, clawing for even the slightest ledge to grab hold of. All I managed to do was catch a fingernail against a small bit of rock, which pulled my nail backward until it snapped off. That should have hurt, but by the time I realized what had happened, the pain was drowned out by something else.

As soon as my feet hit the water, my body became overcome with an intense sensation of fear. I don't mean to say I was simply afraid in the way one would normally be in that situation. I felt a palpable reaction all over my body. If you have a fear of heights, you'll understand how your body shuts down when exposed to a steep fall. It was like that but a hundred times more intense.

My stomach quivered. My legs turned to jelly; my arms felt like they were no longer under my control. The water was only knee-high, yet I was fighting for every breath. I couldn't stand; I couldn't swim.

I felt *it* on my skin like sunshine bearing down on me. Except it wasn't a bright light. It was the darkness itself that pressed against my skin. The force was coming from something in the darkness to my right. My body refused to even breathe in that direction.

But what was it?

I could feel a power radiating from something in the darkness. I couldn't even look in that direction with my eyes closed, the feeling was so intense. Luckily, being able to feel the direction it was coming from meant that I could move away from it.

I struggled. I couldn't walk, not at first. I was stumble-falling in the direction away from the pain, from the fear.

But why was I running?

A dark clarity rose from inside me. Thoughts were being put in my head.

Why was I splashing through the water so pathetically? Why not just stay and be consumed?

I had nothing to live for. My family—Mom, Dad, Grandma, Grandpa—they were gone. My death would mean nothing. What was I fighting against?

The others needed to escape to get back to their families, but I didn't. I could give up. Just stop. What joy. I could just stop fighting. I was unimportant in the grand scheme. Heck, I was unimportant even in the lesser scheme. I was of no help. I was useless.

These thoughts rushed through my mind. I was powerless against them. I felt a crushing weight on my chest. It was like I would never be able to move on from this moment. I kept waiting for each thought to be my last.

And yet, my feet kept moving.

Why?

Stripped of my human desire to live, what was left that kept me moving away from the inevitable?

I struggled forward, tears in my eyes. I breathed only when I remembered to. Why was I even trying?

With every inch I trudged forward through the water, my mind cleared a little more. The pain, the fear—they began to ease. They didn't disappear, not by a long shot, but they became distant. They wormed their way back down where they had come from.

As I made it farther from the area of influence of the darkness, I realized that I heard voices in the distance, back the way I had come from.

"I don't know what to do," Anna screamed. "Tell me what to do!"

"Anna!" I screamed. She didn't answer me. I didn't think she even heard me.

"I can't keep going," she said. "I can't keep going."

"Follow my voice!" I screamed. She didn't show any sign of hearing me. She kept muttering to herself. I heard weeping farther in the distance. It was Camden. The sound was interspersed with splashing as he struggled to move in my direction.

"Sean?" Dina yelled. "Where are you? Sean?"

Dina was talking to someone, but I couldn't say who.

Even with my eyes closed, I could see my close allies on the red wallpaper when I looked in their direction. All of our statuses were lighting up like a Christmas tree. Every single status was flickering on and off. Not just the obvious ones, like Unscathed or Incapacitated. Mutilated was flickering, and so were Infected, Hobbled, Fight Scene, Off Screen, and the rest. Even our Dead status flickered.

Being near the thing in the darkness was completely short-circuiting the very magic that made Carousel run.

We were all in a Chase Scene, but with what? An invisible force? An emotion? "This way," I screamed. "Come this way!"

I was still afraid to open my eyes. Whatever lurked in the darkness still held such power over me, even from a great distance.

"Why won't he look at me?" Nicholas sobbed. "Why won't he look at me?"

He was still back where we had been dumped out, by the sound of it.

I heard splashing, someone fighting the water. Did I dare attempt to go back and save them?

No. I limply rested on my knees. Tears rolled down my face. I couldn't go back. I couldn't.

"Sean, don't run away from me like that. You can't run away from me. It's dangerous."

There was a pause like she was waiting for a response. I swear, in the distance, I thought I could hear the chains of a swing set.

"I know, baby, but what if I can't find you?" she asked. It sounded like she was reliving a memory or something like one. Her voice was soft, nurturing. Nothing like the Dina I knew.

For a few moments, she was silent. I didn't know what was happening in her mind, but it sounded better than what was happening in real life.

I sat and listened to the others struggle. I couldn't bear to go back and find them. The radiating fear and pain were something I could never take willingly, as ashamed as I am to admit it. Even from a distance, my Incapacitated status flared just by thinking about walking back in that direction.

"Sean! Don't go, baby," Dina screamed through tears. "Don't go."

Then there was silence. Whatever daydream she was caught in was over.

"I'll find you," she said quietly.

Her status on the red wallpaper was cleared. No Incapacitation, no injuries, nothing. Her Encouragement from Beyond trope appeared to be enough to snap her out of the mental panic that had befallen us. It was odd, though. Did her character have a kid that was set up in a different scene? She hadn't said anything.

She had stood up. I could hear her walking through the water.

"Hello," she screamed.

"Over here," I yelled back, forcing myself to remember to breathe.

"I'm here," Anna said weakly. She had made it as far away as I was. She must have been twenty feet to my left.

"I'm okay," Kimberly said softly. She was near Anna. I hadn't heard her speak since we got down there.

"Come on," Dina said. She was near Camden. He had gone from weeping to whimpering. For as close as he was to the force emanating in the distance, I couldn't blame him.

I could hear Dina lifting him up.

"We're not going to die here," she said. She was guiding him toward me in the darkness.

"Riley?" she said as she got close.

"Right here," I said.

She brought Camden close. He had started breathing normally. I grabbed onto him when he got near and helped lower him down beside me.

"My brothers and sisters are going to come here looking for me," he said to me as soon as he realized it was me. "There's nothing I can do. They're going to get stuck here too. What do we do?"

I didn't know what to say.

"It's okay," I said. "We'll get out. We'll find a way."

What had I just given Antoine grief for? Promising too much to Kimberly. Here I was, doing the same with Camden.

Dina waded back in the direction she had come and retrieved Nicholas, who was still repeating "Why won't he look at me" over and over, even for a few minutes after he had gotten to safety.

As Dina went back again for Corey, our long-haired hippie NPC companion, I started looking around the cavern.

It took real bravery to even be able to open my eyes. I know that makes no sense, but it felt like life or death.

I looked in the direction I had been crawling. There was darkness. Behind me, the terrifying force emanated toward us.

I heard splashing. Dina had found Corey. I heard him take a deep breath as she brought him above water. That was a close one.

"I was almost there," he said in a strange, uneven voice.

Anna and I had barely made it on our own. Dina had managed to help the others. That was good news, though by helping us she lost some Outsider buffs for the Finale. Oh well.

"How was this supposed to be a simple, fun storyline?" I asked. Chris had described it that way. Fun. He used the word *fun*.

No one answered me.

There is no way that this was the same storyline he was talking about. Our group almost drowned in two feet of water because we lost the will to live. Something was different.

Something was wrong.

Storylines could change from one iteration to the next. In the Delta Epsilon Delta storyline, the killer changed every time you played it. What had happened to make this storyline like this?

We were off-screen again.

Judging by the sounds of sloshing water in the distance, the cave system was huge. Hundreds and hundreds of feet in every direction.

"What is an Unknowable Host?" Anna asked.

I didn't know what she was talking about at first, but then I realized that I had worked so hard not to look in the direction of the terrible force that I had not looked it up on the red wallpaper.

UNKNOWABLE HOST (DECEASED)	
Plot Armor: 150	
Tropes	
EVIL NEVER DIES	It only changes form.
NOT YOURS TO CONTROL	Characters who encounter this being's power will misunderstand it in their attempts to harness it, to disastrous ends.
MINION MAKER	This creature is able to summon or create low-level monsters to do its bidding.
DARK AURA	This being has an aura with wide-ranging effects, from fear to some combination of status ailments. Bypasses stats on first exposure.
23 additional tropes not perceptible	

This entity in front of me must have been massive. I mean the size of a sky-scraper. If the revolting feeling in my mind when I looked at it was any indication, it was hundreds of feet from one side to the other. I couldn't see it in the darkness, but I could still feel it.

"It's dead," Dina said.

It sure was.

I told them about its tropes. Truthfully, there were many more that I couldn't read because of our level differential. I could only imagine what this thing could do or could have done when it was alive.

Off-screen, NPCs usually stay quiet. There are cases where they continue to play their parts, like the paramedics after I got stabbed. You can speak freely around them off-screen and they will just ignore you. They rarely try to interact with you.

This broken storyline was an exception. Almost all of our interactions were off-screen. Even then, nothing prepared me for Corey the eco-warrior. He continued to ramble on about pollution and nuclear waste and who knows what as soon as Dina dragged him away from the Unknowable Host.

"He has not stopped talking since the story started," Dina said. Corey ignored her.

His theory seemed to be that the thing in the darkness was radioactive waste dumped by the company. Maybe he was rehearsing his lines. Maybe he just really loved his job.

"We're going to have to have a talk with Chris," Camden said.

No kidding.

"You have any idea what's going on?" Anna asked.

"Well, Hesper Senior offered his kid to the dead thing. I'm guessing he doesn't know much about it. I assume he gets something as a reward. Maybe health, money, I don't know. Could be he owes the thing already and is paying it back, but . . . I'm not sure."

It felt like Hesper didn't know what was going on down here. The entity's tropes suggested that Hesper misunderstood something crucial.

"Could explain how they pulled so much gold out of this place," Camden suggested. "Assuming that part was even true."

It could. Given the uncomplicated nature of the storyline so far, I could believe it was that simple.

The Off Screen status started to flicker again, never staying lit for more than a few seconds. What was going on?

"I need to look at it," Corey said as soon as the camera returned. "We need proof of what they dumped down here. If it's radioactive, they'll go down for good."

"If it was radioactive, we would be cooked by now," Camden said. "We wouldn't even make it out of the cave."

"I need to see it," Corey responded.

"No!" several of us screamed. We were all terrified to look at the creature.

Corey ignored us. "I've got my flashlight here somewhere. I just need to see it!"

He wasn't just being stubborn. There was something wrong with him. Unfortunately, I didn't have the tropes to learn things about NPCs.

"How much water did you drink?" Dina asked.

"I need to see it," he said. I could hear him digging through his pockets. He grabbed onto something, and I could hear him clicking on his flashlight. It wasn't working, but that didn't mean it never would.

"Close your eyes!" I screamed.

I warned everyone in the nick of time, too, because a few seconds afterward, I could see light through my closed eyelids, and I knew he was looking at whatever that dead thing was.

Corey dropped the flashlight in the water as he let out a yelp of pain.

"Oh dear god," Dina yelled. I wasn't sure why at first; maybe it was just a reaction to his behavior.

No. It was something else. She had noticed it before me.

Corey the NPC had changed. He was now Corey (Possessed). Plot Armor: 3.

He was an enemy. Unlike most possessed enemies, he had no trope that would disguise him from us on the red wallpaper.

COREY (POSSESSED)	
Plot Armor: 3	
Tropes	
EYES OF THE HOST	This creature is a scout for the enemy.
HIVE MIND	This creature's mind is linked to that of similar creatures.
IMMORTAL SERVANT	This creature will not die of natural causes.
GRADUAL INFECTION	After this creature is infected, it can take several scenes for them to completely turn.

Truthfully, he was likely infected when he almost drowned, but he was still an NPC then. We would not have been able to tell. Now that he had laid eyes upon the creature, he was a full-on minion. The Plot Cycle clicked to Second Blood. We still didn't know what First Blood was. In this strange storyline, there may not have even been one.

"Corey," Dina said. "You okay?"

He took a moment before answering.

"Yes," he said. "This isn't so bad." His voice was dreamy, if slightly monotone.

Corey was definitely gone. His Gradual Infection trope oversold how gradual the infection would be.

"We better go," Anna said. She sounded like she was feeling better. Not perfect, but better.

We had to let Corey come with us. Our characters wouldn't know he was an enemy—not until he attacked us, of course. Then he would have to get the chop.

Exploring a cave in utter darkness was one of the most nerve-racking things I had ever done. The water made things even worse than the darkness. I could hear splashing in the distance. Was that simply the water flowing down the sides of the cave or was there something over there?

Eventually, we turned a tight corner and, as we did, we saw a small round beam of light shooting down from overhead. The hole in the ceiling was perfectly round. It was manmade.

"Is that—" Anna started to say. She didn't finish her sentence because as we walked closer, it became exceedingly clear what we were looking at.

It was an old-fashioned well.

The lighting was like something out of a movie. The bright light did not diffuse through the darkness—no, it stayed a beam all the way down to the ground. It looked like a spotlight shining in the darkness.

A long, thick rope hung down from the center of the hole, stretching fifty feet down until it ended at a small wooden bucket. The bucket hung over the water, hovering right above it without touching it.

In this small circle of light, the water was clear and blue.

"That rope looks brand new," Dina said.

She was right. This wasn't an old, rotten rope. This had been replaced recently. The bucket also looked well maintained.

"Oh lord," I said. "Look."

I pointed to the ground beneath the bucket.

Glistening in the spotlight were countless coins. Thousands of them. Coins of all shapes and sizes. Gold, silver, copper. Most were old, some were even older; most were the kind Carousel gave away, though one or two looked much older. Their lettering had mostly worn away, but they were not modern or written in English.

There weren't only coins. There was also jewelry with rubies, diamonds, and emeralds.

"Treasure," Nicholas said. That was the first thing he had said in twenty minutes.

"It's a wishing well," Kimberly said.

That made sense. I looked up toward the circular hole at the top. I couldn't see through to the other side. What I could see were roots; hundreds of wispy roots poked through the ceiling above. I could only see near the well, but I was sure they were all over.

"I think we're under the forest," I said.

Camden retrieved his character's folder, now soaking wet and falling apart. He found a map of the cave and estimated our location.

"Yeah," he said. "We should be right under the forest on the west side of the property."

Anna, Dina, and I looked at each other. We knew what that meant: Stragglers.

"We could climb out," Nicholas said. "This rope looks sturdy."

"Maybe you can," Dina said. "I couldn't."

We knew why we shouldn't climb that rope. It would lead to the forest with the Stragglers. We didn't want a repeat of the last storyline; our characters didn't have any idea. Luckily, not being able to climb a fifty-foot rope is a pretty good excuse.

"Yeah," Anna said. "Let's find another way."

Nicholas kept his eye on the rope. "Okay," he said hesitantly.

It dawned on me in that moment that he was still wearing his climbing harness from earlier that day. The first story with the Stragglers took place in nine or so years. He was wearing the exact same outfit he had worn in that story when he escaped with us in the truck.

That reminded me.

"I get this feeling like we aren't alone," I said. "I feel like we're being watched. Whatever that thing in the darkness was, I don't think it was here alone. We need to get out of here."

Cinema Seer couldn't buff my allies if I didn't make predictions.

The others nodded. They suspected we weren't alone too.

CHAPTER EIGHTEEN

THE SERVANTS

We began moving away from the light of the wishing well. There was something deep inside me that truly did not want to leave the light. The darkness ahead of us was surely safer than the darkness behind us but it was still darkness.

Nicholas kept looking behind us as we walked; his eyes appeared to be focused on the glittering gold beneath the bucket. I didn't know what, if anything, would happen if he tried to take it. If there was an enemy trope associated with it, I should have been able to see its presence even if I couldn't identify what it actually was. The same thing had been true about the pumpkin displays in *The Final Straw II*.

At the end of the day, when you find treasure in the same cave as a dead eldritch deity, it's best not to take it.

The Off Screen light was still misbehaving, though not as bad as it had before. It flicked on every few seconds.

As we moved forward, I could have sworn I heard a clicking sound ahead.

"Stop walking," I said quietly.

Everyone stood still and listened. Sure enough, the clicking continued.

We looked in the direction we thought the sound was coming from. Nothing appeared on the red wallpaper, which meant that it wasn't likely to be the deity from before. Spotting enemies on the red wallpaper generally required getting a visual. The deity had been an exception, probably because of its aura.

All of us had flashlights except for Corey, who had lost his. Up until that point we'd been hesitant to shine them into the distance out of fear that we might somehow have gotten turned around and that we were facing the Unknowable Host again.

Slowly, Anna raised her light farther and farther out across the water.

Twenty yards ahead of us, we saw the source of the noise.

It was a woman.

She was wearing a threadbare nightgown and holding one of those old heavy-duty metal flashlights. The bulb had burned out, but still, she clicked it off and on.

As soon as she came into view, she appeared on the red wallpaper.

Martha Hesper (Possessed). Plot Armor: 3.

She had the exact same tropes that Corey did, though she was further along in her infection. She didn't react when the light shined on her.

Not hard to guess who this was. Some tragedy had befallen Gerald Hesper's wife around thirty years ago, according to Corey's rant earlier. Thanks to her Immortal Servant trope, she was alive. In fact, if she weren't so pale and gaunt, I would almost say that she looked like she was still in her early thirties—the same age she presumably was when she got here.

Every instinct told me to run away. The problem was that we couldn't go off of instinct alone. Our characters would probably be very spooked by this woman, but how certain would they be that she was an enemy? That was the question. Could we run from her, or did we have to feign concern? More importantly, what was the best decision for the story?

As I considered this, Anna decided for me.

"Hello," she said. She began walking toward the woman. Anna was a very kind and considerate person. I hoped that wouldn't come back to bite us.

We followed her. Martha Hesper did not move. As we got closer, I could see her more clearly. Her wrists must have been bound with rope when she was brought here. It had been so long that the rope had frayed and rotted. Her hands were no longer bound but the ropes still hung limply from her wrists.

The Off Screen light still flickered.

"That can't be," Nicholas said. "No . . ."

It looked like Nicholas had finally figured out who we were walking toward.

"What?" I asked. I could guess what he was talking about, but we had to let the audience know somehow.

"That looks like . . ." he started to say. "But it can't be her . . ."

He recognized her as his mother.

"It's Martha Hesper," Corey said. He had a strange blank smile on his face. There was very little left of the anxious, paranoid man that had entered the cave. Only a small sliver of his personality was still there.

"No," Nicholas said. "Her plane went down when I was a baby."

"Well, this is one reason to seal up the mines," Dina said.

"It looks like . . ." Nicholas started to say. He pulled his wallet from his pocket and flipped through it to find a small photograph. He stared at it in disbelief. "This can't be real. That can't be her."

Through all of this, Martha Hesper didn't respond to anything. She had stopped clicking her flashlight, though.

"Tell us exactly what your father's relationship is with this mine," Anna said.

Nicholas furrowed his brow. He was having a very difficult time figuring out what was going on.

"Dad found the mine when he was digging for gravel. He thought he might be able to turn his luck around. Took a couple of years to get the mine set up properly and to get the equipment needed for this type of operation. Gravel is a lot simpler; he didn't really have to go underground.

"Couple years later, he starts finding gold and jewels. The mine is worth millions. But he has a bad run of luck. One of the banks where he kept his money collapsed. Come to think of it, one of his other mines collapsed too. A factory he owned burned down.

"Between that and the cost of equipment and the price of labor after his workers unionized, he ended up going bankrupt. Couldn't catch a break. He showed me one of his old accounting books. After pulling up hundreds of thousands of dollars in jewels and just over a million in gold, he didn't make a dime.

"Then my mother—then she . . ." He looked up at Martha Hesper. "Dad was devastated. He sealed up the mine and let the company go bankrupt. It got bought by some other holding group. We were just able to buy it back with some investor funds. It was our big project."

He turned away from us and ran his fingers through his hair.

Click.

Click.

Click.

Martha had begun clicking the flashlight again.

"What do we do?" Corey asked.

"We find a way—" Anna began answering, but just as she did, she was interrupted.

"He doesn't speak," Martha said.

"Why doesn't he speak?" Corey said.

They both started to breathe in and out quickly.

"What are his commands?" they both asked. "We must wait. We must wait."

"Corey?" Dina asked. She looked at us. "He must have hit his head on something. He's acting funny."

He was. His infection was taking hold.

Sometime during this conversation, Second Blood was struck. I still wasn't certain what First Blood was, but I hoped it wasn't Kimberly.

We went off-screen for real—no flickering.

"There we go," Dina said.

"What is going on with the camera?" Kimberly asked.

I had a theory, but I wasn't ready to say it just yet.

"Maybe we took the wrong path somewhere," Anna suggested.

"So, the servants are just waiting for orders, but their master is dead?" Dina asked.

"That's my take," I said. The Unknowable Host was still acquiring servants passively even though it was dead. I wondered what else it could do while dead.

"Mine too," Anna added.

"Did anyone swallow that water?" Camden asked. "I can't remember if I did."

"I think we'd already know if you did," I answered. "Do you feel the desire to gaze upon Carousel-Cthulhu?"

"Definitely not."

"Then I think we're fi—"

"It's got to be nuclear waste," Corey said. "That's all it could be. Just nuclear waste. I'm already dying. Drifting away."

"Hmm?" Dina said.

Corey stood still. I shined my flashlight over at him. He didn't react. A tear fell down his cheek into his beard.

"When is it over?" Corey asked. "Is it over soon?"

No one answered for a moment.

"Yes," Anna answered. "It's over soon."

In response, Corey gently sobbed, though most of his face stayed wooden. We all looked at each other.

"It was nuclear waste. That's how it ends. Nuclear waste. That's what Hesper's hiding down here. That's all. Maybe it's just radiation? I took a picture. Barrels of sickly green nuclear waste. Report him to the government. That can be it? That can be it? Right? Next time?"

"What the fuck?" Dina said.

"Is he . . ." Anna said. "Is he talking to us?"

I had no idea who he was talking to. He was losing it. Not just within the story.

In an instant, Corey's expression changed from one of horror and confusion back to a gaunt, blank look the same as Martha's.

"How can that be my mother?" Nicholas asked. "She's my age."

"And how long has she been your age?" I asked. "You see those restraints on her wrists. I don't think she came in here willingly. Those things have rotted off."

Nicholas was clearly having a very difficult time coming to terms with what he was seeing.

Meanwhile, Martha's clicking got faster and faster.

Anna took notice of her. She shined her flashlight over at Martha. I only just noticed that Martha had her broken flashlight pointed behind us. She clicked faster and faster.

Was she trying to show us something?

We turned slowly and lifted our lights to the water behind us.

Hundreds, thousands of bright green eyes reflected back at us. They came in all sizes—small ones barely sticking out of the water, larger ones hovering above the water.

I squinted to try to see what we were looking at.

DEER (POSSESSED)	
Plot Armor: 3	
Tropes	
TEETH OF THE HOST	This creature will eat for the enemy.
HIVE MIND	This creature's mind is linked to that of similar creatures.
IMMORTAL SERVANT	This creature will not die of natural causes.
GRADUAL INFECTION	After this creature is infected, it can take several scenes for them to completely turn.

A possessed deer stood closest to us. It might have been a hundred yards away. Behind it were dozens of other deer. And dozens of wolves. And hundreds of squirrels, rabbits, and all manner of woodland creature. They weren't moving. Some of the small creatures simply floated on the top of the water. Others had sunk down into the water but still didn't seem too bothered by it.

Anna, Dina, Kimberly, and Camden had each gotten a boost in Savvy and Grit. My Cinema Seer ability was activated by us finding Martha and the animals.

Martha and Corey each had a trope called Eyes of the Host, which made them scouts for the eldritch entity. The animals were the Teeth of the Host; their job sounded a little scarier.

"I guess we know what happened to all the missing animals Corey was monologuing about earlier," I said.

With the Unknowable Host dead, was it possible that his servants would not attack us? Truthfully, if I didn't know any better, I would say that they were all wondering that exact same question.

Martha had tried to warn us they were over here. It appeared to be some sort of subconscious message from the woman still trapped inside. She wouldn't have done that if we were perfectly safe.

The animals didn't move.

I shined my flashlight at Martha.

"Where's the way out?" I asked. She didn't respond.

"Nicholas," Anna said. "You have to ask her. I think she knows who you are."

Nicholas was frozen as he watched the animals slowly move toward us. He turned his head slowly toward his mother. He was struggling to find words.

"Which way?" he managed to get out. "If you are who they say you are. Please."

For a moment she did nothing.

Then she slowly moved her flashlight and pointed it in a direction opposite the animals and to the right a bit. She started to click her flashlight again.

"Thank you," he said. "Come with us."

She didn't respond in any meaningful way. She stood still and stopped clicking her flashlight. We started to move in the direction she had pointed. Corey stayed with her.

"What's going on?" Kimberly asked as we waded through the water.

After a moment, I realized she was looking at me.

"I think we're behind the scenes somehow," I said. "Those animals are just standing by. Something went wrong."

This part of the cavern grew narrow, and the water started to get shallower as we moved forward.

I could see what she was calling the exit. There was a steep incline ahead of us, though not quite as steep as the one that we had entered through. We would be able to climb it.

We started the climb; rocks cascaded beneath our feet with every step. This area was not natural. These rocks looked like they had been chipped away by human tools. This was the result of the mine.

At the top of the steep incline, there was a small crevice just big enough for us to squeeze through. We each climbed up into the area above.

On-screen. This time, there was no flickering.

As soon as I got through the crevice, I went to stand up and knocked my hard hat against the ceiling. This area was under five feet high. We would have to crouch if we were going to move through this tunnel.

I shined my flashlight back and forth. We were in a small tunnel with mine-cart tracks. Sitting in front of us was an empty minecart. Except it wasn't an ordinary minecart—this was a handcart. It had a handbrake and one of those double-sided handles that two people would grab hold of and take turns pushing down in order to make the minecart move along the tracks. The metal had been painted industrial yellow but had mostly been worn off from use.

There were two shovels and a pickaxe in the cart.

We started hearing haunting howls behind us. The animals had woken up.

A sign was hung on the outside of the handcart: "Use with Caution."

"You've got to be kidding me," Dina said when she saw it.

It was clear what we were meant to do here. We were back in the script it seemed. The tunnel was too short for us to run through. We were meant to ride out.

We piled into the minecart. Camden operated the brake. Kimberly and I took turns pumping the handle to make the minecart move forward. After thirty years you'd think something like this wouldn't be in working order. This one, however, came to life with a loud creak. Grease dripped down the mechanism as we pumped it. It almost looked like the handcart had been maintained recently. A white hard hat was lying on the floor of the cart.

This device was used to get miners from one side of the mine to the other, quickly, without having to dig a tunnel large enough for a man to walk through.

It wasn't designed to be faster than a possessed wolf.

Luckily, after we got started, it turned out that the direction we were moving was downhill. The cart started to move faster.

Camden was ready with the brake, preventing us from getting too much speed built up. We started racing along the tracks. Eventually, we left the short tunnel behind, but by that point in time we were going so fast that we couldn't exit the cart.

We broke out of the tunnel into a larger cavern, where the tracks curved around the side. The animals followed us, snarling and snapping anytime they managed to get close. Anna, Dina, and Nicholas held the shovels and pickaxe. They smacked any animal that got near us.

The tracks around the caverns were designed by a madman. They went in large circles and in hairpin turns that we barely made it around. To add further problems to this, we could barely see where we were going. All we had were our flashlights. The lights in the mine were not on.

It wasn't exactly a roller coaster, but I got the feeling it was meant to be for our entertainment, not the audience's. It was like an amusement park dark ride.

Perhaps this is what Chris meant when he'd said that it was fun, but I was still skeptical. On balance, I would say that this hardly made up for the dead entity that made me question whether my life was worth living. Of course, I wasn't sure we were actually supposed to have encountered the dead god. I think that was where things had gone wrong.

Anna smashed her shovel against the head of a wolf as it snipped at her.

"Look," she said, pointing beside us.

I looked. It was Martha Hesper standing beside the tracks as we passed. She had left the cavern. She just stood there. She didn't attack. It was like she was only there to be a jump scare.

After more distance, we saw Corey doing the same. Then we saw the foreman who had worn the white hat earlier that day. He must have gotten infected at some point in time. He was bloody and covered in bite marks.

There were more. Miners mostly. They were spread out throughout the ride, looking gaunt and pale and ghostlike. We hadn't seen them in the cavern below, though we had not explored it fully. The human enemies only showed up for glimpses and then disappeared. None of them attacked.

"Over there," Dina said, pointing across the cavern. "I know where we are. That sign. That's the air shaft where Corey and I entered."

Camden pulled the brakes as we got close. A high-pitched squeal echoed through the cavern.

The animals were hot on our trail. We had to move quickly.

The air shaft was steep, but it was so narrow that you could put your arms to the side and help yourself climb to the top.

Soon, we emerged from the mines. Judging from my surroundings and the directions we had taken underground, I would've said that we were in the wilderness refuge. After we exited the air vent, Dina and Camden moved a large metal grate over the opening. The animals would be able to move it if enough of them could get to it, but with the narrow shaft, that seemed unlikely.

That was the Finale. The End would come soon, but it wasn't here yet.

The minecart chase was closer to the tone I was expecting from this storyline than the Unknowable Host was. The question was: why had we been forced to take that detour?

That couldn't have been in the script.

CHAPTER NINETEEN

WHAT DOES IT WANT?

The storyline was nearly over, yet we hadn't reached The End yet. There was something further to get done.

We raced back to the mine entrance where Nicholas's SUV was parked. When we arrived, we saw that the workers had left.

Off Screen.

So, we were back to that.

Hesper was sitting in his wheelchair at the entrance to the mine. His guards were carrying boxes as they walked past him and disappeared into the area where the elevator was. Hesper had one of the boxes next to him. He was reaching into it and messing with its contents.

"What are they bringing in?" Anna asked.

Hesper lifted one of the items out of the box as if to examine it. I saw it glinting in the sunlight.

"It's gold," Dina said. "Boxes of gold."

"Why would he be bringing boxes of gold *into* the mine?" Kimberly asked.

That was a good question. He had clearly thrown his wife into the caverns in exchange for something. Was it gold? Success? Who knows.

"Maybe he's trying to return ill-gotten gains," I suggested.

Nicholas shook his head. "I don't know what he's doing but he didn't have any gains. Not from this mine. He went bankrupt after this venture. It was his most embarrassing personal failure. He was humiliated. And then our plane went down. The crash put him in a wheelchair and killed my moth—"

He stopped talking as he realized that the story he had been told must not have been true.

"I'm going to trap them in there," Nicholas said.

"What?" Anna said. "We can leave now. They aren't going to stop us."

Nicholas ignored her.

"We need to jam the elevator," he said. "Then we can have a talk."

"They have guns," Anna said. "We should just leave."

Finally, Nicholas acknowledged her. "And what happens when they discover we have escaped? You think they'll just let us be? They threw us into that pit to die. Threw his own son . . . They're not just going to let us walk free."

That was probably true, but it didn't really affect us. Still, our characters would likely be motivated by that logic. It was clearly scripted as much as anything was scripted in this broken storyline.

"We just need to see if there's an emergency shutoff," Camden said.

"Do you want to get that close?" Kimberly asked. "They have guns."

"We'll wait until the elevator has lowered some and then jam it up," Nicholas said, looking around for some means of doing so.

"That might work," Kimberly suggested as she pointed to the earth mover that had been used to unseal the mine.

Nicholas's eyes lit up.

Nicholas scurried toward the earth mover. He got into the operator's seat and found its key. As Hesper and his guards started moving into the elevator, he started trying to turn the machine on and get it moving, yet he clearly didn't know how to operate it very well. He started moving forward clumsily, lowering the jackhammer attachment on the front of the machine into the ground by accident.

"Let me do it," Kimberly said. "My dad had a construction business. I know how to operate it."

Her Savvy jumped up as her Convenient Backstory ability kicked in. I didn't think it would work off-screen, but then again, I didn't think we were supposed to be off-screen in this scene anyway. The storyline was still broken. In fact, I noticed that the story went off-screen for anything involving Hesper, as if he and the big dead thing in the mine were somehow being hidden from the audience.

After a few more failed attempts at operating the contraption, Nicholas finally relented and let Kimberly try. Thanks to her ability, she was able to make it work well enough.

"It's now or never," Camden said. "Hesper is about to get back on the elevator."

Of course, we couldn't just walk away. Not really.

We needed a final word from Hesper. An explanation.

Kimberly's Savvy was pretty high right now. Odds were that her plan to use the earth mover would work. It wasn't too far-fetched even by real-life standards. By movie standards it was practically guaranteed.

One of Hesper's guards wheeled him around into the elevator to join a stack of boxes and his other guards. The mine elevator was slow compared to a normal elevator.

As soon as the metal gate closed and the elevator started to descend, Kimberly kicked the earth mover into gear and drove it as fast as it would move down toward the entrance to the mine. From there, she didn't slow down much at all. She lifted the scoop of the earth mover so that it would knock into one of the support beams for the elevator and bend it over into the motor relay.

Crunch.

Rerereererere.

The motor was bound up and could no longer lower the elevator. Smoke started to pour out of the motor. As I ran up to the mouth of the mine, I could smell the internal components of the motor burning. The elevator car had gotten stuck. The top of it was just below ground level. Hesper and his men were trapped just far enough underground that we didn't have to worry about getting shot.

The elevator supports were bent, and the brakes had locked up.

Kimberly backed the earth mover up and waited to ensure the elevator was stuck before shutting it off and getting out.

Nicholas ran up behind me. "Dad. What the . . . What did you do?"

"Nicholas," Hesper said. "What are you doing here?"

He sounded surprised.

"What am I doing here?" Nicholas asked. "What are you doing? What did you do to my mother?"

Hesper didn't respond for a moment.

"Your mother died in our plane crash," Hesper said. He said it without emotion.

"She's still down there," Nicholas said. "I saw her. You tied up her hands."

More silence.

"Son, listen to me. This is all a misunderstanding. Just help me out of here and I'll explain everything."

"Explain everything now," Nicholas said. "Explain it and then I'll see if I'll help you out of there."

Hesper yelled out in frustration. "Just do as I tell you."

Nicholas didn't answer. "You just tried to kill me. I'm never doing anything you ask me again."

"If it wasn't for me, you wouldn't be here," Hesper said.

"Why do you always say that?" Nicholas asked.

More quiet contemplation.

"You weren't what I asked for."

Nicholas looked taken aback. "I never asked for a father like you either."

Hesper started to laugh. "I don't mean like that."

For a moment he stopped speaking. Then, he took in a deep breath.

"The first thing I put in was a gold watch," Hesper said. "I told people it was a ten-thousand-dollar watch. It wasn't but it was still more expensive than I could afford. I scraped it while trudging through the mine looking for the copper ore my idiotic geologist said would be there. Every rock without pay dirt was a reminder of my failure. And then I scuffed my watch. It loosened the strap too. I could have had it fixed but I was frustrated.

"A crack had opened up in the mine wall a few weeks earlier. We had dug too far to the west. I threw my watch in just to hear it crash against the rock below. Of course, all I heard was a splash. I regretted it immediately. I wanted my watch back, but what could I do?

"I continued looking for copper ore and found none. I fired my crackpot geologist. The company he worked for tried to get my business back. I didn't have any money to pay them, but they didn't know that. One of the owners visited my office and gave me a gift. He said that it retailed for over ten thousand dollars and that it was a token of his appreciation for our long-standing business relationship. When I opened it, it was the very same kind of watch I had just thrown into the mine. I thought it was a cosmic joke.

"But it ate at me. Somewhere in the back of my mind, I knew it was more than a coincidence. I couldn't fight the urge to throw something else into the cavern just to see if I could get more back. We had been looking for copper in the mine. I went to the bank and got my last hundred dollars out in one-cent pieces. They were made of pure copper back in those days. I threw them into the mine. The next day, one of my guys finds a vein of copper.

"I just knew it wasn't a coincidence. I went to the bank and got every loan I could and turned it all into gold. I tried one piece at first, and then, when that worked, I put the rest in.

"Within a few months, I had turned things around. I was pulling more gold out than I could even believe. Every ounce I threw in turned into five ounces in the mine. But the happy days didn't last. It came time to tally things up. Costs, labor, interests on my loans, repairing equipment, lawsuits, and one of my mines down south had collapsed. My bank went out of business because of fraud, and I lost millions. After all was said and done, I only had a hundred dollars left. And that isn't including the cost of opening the mine to begin with."

He started laughing.

"I was broke. Ruined. The grand fool I was, I mined out every single bit of gold I could find. I should have left some in and then sold the mine to save on time and expense. After finding out that even with my unending supply of gold I wasn't making any money, I . . . I got frustrated."

He paused for some time.

"When our plane crashed into the lake, I thought I would die, but I didn't. I was so disappointed. Instead, I was injured. I couldn't feel my legs. Your mother made it out alive. We searched for you for days, but your body was long gone. You were too young to swim.

"Your mother was crazed over losing her baby. I was enraged. I wasn't fortunate enough to be successful nor was I unfortunate enough to die. I decided to ask the mine for one last favor. Your uncle, whom I had shown the mine and its magical properties, helped me. I couldn't shake this feeling that the waters wanted something more personal, more substantial. I dreamed about it at night. With a sudden realization, as I lay in my hospital bed, I knew the water didn't want to trade gold for more gold. It wanted something more. That had to be it.

"So your uncle and I gave it your mother. I asked for my legs back. Pleaded with it. It wouldn't tell me what it wanted. It wouldn't tell me anything. All I heard were splashes. Your mother cried out for you. She was never so interested in being a wife as she was in being a mother. You should know that.

"I waited in vain for my miracle and it never came. I could not walk. I left the mine defeated. When I returned to the hospital for treatment, hoping perhaps that the doctor would give me some miraculous news, I was instead greeted by the police. A fisherman had found you on the shores of the lake. You were alive. After days and days, you had been found alive. It was impossible.

"You were not what I asked for. Why would it not tell me what it wanted? I would have given it anything. See, I think my mistake was that I didn't get Martha's consent. I think that must have been it. She did not walk into the mines willingly. But you did. I was certain that would be enough, but apparently, it wasn't. Why won't it just tell me what it wants? I tried to figure out how to profit from the mine, but I couldn't.

"Soon, some government agencies started asking about pollutants. I couldn't have them poking around, not with your mother down there. I sealed up the mine, planning to open it in a few years once I had a better plan and some more money.

"After some worse luck, we lost the company to bankruptcy. I put the past in the past, but this has been eating at me for thirty years . . . What does it want?"

Hesper had a madness in his voice. A crazed obsession. I knew that the Unknowable Host could passively create servants, but it was more than that. I think using its power also infected you in a different way. One of its many unreadable tropes must have caused this.

It was nice to have a bad guy not try to justify himself or convince you to go along with their plan. It was a change of pace.

Nicholas could not comprehend what he was hearing.

He didn't have very long.

Outside of the mine, the sound of a motor starting up echoed through the gravel pit.

"What's that?" Anna asked.

No one knew.

We began running out of the entrance of the mine. As we did, water started to trickle down into the entrance. At first, it was a single stream, but it grew and grew until a small river of water began splashing its way down the entrance.

"The water pump," Camden said.

The mine drainage system was situated outside and up around to the left. When we turned and got a view of it, we found Corey smashing the controls with a blank expression on his face. The pump wasn't just blowing water back into the gravel pit, where it ran down into the entrance of the mine, it was blasting water everywhere, dozens of feet into the air. Much of it was getting out onto the fields to the east.

When he caught sight of us, he turned. "We weren't supposed to stop the spread," he said. "I think this is what he wants."

Corey smiled.

We heard yelling from inside the mine. The water reached Hesper. Hope he wasn't thirsty.

"What do we do?" Kimberly asked.

"We leave," I said.

"Any of that water that doesn't get back in the mine is going to end up in the water table," Camden said. "I'm guessing that's how the animals got possessed last time."

"We need to go," Anna said. "Look."

She pointed out to the field next to the gravel pit. The animals had made it out of the air shaft. They stood watching us. They didn't attack. That part of the story was over.

"What about the machine?" Dina asked.

"It's gas powered; it'll run out in a few hours," Camden answered. "Besides, I don't think those animals will let us near it."

With the workers all gone, there were far fewer vehicles near the gravel pit. Nicholas's SUV was still there. We loaded in, but before Nicholas started the engine, he paused. He handed the keys to Kimberly.

"What are you doing?" she asked.

"I'm going back to get my inheritance and my mother," Nicholas said. "Go home. I'll be back in a little bit."

He leaned over and gave Kimberly a kiss.

He ran away from the SUV back to the table where we had gotten our climbing gear. He started grabbing things off the table. I didn't know what he was getting but he seemed to have a good idea of what the equipment was.

"Is he going back in the mines?" Kimberly asked.

Surely not.

Nicholas gathered all of the things that he needed and tossed them into the back of the truck near the table. He opened up the door and fished a key from his pocket. He turned on the truck and started to drive away from the entrance to the mine. He drove west.

"He's going for the wishing well in the Straggler forest, isn't he? The money at the bottom?" Camden asked. "I wonder what the deal was with that."

"I think we'll find out soon enough," I said. As I watched him drive away, I noticed something familiar. "You guys recognize that truck?"

"Isn't that the same one Akers had?" Anna answered.

"I think it will be," I said as the needle on the Plot Cycle clicked to The End.

CHAPTER TWENTY

THE AKERS PLOT

Suddenly, we were back around the campfire. At least we had all made it out this time.

"What was making the animals act so weird?" Jake asked. "Why would they attack like that?"

Why would they attack? Had he not been paying attention?

"No one knows," Akers answered. "Some say it was the ghosts of all those who had died in the mine. Others say it was a disease. Me, I think that nature itself got upset at the scarring of the land and decided to take revenge. I suppose we will never know."

I looked around at my friends. We were all confused.

The story was pretty clear about why the animals attacked. Wasn't it? They were possessed by the eldritch entity in the cavern.

It was true that at many moments throughout the story, we were off-screen. The most notable of which had been when we were around the Unknowable Host and the Off Screen light was blinking continuously.

It was like only we were shown the dead thing in the mines. Only we knew about the entire Hesper plotline. That left two likely possibilities. One: the storyline was broken. This seemed unlikely because surely one of the other teams would have seen it and Chris would never have recommended the storyline. Two: someone pulled some strings to show us something.

"You know," Akers said, "I think we have time for one last story. This one is really the last one, though. This one took place over two hundred years ago when a settlement near my family's claim started getting attacked by horrifying creatures in the night."

In an instant, I was sitting on a wooden bench on top of a large wagon. I could hear the clip-clop of a pair of horses in front of me pulling the wagon. I slowly realized that their reins were in my hands. I had no idea how to direct a horse, but I don't think it mattered. The horses were NPCs; they knew where to go. I just had to pretend like I was directing them.

The roads were dirt, the scenery forested and largely untouched. No barbed-wire fences, no buildings.

"It isn't fair that we were sent to fetch Cousin Walter. We should be back with the others. I wanted to see what happened to the settlement across the vale in the night. I can only imagine that it has been laid to waste," a young man said.

I only realized that he was sitting next to me when he spoke. I needed to say something.

"We do as we're told," I said.

"We always do," the young man said.

I looked at him. He might have been sixteen. Dark hair and a mischievous smile. On the red wallpaper, he was called Douglas. He was a standard NPC.

"I told grandfather that I loathed Walter," Douglas said. "He teases me so. He calls me Doug. What kind of name is that?" he huffed. "A terrible name."

"Walter is family," I said.

"That's what Grandfather said. He went after me with a rod when I told him I would not come."

I examined myself. I was not wearing my hoodie. I was wearing a loose white cotton shirt and . . . pants unlike anything I had worn before. I had no sunglasses or headphones. I was dressed like something between a pirate and a pilgrim. So was Douglas.

What year was it?

On the red wallpaper, I could see my role was to be Douglas's brother. I was tasked with keeping him in line. That was it. That was my whole role.

My friends and Dina were nowhere to be found.

"The settlers got what they deserved. We had a claim to the whole vale before they arrived," Douglas said. He twisted his face into one of disgust. "I cannot fathom why Grandfather permitted them to build so close to our land."

My job was to be a stand-in so that Douglas could catch the audience up on exposition, apparently. I had nothing to contribute to this conversation. I had no idea what he was talking about.

"Grandfather has his reasons, I'm sure," I said.

"Perhaps. I do not think it will matter soon. Their settlement will not last another night like last night, I am certain," he responded.

Off Screen.

Douglas stopped talking and sat still as the NPC horses continued to drag us along on our path. It was nice to see NPCs acting like actual NPCs again.

Our trek took us from a narrow wagon path to a larger, more established road. There were some forks that could have taken us in various directions. Still, there was no one to see for miles. The area was all wilderness.

Some of the landmarks were recognizable. We saw a sign directing us to Culling Creek, which was the area where the church had been in the Grotesque storyline. Mostly, though, evidence of human civilization was few and far between.

Eventually, we were let out into a large clearing that had been crossed every which way by wagons and cattle. On the other side of it was a wooden building with a water trough and horse posts along the front. Two people sat outside the building along with some large parcels bound with ropes.

One of them was a man dressed in a cloak, breeches, and a strange sort of hat that would have gone out of use hundreds of years ago. On the red wallpaper, his name was Walter. He was probably a few years older than me. Next to him, sitting on top of a crate, was a woman in a conservative dress and a crude bonnet. I recognized her immediately. It was Dina.

She had her eyes on us the moment we approached the clearing.

Her role was to be Walter's new wife and a newcomer to the Akers's claim.

As we approached, Walter finally noticed us right as we came upon them. He grew a large, cheerful smile and waved to us enthusiastically.

"Cousins," he called out as we arrived. "Time has treated you so well. Young Doug, you have grown tall since our last meeting. Soon, you'll be strong enough to best a bear in a wrestling match!"

Douglas barely acknowledged Walter and jumped off the wagon. He started loading the parcels into the wagon.

"Riley," Walter said. As I stepped down off the wagon, he embraced me in a hug. "I would like you to meet my new wife. We met at the delta and were married within a fortnight. Isn't it wonderful? This is Dina."

I looked over at her. "How do you do?" I asked. "I'm sure the family will be thrilled."

"Oh yes," Walter said. "Grandfather had threatened to wed me to a donkey if I didn't find a suitable wife. I am certain he will be pleased."

"Hello," Dina said. She smiled politely. I sensed that she was not loving her colonial clothing.

"Rope, nails, wax, leather," Walter said. "That and more. Everything Grandfather requested. It took me some time to procure it all."

I looked it over. "You have arrived at a time when the supplies are much needed," I said. That sounded like something that would be true.

We began helping Douglas load the parcels and packages onto the wagon. It was barely large enough to fit it all. Soon after, we all boarded the wagon and started our journey back. Luckily for me, the horses knew the way.

The trip back took almost all day.

When we arrived back at Akers's property, I hardly recognized it. In the present, it was a giant scraggly plain with two forests on either side. But hundreds of years ago, it was a lush green valley paradise. The land had not been cleared for farmland yet, though there were a few plots here and there growing wheat, tobacco, and other staple crops.

We were back on a narrow path. No road, just two ruts that the wagon wheels fit into perfectly.

"I am so excited to be home," Walter said to Dina. "The delta was exquisite but there is no place on earth like this valley. I am so excited to show you our new home. I built a cabin just before I left. Little did I know that I would soon be housing my own family there."

"Sounds wonderful," Dina said.

"Oh yes," Walter agreed. "At night we build a campfire and commune with each other under the stars. Uncle Timothy has mastered the art of wine making. We have many fine summers to come."

As we pulled farther down the road, we approached a small, humble house with two men outside hammering wooden planks over the windows.

"Hello there, Mark," Walter said. "Say, why are you battening down the hatches? There haven't been thieves about, I hope?"

The NPC, Mark, a long-bearded red-headed man, called back, "Ahoy, Walter, you back from the delta already? Have to make safe from the beasts."

"See you tonight," Walter called back as the wagon kept going. I didn't know how to stop it. The horses were in charge. "I will tell you all about my travels," Walter yelled behind us.

Walter looked back at Douglas and me curiously. "Have there been bears or wolves in the vale?"

I had no idea what was going on. "Douglas could say more than I could," I said.

Walter looked expectantly at Douglas.

"Mark is a fool," Douglas said. "The beasts have only attacked the trespassers to the east. We have no reason to cower in the dark."

"Beasts have attacked the settlement to the east? Do they need our assistance? I have two strong hands if they are of use," Walter said.

At this suggestion, Douglas absolutely fumed. "We should not expend our efforts on their behalf. This is our valley. They should leave."

"Douglas," Walter said. "That is no way for us to be. They have not, to my knowledge, ever done us any harm."

Douglas turned from Walter and said nothing more.

"I should like to speak with Grandfather," Walter said. He reached his hand over to Dina's and held it. "I have a new wife to protect. These beasts need to be dealt with."

As we got farther down the road, we came across more and more houses being boarded up. At the end of the road, there was a larger collection of houses surrounded on all sides by the beginnings of a fifteen-foot-tall wooden barricade. The barricade was simply trees stripped of their limbs and sharpened at the top. The barricade was far from being completed, but men and women were busy at work constructing it.

"What does Grandfather have them building?" Douglas asked. "And who is that?"

I followed his gaze toward the center of the collection of homes. There was an older man named Theodore Akers on the red wallpaper. He had a sturdy build despite his age, and the way he moved was like that of a younger man. As we got closer, I could hear his booming voice.

He was talking to two gentlemen who wore green cloaks. The cloaks had seen better days. One of the men was Camden. His role was the son of the leader of the Lord's Glory settlement. The other man was simply called Brent on the red wallpaper.

Theodore Akers glanced up at us as we approached, and a smile grew on his face.

"Blood of my blood. Walter, you've come home," he said.

Walter energetically jumped down from the moving wagon and ran to his grandfather. The senior Akers wrapped him up in a big bear hug.

"Grandfather," Walter said. He pointed back to the wagon. "I have news."

Theodore looked to the wagon, spotted Dina, and looked back to Walter. "You've found a woman to marry?"

"I already married her," Walter responded with a big grin.

Theodore grabbed his grandson up in another hug and then quickly moved to the wagon to reach his hand up for Dina's so that he could help her down.

"May I help the newest Mrs. Akers down?" he asked.

"You may," she said.

"And may I know your name, my dear?"

"Dina," she answered with a smile.

Theodore smiled. "A beautiful name. I am so glad to meet you. Come, I would like to show you your new home."

He helped Dina down as various NPCs started unloading the wagon in the background.

"Thank you for retrieving them, Riley," Theodore said. "Please help our guests with whatever they need."

"Yes, Grandfather," I said.

Theodore, Dina, and Walter walked off on a tour around the homestead.

The area was very well developed to my eye, boasting many homes, barns, storehouses, and other buildings you might expect in a small town. Children played and men and women worked on constructing the barricade. The people who walked around the Akers's property were likely related to my character.

There was little sign that this place would become the haunted land that I had entered hours ago. I didn't even know where the Straggler forest was—or, rather, the forest that would become the Straggler forest.

I approached Camden. He acknowledged me with a tight smile.

"I'm supposed to give you whatever it is that you require," I said.

The man next to Camden, Brent, said, "We are much obliged. We are in a desperate situation over at Lord's Glory."

"I have only just heard. Am I to understand that you were attacked?" Eventually, I was going to get one of these NPCs to tell me what was going on.

Brent nodded his head. "Creatures in the night—horrifying, ungodly things. They destroyed much of our home and raided our livestock. I don't know how our settlement is to continue without your family's generosity."

Off Screen.

Going off-screen meant that I didn't actually have to help them, which was great because it sounded like a huge distraction.

Wordlessly, Brent walked over to a horse that had a very small wagon hooked up behind it. NPCs started to load a small amount of material onto the back from the supplies that Walter had retrieved.

"What do you have?" Camden asked.

I shook my head. "My whole job is to follow this little kid around," I said. "All I know about you is that you're the son of the founder of the Lord's Glory settlement, whatever that means."

Camden nodded. "I don't know much more than that. That settlement was ravaged last night. Whatever those creatures were, three settlers disappeared. Some houses got knocked down."

"This doesn't really make sense," I said. "When Old Man Akers told us about the Straggler curse, he never mentioned monsters attacking in the night. You think he would have brought that up. This should be around the time the forest became the Straggler forest, right?"

Camden shrugged. "This whole storyline has been weird. Hopefully, this part is better."

"Are Kimberly and Anna with you?" I asked.

He nodded. "I haven't been able to talk to them much. I'm not allowed."

Brent waved for Camden to come to him.

Theodore, Dina, and Walter joined them. I ran to catch up. Douglas wasn't far behind.

On-screen.

"Riley," Theodore said, "I want you and Douglas to go with Brent and guide them through the forest to the west. Their food stores have been greatly diminished. Help them gather food from the abundance of the forest. They will be sending five of their best foragers over to take absolutely as much as they can carry. Understood?"

Douglas got a sour look on his face but said nothing.

Theodore gave Douglas a strict look. "Do as I tell you. We need to show compassion now more than ever. Don't you understand that?"

Douglas marched away in a fit.

"Go look after him," Theodore said to me.

I ran after Douglas and caught up to him.

When he saw me, he said, "We are going to risk everything to help these strangers. It makes no sense."

"We may need their help," I said. "What if the monsters attack us? They could help defend us."

Douglas had a strange look on his face. "I hope the monsters chase them out of the valley."

I didn't know where to steer the conversation, so I asked him something that I had been curious about since the Straggler storyline. "Do we need to get permission to enter the forest to the west?"

Douglas looked at me with a raised eyebrow. "Grandfather just told us to go there. We have permission."

"No," I said. "Don't we need permission from the forest itself?"

Douglas looked at me like I was speaking a foreign language. "Why would we need permission from the forest? It is our forest. We can do as we like."

Hadn't Akers said that the forest was magical and required permission to enter and harvest things from it?

"Permission from a forest?" He laughed. "What kind of nonsense is that?"

CHAPTER TWENTY-ONE

THEY COME IN THE NIGHT

I don't know why he helps those settlers. Every chance we get to let them either die off or abandon their settlement, he saves them. He gives them our food, our supplies," Douglas said.

We were alone at a trailhead leading into the western wood. I was apprehensive about entering. If I understood the geography correctly, this was the Straggler forest, or at least it soon would be. All I knew was that I didn't want to be inside of it when it became cursed.

"Maybe he's just being kind," I said. I didn't really need to say much to make Douglas go off on long tangents about how much he hated the settlers to the east. It was a subject that he could speak on for hours. Every moment we were on-screen he would strike up some new angle on why the settlers were dangerous or otherwise unacceptable.

"They can barely tan a hide," he said. "It's a wonder they didn't freeze last winter. They cut down so many trees for firewood that their forest is ravaged, so now they have to come over to ours."

While we waited, Dina broke away from whatever she was doing and came to join us. "Theodore said that you might show me the forest to the west," she said. She held up a basket that she'd been carrying. "I may not know how to build a fortress, but I can pick berries and mushrooms."

Off-screen, Douglas would just stand around and throw sticks and rocks at trees in the distance.

An older woman dressed in many layers of fabric and a hand-knitted shawl set out on a path toward us. She moved slowly. So much so that I wasn't even sure she was walking toward us. I thought maybe she was just out for a random NPC stroll so that she could be in the background of a shot somewhere.

On-screen.

"Douglas, Riley, care to aid an old woman as she searches for barnok berries?" she asked as she drew near. "This late in the day I'm afraid to wander off. They say that there are terrible creatures about."

"They won't hurt you," Douglas said. "I think they're only after the settlers across the valley."

The old woman smiled. "I've never known a beast to have such discerning taste."

Douglas didn't respond.

"We'll go with you," I said. "But Grandfather has us waiting on some of the settlers. He wants us to help them gather some food."

"Terribly generous of him," the woman said. On the red wallpaper her name was Esther. She was an ordinary NPC as far as I could tell.

"Foolish you mean," Douglas said. "They will raid it as they have the forests to the east and we will all starve."

Esther smiled. "I was worried that my father's pessimism had been bred out of our family. Then I realized that it is alive and well in you, Grandnephew. In fact, I recognize quite a few qualities of his in you. He used to think that we would starve every winter and be overrun by pillagers every summer."

Douglas threw a large rock at a tree in the distance. "What else but pillagers would you call the settlers to the east?"

"Fools," Esther said. "Harmless fools."

Douglas smiled. He liked hearing the settlers referred to as fools. "Fools indeed. Last year, they cleared a parcel of land that had a dozen berry bushes," Douglas said, looking over to Dina to gauge her reaction. "Cleared through them with axes and fire. Didn't even know what they had done."

"Our family was no better when we first came," Esther said. "My father had been a rich man when he purchased this land outright. A merchant. Spent his fortune making up for one mistake or another out here his whole life. Of course, Theodore thinks he buried his treasure on the land somewhere and never told anyone . . ."

She started to laugh.

"Our family never hunted an entire herd of deer only to let the meat spoil, did they?" Douglas said. "The Lord's Glory settlement did. Thought they would leave it to dry, turn it to jerky. They left it to rot. Grandfather gave them much of our dried venison so they wouldn't starve that winter."

"My brother is a generous man," Esther said. "I haven't any idea where he learned that from."

Douglas's face remained in the same sour position that it had been in. "Then when their goats and sheep died off for no reason, Grandfather gave them some of ours for milking and shearing and they ended up eating those too."

He really wanted Dina to dislike the settlers as much as he did.

Esther laid a hand on Douglas's shoulder. "You are giving them no grace at all. They have had many ill-fated summers. They do what they must to survive."

"They could leave," Douglas said. "They could leave this place and return to whatever place they are from."

Esther shook her head. "They came here seeking peace. They came here seeking God. We have no right to deny them that. They have not infringed on our claim."

"Close enough. Timothy says they practice a strange religion. That they worship a strange god," Douglas said.

"Hush now," Esther said. She turned to the east. "You are working yourself into a dark place. We should not speak of this when they arrive."

Douglas glared at Esther behind her back.

Worshiping a strange god? Did that mean that the Lord's Glory settlement was a cult? I would need to figure out which Lord they served. Perhaps he was taking "the long sleep" in a cavern below us.

"We need to stay away from Great-Grandfather's well," Douglas said. "We don't want them to learn where it is."

"True," Esther said as she leaned toward Dina. "They might try to drink from it. The water is foul, though you cannot tell that from the smell."

"I see," Dina said. "I'll be careful."

"It was his favorite spot," Douglas said.

"Oh yes," Esther said. "He used to go there to pray. My father would pray for hours. And we needed it. We had our fair share of setbacks."

Douglas looked to the ground contemplatively. "He used to take me out there. Before he passed. He wouldn't let any of the others go with him when he prayed. But he would let me."

I thought Douglas was quite fond of that memory.

"That's very nice," Dina said.

"The settlers would probably try to pray to their god there," Douglas said. "We can't have that."

In the end, we didn't have to wait that much longer for the settlers to send over the five they had selected. Those that came carried huge baskets. I didn't think they would have time to fill them before the sunset.

Anna, Kimberly, Camden, the NPC Brent, and another NPC were those selected. The final NPC had no name at all on the red wallpaper but was merely called Gatherer. She didn't talk much.

We were on-screen, so I couldn't talk with my friends about anything they had experienced yet.

"We do not have long," Brent said. "We will not take much. We would gather from the forests to the east, but the beasts came from there last night."

Douglas didn't answer. He simply started walking down the trail into the woods.

"We're happy to help," I said. Then I turned to follow him.

Off Screen.

We followed Douglas. The group moved at a slow pace to accommodate Esther. Douglas would occasionally get far out in front of us and then have to circle back impatiently. He didn't have any dialogue when this happened. Unlike the last miniature story, the NPCs behaved like proper NPCs here.

As soon as I could, I fell back to Anna, Kimberly, and Camden.

"Are you guys in a cult?" I asked.

"Yep," Camden said with a faint grin.

"They won't even let me speak to any of the men there," Kimberly said. "I'm not using Pregnancy Reveal in this one to save my life. They would probably lock me in the barn with the dairy cows."

"Last night the settlement got absolutely torn to pieces," Anna said. "They worship some hooded figure. I don't know much about it. Even with my A Kind Face trope, they won't talk to me. Camden has to talk."

"Wish I'd put a few more points in Moxie," Camden said. "They're really freaked out. They think that these monsters are an attack from the devil."

"What are they?" I asked. "Based on the descriptions I've gotten they could be anything."

Camden shook his head. "No one has seen one. People can hear them. Men just go missing."

"Carousel must be waiting to reveal what they are until First Blood," I said. "I've just been following that kid around. He really hates you guys."

"They call you Outsiders," Kimberly said. "They think you are sinners because you play music and don't pray. But they think you are kind."

They had better.

"Kimberly and Anna are sisters contemplating leaving the settlement," I said. I decided to take the opportunity to clue them in on their roles in the story.

"That makes sense. My character has a coin purse that she keeps hidden," Anna said. "Camden's fake dad is a jerk."

Camden's character was the son of the settlement's leader. He nodded in agreement with Anna's statement.

I wasn't quite sure how our characters' arcs would intersect again. Maybe my character would have to help Anna and Kimberly escape? Hopefully, I had something to do other than babysit Douglas.

We spent an hour or two gathering berries, mushrooms, and nuts from trees. Douglas was very careful not to let anyone out of his sight. Sometimes we were on-screen. Sometimes we were off-screen. I got the feeling that this was just going to be a montage. There was no dialogue.

The NPCs weren't really gathering much into their baskets. They were miming it. No one would be able to tell.

The sun did eventually begin to set. I waved goodbye to my friends as they set off across the valley back to their settlement.

"There will be no bonfire tonight," Theodore said. "All must be ready to take up arms in case the devils that plague our neighbors decide to turn to us next."

The entire Akers clan had gathered behind the newly constructed wall encircling several buildings at the center of the property. Their weapons were simple: axes, blades similar to machetes, pitchforks—the exact type of weapons you might expect to find in a place like this.

"We will divide up watch to ensure that we all get rest. We have a long night ahead of us. Bring the children and elderly into my home and lay them to sleep. The rest of us will take turns patrolling as our watch comes up."

I was given a metal pitchfork and first watch.

"Keep an eye on Douglas," Theodore reiterated when he saw me. Crystal clear. Why did this kid need so much supervision? Was he killing the neighborhood cats or something?

Small stands had been built along the inside of the wall so that the men posted on them could survey the area. Unfortunately, many of the buildings on the property weren't within the walls. It was simply impractical to hope to build a wall big enough in such a short time.

Walter, Dina's NPC husband, patrolled the area with a musket, ever vigilant.

"This is a waste," Douglas said. "They aren't going to attack us."

"You don't think so?" I asked. He had stated this multiple times. I was starting to get curious about why he was so certain.

"Our family has been here for generations," he answered. "If they were going to attack us, they already would have."

Still, I thought there was something he wasn't telling me.

Night had fallen. Hours had passed with no sign of any monsters.

Then there was a cry. An inhuman cry echoed across the valley and sent a chill down my spine.

It was followed by another and another. Each of them was coming from the east.

A howl in pain rang out with them.

In the darkness, I couldn't see far. My eyes scanned the walls waiting for one of those cries to be closer. Douglas listened too. We were off-screen, but still, he almost had an amused look on his face.

The carnage across the valley must have carried on for thirty minutes. The camera returned sporadically to get folks' reactions to the sounds. Then, all was silent for a while.

"I think the settlement must be gone now," Douglas whispered.

I could only hope that my friends were okay.

The Akerses on watch stood silently. Each face was more terrified than the last. The quiet grew more and more stressful. Even the livestock, which had been corralled within the fortress, did not dare break the silence. My ears strained to give me information about the outside world.

For the longest time we waited, the NPCs around me visibly shaking.

I didn't know if it was my imagination, but I swore I could hear creatures walking outside of the fence. I tried peeking out through gaps between the logs, but I wasn't able to see anything.

For ten minutes I waited.

Then I heard something outside. It was like the sound of teeth chattering.

Crash.

Glass broke in the distance. Someone forgot to cover a window.

"No," Douglas said. "It couldn't be . . ."

"They're here!" one of the men called from atop a stand looking over the fence.

Quickly, all of the NPCs that were supposed to be asleep were called by those who were awake and came from the buildings within the impromptu fortress, readying themselves as they walked.

"It can't be," Douglas said.

But it was.

Loud crashes started echoing around the fortress. Doors and windows were being broken in the houses that hadn't been walled in.

Something started to bang against the gate.

CHAPTER TWENTY-TWO

THE CLOVEN WOMEN

They're just . . ." a man yelled from atop one of the viewing platforms. I couldn't see his face, but I could hear the confusion in his voice. "They're . . ."

"What is that you say?" Theodore called out.

"There are no monsters," the lookout said. "There are women wandering about. Maidens."

Whatever was outside struck the gate again. The lookout should have been able to see whatever it was, but something had transfixed his attention in a different direction.

The animals in the corral had started making noise. They pushed against the sides of their enclosures.

Off Screen.

This mini storyline seemed to be functioning normally. I assumed that if the camera was not on us, it must have been on the other side of the valley. I could only imagine what Anna and the others were going through.

The needle on the Plot Cycle struck First Blood.

With the camera elsewhere, the gate was not going to open. The NPCs were stuck on a loop of waiting for the gate to break down so that the scene could continue. Men stood their ground, holding their weapons up in attack position against the unseen enemy.

Among us there were only three muskets in total. Walter, Dina's character's new husband, held one and the other two were in the hands of men perched on top of two of the buildings within the newly built walls. I predicted that they would be useless.

Douglas stood next to me in fear and confusion.

"What is happening?" Douglas said to me as soon as we were on-screen again. "It cannot be. Why would they . . ."

He was drowned out by the louder banging on the gate. Men had been stacking anything they could find in front of it. Whatever was on the other side was strong enough to send anything they stacked flying. Wood was splintering off the other side with every blow.

I racked my brain for some prediction that I could use for Cinema Seer to buff Dina, but I could think of none at the moment. Our part of the plot had very little information about the monsters. Anna and the others might have known more than me at this point. Luckily, Dina already had a huge Grit stat, so she likely wouldn't be able to use the buff that much anyway.

"Ready yourselves," Theodore cried. He had a hard look in his eye. A focused look. Even at his age, he stood tall and tried to project bravery for his kin.

I had my pitchfork prepared. It would take a lot of work to make any real use of it. I had not foreseen a direct fight like this. I always thought I would be able to sneak around and avoid danger. At the very least, I expected any fights to happen in the Finale with Anna around so that she could buff my Mettle.

So much for that. I had focused so much on making my Oblivious Bystander strategy work that I had neglected to prepare for an actual fight.

"They need our help," the lookout said from atop his perch near the wall. He was looking at something beneath him. He didn't look scared or confused anymore. He was almost smiling.

He jumped off his stand over to the other side of the wall.

"Jeffrey!" someone from the crowd yelled.

Moments later, we heard the NPC, Jeffrey, screaming as something struck him so loudly that I could hear his bones breaking. This sent the Akerses into a fearful uproar.

Bam.

Crack.

They would be through the gate soon.

Dina gathered beside me. Her stats were better than mine for a fight. Not that much better, but still.

Bam.

The gate blew open. The boards and crates that had been used to hold it closed were no match for the creatures outside.

As the gate crumpled from the last strike, I saw . . . nothing.

Nothing at all but a shadow fading into the tree line.

But I heard something. Whispering. I couldn't discern actual words, but I could hear them coming from a distance. It was a fascinating sound. So pure and sweet. I couldn't place it. Had I heard it before when I was young and things were better?

Dina grabbed me by the back of my collar. Suddenly, I looked around to realize that I had walked five steps forward without even knowing it.

"What are you doing?" she screamed.

"I . . . I don't know," I said.

Something was pulling me forward. It was pulling several of the men forward.

"Stand your ground!" one of the women in the back screamed as half a dozen men began slowly walking forward.

I heard whispering again. It was different. This time, it had no effect on me. In fact, it sounded closer to an animalistic bray than human speech.

But the handful of NPC men were still mesmerized by it.

Those affected inched their way toward the smashed gate. Those unaffected did everything in their power to stop them from leaving.

"They weren't trying to get in," I said. "They were trying to let us out."

Sure enough, just as I said that an older man on the front lines broke free from his kin and started running out into the darkness, following the tantalizing whispers.

As he ran, he threw down the spear he had been holding and yelled out, "I'm coming! All will be well."

It wasn't, though. He started screaming as something crushed him in the darkness.

This was how we spent much of the next few hours. The camera jumped back and forth between us and other things. When it was on us, the whispering would return and one of the NPCs might break for the exit while another tried to throw up a barricade.

There were more screams coming from across the valley whenever it was their turn to be attacked.

Even I was not spared the hypnotic effect of the whispering. Sometimes the whispers sounded rough and unappealing, other times they were soothing and beautiful. Dina was there to stop me when I couldn't snap myself out of it.

My theory was that there were multiple monsters in the shadows. Some had lower Moxie, so their whispers didn't work on me. Others had enough Moxie for their spell to send me stumbling toward the exit without a thought.

Dina and the other women were completely unaffected.

First Blood was long gone by the time we made it to the midpoint of Rebirth. We had lost several NPCs by that point.

The monsters' calls were strong, but it appeared they could only affect one victim each at a time. By that logic, there must have been six of the creatures waiting for us out in the dark.

I heard the whispering again. This time, it was so strong I was almost out of the broken gate before Dina could stop me.

I "woke up" with Dina and an NPC wrangling me to the ground.

"I'm fine," I said. "I'm better."

That one was powerful.

I could almost feel its whisper like it was a physical force in my ear. I looked out into the wood where the beasts hid.

It must have been time for the reveal because as I lay there with Dina's arm clamped around my neck, I saw a woman walk out of the forest. Five more followed her.

They were women. Just women. The lookout had been correct before his demise. They were pretty. They wore long dresses that draped down over their feet.

"Oh god," Dina said with a quiver in her voice.

What was she so shocked about?

Most everyone had the same dumb, confused look on their faces that I probably did. We shuffled back into the ruined fortress. I retrieved my pitchfork, which I had dropped moments earlier on my way out toward the forest.

There were six of them. They didn't seem threatening. Yet I felt a familiar force on my mind like I had with the Stragglers. I could tell I was being manipulated, but I couldn't tell how.

"You got anything?" Dina asked me. I could see the fear in her eyes. Whatever it was she saw scared her deeply.

But why? They looked harmless.

Shit, I needed to think. Dina had wanted me to use Trope Master on them. In the moments since then, I had almost forgotten. My mind was fuzzy. I focused on the one that stood in front of the others.

CLOVEN WOMAN	
Plot Armor: 22	
Tropes	
SUCCUBUS	This creature targets men, usually through seduction.
VIOLATED LORE	This creature is acting outside of its normal behavior. This includes ignoring some of its tropes.
PALE IMITATION	This creature is an artificial or false version of a traditional monster or entity.
JUDGMENT CALL	This creature only kills those whom it has deemed unworthy or immoral.

UNDETECTABLE	This creature warps the minds of its victims so that they will not notice that it does not belong, despite all the evidence.
THE EVIL VERSION	Many folklore creatures have versions that are good, neutral, and evil, depending on story and context. This creature is the evil version.
WHISPERS IN THE DARK	This creature can sense a player's or NPC's vulnerabilities and manipulate them via hypnotic whispers.
NON-COMBATANT	This villain cannot be attacked on-screen until it attacks the player or is otherwise identified as hostile. Attacking it will not be effective, nor will it change the story. It will cause the player to go off-screen for a time.
ARMS OF THE HOST	This creature will take up arms for the enemy.

That was a lot to process in a small amount of time. At the time, the thing I noticed was that it was a Non-Combatant, which made sense. Whispers in the Dark was familiar. The stronger Grotesques had the same trope, but for them, it manifested differently.

Non-Combatant might have been useful information, though. What it meant to me was that the Cloven Woman probably didn't need a lot of Grit if its build was logical. Why invest points into Grit when you cannot be attacked?

We might stand a chance.

One of the Cloven Women, the one that appeared to be the leader, walked forward to the nearest man, the red-bearded cousin I had seen earlier. She made eye contact with him. He did not attack her as she got close to him. He was under her spell. She had the highest Plot Armor among them.

"Run!" a woman screamed from behind me.

"Kill it!" Dina yelled.

Several of the faster-thinking Akerses stepped forward to try to intercede, but they were too far away.

The red-bearded man did nothing but look back at us strangely as she approached.

As she neared him, she reached her hand up to the side of his face, caressing it. Then she grabbed his beard and pulled hard. He fell forward onto the ground. Then she stomped his head. It might as well have been an egg under her foot.

Everyone screamed at the sight of it. Whatever men might have been entranced by the women suddenly snapped out of it and started to attack.

The creatures were strong and fast, but they were wary of the weapons facing them. The muskets fired upon them every time the guns could be reloaded. If the shots hit, they would only leave scrapes. Nothing substantial. None of the shooters had good enough Hustle to get a good shot in.

Walter shot his musket at one of the Cloven Women as she threw three men across the ground into the wall. His shot did nothing. She didn't even turn to him.

The leading Cloven Woman caught sight of Douglas and began approaching. In the background, the other monsters threw men around and stomped them to death every time the camera returned.

Dina and I raised our pitchforks. Douglas had a crude spear that he held out in a panic.

She moved forward, trying her best to dodge the points of our weapons.

"This shouldn't be happening," Douglas said. "This isn't what I wanted."

The Cloven Woman lunged at Douglas, but he dropped back behind Dina and me. In the corner of my eye, I saw Walter frantically trying to reload his weapon.

The Cloven Woman still had her eyes on Douglas as she lunged around Dina, attempting to grab him. She wasn't even trying to get at Dina, despite Dina being in arm's reach.

But Walter didn't see that.

"Dina!" he yelled. In an instant, he jumped between Dina and the monster, trying to point his musket at the attacking woman's head.

The woman struck him so hard that his musket went flying. He was cast to the ground with a thud. Then the woman lifted a foot and stomped Walter's chest with a sickening crunch.

Her . . . foot?

As I stared, I realized that she didn't actually have a foot. She had a hoof. A cloven hoof.

The wool was lifted from my eyes in an instant. How had I not seen?

This monster wasn't a woman, not a human woman. She was a terrifying hybrid of woman and beast. Deer, goat, I couldn't tell which. Her eyes were large like a doe's eyes and her look was wild and untamed.

Her magic had stopped me from seeing that.

Now that my head was clear, I jumped toward the musket that Walter had dropped. I picked it up and aimed it at the Cloven Woman. My Hustle was surely high enough to get a hit.

Bam.

She screamed out an animalistic yelp in pain as the shot tore across the bridge of her nose and struck her left eye.

As high as my Hustle was, my Mettle wasn't enough for the kill. It was enough to blind her, though. The Cloven Woman pounced on me and drove her hoof down onto my leg. I was able to move it out of the way enough that it only made contact with my foot, crushing three of my toes.

The monster still screamed out in pain from her lost eye.

I screamed out in pain because of my crushed toes.

However, its pain didn't last long, because Dina drove her pitchfork into the beast's back.

As I suspected, the creature had low Grit. Together, we were strong enough that it fell to the ground, dead.

As I looked back at the other women, they saw their dead leader and drew back. The other Cloven Women still looked like humans to my eyes, but I found that if I intentionally focused on their hooves, suddenly I would see their true form. Just glancing at them wasn't enough. You had to look at them purposefully.

Off Screen.

The women didn't leave. Instead, they pulled back into the shadows and started whispering again.

The screams across the valley were getting closer. That meant the survivors of the Lord's Glory cult were running this way.

And bringing more monsters with them.

I noticed that Second Blood had passed. We were in the Finale and the needle on the Plot Cycle was ticking along steadily.

The final battle was coming.

CHAPTER TWENTY-THREE

THE SECRET

All of the short stories within this storyline had gone by quickly, but this one even more so because I wasn't even in the main plot. Anna, Kimberly, and Camden had taken care of that. Dina and I had been in small snippets of screen time. That was about to change.

I could hear the sounds of travelers in the night—more than eighty people, by my guess—making their way through the woods toward us. They were screaming, praying, pleading . . . and dying. Every few seconds, I would hear the echoes of a man screaming along with the sickening sound of him being stomped to death.

It made sense, then, that when I finally saw the fleeing survivors of the Lord's Glory settlement, it was mostly women left. There were nearly thirty of them. There were only five men among them; Camden wasn't there. There were dozens of children with them, ranging from infants to teenagers. The babies and toddlers cried inconsolably.

Theodore Akers walked to the edge of the broken gate.

"Who goes there?" he called out. "Are you of the Lord's Glory settlement?"

One of the women moved to the front of the group. It was Anna.

"Please," she said. "Our homes are destroyed. Please help us. The Lord's Glory settlement is gone."

Theodore hesitated. The monsters looked like young women to his eyes, after all. He wouldn't have known if these were more of the same.

"Look to their feet," I shouted. "The women that attacked us had cloven feet."

This was news to most of the men in the camp, as well as some women. They had been completely fooled. Theodore looked back at me with a furrowed brow.

"Our attackers had the legs of deer or goats," I said, hoping to convince him. "Look at their feet. If they are human, you will be able to tell."

Theodore wasn't sure.

"He tells the truth, Theodore," Esther, his sister, called out. "They are the Cloven Women of legend. They have the feet of a doe. They lure careless or violent men from campfires and kill them unseen."

The other Akers family members who had seen the beasts' true nature chimed in with support.

Theodore relented.

"Well, come in," he said. "Hurry. And show us you are human."

The refugees did. They began running in.

I spotted Douglas backed into a corner. He would make eye contact with me every time I looked at him. I suspected the script needed us to clear the air before the final battle commenced. Douglas had a confession to make.

As NPCs began roughly rebuilding the gate, which amounted to stacking things back in front of the entrance, I approached Douglas.

"What did you mean when you said this wasn't what you wanted?" I asked.

Douglas was distraught. "I couldn't have foreseen this, brother. I only wanted to do as our great-grandfather did. I was charged with protecting this land. He said Grandfather Theodore was too weak to do it."

"What did you say?" Theodore yelled. He joined us as soon as I had initiated the confrontation. Many other Akerses joined him.

"I . . . Grandfather," Douglas whimpered. "I was doing as I was told! I only made my wishes to help us!"

Theodore looked at him with disgust.

"My father?" Theodore asked. "He showed you the well?"

Douglas nodded.

I wasn't sure if my character knew about the properties of the well, so I didn't say anything.

"We had it sealed," Theodore said. "You opened it back up?"

Again, Douglas nodded. "I only wanted to push them away. It doesn't listen," he said. "I can't figure out how to ask it to do what I want. I do not know what to offer it. I asked it to turn their milk sour and it did, but then they slaughtered their milking goats as diseased, and you offered them some of ours. Everything I did to run them away you ruined!"

"You fool. The powers of that well are not to be meddled with." Theodore said. "My father spent his life and his fortune at that well and all it brought us was heartache and pain. It always takes just as much as it gives. No more, no less. You have doomed us."

Douglas, like his great-grandfather before him and Hesper after him, had taken to offering things to the waters underground—to the Unknowable Host.

Like Hesper, he could never get what he wanted. In a sense, he would always break even.

Theodore approached his grandson and struck him upside the head.

"I'm sorry!" Douglas cried. "It was my job. He said you wouldn't want to know."

"His mind was gone!" Theodore said. "His heart was devoted more to the well than to his family. Now he's done the same to you."

Douglas fought back tears. He approached Theodore and said, "I can fix it. I can go wish this all away."

"What was it that you wished for?" I interjected.

Douglas looked down at the ground. "I wished that the men across the vale would be driven away."

The men.

The power in the cavern took him literally. It summoned creatures that would target the men. That's Wish-Making 101 in movies.

"I can undo it," he said. "Just let me go back to the well."

Theodore looked at Douglas with a mix of fiery anger and sheer disappointment.

I had an idea.

"Let me take him," I pleaded with Theodore. "We can saddle horses and have this madness ended before sunrise."

Truthfully, a horse was the only way I would make it to the well. I was Hobbled, after all.

Theodore wasn't sure.

"We need men here to defend the keep," he said.

I shook my head. "No, we don't. The monsters only attack men. It is women who should defend us. If women are on the front lines, the monsters will not kill them."

I finally had a prediction for Cinema Seer. It was something substantial too. My biggest problem with that trope was that my predictions could be so inconsequential that even if they came true, my allies wouldn't get a buff. This was different.

It was a risk, though. Attacking men didn't mean they couldn't attack women, but I was fairly certain. The one Dina and I killed had completely ignored her.

Esther limped her way into the conversation.

"Brother," she said, "these creatures only have wrath for men. Don't you see? They have no love for men, but in legend, they are protectors of women. I do believe your grandson is correct."

Theodore was uncomfortable.

"How will I forgive myself if I send women into battle while the men hide?" he said. "What if he is wrong?"

"If he is wrong," she said, "you will not be here to forgive yourself or otherwise."

Theodore reluctantly nodded. He turned and began instructing NPCs to arm the women.

"One more thing," I said. "We need cotton or wax. Anything that can clog a man's ear."

When the Cloven Women attempted to lure the men out, the air was thick with their whispers. They had the same trope that the Grotesques had: Whispers in the Dark. The difference was that the Grotesques' trope manifested differently. Theirs caused impulsive thoughts. The Cloven Women actually whispered.

If we couldn't hear them, they couldn't hypnotize us.

This sort of thing always worked in movies. In real life, blocking your ears only muffles things, but in the movies, it blocks sound completely, whether you are blocking a siren's song or a hypnotic suggestion from your girlfriend's racist parents.

"We have wax," one of the NPCs suggested.

Of course—that was part of what Walter had brought back with him from the delta.

Theodore nodded his head. He rested his hand on my shoulder in a show of approval. I got the feeling that my character wasn't one of his favorite grandchildren. He had over a dozen, after all. Maybe I could change his mind tonight.

"Do as he says," Theodore yelled. "Men, block your ears. Do not allow any sound through."

One of the NPCs produced a slab of orange-yellow wax from inside one of the buildings. The men began breaking off portions and stopping their ears with the stuff.

In the movie *Get Out*, the main character used chair stuffing, but we were using wax just like they had in *The Odyssey*.

Off Screen.

As the NPCs worked on repairing the gate, distributing wax to the men and weapons to the women, and saddling the horses, I found Anna and Kimberly. Dina soon joined us.

"Where's Camden?" I asked.

Anna shook her head. "We had to leave him. His leg is broken. He thought hiding was his best chance of survival."

"Dammit," I said. "Did you hear about the well?"

Anna nodded. "We'll go with you," she said.

I nodded. "I think Carousel wants you to. The NPCs are saddling up five horses."

"What happened with the cult?" Dina asked.

Anna shook her head. "The leader has been trying to get their deity to listen for years, but the results are only so-so. He thought the land was cursed. He figured that if he did some ritual to cleanse the land, his god would listen to him again. He was going to sacrifice us as virgins."

We had a brief laugh at that.

"Camden freed us just as the monsters attacked. It was a bloodbath. They were disappearing left and right. There were originally two men for every woman. They scattered. I don't know how many survived."

"Just for the record," Kimberly said, "I thought of plugging the men's ears earlier but none of them would talk to me."

Guess they got what they deserved.

The battle was set. Douglas and I had mounted horses. For our protection, we brought with us three women randomly chosen from among volunteers. Kimberly, Dina, and Anna all volunteered. We were briefly on-screen for this moment; we needed some explanation for why they were coming with us. We reverted to off-screen as the NPCs moved into place and the monsters regrouped to attack.

Between us and the gate, a line of women held their weapons. The men stood behind them ready to step in if my prediction was wrong. I could still hear through the wax somewhat, but the NPC men couldn't. They were method actors.

On-screen.

The newly rebuilt gate crumbled in one hit. It wasn't a barrier at all to the monsters.

There were whispers in the air, but as long as I pretended not to hear them, they had no effect on me. As far as the audience was concerned, I couldn't hear anything.

After none of the men were affected, the Cloven Women decided on a direct assault. They moved in through the gate a few at a time. They stared at our formation—with the women in front, they hesitated to do anything.

They began whispering again, but not to us. They were communicating with each other.

Soon, the wooden walls of the fortress were inundated with heavy blows as the Cloven Women tried to break them down. The walls consisted of heavy sharpened logs driven deep into the ground. They were much sturdier than the gate. They wouldn't last forever, but they would buy us time.

The monsters approached the front lines of NPCs. When they did, they were met with a flurry of swinging weapons warning them off.

I sensed an internal struggle in the eyes of the Cloven Women. Their lore said they were protectors of women, but then they had a trope that stated they would act outside of the rules of their lore. They demonstrated that by attacking the settlements. That was against their nature as Esther described it.

They were supposed to punish young men who chased after or otherwise harmed women. They weren't meant to kill all men. But they had thrown that part of themselves to the side under the influence of the Unknowable Host. After all, it was the Host's power that had brought them here, pulled straight from a fairytale.

Would they be willing to harm a woman under the deity's influence or would their original nature prevail?

Despite a desperate rage building in their eyes, they resisted.

They refused to harm a woman.

Kimberly, Dina, and Anna all received a buff from my Cinema Seer ability. It was a three-point boost. Two in Grit, one in Savvy.

The women began driving back the monsters. The cloven creatures had no choice but to move back as their sisters continued trying to break the walls of the fortress. As soon as they were clear of the now open gate, it was time for the rest of the plan to go into motion. I willed my horse forward. I didn't actually know how to ride a horse. Luckily, as I had learned earlier when driving the wagon, these horses were NPCs. They didn't need me to tell them what to do. I just had to hold on.

That was quite difficult to do.

Douglas and I were out the gate right behind a few of the armed NPCs. They gave us just enough room to squeeze through and make our way out.

The horses were more than happy to get away from the Cloven Women, so they ran fast and free in the direction of the well.

I thought we were home free until I learned something the hard way: the Cloven Women were fast too.

In fact, they were as fast as a deer.

The race in the moonlight was on.

CHAPTER TWENTY-FOUR

A LESSON IN WISHING WELL

Even though the horse ran with even, graceful strides, every hoof strike sent a jolt of pain up my leg from my shattered toes. An onlooker might have thought I had ridden a horse all my life as I guided the creature through the trees and over obstacles. Of course, that couldn't be further from the truth. The NPC horse knew the way. I was a passive rider. Pulling the reins did nothing except help me to hold on.

Douglas rode ahead of us. He was the only person that knew the way to the well. I watched his face, looking for some trace of the madness that I suspected lay underneath his foolish angst. Invoking the power of the Unknowable Host came with a cost, after all. It had driven Hesper to sacrifice his wife and attempt to do the same to his son. Douglas continued to invoke that power time and time again even as every wish turned back on him.

As I watched, I saw his hand hover over his right ear several times. He was picking at the wax plug—the only thing standing between us and the Cloven Women's spell. I couldn't tell him to stop; he wouldn't be able to hear me. Instead, I just watched as he touched it, rubbed it, and fidgeted with it every moment that he could get one of his hands off the reins.

Shadows danced alongside us as we rode. The Cloven Women weren't attacking directly, but still, we kept our weapons at the ready. Truthfully, I wasn't sure if I was coordinated enough to use my pitchfork while riding a horse. Luckily, the threat of it kept them at bay for a time.

Douglas held out his hand, directing us to follow him through a tight footpath that weaved between some large trees. The horses followed him without missing a beat.

I could hear very little but hoofbeats and heartbeats echoing inside my ears. Everything outside was muffled.

I saw a hand waving in the corner of my eye. I ducked down, believing it to be the hand of one of the Cloven Women, but I soon saw that Anna was trying to get my attention. I looked over at her. She mimed that she had seen Douglas messing with his earplugs. She was mouthing something. I couldn't tell what.

I could see the creatures moving behind us to the left and right. The horses were faster than them, but only just.

We broke from the footpath into a clearing. Ahead, we saw a cobblestone path leading up to a well sticking out of the earth. A large rock lay leaning against the side of the well; that was probably what had been used to seal it before Douglas moved it.

Someone had spent a lot of time creating a stone pathway, a bench, and a flowerbed around the well. All of it had become overgrown and run down with time, but I imagined that Douglas's great-grandfather had really devoted himself to this place. It was his temple.

We were a hundred yards out from the well when Douglas reached up to his right ear and rubbed it for the twentieth time. This time, the wax plug lodged within it came dislodged and fell from his ear down to the earth.

His horse slowed down almost immediately. He mindlessly dismounted before his horse even came to a stop. He fell to the ground, undeterred. Anna was yelling something that I couldn't make out. Douglas looked at us, then past us. He started walking forward, then running.

"Stop him!" I yelled.

Anna reached out to him to no avail. The horses turned toward him but steering them toward an unscripted goal was a fool's errand. Horse riding likely required a special trope. Luckily, we had someone with a trope that could do the trick.

Kimberly handled her horse with grace and skill. She must have used her Convenient Backstory ability. I wasn't able to hear her do it. She had rerouted her path so that she rode right past Douglas. She swung the end of the crude spear she was holding like a club and crushed Douglas's nose with it. He stumbled backward onto the ground.

I jumped off my horse and fell forward onto him. I quickly removed the stopper from my ear and shoved it into his. The pain in my foot was immense. At this point, getting him back to that well was too important. I wasn't sure if someone other than him could undo his wish. I wasn't sure anyone else would want to, with the effect it had on people who tried.

Suddenly, I heard the sounds of the night again. I quickly put my finger in my ear to ward off the spell of the Cloven Women.

Douglas was dazed. He stood up and Anna beckoned him forward back to his horse.

All around us, I could see a dozen or more of the Cloven Women arriving at the tree line.

"Hurry!" I screamed as I scrambled back to my horse. My injured foot was useless. Stepping on it sent a shock through my body. I fell down to the ground before I could make it. Fighting against the Hobbled status required Grit, a stat I had woefully neglected.

As the others rode off toward the well, I struggled to even stand. My foot had swelled, and my joints were stiff and unbending.

My horse took off toward the well as soon as it saw the other horses going. I was alone, failing to stand in the middle of a clearing. I could hear the others screaming as they realized I had been left behind.

The Cloven Women started running toward me.

I tried crawling away, but I knew if they got to me, that would be pointless. My pitchfork had fallen somewhere when I jumped off my horse. I only had one hand. The other had to block out the sound of the monsters' whispers.

It didn't really matter. They were beyond whispering. They weren't even trying to project their human forms. They were pure monsters now.

I really only had one thing going for me: I was not the male with the lowest Plot Armor near the Cloven Women. Normally, I could count on being targeted because of my halved Plot Armor. It was even lower than normal now, as my Hustle had been cut by being Hobbled. Still, with Douglas nearby, an NPC with three Plot Armor, the monsters would *technically* target him first.

Of course, that didn't mean they would ignore me. That would be too much to hope for.

The first Cloven Woman to reach me was small. She kicked me as she passed by, which dislocated my shoulder on contact. The second creature picked me up and threw me. I couldn't do anything to stop her.

I could hear someone yelling my name. I thought one of them, maybe Dina, was trying to get to me.

Something hit my face. A hoof? It could have killed me if it tried. My nose was broken. I wasn't sure how long this could go on. Whenever the Mutilated status clicked on, my Plot Armor would drop even further, perhaps even enough to lower me below Douglas and permit a kill.

I was Incapacitated by the blow as I lay on my back. I blinked rapidly to try to wake up my senses to the world around me.

I could hear them running over me. Most of their hooves dodged gracefully around me. Others stepped on me—my legs, my chest, my stomach. Still they wanted Douglas. One made an effort to stomp on my dislocated arm as she passed by with the herd, snapping it like a twig.

I lay there, unmoving.

My mind drifted into a dazed dream as I waited for the story to end. The needle on the Plot Cycle was nearly to The End. I didn't know how long I lay there.

The final battle, a race to the well, was over. Whether I lived or not, we would beat the storyline. After all, the Cloven Women would not attack my remaining teammates.

I heard something walking up near my head.

A Cloven Woman? One of my friends?

No.

I opened my eyes.

It was a deer.

I turned my head and looked up toward the well. My friends were running toward me. Around them, a dozen or so deer pranced off into the forest. The Cloven Women were gone.

I could hardly move. I had some broken ribs, I could tell.

"Riley!" Anna screamed as she got to me. She was crying. I must have looked pretty bad. I had taken a hoof to the face.

She stooped down beside me. I looked up at her. One of my eyes was swollen shut.

"It worked?" I mumbled. I realized as I tried to speak that I was missing teeth.

"They disappeared," Douglas answered from somewhere I couldn't see. "Riley, I . . . did not know this would happen. I did *not* ask for this."

He started to cry for a moment while repeating that he didn't know this would happen.

Off Screen.

The final battle was over, yet the storyline did not end. We waited for a while hoping to see the needle move forward but it didn't. Eventually, Douglas remounted his horse, and he went and found wherever it was that mine had run off to and brought it back so that I could be lifted up onto it. Apparently, we weren't going to get the easy way out. We had to go back to the Akers plot.

The ride back was a lot slower than the ride there. It was still dark outside, but sunrise must have been just around the corner.

On-screen.

While riding through the thick forest, we heard someone talking.

"Who is that?" Anna whispered.

I wasn't sure. It was a man's voice.

"Not a bad place to build," a man said defiantly. "Plenty of lumber here."

"Quiet down," another voice said. "Are you trying to attract those monsters?"

We rode along until we spotted the source of the voices. Beyond the thick brush, there was a small opening where the decrepit remains of a covered wagon sat thick with moss. A group of men lay underneath it in hiding. They had stacked up sticks and other debris to try to hide themselves, but I could hear them. What's more, I could see them on the red wallpaper as I stared at them.

They were NPCs. Nothing special. Only one of them had a name: Cooky. I assumed it was a nickname.

As we rode by, the men stopped whispering to each other.

"Who's under there," Douglas cried out.

The men didn't answer for a moment.

"Refugees," a voice said. "Only refugees."

I couldn't see Douglas's face, but from the sound of his voice, I could tell he wasn't happy. "What are you doing on our land?" he asked.

"No disrespect," the voice said. "We have come from the Lord's Glory. There are monsters about. When we heard them start to attack, we fled. Please, do you know if the Lord's Glory survived?"

"This isn't your land," Douglas said. "You shouldn't be here."

"We fled for our lives," the men pleaded.

"I told him this would happen," Douglas said as he turned to me. "That they would use this as an excuse to take our land. He'll have to listen now."

Douglas was obsessed.

Anna and Kimberly stayed quiet. Their characters were trying to flee the cult, so they must not have felt compelled to try and help its members.

"Let's go," I said to the best of my ability. "I need to get back."

"And just leave them here?"

"Yes!" I said. It was difficult to talk, let alone talk loudly.

I could hear Douglas mumbling to himself. Soon he urged his horse forward quickly. I thought about saying something to the refugees hiding underneath the old wagon, but my mouth hurt, and I just didn't care. The storyline was over. The others must have had the same idea.

Kimberly nudged her horse to move forward. The other horses followed.

Off Screen.

When we arrived back at the Akers plot, we noticed that Douglas was not there. Neither was Theodore for that matter. Douglas had ridden in this direction; I had assumed he was coming here. NPCs started caring for the horses and one of them began tending to my wounds. The storyline just wouldn't end.

We sat together, all of us, while the NPCs around us worked on repairing the damage from the attack. They had survived; the Cloven Women had followed us.

On-screen.

Douglas arrived on horseback. Something about him had changed. I couldn't see what, but then, I was not at my sharpest. My mind and body ached with pain as I lay back on a bale of hay.

He sat down near us.

Off Screen.

There was a scene change. I could tell because all the NPCs stopped what they were doing, and the sun began rising in the sky. The NPCs moved into their new places. About fifteen minutes later, we were on-screen again.

"I took care of it, brother," Douglas said proudly.

"Took care of what?" I asked.

He came close and stood over me.

"I went back to the well. I told Grandfather about the trespassers in the wood. That they even said they were planning to rebuild there. He didn't care. So, I went back."

"What did you do?"

He started to laugh, a nervous, crazed laugh.

"I asked the well to curse any trespasser who entered without permission," he said. "To make them wish they had never come."

Of course he did.

"Someone had to protect this land, this family," he said as he held out his hand. There was a bloody cut on his palm. It hadn't been there before. "I think I figured out what it wants—"

An NPC approached and cleared his throat. He was one of the Akers cousins. I didn't catch his name.

"Have either of you seen Grandfather?" he asked.

We said that we hadn't.

"That's strange," he said. "He went to help some displaced settlers from the Lord's Glory." The NPC looked west and scratched his head. "He said they were in the western wood. I'll have to go find him." As he spoke, the needle on the Plot Cycle clicked over to The End. "It's not like him to get lost. He was supposed to be back hours ago."

CHAPTER TWENTY-FIVE

THE BAD LUCK MAGNET

For the final time, we appeared back in front of the campfire. Camden was gone. He had either died or had hidden for so long that he was Written Off. Either way, it was just the four of us, Dina, Kimberly, Anna, and me. My injuries had healed, so I was no longer in terrible pain.

But something else had changed. When I had been in the last story, I had noticed there was something off about Douglas, the young character who had been so obsessed with removing perceived trespassers that he had, apparently, created the Straggler curse itself.

There was something about him I couldn't put my finger on, something being hidden from me.

He had offered his own blood in exchange for his last wish—the morbid conclusion of the same years-long eldritch-entity-induced mania that had corrupted Hesper.

He was no longer an NPC. He was an enemy. I didn't find that out until being transported out of the story. Over two hundred years had passed between that story and the present. And yet, Douglas was still here. He had been here the whole time.

DOUGLAS "OLD MAN" AKERS	
Plot Armor: 35	
Tropes	
UNRELIABLE NARRATOR	There may be a kernel of truth to this villain's tale, but it is best not to take them at their word.

TELEGRAPHED REVEAL	While an astute observer will know there is something strange about this character, the specifics will be hidden from the player until the end of the story. The red wallpaper and insight tropes will not help you here, though logic might.
CURSE OF LIFE	This villain will wander the earth until they remove their curse.
MOUTH OF THE HOST	This villain will speak for the enemy.
NARRATOR	This character can tell stories that the players must play through.
NON-COMBATANT	This villain cannot be attacked on-screen until it attacks the player or is otherwise identified as hostile. Attacking it will not be effective, nor will it change the story. It will cause the player to go off-screen for a time.

"What were the creatures in the dark?" Jake, one of the two teenage NPCs from the beginning of the story, asked.

Douglas Akers laughed. "No one knows. Some say they were sirens, attacking the cult for the way they treated the women. Others say it was spirits of the land, offended that the cult worshiped a foreign god on their soil. I couldn't say for sure either way."

Again, it appeared that the story Akers told Rudy and Jake was different than the one my group had played through.

"But when you come out late on a night just like tonight," Akers continued, "and you are very quiet, you can almost hear the whisp—"

Akers stopped talking.

He slowly looked away from Rudy and Jake, turning his head over to Anna, Kimberly, Dina, and me.

"Wait," he said. There was a twinge of . . . desperation, I thought, in his voice. "No. You weren't supposed to see that. That wasn't what happened! How did you see that?"

He stood up.

"That couldn't be what happened," the old man put a hand over his face. "It wasn't my fault. This land is cursed five times over."

He fell to his knees.

"The forest cursed the settlers because they did not ask permission!" he screamed.

The scenery changed, melting away.

We were back inside the Straggler forest right in front of Old Man Akers's cabin. It was the scene where he had explained the Straggler curse to us.

"The settlers didn't listen. They took more than they were allowed! That's why they were cursed." His voice came from somewhere above us. The Old Man Akers in front of us was looking around, wondering where the voice was coming from.

From all around us, Stragglers began appearing from the surrounding area. They were not the same Stragglers we had seen before. These were mostly members of the Lord's Glory cult. I could tell from their clothes.

But they weren't all cult members.

Among them, several members of the Akers clan stood. In the center was Theodore Akers, the patriarch of the family who had gotten trapped there when Douglas created the curse.

"No," Douglas cried. "I didn't mean to! I didn't ask for this."

Unlike the other Stragglers, which stepped toward us menacingly, Theodore Akers did not. He stood still, unwilling to attack.

"The old man always thought he was so noble, didn't he?" Douglas Akers continued to narrate. "Well, it took fifty years for that to change. Time changes all."

The Stragglers changed. Now they were gaunter, more decrepit. Their clothes had worn out. Theodore Akers had lost weight. Now, desperation appeared on his face. His time as a Straggler had stolen his restraint and better nature. He attacked along with the rest of them.

We ran toward the place where we knew the exit to be.

Our Hustle stats were higher than the Stragglers'. We soon left them behind as we ran to escape. It turned out that running was a pretty good strategy if you knew the rules before entering.

Before we could get to the exit, Akers spoke up again. "But then you would know all about escaping the Straggler curse, wouldn't you? You left your friend in the forest to rot. Ever wonder what a hundred years cursed to wander in a forest will do to a person? Let's find out."

Suddenly, a Straggler appeared in front of us, sitting down against a tree. He was gaunt. His clothes were worn down to threads. The muscles that had once made up his frame had now atrophied away. He barely had the presence of mind to look our way.

It was Antoine.

Kimberly ran toward him screaming his name. Anna pulled her away; he was an enemy now. We could only save him by ending the story.

We emerged from the Straggler forest. We were free.

For a moment.

"And the mine where all those poor men died, their lingering spirits reaching out and possessing those who come near, man and animal alike—you didn't like that story either, did you?" Akers said.

We were transported again. This time, we were back in the mine.

"How did you find the cavern beneath the well? Why did you go there? You were just supposed to ride the minecart and escape. There was no evil entity in the mines. No waters brimming with power. It was only the possessed, that's all."

Sounds started to stir behind us. Clawing, scuffling.

"Run!" Anna screamed.

We didn't have to be told twice. We ran forward along the underground tunnel as the possessed animals from the mine story chased us.

"That man from the forest wasn't supposed to be there. How did you know about him?" Akers asked.

The area in front of us opened up. There were trees there now, like those from the Straggler forest. Standing amongst them was Nicholas. He was a Straggler again. Beside him was his mother, still possessed, still the Eyes of the Host.

They didn't attack us but watched us as we ran by.

As we ran, dozens of possessed people began appearing around us and grabbing for us. They were miners, mostly. Corey, the activist NPC who had been with us in the cavern below, also appeared. He lurched out at us as the others had done.

"Why did you go off track?" Akers repeated. "What did I do wrong? You weren't even supposed to see the monsters hiding in the shadows, but you did."

Suddenly, we were out of the mines.

We were running through dark woods. Something in the darkness whispered to me. I covered my ears as I ran. If they attacked, I was helpless.

But they never did. I never saw a single Cloven Woman. All I saw were figures moving about in the shadows.

We ran out into the clearing where the well was in the Cloven Women storyline. The young Douglas Akers was at the well. He was slicing his hand and letting blood drop down into the well. I could hear Akers's voice even with my ears covered. He was distraught.

"This couldn't be what happened," he said. "This mustn't be what happened!"

And then we were back around the campfire.

Akers had collapsed onto the ground. He was sobbing.

"That is not what happened," he said. "That is not the story! I can change the story. Please let me change the story!"

Around us, the monsters were gone. Rudy and Jake were . . . all over the place. Maybe they had gotten attacked while we were running from Akers's narration.

We turned and ran away from the land. As we did, the Plot Cycle hit The End for the final time.

Akers had made up a story to conceal his past deed. Why had we somehow seen something different?

* * *

We waited at the entrance to the property for half an hour. Camden got to us in ten minutes. He explained how he had survived.

"Luckily, my leg was broken, so every time they whispered to me, I would try to walk out to them, and the pain would snap me out of the trance. Then I hid under the fallen church. Used a pole as a lever to lift up a piece of timber and lower it back down on my foot to pin myself down under there. They couldn't see me. I couldn't leave. Then I passed out from the pain."

He wasn't sure if he died or not. He just woke up on the ground when the story ended.

"Clever plan. Still got Written Off," I said.

"Success is all about lowering your standards," he responded. "I thought you would know that."

Antoine still hadn't showed up. We were talking about going in to look for him, but we weren't sure if the Straggler forest was operational still.

So, we waited.

"There," Dina said finally.

Antoine shuffled toward us from the western side of the field.

"Something's wrong," Dina said under her breath.

She was right.

As he drew near, he looked exactly as he had when we had entered the storyline, young and healthy, but his face was blank, trapped in a thousand-yard stare. His legs marched forward in an uncoordinated manner as if his mind barely had the will to move them.

He was crying.

"He's Incapacitated," I said. His Incapacitated indicator flashed the same as mine had when I was stabbed. For me, it was because I was in great pain and had lost blood. Why was his going off? We had just been healed at the end of the storyline.

We ran across the field to him. As we drew near him, I saw the distant, broken look in his eye.

Oh no.

As Kimberly got to him, she grabbed him in an embrace, and he fell to his knees. Camden and Anna helped catch him from falling all the way over.

Tears rolled down his cheeks slowly in a continuous stream. He barely even registered that we were there. How long had he been in that forest?

He raised his hand. Crumpled in his fist was a ticket. I couldn't read what it said.

"Look at his tropes!" Dina said. "Oh my god, look at his tropes!"

Her Outsider's Perspective ability had alerted her to them. I did as she said. Sure enough, there was something very strange: Antoine had two tropes equipped that he had not possessed when we entered the storyline.

Where had he gotten them? They were two of the most potent tropes I had ever seen in Carousel.

Bad Luck Magnet Type: Rule Archetype: Any Stat Used: N/A
Sometimes, one character has all the bad luck. They fail at everything they attempt and make the other characters look competent by comparison. With this ticket equipped, the player will be first in enemy targeting priority, regardless of Plot Armor. All of their stat checks will fail. On the other hand, allies will receive a buff in every stat check as long as the player with this ticket is alive and not Written Off. If an enemy casts a spell or aura on the party in any form, the player will be affected first. If equipped to a Wallflower, the buffs to allies will last the remainder of the storyline if the player survives to the Finale. Some people are born with all the luck. You should invite them to your funeral.

Failing every stat check was the same as having a zero in every stat. On the bright side, this trope effectively buffed every ally in any stat they used while they were using it.

Wait . . .

You Were Having a Nightmare . . . Type: Perk/Healing/Action Archetype: Any Stat Used: Moxie+
In horror movies, the audience often has a view into the character's memories and nightmares. At the end of the sequence, the player wakes to realize that the scene the audience has just witnessed—usually in a montage or in flashes—was actually just a nightmare. Traumatic Memories: With this ticket equipped, the player can temporarily repress or, at its greatest strength, permanently heal mental trauma by pretending that a traumatic event was actually only a nightmare that the player has been woken up from. Doomed Sequences: The paramount application of this trope will allow the player to undo entire sequences within the storyline by presenting them as simply being a dreamed event, thus healing allies and giving the players a second chance.

The player must be a main character and have interacted with the enemy of the storyline before using this trope. The story can only reset to the midpoint of Rebirth. This application will fail if not perfectly executed and in line with the narrative.

Be warned: unless the player has established Psychic abilities, the second version of events will be completely different than the original version.

The player must be "woken up" by an ally whom they have an established connection with. Its effectiveness will depend on both of their Moxie stats. Wake up from the nightmare of the past. Wake up to the horror of the present.

That one was . . . really good. If used perfectly, you could undo Second Blood and a botched Finale. That was incredible. Of course, Antoine surely didn't have the Moxie to pull that off, but still, he could use that trope to—

"Look at his nightmare trope!" I exclaimed. "Look. It can heal mental trauma. Read it!"

Kimberly was kneeling down over Antoine. She was tearfully trying to comfort him. She had been so preoccupied that she had not paid any attention to his tropes until I drew attention to them.

"How did that—" Kimberly started to ask. She read the trope on the red wallpaper. "What do we do?"

Antoine moaned dully. Somehow, he must have been a Straggler for ages. Surely Chris would have warned us about this.

"Will that trope even work?" Dina asked.

"Yes," Anna said. "It has to."

Healing tropes of all kinds tended to work outside of storylines, especially the mental health perk tropes. All of the veterans had their favorites. Reggie used one of his alcohol tropes regularly. Valerie always had her little candy "pills" on her. No one went through these storylines without losing some portion of their sanity. Tropes like this helped you get some of it back. Though, I couldn't remember seeing a trope that claimed it could permanently cure trauma at its highest power. That was very powerful.

"What do we do?" Kimberly asked again.

"Do we need to get him to a bed?" Anna asked. "It says he has to be woken up."

I shook my head. "Just lay him down. We don't need it to be perfect. It just needs to be good enough for now."

"Lay him back," Camden said.

Kimberly helped lower him to the ground.

"Close your eyes," Kimberly said. "Just lay down."

Antoine looked over at her. He suddenly appeared to recognize her. He breathed quickly.

"Close your eyes," she said. She gently placed her fingers over his eyes.

He did as she said. Still, tears leaked out the corners of his eyes.

Kimberly took a few deep breaths and tried to calm herself. She was going to give everything she had to this. In a storyline, this would probably not work. Antoine randomly sleeping in a field would be an awkward fit for most narratives. But we were outside of a storyline. That shouldn't matter as much.

I hoped.

I didn't know where this trope had come from or how he had gotten it. I wasn't even sure it would work. I just had to wait.

Kimberly placed her hand on the side of Antoine's face. "Wake up," Kimberly said softly. She moved her other hand onto his shoulder. "You're having a nightmare."

Antoine's eyes shot open. He breathed in a deep breath. He looked around at each of us.

He grabbed Kimberly up in a hug. All the while, he was crying and laughing with pure joy and relief. He whispered over and over under his breath, "Are you real? Are you real?"

This continued for several minutes. Antoine would cycle between fits of joyful relief and horrified tears. The trope hadn't healed his mind completely—we were far too low level to expect that—but he wasn't catatonic anymore.

"I am so sorry," Kimberly said. She had been crying too. "I am so sorry. I didn't mean to leave you behind."

Antoine pulled back from her and said through a lump in his throat, "You didn't . . . It wasn't your fault. It was him."

He pointed a finger back across the field in the direction of the gate.

Placed there, where he had not been before, was Silas the Mechanical Showman.

CHAPTER TWENTY-SIX

SECRETS OF CAROUSEL

I had never seen Antoine like this. Even when he had stab wounds and broken ribs, he stood tall and pretended it didn't bother him. At that moment, he was completely vulnerable.

It took a while to get the story out of him. He didn't remember some of it. Maybe it was because he was in the forest for so long. Maybe because it was now, partially, a fading dream. As he spoke, he would pause for a few seconds. He might have been haunted by the memory or simply been trying to remember. I wasn't sure.

"Someone told us to meet back at the cabin, but I didn't want to go," Antoine said, his voice filled with uncertainty. "I don't have any insight tropes that could help me tell the difference between a Straggler and my friends. The old guy said that you would be okay if you were all by yourself. I decided to make a break for it. I figured I'd just take myself out of the equation. As long as I didn't bring any Stragglers with me, it shouldn't matter.

"It would have worked too. I must have been almost out of the forest when I heard him. Silas. Appeared right beside me. He said I'd won a ticket. Riley's always talking about how he got his Oblivious Bystander trope in the middle of a storyline, so I figured that's what was happening to me. Like Kimberly's trope at the high school. I pressed the button and he spat out two tickets. And then he disappeared as soon as I grabbed them. Suddenly, there were six Stragglers on top of me.

"I tried to get away, but I couldn't outrun any of them. I couldn't figure it out at first. I didn't know anything about that damn trope he gave me. That stupid trope . . . No matter how fast I was running or where I went, they were right on my tail. I ran to where I thought the exit was supposed to be, but I could never find it because they were with me. I was panicking. Thirty minutes later, and suddenly, I look at the red wallpaper and I had become a Straggler. No more confusion. I knew what I was and what had happened.

"I kept waiting for the storyline to end, but it didn't. I watched the Plot Cycle. The needle was stuck right before The End. It would almost get there but then it would click right back, ticking back and forth but never actually getting to The End. It was like it was broken.

"I don't know how long I was there. The sun never rose. I never had food or water or sleep. I couldn't. The curse wouldn't let me. I just kept waiting for the story to end. I don't even remember when it did. Suddenly, I woke up and I was lying in the field with you."

Kimberly wrapped him up in a hug and cried into his shoulder.

"What the hell," Dina said.

"Why would Silas do that to him?" Camden asked. "Give him a trope that would guarantee he ended up getting stuck there?"

"I don't understand," Anna said.

I had an idea, but I didn't want to say anything until I was sure.

I turned from the group and marched back to the gate to where Silas was. Dina followed. The others stayed with Antoine.

"So, you're interfering directly now, huh?" I asked as I saw the mechanical man.

"You won a ticket. Hehehe."

I nodded. Of course. He wasn't going to just come out and talk to me.

Dina was quick to press the red button. She got a stat ticket, a trope, and something else, along with a handful of coins.

"I knew something was wrong with that storyline," I said. I had to assume that Silas, or whoever was controlling Silas, could hear. "Chris wouldn't send us on a busted storyline. You did it, didn't you?"

Silas didn't respond. His mechanical arms continued to move, and his little silver flashlight turned on and off.

"Riley," Dina said. She held up one of her tickets. "Look."

I took a quick glance at it.

Wait a second.

I pressed the red button and got a stat ticket, a trope, and . . . something else, along with some coins.

The something else was a ticket that read:

Congratulations!
You found Secret Lore: Secrets of Carousel #6: The Dark Water

---

Bring this ticket to the Carousel Public Library to collect your prize. Collect ten for a huge reward!

"Beneath the stygian depths of those accursed lands lies the cadaver of an unfathomable abomination, decayed and desolate, hailing from a plane beyond the grasp of mortal comprehension, where time and space intertwine in grotesque amalgamation. Those audacious souls who dare to feign dominion over the lingering puissance shall forever remain oblivious to the insidious sway it holds over their very thoughts, for their consciousness becomes mere puppetry, enmeshed in the service of an enigmatic primogenitor. In solemn silence, its devoted thralls patiently await commands that shall never come, forever trapped in a maddening cycle of anticipation and despair. A malevolent force permeates the air, subtly and insidiously, causing dreadful transformations and disfigurements to all that bask in its baleful aura. The indigenous populace once believed that the accursed land was besieged by a multitude of evils, yet their misconception betrays their feeble understanding; for in truth, a singular abhorrence reigns supreme, exerting its insatiable dominion over the forsaken territory even in death."

"In Carousel, I envision a haven for souls of every stripe. Without each member of our growing community, we wouldn't be the town we are today."
—Bartholomew Geist, Founder of Carousel.

Secret Lore . . .

We had been in a secret version of the storyline. But how? And what was different about our version? Did the other players not know about the dead entity underground? We needed to get back to Chris and the other players so that we could ask them what had happened in their versions.

This didn't sit right with me. Finding something significant by *accident* . . . Something was off. Carousel had forced it. I needed to figure out what it was.

Eventually, Antoine, Kimberly, Anna, and Camden made it all the way to the gate.

"Is it talking?" Kimberly asked.

I shook my head.

"Can it even hear us? Is it just a machine or is there someone there?" she asked, enraged. "Hello! Why did you do this?"

"You won a ticket. Hehehe," Silas said.

Camden pressed the button. He got the same things Dina and I did. So did Anna afterward. Kimberly eventually came around. Antoine was hesitant to press the button, but he powered through; I could tell that the sight of the machine affected him.

They all got the same Secret Lore ticket and a trope. They also all got a good number of stars on the red wallpaper, but no one cared. No one wanted to think about how good our performances were after what happened to Antoine.

Kimberly got two stat tickets instead of just one.

After Antoine got his rewards, which included twice as much money as everyone else, Silas started to speak again.

"The stories can be pretty gruesome here in Carousel, but at least you get to be the star of the show!" he said. "Hehehe."

"What the fuck does that mean?" Antoine asked with a mixture of anger, sadness, and desperation.

Silas didn't answer, but still, I had a hunch.

"I think he can only talk in prerecorded quips," I said. "He can't just talk to us straight up."

When I said that, Silas turned his head to me and said, "Aren't you a smart cookie? Be careful—some of the monsters around here have a sweet tooth! Hehehe."

Then he disappeared.

I received a blue ticket:

Location Scout
Type: Insight
Archetype: Any
Stat Used: Savvy
Before any movie can begin production, the filmmakers must find locations for the shoot. Finding the perfect venue to shoot the film is important for making the movie come to life.
With this trope equipped, the player will receive a list of all primary filming locations within the storyline. The higher the player's Savvy, the more expansive the list becomes. If equipped to a Film Buff, the player will be able to scout a limited amount of this information *before* entering a storyline.
At higher levels, the player will receive locations that the story *can* go, not simply the places it *will* go.
Of course, even if you know where the film takes place, your final location will probably be the morgue.

Kimberly received a red ticket:

That's What I Said!
Type: Action
Archetype: Any
Stat Used: Moxie

Some characters get no respect. Even when they have a good idea, they get overlooked and have their ideas stolen by someone else.

Normally, a plan's success or failure is a result of two factors: the innate plausibility of the plan and the Savvy stat of the person who came up with the plan. A player with this ticket equipped can have their plans and ideas "stolen" by higher-Savvy allies, with the ally seemingly rephrasing their very same idea. When this verbal exchange occurs, the plan's success will be gauged by the ally's Savvy.

Ally: "We should sneak in through the window and surprise them."

Group: "That's a great idea. You're so smart."

Player: "Wait, when I said that you said it was stupid!"

Camden received a green ticket:

The Immobile Genius

Type: Buff

Archetype: Scholar, Doctor

Stat Used: Savvy

Why is it that smart people in movies are always unable to enact their plans themselves? They always have to explain their plan to some good-looking, cool character who then has to go complete the mission while the actual smart person sits back and waits.

When the player equips this ticket, they will be able to send allies off to enact a plan instead of doing it themselves. In doing so, the ally will gain a temporary Savvy boost proportionate to the player's Savvy. Any knowledge passed to the player to perform the task will appear on their red wallpaper. If the player has been Hobbled or Captured, the buff will last long enough to rescue or otherwise assist in relocating the player.

"Now listen to me very carefully: when you get there, you need to flip the switches in the correct sequence, or we're all doomed."

"So you're saying there's no pressure?"

Dina received a blue ticket:

Outside Looking In

Type: Insight

Archetype: Outsider

Stat Used: Savvy

In a world filled with action and attention, it's challenging to avoid the spotlight. However, there are moments when observing from the shadows can provide a clearer understanding of the situation.

Equipping this ticket grants the player the ability to discern ideal spots to linger, granting them a vantage point to observe events without actively participating in the narrative.

Not all characters are destined to be in the limelight.

Anna received a purple ticket:

Along for the Ride
Type: Rule
Archetype: Final Girl
Stat Used: Savvy

In a group, members with less Plot Armor can be picked off one by one, but when they travel together in a vehicle, their fates are tied together.

With this ticket equipped, when allies are gathered together in a vehicle or similar, the entire vehicle will be considered to have the player's Hustle stat. In the Finale, it will also have their Grit.

A huge percentage of people in modern society die in car wrecks. In Carousel, they usually die right afterward.

Antoine received a red ticket:

Time-Out!
Type: Action
Archetype: Athlete
Stat Used: Grit

In a movie, a fight can often last so long that the camera can cut away to give the audience a break. When the camera cuts back, the fight is still going, often having changed location as the combatants throw each other around the scenery.

When equipped, the player can call time-out in the middle of a fight just by saying or signing it. They will go off-screen the very second the player starts to do this. The enemy will be far less aggressive off-screen, though they will still fight and will not be killable during this period. The player can flee; however, the fight will resume as soon as the time-out ends, regardless of the player's action. The higher the player's Grit, the longer the break.

Don't be afraid to take a breather. Just know it may be your last.

CHAPTER TWENTY-SEVEN

A THEORY

We made it back to Dyer's Lodge before sundown.

Antoine was still visibly withdrawn and distant. His eyes were red and watery. It was enough that when we walked back into the lodge, people noticed. Dyer's Lodge was never the happiest place on earth, but most people breathed a sigh of relief when they walked through the doors.

"Is he . . . hurt?" Grace asked as we walked by her. She was on the couch reading a book but looked up as soon as we came in.

"Bad run," I said quickly as we walked by.

Antoine was looking for Chris. I didn't know what answers he might have; at this point, we knew our version of the campfire storyline was highly unusual. Still, we needed confirmation. We needed to know what exactly had happened differently.

I already had my suspicions.

"Chris!" Antoine yelled as we moved to the center of the entryway.

Players looked up from all over to see what the ruckus was about. Chris was upstairs in the nook where all the unsolved treasure maps and riddles were kept. When he saw Antoine, he immediately knew something was wrong. I thought he had insight tropes to help with that, though I didn't think to look at the time.

"What's wrong?" Chris said. He ran down the stairs two at a time. "What happened?"

"I got trapped in—" Antoine started to say. The very thought of what he had experienced brought back a flood of emotion that caught in his throat and stopped him from talking.

Chris grabbed Antoine and led him to a nearby couch.

He looked back at us. "Tell me what happened now."

Anna, as usual, spoke for us. "He got trapped in the storyline we went into. The Straggler forest. He was there for . . . we don't know how long."

"Stragglers? What?" Chris said. "That doesn't make sense."

A crowd of concerned players surrounded us. They began whispering to themselves. One thing that was evident was that they had all done the Akers campfire storyline before.

"I was caught by the Stragglers," a man in the back said. It was one of Reggie and Grace's teammates, one of the Bruisers. "I was only there for a half hour. Barely even realized I had been caught before the game ended." He chuckled to himself at the thought.

"Our storyline went wrong," I said. I had wondered if the axe murderer might be upset by my mentioning it, but I didn't hear a peep from him. "He was stuck in the first storyline in the anthology after the rest of us left. Old Man Akers said he trapped him for a hundred years."

At that, the people surrounding us were confused. The crowd parted ways and Arthur came through.

"Tell me everything," he said to Anna.

So she did.

She told him about leaving Antoine behind in the Straggler forest, the strange second storyline in the mines with the Unknowable Host and Hesper, and the final storyline with Douglas and the Cloven Women. Then she told him about Silas the Showman interceding to make Antoine fail.

Arthur was interested but offered no answers. "How do you know the storyline broke?" he asked. "Maybe this creature just had a powerful trope."

The others in the crowd liked that theory more. It was safer.

Now that they understood his condition a little better, they started to offer solutions. A Doctor Archetype named Jordan gave Antoine a pill to make him fall asleep right there on the couch. They figured that actual sleep combined with his new You Were Having a Nightmare . . . trope would help him shake much of his mental fatigue. It might not be permanent, but if not, the other players offered to share some of their mental health tropes until he was able to manage.

Antoine was soon asleep. A peace spread over his face, but even that was interspersed with fear and shaking. Kimberly sat near him, ready to wake him and activate his trope at the slightest turbulence in his sleep. Chris stayed with them for hours. Hearing about what his little brother had experienced had devastated him.

The conversation continued elsewhere so as to not disturb Antoine.

"You guys are just being paranoid," Todd said with a smile. "Silas does that type of thing all the time. A year after I got here, he appeared to me in a storyline that starts on a plane and gave me a Comedian trope called Rubber Bones that gave me higher Grit but made me more accident-prone. My parachute didn't open all the way. I got horrifically injured, but I also got a background trope called Near Death Experience that I still use to this day."

Other people had similar stories.

If they expected us to believe that everything was business as usual, they weren't doing a good job. I refused to believe this was normal. Silas sabotaging a player to this degree went against the rules Carousel had established. It had its version of fairness that wasn't really fair, but this was too far.

After a minute of discussing Silas, they all started recounting their experiences in the campfire storyline. One thing remained constant: the Straggler forest. After that, you would get two different mini storylines. We didn't have to worry about spoiling the story because everyone had already done it. Some of the stories actually did sound fun as Chris had promised.

"We got the mines," Grace said. "Didn't see any undead god, but we did the minecart race thing. Barely managed to fit my boys in the cart. Then we did the mutant bat hunt with the rifles. Bruisers don't have Hustle, though, so they just smacked them with tree branches."

This elicited some laughter.

"We repeated it a dozen times trying to get the treasure hunt one," Todd said. "We got the minecart race, the dirt bike race with the ghost horses, the bat shootout, and a few others. We also got the one set in the past with the monsters whispering in the dark, but there was nothing about a wishing well."

As they told their stories, it became clear that none of them had heard of the wishing well. To them, the Cloven Women had been a glorified game of flashlight tag. They ran through the dark woods trying to avoid getting lured away by unseen voices with few of them having actually seen what killed them if they died.

More significantly, none of them had seen the Unknowable Host, or Hesper for that matter. No one remembered the owner's son, Nicholas, being there. In fact, the mine owner was usually a role for the players to play.

It wasn't like this was a niche little storyline either. On the contrary, many had played it multiple times trying to find new mini-games and hoping they would get a storyline with otherworldly moonshiners and buried treasure. Only a few had succeeded.

That was the reason Chris knew it so well. He had gotten the treasure years earlier.

After they had told their stories and the mood started to calm, I showed them the Secret Lore ticket. "Has anyone gotten one of these?" I asked.

They seemed vaguely familiar with them, but most had only heard of them secondhand. The former generation had dismissed them as being tied to high-level storylines and they had believed them to be inaccessible. They were apparently wrong.

Upon passing around my Secret Lore ticket, one of the players laughed. "I got one of these. A million years ago. Sure."

It was Lukas Lewandowski, our craziest Hysteric. He had been our First Blood in the *Scrunchies* storyline. His poster on the red wallpaper showed him screaming at an axe that was lowering into the frame. "Lukas Lewandowski is *The Hysteric.*" Plot Armor: 44.

Every morning, he could be seen draining an entire pot of coffee into an insulated jug and walking around camp with it, taking big swigs every few minutes.

"What do you want to know?" he asked, eager for attention.

Anna looked down at Antoine on the couch and decided to take the lead. "Did the storyline mess up?" she asked. "Did the story go off-screen or did any of the NPCs act funny?"

"Yeah," he said. "Well, the last part. I don't know about anything messing up. The story went off the rails for a bit and we were off-screen for it. It's actually an interesting story."

He took a big swig from his jug of coffee.

"We were just fooling around. This was over a decade ago, mind you, so my memory isn't fresh. We were trying to see how much we could power up one of my tropes, called Too Pathetic to Kill. It's Moxie based and prevents you from being killed as long as you act, well, pathetic. Harmless. But its odds of working go down every phase of the Plot Cycle.

"We had a plan, though. We would get a bunch of strong buffs and buff my Moxie through the roof. Then we would go to a storyline and see if we could make me immortal. We tried it a few times. It worked pretty well. The problem was, if I ever tried to help or fight, or ever acted brave, it would stop working permanently. So not viable in most storylines.

"But that doesn't matter. We decided to clear through a—" He paused, closing his eyes and lifting his finger while he was in thought. "I'll be vague because of spoilers. We decided to clear through a particularly tough storyline. It was way over my level, but I had some heavy hitters with me. A home invasion slasher. There are plenty of those out there, right? Anyway, this one was weird. I tried acting all pathetic, sad, pitiful—things that had worked before.

"Except in this storyline, they didn't work. Not even a little. My Moxie should have been high enough, but still, these slashers didn't even hesitate to kill me. So then we tried to find out why. We tried everything to figure it out. Maybe they've got a ridiculous Moxie to counter mine? Too high for the trope to work? Nope. Brought in an Eye Candy to check. Their Moxie was super low.

"Maybe they had a trope that prevented it from working. That's our next thought. Nope, got an Outsider—he's gone now—with a betrayal trope called Evil All Along—" He looked over at Anna. "What? You furrowed your brow."

"What's a betrayal trope?" she asked.

I wished she hadn't distracted him.

Lukas held up a finger and closed his eyes for a moment while he thought about the best way to explain it. "A betrayal trope allows you to betray your team for some benefit. There are a bunch of them. Some are useful, some less so. I've got a Hysteric one that allows me to betray someone in First Blood and get them killed by the bad guy, but guarantees I get killed as Second Blood. Pretty good blood control."

Lukas was the only person at the lodge who called manipulating First and Second Blood "blood control."

"Anyway, this one was a good one. It allowed an Outsider to betray their team and reveal that they were on the side of the bad guys the entire time." He smiled a big smile. "In doing so, the Outsider can then see the enemy's tropes because they're on the enemy's side. They can sneak over off-screen and tell you everything. Course, then you have to kill them in the Finale, but still. It is really useful to know the enemies' tropes."

I'd have to agree with that.

"Anyhoo, that didn't work. He said they were all normal slashers. No tropes to explain how they were resisting my trope. It was infuriating. There was no explanation. But we didn't give up. We kept trying. We were obsessed at this point."

Lukas stopped talking for a moment to gulp down his coffee.

"We decided to pull out an old trick from treasure hunting. We invited a player who had a Departed Advanced Archetype. Departed become ghosts when they are killed. Couldn't get him to come until we told him the betrayal trope didn't work. Then he was suddenly interested. I forget his name. He . . . well, he's been gone now for many years.

"He comes with us. Gets killed for First Blood and then he's a Departed, floating around unseen, looking for some explanation for why these killers are resisting my trope. But the story was just a slasher without any supernatural elements, so of course he couldn't reveal himself without altering the story more than it already was. But he could give us hints off-screen. Then he found it: there were other ghosts there. The strangest thing was these ghosts had ninety Plot Armor in a sixty Plot Armor storyline. They must've had tropes that blocked even most Psychics from detecting them. Must have had a trope that countered mine too.

"Turned out this simple home invasion storyline wasn't actually just a slasher: it was a haunting. The victims were responsible for a bunch of people dying and were being haunted. The killers were all possessed, but the ghosts were so strong no one could detect that. On that run, the story went in a whole different direction. We had played through this storyline dozens of times at this point, mind you. It had changed completely.

"By the end, we had to escape as the ghosts killed the NPCs that had killed them years earlier. Mind-blowing. As you said though, we were off-screen for some bits, but I didn't think too much of it at the time. If you play through the storyline today, you would never think there was anything supernatural involved, but there is.

"When we finished the storyline, we got one of those tickets, talking about some massacre in Carousel years ago. Traded it in for a treasure map a couple of years later. Still, it was quite exciting at the time."

After a while, everyone dispersed. I found myself on the back deck watching the sunset. I figured that the others wouldn't know much about the problem. If they had, that would have come up at some point. Even Arthur didn't seem too interested once we described it. They all explained that NPCs often keep talking off-screen to help push you to the next scene or just in case the camera came back on suddenly. They said the camera could have been cutting in and out due to one of the creatures' tropes.

I don't want to say they dismissed it, because they didn't, but they certainly didn't seem as alarmed about it as we had. They were interested, but it wasn't the game-changing revelation I had expected it to be. If anything, they were more interested in the Secret Lore ticket than the weird effect on the red wallpaper.

Soon, Dina, Anna, and Camden joined me on the deck. They were all tired and confused; I could see it in their eyes. Camden slumped down into a chair near me.

"What do you think?" he asked.

I shrugged. "A million things," I said. "They seem to think the flickering was just one of the Host's tropes messing with us."

"Well, they'll see it for themselves soon from the looks of it," he said.

Inside, many of the veterans had rearranged some couches and brought in a chalkboard to devote to the Secret Lore investigation. The energy inside was electric. Soon, they would be running the campfire storyline for themselves to try and reproduce our run.

Dina watched them. She actually looked happy to see them working.

"Looks like they're going to figure things out for us," she said. "Finally, they're doing something useful."

Anna shook her head. "You're not being fair," she said. "You heard them talking. They thought all of the Secret Lore was locked behind high-level storylines."

Dina didn't respond.

"You all think the Secret Lore will show us the way out?" Camden asked after a beat.

No one said anything at first. It was too early to guess.

"Maybe," I said. "I couldn't say."

I must not have sounded too confident.

"You don't think so?" Dina asked. "It has to be important."

I shrugged. "It may be important, I don't know."

"But you don't think it's the way out?" she asked as if it were an accusation.

From the moment I picked up that lore ticket, I couldn't shake the feeling that there was something off. Antoine's suffering aside, this whole thing was too easy.

"I just have a weird feeling about it," I said. We hadn't had much time to discuss this.

"So?" Dina asked.

"I don't pretend to be a movie critic or anything, but I do know some things. In a story, the main character can stumble sideways into a B plot, but they can't stumble forward in the A plot," I said. "We went out on some random storyline and just happened to uncover a huge plot development? That isn't how it works. We are supposed to seek things like that out."

"Does everything have to fit perfectly?" Dina asked. "We're clearly being led this way. We can't just ignore it."

She was taking my musing a little too seriously.

I was assigned Film Buff for a reason. I didn't want to argue with her, though. I shouldn't have said anything.

Camden spoke up. "Silas interfered. We didn't stumble into it. Silas showed it to us at a huge cost to Antoine. Whatever he did, it was his doing."

"Fine," I said. "It's just a theory. I think we need to keep our eyes open is all."

Anna changed the subject after that.

I should have waited to bring up my reservations.

The veterans inside were dissecting what we had told them and were making battle plans. I was actually looking forward to seeing them in action.

More than anything, I couldn't wait for them to go through that same storyline, if only so they could see the Host for themselves. I wondered if they would explain his effect away then.

I went inside to watch them discuss their plans. They hadn't been able to share much with us in that regard on previous storylines, because they hadn't wanted to spoil important stories and cause us to miss out on experience and loot. Now, we could actually learn from them.

And I couldn't wait.

CHAPTER TWENTY-EIGHT

THE BRAINSTORM MONTAGE

By the next morning, much of the lodge had developed a fascination with the concept of Secret Lore tickets. They wanted to get Secret Lore tickets of their own.

Not the whole lodge, of course.

"Those things are a waste of time," Arthur warned us as he and the other high-level players prepped for their own mission. "The players that were here when I got here obsessed over those things for years and all they ever got was a few trinkets. They're all flavor and no substance."

"We should pack it up, then," Roxy, the Femme Fatale, whispered to Grace with a smirk after Arthur was out of earshot. "Those folks never missed anything."

"Don't speak ill of the dead," Grace said, while still laughing at her remark.

We had arranged the couches in a big circle with a couple of coffee tables in the middle. Arthur took the stairs up to where he, Adeline, Chris, Todd, Valerie, and a couple of other strong players were running through their plans. Something involving a travel agency.

Grace had the lodge's corded telephone in her lap. The receiver was in her ear. She was on hold.

"No, I'm still here," she said into the phone. "What do you have for me?"

She listened intently as the person on the other end spoke. She had a notepad and pen in her hand. She pretended to write things down on the sheet but didn't need to. She had a trope that would transcribe information like that onto the red wallpaper whenever she mimed writing it down.

"Uh-huh," she said. "Thanks, Harvey. You're the best."

She hung up the phone.

"My friend at the station says that a Nicholas Hesper went missing near the property in question about a decade ago. Made a point to tell me how strange it

was that there was no follow-up. The case file was empty. Wasn't even a search."
She smiled as she spoke. "Harvey drew special attention to Nicholas above the
other missing people. Definitely confirms that he's important."

Grace was a Detective Archetype. She had a trope called My Friend at the
Station that allowed her to call her titular cop friend for information on a storyline. It was a scouting trope, so it could be used without even being in a storyline,
much like my I Don't Like It Here . . . trope.

Around thirty veteran players had taken an interest in finding these tickets. Lukas, the Hysteric who had found one over a decade earlier, had suddenly
stepped in as our resident expert on the subject, despite having admitted that he
had never managed to find a second lore ticket.

Apparently, about twelve years earlier, the players had stopped being interested in Secret Lore. Rescue tropes had just disappeared and there was a period
where players were failing storylines left and right before they adapted to a more
cautious style of play. As I understood it, players used to routinely play storylines
even ten levels over their Plot Armor, and their style of play was risky as well.

None of that was done anymore.

When the dust settled, the remaining players deemed Secret Lore too dangerous to be worth it, especially since they could not find any Secret Lore storylines
in the lower levels. Until we found one, that is.

Lukas listened to Grace's information intently.

"Yes, Grace," Lukas said, sipping his coffee. "That's good work. Definitely
good information."

That's what he did. He agreed with everyone. Even when people were arguing, he agreed with both sides.

The first step of their investigation was retracing our steps, so to speak. The
idea was that stumbling onto a Secret Lore ticket is not very useful. They wanted
to find out how a player might detect the presence of such a ticket in the first
place. Relying on luck was not enough. They wanted to be able to find more
tickets afterward, after all.

"What do you have, Lara?" Grace asked.

Lara, the Psychic Archetype, was cycling through her binder of tickets, trying
to find a scouting trope that would give her new information.

"Nothing," Lara answered. "I can't find anything that helps me detect the
presence of the being they describe."

She was clearly growing frustrated.

"It was really high level," Anna said. She sat on the same couch as me. Dina
and Camden were nearby. Antoine and Kimberly were off together trying not to
think about the Straggler forest.

"It would have to be," Lara answered. "It just looks like a normal storyline
to me."

I furrowed my brow. "It's weird. In stories, Psychics usually tune into eldritch entities before anyone else. It's strange that you can't see it."

"It was the same way with the ghosts in the storyline I found my ticket in. Psychics didn't even know they were there," Lukas said. "Carousel knows that Psychics are overpowered, so it gave them a weakness, I bet."

Lara glared daggers at him.

Grace stood up and stretched. "Maybe when Garrett gets back, he'll have something."

Garrett was a Soldier Archetype who floated around from team to team. He had a handful of abilities for scouting out enemies.

The other players weren't as concerned with finding out information. They were focused on figuring out how to trigger the Secret Lore version of the storyline as painlessly as possible. They interrogated my friends and me for hours. They wanted to know every single detail.

We were pretty quick to conclude that getting Nicholas, the NPC and Straggler, out of the forest was essential.

The first trouble with trying to get Nicholas out of the forest was the fact that the Straggler curse made it difficult to know friend from foe. A further and bigger problem was that when they did get Nicholas out, they would be leaving behind a player who would end up in the same boat as Antoine. Nobody wanted to risk being stuck in that Straggler forest for who knew how long.

Those were only the first two problems. On top of that, we stressed to them exactly how mentally taxing being in the presence of the Unknowable Host was.

They said that they were taking it seriously but most of them appeared to think that it was nothing they couldn't handle. I wasn't sure about that, but I didn't know what other kinds of horrors they had come across. They took mental health tropes just in case.

Truthfully, a problem we didn't speak about much was whether you could spoil a secret storyline and make it so that other players couldn't trigger it. Roxy seemed to think you couldn't, that spoilers didn't matter after you'd played through a storyline. There were lots of times they would discuss completed storylines and variations of those storylines and it didn't seem to matter. I hoped she was right. If she wasn't, all of their efforts would be in vain.

It was interesting watching them work on the problem. Up until this point, we had never been able to sit in on their prepping sessions. They were worried about spoiling important storylines for us, so we just weren't included in those conversations. This time was different. We couldn't be spoiled on this storyline because we had already run it.

We actually had a seat at the table for this one.

They planned out how to find secret treasure and other consumables. They theorized about how to get a perfect run in a storyline, a feat that was heavily rewarded.

The first strategy they came up with to avoid getting stuck in the Straggler forest was something called Scared to Death. It was a Hysteric trope. The way it worked was simple: when you are confronted by an enemy, you pretend to have a heart attack or a stroke, and then you die. You actually die. Your death will count as First Blood if you time it right.

Their thought was that if five players entered the Straggler forest and then one died of a heart attack, four players could leave along with Nicholas without anybody having to worry about staying in the forest for who knows how long.

Lukas thought of this plan himself. Not only was it his trope, but Lukas had a few screws loose and was always willing to die.

The problem with this plan was that it left too much uncertainty. If there was no one to pass his curse on to, would Nicholas be allowed out of the forest? Or was the whole thing about the number that entered always having to be the number that left literal? Could it be that simple?

Luckily, Roxy had a better idea.

She observed that the only time an NPC was brought into the forest was when one of the players started the game as a Straggler and would need to pass their curse onto the NPC to get out. This was what Dina had done to the NPC Roberta.

"But what happens if we bring in an NPC of our own?" Roxy suggested.

She presented the group with three of her tropes that could do just that. One was an Eye Candy trope called Carry the Bags, which allowed her character to have a hired assistant or servant. Her second, Hired Muscle, worked the same way, but with a hired bodyguard.

Her final trope was called Meet My Mark, a Femme Fatale trope that allowed her to enter the story with an NPC on whom she was running a scam. Usually, the NPC in question would have money, information, or access her character was trying to get from them that would further the storyline.

The first two cost money to use and limited the player's role to something that could conceivably have a servant or bodyguard. Not a big deal. The third was a risk because she would have to be a Femme Fatale Advanced Archetype to use it and doing so might alter the storyline so much that the secret ending wouldn't trigger. Advanced Archetypes had that problem.

"That is stone cold," Reggie, Grace's Bruiser brother, said.

It was quite coldhearted. But it was a good idea.

"Think about it," she said. "We need someone for the Straggler to pass his curse to. Why not an NPC?"

No one could argue with that.

The problem then was making sure Nicholas got out in the first place. This one was solved pretty quickly, funnily enough. One of the Bruisers had an Advanced Archetype called Bounty Hunter. The Bounty Hunter had all sorts of tropes for finding and capturing NPCs or enemies. One of them, It's Just Not Your Day, was a rule trope that guaranteed the player would run into their target at the beginning of the story. The Bounty Hunter would alter the story, so that ran the same risk as any other, but in the end, they tried it.

Other players had to figure out their own ways. Lara used one of her Psychic Occultist tropes to scry for Nicholas and another trope to ward off Stragglers that weren't Nicholas.

Others simply planned to wander around until they found him and then drag him out with them. It's not like he would argue. It turned out that there were more tropes that could bring an NPC into a storyline with you, though they were usually for very specific use cases.

It took them three days to make it work. Making sure that the right Straggler got out was the biggest hurdle, in practice.

Roxy and her team ran the storyline and managed to nab Nicholas from the Straggler forest. But there was a problem. When they returned to the lodge, they let us in on the bad news.

The secret route didn't trigger. Something was missing.

To make matters worse, the storyline took five hours on average to reset, so they could only try so many times in a given day.

"I knew it wasn't going to work," Garrett, the Soldier, said. "There is something else going on here."

I was eating lunch when another deflated team returned with their heads hanging low. Lara was sitting at the table near me, trying her Psychic tropes again. Her frustration was growing with every failed vision.

"Did you know that you should not trust your eyes in the Straggler forest?" she asked in a huff. "That's what this stupid Harbinger trope has told me twelve times now. Not a thing about the dead god. I thought you said Psychics should have a connection?"

Lara was usually calm and collected. She was clearly very frustrated.

The vets were not pleased with the lack of forward progress. They kept asking for us to go on the storyline with them to see if anything about us specifically triggered the storyline.

Each team had developed a way to get Nicholas out, a way to not leave a player in the Straggler forest, and a mental health trope to ensure they survived the encounter with the Unknowable Host.

Eventually, they came to the conclusion that they needed me to be there with them on their next run, a prospect I was not happy about. The aura of the Unknowable Host was still messing with me days after the fact.

They figured that I was the only thing they couldn't replicate. I was the only Film Buff, after all.

"You won't even have to do anything hard," Roxy suggested. "We'll take care of you just like with the Grotesques."

Did she not remember what had happened to me on the Grotesque storyline?

I really didn't want to go. At the same time, I didn't want to disappoint the other players. I told them I would think about it.

A breakthrough came just in time. They had their own copies of every single trope that my friends brought on that storyline. They tried them all. What they didn't have were Film Buff tropes.

Of course, the real prize was my Trope Master ticket. It was the ability that would allow someone to detect the Unknowable Host indirectly. One look at a possessed animal or a Cloven Woman's tropes would hint to you that something more was going on, that something linked the storylines together.

The question was, was it possible for them to replicate that ability without just bringing me with them?

We knew that there was an Outsider ability that would allow you to betray your teammates in order to join the bad guys and get a look at their tropes. The problem was that there were no Outsiders at the lodge who had that ability anymore.

But there were other abilities that worked similarly; they just were not the kind of trope that you would bring on a storyline like this.

For instance, Lara had a Psychic trope called Fatal Connection that allowed her to have visions through an enemy's eyes after it had Mutilated her. That wasn't a trope that she liked using, for understandable reasons. Not to mention that trying to get it to work inside this storyline would be difficult.

The Stragglers wouldn't mutilate her. Not that it mattered, because they didn't have any tropes tying them to the Unknowable Host anyway. The Cloven Women wouldn't even attack her because she was a woman, let alone mutilate her. The only option would be the possessed animals in the mine storyline.

But then, I don't think it actually mattered how feasible implementing the trope was.

My theory was that having a trope that would allow you to see the enemies' tropes would be enough. You wouldn't actually have to use it. After all, I had not detected the Unknowable Host until after I had seen it. Having the trope was important but using it might not have been. I think you just needed the trope with you.

This secret storyline was meta. It made sense that they needed to bring a meta trope to unlock it.

With this assumption, the veteran players collected tropes that might allow them to see an enemy's abilities and went back to the campfire storyline. It was a meager collection. Seeing an enemy's tropes was a rare gift, apparently, and always required ridiculous amounts of setup.

But it worked.

A few hours later, Roxy, Lara, and the rest of their team came back to the lodge holding their brand-new Secret Lore tickets.

They weren't exactly thrilled about it. The aura of the Unknowable Host was just as hard on them as it was on us. We didn't say, "I told you so."

They suddenly agreed that the Unknowable Host was causing the red wallpaper system to go haywire, along with the NPCs near it, but they still chalked it up to some type of mental trope causing our wires to cross.

The lodge was a quiet, dreary place for a while as people recovered from their run-in with the Unknowable Host's aura.

What a convenient coincidence—my ability just happened to be the key to unlocking the Secret Lore that we just happened to find on a random storyline. This development felt unearned. None of the other players shared my reservations, at least not to the same extent. I added that to the pile of things causing me to be uncomfortable about the situation.

Something felt off. I couldn't articulate exactly why in a persuasive manner.

Within two days, all of the veterans who were interested had managed to scrounge up their own Secret Lore tickets from the campfire storyline.

Then it was time to go to the library. We needed to inquire about the tickets and hopefully find out how we were supposed to find more Secret Lore storylines.

I had never traveled in such a large group. We were doing it together because apparently getting into the library and moving about freely was quite a chore. It was better to do it once for everyone.

"So, here's how it works," Garrett told us as we stood outside the giant stone building. "There are Omens all over the library. Luckily, they're all contained in books, and they will leave you alone as long as you don't open them. Except for one. There is one storyline in that library that'll sneak up on you. And it's a real pain in the butt. But we have a workaround.

"You enter the library, and you find an Omen for a storyline called *The Final Page*. You can use others, but that one is near the entrance and it works well. You've got to run through that storyline; it's a little above your current level but it's nothing you won't be able to handle soon. When you're inside that storyline, you've got to make sure that you find an excuse to burn down the children's literature section. It'll make sense once you're there. You have to burn down the whole section while you're in the storyline; that is very important.

"After you finish the storyline, and the children's literature section has burned down, that sneaky Omen isn't there anymore and you can move about the library freely without worrying about triggering it. That's what we've got to do every time we come here. It's a pain."

Apparently, the team that went up ahead to clear the storyline was taking longer than expected.

Grace suggested that while we waited, we should go check out the job board next to the library. It was in a glass enclosure meant to protect the board inside from the rain. It almost looked like a bus stop, but it wasn't next to the road. The way she described it, the job board held directions to Omens that were related to storylines you had already completed or to tropes that you had equipped. It was largely random but now that we had a few levels we might be able to find something good. The storylines would all be within our level range.

So that's what we did.

When we got there, there were only three jobs on the board.

The sheets of paper themselves seemed like normal ads for a job you might find on the Internet. They didn't really say much about the storyline. One offered a job for a farmhand, another for a security guard of sorts, and the final for a maid.

What was on the paper itself didn't seem to be that important. What really mattered was what was on the red wallpaper.

As I looked from sheet to sheet, I realized that I could see the title and poster for each of the storylines. These weren't Omens, so they didn't trigger any information for me in that way. They just told you where to go.

The first option was *The Final Straw*.

We had been carried through *The Final Straw II* when we arrived in Carousel. Not a bad option. It would be nice to see what was going on in that franchise; we knew so little about it. The poster was of a scarecrow hung up on a wooden stand with some spatters of blood. Interestingly, this scarecrow was not wearing the coveralls that said Benny on them.

The next option was *Subject of Inquiry*.

The poster for this one depicted a bunch of security monitors, most of which were just showing static. There was blood on the screens.

The last option was *House of Fane*.

This showed a long fancy dinner table with people sitting in all of the seats. The people's heads were all turned away from the viewer toward a chair at the head of the table with claw marks on it.

We voted, and after much discussion, we decided to go with *Subject of Inquiry*. We grabbed the flier. But that would come later. Soon, we were being ushered inside. We needed to talk to a librarian.

CHAPTER TWENTY-NINE

MAKE HISTORY PART OF YOUR STORY!

All in all, there were seven teams at the library. Of course, my friends and I hardly counted.

The other teams had been put together strategically, with notable exceptions, and they could adapt seamlessly to different storylines. Players tended to plateau at around forty Plot Armor. Most of the lodge existed around that range. Those that were really dedicated, like Chris and Valerie, might break free and attain a higher level, but most would not. Most never broke level fifty.

There were benefits to that, though. Pretty much all of the players in that range could group together for storylines. In fact, it was difficult to tell which players had come to Carousel together just by looking at their current groups. They end up dividing themselves into teams based on the task at hand.

The library was not a remarkable run for them. They had been there before and believed that they had its eccentricities well understood.

"Don't touch the books unless you are sure they aren't an Omen," Grace reminded us as we walked in. Anna assured her that we would be careful.

"I smell the children's section," Camden said as we entered.

Everyone could. The whole first level of the library had a layer of smoke in the air. NPC firefighters put out the flames and made small talk with a library administrator. It wasn't long until they had left. They were only there as background for the storyline that had just been run.

I stole a glance at the area where the burned-out children's section was. The books were mostly ash. NPCs worked to block off the section from view with a large movable curtain. I managed to see a smoke-damaged red box against a wall. It was a Silas the Showman display, one of several permanent installations around town. Of course, it was not in working condition; Silas had been damaged in the fire. Bad luck for him.

The building was large. Each section had its own room cordoned off somewhere in the stacks. The library had all of the normal sections you might expect: fiction, nonfiction, biographies, genealogy, and so on. It also had a few Carousel-specific sections. Ancient tomes, witchcraft and folklore, history of Carousel, and the Bartholomew Geist Private Collection—which you needed a special key to enter—were among them.

A lot of the rooms were just designed to be settings for scenes in different storylines, usually one-offs. Do you need a scene of a Scholar poring over books searching for some obscure fact? There was a place for it on the second floor called the Leatherbound Vista. That wasn't the name for it on the library map, no, but my Location Scout trope told me it was there. There was also a place for college kids to study together on the top floor called the University of Carousel Group Study Annex.

The library was actually quite pretty in the way libraries often were in movies. There were towering stone pillars and multiple levels with shelf after shelf of books.

But it was filled with Omens, most of which could be triggered by some variation of "touching the book." Some were more generous and actually required you to check out or read the book. Interestingly, most of the storylines triggered by these book Omens took place outside the library. Location Scout assured me of this. In fact, some didn't even have scenes in the library.

Upon asking Roxy about this, her explanation was that while most storylines were ready to go at a moment's notice, others had to be set up. Making sure you could only trigger the storyline from far away ensured that the NPCs could get everything into place before you got on set.

Of course, many of the storylines were directly related to the library and the books involved. I saw a litany of storylines around the library. Most of them were a high difficulty. That made sense. No use putting beginner storylines in a place beginners couldn't get to them.

We found a table on the second floor that was separated from the rest of the library but was on a landing that could look over the librarian's desk. We wanted to watch as the other teams approached the head librarian for information about the lore tickets.

Each team moved separately through the library so that if someone accidentally triggered an Omen, other teams wouldn't have to be involved.

In the Grotesque storyline, everyone who had gotten close enough to the Omen for their Plot Cycle indicator to switch on was subject to be included in the storyline. The theory was that if we divided up the library and stayed separate, we wouldn't have to worry about that.

We were waiting our turn to talk to the head librarian. In the meantime, we decided to read up. I helped everyone find books that were safe to read from the section that we had been allotted. We were eager to see what kinds of information the library held. I half expected the books to be blank. Why go through the trouble of writing enough books to fill a library if they weren't part of a storyline? I was wrong. The books were all real.

Though, they were a little strange.

"I found a President Eli Morris as the twenty-eighth president of the United States," Camden said, holding up a book that claimed to be a US history textbook. "I don't remember learning about him in school."

"That's not right," I said. "We all know that the actual twenty-eighth president was . . . uh . . . you know."

"And the section on the Salem witch trials is a trip," he said. He flipped it around and showed me what looked like a pilgrim woman absorbing the souls of some townspeople. "It talks about it like they were actual witches."

The actual Salem witch trials were famous in the real world for being false accusations. He handed me the book, and I scanned the page. Sure enough, the entire county around Salem was abandoned to keep the "coven" separate from the rest of the country. However, when they checked on those lands years later, they were unable to find any evidence of inhabitance. The section concluded that the witches had either died off, left with the townspeople, or simply never existed.

"Maybe it's randomly generated," Camden suggested. "Or maybe that's just what happened in the fictional version of the US that Carousel is set in."

I shrugged.

"It might have been made for a specific storyline," Anna theorized. "One with witches."

That seemed possible.

"Here we go," Antoine said, lifting a book onto the table. He seemed better after a few days' rest. Or, at least, he had gotten better at hiding his trauma. "This book references a *Catalogue of Eldritch Entities*. Maybe that would work. You guys said it was an eldritch deity, right?"

We were still trying to figure out how a player might have found the Secret Lore in the campfire storyline on purpose. Stumbling onto them was unreliable. If we were going to find ten, then we needed to understand how to track them down.

"None of these people exist," Kimberly said, as she looked through a celebrity gossip magazine. She had gotten bored of looking through historical texts, so she'd picked it up off a rack downstairs. By this point, we were all burned out on studying.

We slogged through more of Carousel's collection of alternate histories. These books didn't line up with reality or each other. The problem was that none of it tied directly to Carousel. We were in the wrong section.

"We need to go to the History of Carousel section," Anna said. "Did they say how long they would be?"

I shook my head.

Grace and her team were in the room that contained the actual History of Carousel section itself. It was thought that there would be something more substantial in there.

"If there's something in there, Grace will find it," Camden said. "Her Savvy is higher than mine, and she has Eureka too."

His Eureka trope allowed him to sift through books quickly to find relevant information. According to him, it wasn't as useful here in the library where most things were higher level than us and he had no idea what it was we were looking for.

"Why is it taking so long?" Kimberly asked. "Are they asking the librarian her life story?"

I looked down at the current team interrogating the head librarian for information about the Secrets of Carousel.

They were using insight tropes to try to get as much information as they could about the tickets. One team at a time, they would present their Secret Lore tickets and ask her about how they might get more. Later, we would all discuss what we learned.

On the red wallpaper, the librarian was called "Constance Barlow, head librarian of the Carousel Public Library." She had fifty Plot Armor. Like all of the other level-fifty NPCs I had met, she had tropes that I assumed were enemy tropes. They were grayed out and unreadable, just as the others had been. I chalked that up to my low level.

"What are we going to say that others haven't?" Anna asked.

"Maybe we won't have to," Dina said. She had been silent for much of the time we were in the library. "Maybe she'll tell us something different because we were the first ones to discover it."

"Maybe," Anna said.

All we had left to do was wait.

Forty-five minutes later, all the other teams had finished trying to get information from the librarian. We got the nod. Most of the teams left the library altogether after their turn. They had combed through this place time and time again in the years before we got here.

It was about time. The smoke had cleared from the fire in the children's literature section. Soon, the section would reset, and we might find out exactly why the other players worked so hard to avoid the Omen that lurked there.

We made our way downstairs to the head librarian's desk. Hers was placed in a position of authority behind all of the check-in counters where ordinary library worker NPCs sat with friendly smiles.

When we arrived at her desk, she turned to us and smiled. She transformed into a cheerful woman, not anything like the stern image that the term librarian might evoke for some. It looked like she was putting on an act, though. She wore glasses and a blue blouse. Her hair was tied back in a bun. Books surrounded her, piled up on her desk.

"Hello," Anna said as we approached.

Constance smiled brightly. "So many tourists! Today is a busy day! Welcome to the Carousel Public Library!"

Anna took her Secret Lore ticket from her pocket and held it up. "Can you help us with this?"

The librarian glanced over at the ticket.

"It's great to see the Secret Lore Rewards Program is still drawing in participants after all these years. The program is a joint project between the library and other institutions of learning in Carousel. The project's motto is 'Make History Part of Your Story.' Isn't that clever? Beverly Canton from the Museum of Natural History came up with that. She's a hoot. I just think it's so fun." She smiled at each of us in turn. "I trust your vacation in Carousel has been captivating?"

Anna nodded and forced a smile.

"Wonderful," Constance said. "If you would like, you can trade that in for a prize now or collect ten for a secret reward."

The whole lodge had discussed this. Lukas had traded his in after several years and had only gotten a treasure map, something that the higher-level players collected with some regularity. We were going for the big one.

"We'd like to save them," Anna said. "The secret reward sounds tantalizing."

"I would do the same thing in your position," Constance said. "You know, it's great to see young people with such an interest in history."

Anna glanced back at the rest of us, then leaned forward and said, "We were wondering if there was a way to find storylines with Secret Lore."

The librarian smiled.

"Of course," she said. "History is all over. You'll find its tendrils everywhere you look. I'm certain you will find another if you keep your eyes open."

The other players had tropes they could use at this point to try and get more specific answers. We had nothing. None of our information-gathering tropes could help in this situation. Most of ours were designed to be used in a storyline.

Dina stepped forward. "Are you sure there isn't any other hint you could give us?"

Constance smiled. "You tourists really are curious today, aren't you? Well, fear not. I am certain that the clues will come to you now that you know what to look for."

That was actually reassuring.

"I am glad to see you here. I hope you will be back," Constance said. "If I were you, I would be sure to collect ten Secret Lore tickets before you leave town."

She stood up and began walking away from her desk.

"Now, if you will excuse me," she said. "We are about to open up our new children's literature wing. It's a very exciting day."

That was our cue to leave.

As we turned to go, she cleared her throat and added, "Just remember, the motto is 'Make History Part of Your Story.' Just a *part*. There's so much here to see in Carousel. I wouldn't want you to miss anything."

She paused as if evaluating whether to say more. Then she smiled before walking away.

CHAPTER THIRTY

BET YOUR LIFE ON IT!

As night fell, my friends and I found ourselves on the back deck watching the sun go down. We didn't talk about much. We had had a busy day and there were veterans around steering the conversation.

Antoine was the quietest. It was hard to see him like that. Ever since we got there, Antoine had made it his own mission to reassure us and to encourage us that we would be able to get out of this place. I thought he was being too optimistic—naively so. Anna said it was because he felt guilty about getting us trapped in Carousel. He wanted to believe that he could fix it.

He didn't talk like that anymore. Kimberly had picked up the slack. Where before she was the one worried about what was going on back home, what her parents were thinking, and how long it would take for us to get out of this place, now she was a beacon of positivity. She tried to soothe Antoine by encouraging him and telling him that this was just a minor setback and, thanks to his new trope, he would forget it all in time.

Antoine wanted us to believe that he was over it, but none of us did.

Inside, the veterans had put up a chalkboard where they wrote all the information they had gathered about Secret Lore. Right then all it had was the information that they had been able to ascertain from talking to the head librarian. They had gotten a lot more information than us, but still, they only had a few leads.

The only real storylines with Secret Lore that we actually knew about were the campfire storyline and the one that Lukas had played through. No one had investigated that one yet. They were taking their time and being methodical. It was way too high level.

Grace was looking into any records of Secret Lore from the previous generation of players. She had read the *Carousel Atlas* backward and forward. The atlas was the grown-up version of our Carousel field guides. It was more dangerous because it had spoilers, or so we were told.

Most of the veterans had gotten information from the head librarian, but a lot of it was redundant. The unique pieces of information were posted as follows. The players included their names and the trope they had used to acquire the information in case anyone else wanted to take a crack at it.

Sam
Trope: Rumors of the Lost City
Info: I learned some possible prizes: treasure maps, money, consumables, Excursion Train tickets, weapon upgrade trope, Private Showing tickets, tropes, maybe stat tickets but not clear.

Sam was an Adventurer Archetype with a Plot Armor of forty-eight or so. He used a trope that encouraged NPCs to tell him information about valuable treasure both in and out of storylines. The trope was very powerful and even worked for something like this, where the treasure he was seeking was a prize.

Lara
Trope: Are You Ready to Listen?
More hints will appear to us in the next few weeks. Everyone keep an eye out.

Lara was flummoxed trying to use her Psychic tropes. She said that something was blocking her. It made sense. If you were a Psychic and you could use your full power set, this entire endeavor would be trivial. She did manage to use a generalist Psychic trope that assured her more information would make itself known to the players.

Grace
Trope: What Were You Going to Say?
Info: One of the storylines at the Botanical Gardens has Secret Lore.
Trope: Human Lie Detector
Info: She said there was no way to trace the information about the campfire storyline back to some clue in Carousel. She was lying.

Grace was a Detective Archetype and used a couple of her tropes to narrow down the location of a storyline with Secret Lore. She was also able to figure out that our attempts to dissect the campfire storyline were logically sound.

Bella
Trope: The Implication
Info: Check out the Natural History Museum for leads. The basement level has something, but I don't know what.

Bella was a Bruiser who specialized in the Bully Aspect. She managed to threaten the librarian into giving up some information.

Oliver
Trope: Professional Courtesy
Info: Other NPCs involved in the Secret Lore Project are the curator at the Natural History Museum, someone at the Botanical Gardens, the lead astronomer at the observatory, and someone at a dig site of some kind.
Trope: Call It a Finder's Fee
Info: There is something about Secret Lore and an antique vase.

Oliver was an Antiquarian. I wasn't super familiar with his tropes, but they mostly revolved around antiques and cursed items. From the second trope, it sounded like he'd managed to bribe the librarian.

Lukas
Trope: "They" Don't Want You to Know
Info: (Note from Grace: don't trust this information)
• All of the Secret Lore is in supernatural storylines. • The truth was hidden by the mayor. He is hiding his involvement. • The leads are only found inside other storylines. • Carousel is tricking us. This is a trap. • Finding Secret Lore is the only way to escape Carousel. • Some of the players know more than they are letting on . . . • Bartholomew Geist is still alive and laid out clues for us to follow. • Carousel doesn't want us to know the truth. • Carousel wants us to know the truth. It needs our help. • The NPCs are scheming. • We are just pawns in all of this. We are being led around.

In addition to being a Hysteric, Lukas had an Advanced Archetype called Doomsday Prepper. This Archetype had a lot of conspiracy-theory-related tropes, or at least the version that Lukas played did. The way his trope worked was that he would get a lot of information given to him at once but only a small amount of it was actually true. The higher his Savvy stat, the less misinformation there would be, but Savvy was not his best stat. We were advised to take all of this information with a grain of salt.

Roxy
Trope: Just Like Old Times
Info: An NPC related to a secret storyline visits the Casino regularly.

Roxy had managed to coax information from the librarian. I'm not quite sure how.

Ethan
Trope: I used The Golden Boy along with The Eligibility Imperative
Info: Check out the graveyard on Sickle Street.

Ethan was an Athlete who specialized in the Stud Aspect. He used two tropes that gave him a lot of favoritism from authority figures, like a librarian. He had gotten a solid lead.

As we sat on the back deck, the sun faded to darkness. A fog moved over the lake. Grace went around lighting citronella torches and oil lamps so that we could still see. We continued talking quietly among ourselves, theorizing about what the Secret Lore might mean.

Everyone had different theories, but the common element was that they thought it meant we were going to find the way out of Carousel. Some of them were ashamed to have missed something just under their noses—they had been told about Secret Lore before, after all. Others were relieved; if Secret Lore was the way out, that made the world of Carousel that much less mysterious. It made it solvable.

One of the veterans I hadn't talked to too much, Peter, made a joke about how we were going to get to the end and Silas would ask what took us so long.

I wasn't so sure we were home free, but I didn't voice my doubts. It was a rare thing to see people talking about getting out. That kind of optimism was pretty taboo around here. Sure, they would dream about what they would do when they got back home, but hope made people nauseous.

Eventually, Todd joined us. He was one of the higher-level players. He had been part of the group that was still planning out the Excursion Train route, so he had little involvement in the Secret Lore runs until they started working. Valerie had won excursion tickets to any destination within greater Carousel. The highest-level vets were planning to use them for something big.

"You know what's funny about this?" he said. "We were just talking about that storyline the other day. Weren't we, Chris?"

Chris nodded shamefully. I think he still felt guilty about sending his little brother to the Straggler forest, even by mistake.

"When we first got here," Todd continued, "we ran that storyline a dozen times. No joke. One run after the other, trying to find treasure."

"Did you not know how to trigger the treasure hunt variation?" one of the veterans, Sam, asked.

Todd shook his head. "We were the ones who found it. Well, we had help. Winston Ashwood."

"Here we go," Chris said disdainfully.

"They need to know," Todd said. "Winston Ashwood. He was a real character. Psychic Archetype, a Seer. Almost never went out on storylines. He had a trope that let him hear spirit messages or whatever in scrambled radio broadcasts. He'd sit out on the deck all day long wearing a smoking jacket—pipe in one hand, book in the other, listening to the radio for messages to tell the other players."

"Had a Salvador Dali mustache," Roxy added.

"Yep," Todd agreed. "Almost. Strange guy. His name wasn't even Winston Ashwood. His name was Egan Johnson or something like that, something really white bread. He was always so frustrated that you could see his real name on the red wallpaper in parentheses.

"Anyway, Winston Ashwood comes to us one day and says you need to go run the campfire storyline. The third one in the franchise. The one with the Stragglers. We asked him why. Well, he's heard on the spooky radio broadcast that there is treasure there, that there was something very important that we had to go find in that storyline."

"The casino jingle," Chris said.

"The casino jingle," Todd repeated. "He had himself convinced that whenever the radio broadcast messed up and you could hear the Carousel Casino commercial come on that it was a sign of fortune or good luck."

He started singing the jingle:

"Under the neon glow, where the lucky ones go,
Bet your life on it, it's the Carousel Casino.
The stakes are high, but so is the fun,
Bet your life on it, the night's just begun!"

He and some of the other veterans laughed.

"I don't know if there's any truth to it, considering what ended up happening, but every time that commercial came on during one of his prophecies, he would get all excited and tell players to go out and look for treasure.

"So, we go run the campfire storyline again. Nothing. Just a normal storyline. A few days later, he comes back and says you missed something; you've got to find something else. So, we go run it. Nothing. Again. This repeated itself for two months off and on until, eventually, we found the treasure hunt variation with the moonshiners. Even after that, he was still on our butts about it. Guy never quit."

Todd laughed for a bit, but as he slowly stopped, a heavy silence grew.

"You think he was trying to . . . you know?" Sam asked.

I wasn't sure what Sam was asking, but Todd seemed to.

Todd looked over at Chris.

"We always wondered," Todd said. There was something they weren't saying. "Whatever the case, a few days ago we heard that casino jingle on the radio. Right, Chris? Several times. Made us think of him. Reminded us of that storyline too. It's just that it was a big coincidence, us talking about it, and then it turns out it was important."

We sat in silence for a few moments more, but then eventually small talk broke out and we were talking about Secret Lore and our plans once we got back home again. Todd and Chris left, as did some of the other veterans.

Once they were gone, Dina leaned over to Roxy and asked, "So, what was that about? With the whole Psychic dude. The awkwardness."

Roxy, who had clearly been waiting ever since his name was mentioned to talk about it, replied, "He betrayed us. Got a lot of people killed."

She paused, letting her words linger in the air.

"What do you mean?" Kimberly asked. She had largely stayed out of the conversation and only paid attention to Antoine. Now both of them were interested.

"If you're going to talk about that," Grace said, "keep your voice down. Arthur hates us talking about it."

Roxy rolled her eyes. "Arthur just hates hearing about it. That's all."

She leaned toward the rest of us.

"You know how some players don't have to go out on storylines as much, right? They can just stay here and give advice to people using their tropes, and they can get experience from that? Well, Psychics can do that way more than anyone else. This Winston Ashwood guy was here when I got here. That's what he did—he sent people on storylines and gave them Psychic advice.

"Since I didn't have a team of my own, I got put in a group with Lara and a couple of others. One day we go to him asking for advice about what storyline we should do next. He describes where we should go and tells us all these different prophecies about what we have to do once we get there to win. Same old same old. Except he was lying. Lara had Psychic tropes of her own. She had only been here for three months but even then she could tell that this Winston guy was sending us into a storyline we couldn't beat.

"We thought maybe because he was high level he could see things that she couldn't, but she was insistent. She was crying and kicking and screaming, telling us not to go on this storyline that he had just sent us on. So we went to Arthur and Adeline. We described the place that Winston wanted us to go and what he wanted us to do there.

"Turns out, he was sending us on a storyline that was fifteen levels ahead of us. None of us had scouting tropes to be able to figure that out, but Lara had a premonition from one of her abilities. Leading up to that point in time, it had become common for us to lose a group every month. We were dropping like flies; we didn't know what was going on. Normally, we only lose maybe one team per year. We get enough new players to replace all the old ones.

"Not that year, though. Teams were wiped out one after another. So, Arthur starts to interrogate Winston with the help of a Detective Archetype and a couple of Bruisers who all have tropes that will work outside of the storyline and can help get information out of people the hard way. It turned out Winston had been sending people on storylines they couldn't beat for years."

"Oh my god," Kimberly said. "Why?"

Roxy shrugged. "Lost his mind, I guess. We never found out."

"Well, what happened to him?" Anna asked.

"Arthur never said exactly, but his missing poster is on the community board by the diner if you ever want to go look."

CHAPTER THIRTY-ONE

SUBJECT OF INQUIRY

*I*t was another day before we finally went to the diner we had been hearing about since we'd arrived. If you heard someone talking about the diner, it was usually because they were talking about where Arthur had run off to. He spent a lot of time there.

It wasn't a long walk to get there by Carousel standards. It was on the western edge of town. If you traveled any farther, you might start running into the minefield of Omens that plagued downtown.

We went there late in the evening. The veterans had spent all day researching Secret Lore. Better them than me. I just had to watch. They had become obsessed.

Roxy, the Bowlers, Lara, and Sam had gone with us. Sam was an Adventurer Archetype who, amusingly enough, went out jogging every morning, a rare hobby in Carousel. That was most of what I knew about him.

Before we went into the diner, we first stopped off at the missing persons' board. I had been there just once before. It was attached to the wall of a brick building. I didn't know what it looked like normally, but multiple boards had been added until it covered much of the wall.

The boards were full.

Poster upon poster had been pinned to them. They were posted in chronological order from left to right, with the occasional odd duck that was posted out of order. I could tell because the old posters were yellowed and faded, while the posters on the far right still had much of their original coloring.

Roxy pointed to one of the posters. It showed a middle-aged man wearing a smoking jacket. His dark hair was slicked back, and he had a finely groomed curly mustache.

MISSING
Name: Ethan Jacobs (AKA Winston Ashwood)
Plot Armor: 42
Place Last Seen: Montgomery's Salvage, October 2016
Occupation: Psychic (Seer Aspect)
Reward: 600 Dollars

Along with him were dozens upon dozens of missing posters—more than I could count. Some of them went back over twenty years. If I understood the timeline right, that meant they had been there even when rescue tropes existed. For some reason, they weren't rescued.

"There are so many," Anna said. The sheer magnitude of them had almost brought her to tears. Our reactions would likely be just as strong every time we saw it.

"You know, players used to be able to use these posters to rescue teams that had died in storylines," Sam said. "If you took someone's poster and went to the story they died in and beat it, they would be revived."

"Oh yeah?" Antoine asked. He had mostly been quiet up to that point. We had heard this before, but when the Vets were willing to talk, we listened. When it came to fallen players, they were often withholding on the specifics.

"Yep," he said. "It was before my time. One day, it just stopped working. No one knows why. Now we get this." He gestured toward the wall of missing posters.

Roxy flashed me a glance. We both knew why the rescue tropes were gone. As the others discussed the topic, I stayed out of it.

I noticed that the most recent group of people to wind up on the board had been wiped out just two weeks before we arrived. No one mentioned them. People rarely mentioned specific dead players. We could add that to the list of things the veterans rarely mentioned.

The missing board was a hallowed place. The gravity of all those posters stole your voice and sobered you up just by looking at them. They smiled in their pictures. You might think that they would be screaming, but they weren't. I thought the smiles were scarier.

The restaurant across the street was a welcome reprieve.

It was just called "Diner." There was no horrific pun in the name, save for the letters N and R, which flickered off on occasion.

The diner was wrapped in shiny aluminum siding. Most of the building was visible through large wall-length windows. The floor had a black and white checker pattern, and the seat upholstery was blood red—perhaps the only clue that the restaurant was in Carousel.

As we entered, we heard the clinking of metal tools on the flat-top grill. An NPC waitress read off an order for the cook at machine-gun speed. The order was all in lingo, like diners used to do years ago.

"—side of hashbrowns, smothered, sliced, charred, and slayed."

I didn't know what that meant, but the food looked normal.

The place was full when we got there, but several tables of NPCs just happened to finish their meals as we arrived, leaving us with just enough room to sit. I found it funny that Carousel would script that.

A short-order cook and two waitresses made up the staff, along with the owner, Gloria, who did a little bit of everything. She was firmly in her late thirties. An NPC, of course. Nothing unusual level-wise.

Arthur was at the diner when we got there. We waved at him. He and the owner were having a conversation. I don't know what about, but he seemed to be enjoying himself. That was a rare sight.

The diner had all manner of breakfast food. I got a waffle. Our conversation revolved around Secret Lore; Grace had developed a wealth of knowledge on the subject in the last few days.

"We were told Secret Lore was only found in high-level storylines," she explained. "I've been going through the records from back then—what's left of them anyway—and they had discovered four storylines with Secret Lore. All of them were over level sixty."

"What do you mean, 'what's left of them'?" Anna asked. "What happened to the records?"

Anna had inadvertently found a subject that Grace could lecture about for hours.

"They didn't take good records, for one," she said. "I guess when you think you will be revived you don't put as much thought into it. And then there's the problem of much of the writings from that time just being gone."

She went on about how there were several gaps in the records where years would pass with only a few scraps of paper left to tell what had happened to the players in Carousel at that time.

"How long ago was the gap you're talking about?" I asked.

"The Secret Lore?" she asked. "They first discovered it thirteen years ago. From before I got here. Lukas, as usual, only remembered about sixty percent of the truth. The players back then knew what Secret Lore tickets were when they went to the possessed ghost storyline. If I were to guess, they might have even gone there looking for it despite what Lukas said, but I can't confirm that from any of the information we have."

Thirteen years ago was around the time the players had discovered the rescue trope power-leveling exploit that got players killed and rescuing as a mechanic taken out of the game. The players had discovered that even though using a rescue trope usually made things harder, sometimes they also made them more streamlined. It was high-risk arbitrage. Enemies became more difficult in theory, but were more balanced because they were predictable. It was pretty clever until the axe murderer showed up.

That might be the reason documentation from that era was missing.

I nodded and went back to my waffle. They continued talking about how poor the record-keeping of the last generation of players was and the struggles it had caused in attempting to organize modern-day runs of Carousel. This was a constant point of frustration for the veterans. The Secret Lore hunt had brought back those same old problems.

I didn't talk much for a while; I was lost in thought. I only came around when I heard my friends asking Lara for Psychic advice on our next storyline.

"I'll give it to you straight," she said. "Do you want good information but a lower reward yield after you complete the story, or vague rambling that won't be as useful but won't stop you from getting good loot?"

That was a tough one.

"Vague," Dina said. "I'm not going through one of those things without getting anything from it."

No one argued with that.

"Are you sure that you're all ready to go on another storyline?" Lara asked. "You've had a rough few days."

We had all been through a lot. No one was completely unscathed. But we knew she was talking about Antoine specifically.

"I'm fine," he said. "Why do I have to keep telling everyone that? We need to keep up our schedule."

"You can probably wait a few more days," Grace said.

"I don't want to wait," he said. "I'm going crazy at the lodge."

When I died in the Grotesque storyline, I probably said something similar when people tried to pity me. Going through a rough patch can hurt worse when other people can see you doing it.

"Okay, then," Lara said. "Remember to never suffer in silence."

"I said I'm okay," Antoine said. "Really. I can handle it."

"Hmm?" Lara said. "No, that was your advice for your storyline. Never suffer in silence. You wanted me to do a vague Psychic reading."

She didn't put on the theatrics she usually did when making predictions. Psychic tropes are usually Moxie-based, so choosing not to play the part made them weaker, just as we had requested.

Still, those four words were pretty vague. It's hard to imagine what they might mean in the context of a horror movie. Maybe we were supposed to scream extra loudly.

Antoine nodded in understanding.

We ended up going out on the storyline two days later. I carried the job flyer with me:

Job Title: Security Surveillance Specialist

Company: Keystone Recovery and Security Laboratories (KRSL)

Are you a detail-oriented professional with a background in security surveillance? Do you have previous government work experience that required a background check? If so, we have an exciting opportunity for you at Keystone Recovery and Security Laboratories.

Responsibilities:

- Monitor and analyze security footage from various areas of the research facility.
- Report any suspicious activities or anomalies.
- Maintain logs and records of surveillance activities.
- Collaborate with the security team to ensure the safety and security of the facility.

Qualifications:

- Minimum of 2 years' experience in security surveillance.
- Excellent attention to detail and observational skills.
- Ability to work independently and make quick decisions.
- Strong communication skills.

KRSL is a leading research lab committed to advancing knowledge in various scientific fields. We offer competitive salaries, comprehensive benefits, and opportunities for professional growth.

Other Positions Available:

- Security Guard
- Research Scientist
- Therapist for Test Subjects
- Test Subject Manager

Interested candidates are encouraged to apply with their resume and cover letter. Please inquire within for more details about the available positions.

KRSL is an equal-opportunity employer. We celebrate diversity and are committed to creating an inclusive environment for all employees.

Note: All applicants must be willing to undergo a comprehensive background check as part of the recruitment process.

Important Notice: Due to the nature of our work, we regret that we are unable to consider applicants with certain neurological conditions. Because of this, testing is required. Please inquire within for more details.

Confidentiality Notice: The nature of our work at KRSL is highly confidential. All applicants must be willing to sign a non-disclosure agreement (NDA) as part of the recruitment process. Any information related to our projects, methodologies, and research findings must not be disclosed to any third party.

The location we were directed to was a large white facility on the northwest side of town. Mobile emergency-station tents had been put up all around the facility, but now, some of them were being taken down. It looked like this site had been used for some sort of disaster relief, but I could not begin to guess what for exactly. Ambulances and fire trucks were parked all around. The entire facility was fenced off, but the gates were open.

A woman wearing a suit stood outside one of the gates and made eye contact with us.

She was an NPC with three Plot Armor named Nancy Cartwright. I could see that to trigger the Omen for the story, all we had to do was approach her with the job flier. The movie poster for the storyline was the same as was shown when we first picked up the flier: security monitors splashed with blood. "*Subject of Inquiry*" was written across the top of the poster.

My scouting tropes activated. I Don't Like It Here said the level was set to "This is scaring me." On the difficulty scale, I would rank that pretty high, but it wasn't high enough to make the trope fail. Location Scout told me that all of the shooting locations were in the building. Some had titles like "Corporate Mess Hall" and "Control Room." None of them were called "Torture Chamber" or "Execution Room," or anything like that. There were rooms called "Secure Patient Room," which sounded a lot like a cell in an insane asylum, but I couldn't have expected it to be all sunshine and daisies. There were a lot of hallways, conference rooms, and laboratories.

I told the others this information and we approached the NPC that was waiting for us.

Our character stats:

Player	Plot Armor	Mettle	Moxie	Hustle	Savvy	Grit
Riley	21/2	2	7	4	7	1
Antoine	17	4	3	5	1	4
Anna	19	4	4	3	3	5
Kimberly	16	2	5	4	1	4
Camden	16	2	2	2	7	3
Dina	17	2	2	4	2	7

Our tropes were as follows:
Anna Reed is the Final Girl.

As the **Last One Alive**, she cannot die until the rest of the party is killed.
Her **Who's with Me?** trope allows her to buff allies in the Finale, and **Let's
Not Fight** buffs allies when she defuses infighting.
A Kind Face makes NPCs more likely to reveal important plot information,
and **Shared Experience** allows players to gain loot based on her efforts.
Along for the Ride buffs the Hustle and Grit of vehicles. Borrowed from
me, she also has the **Stick to the Plan** trope, which allows her to get doomed
plans back on track by rallying allies as if victory is still possible.

Antoine Stone is the Athlete.

His **You Were Having a Nightmare . . .** trope allows him to repress or heal
mental trauma (he is not strong enough to use its plot-resetting powers yet).
It's Part of the Uniform gives him higher Mettle when attacking with sports
equipment.
Gym Rat buffs Mettle and Hustle by revealing athletic backstory.
Just Walk It Off heals the Hobbled status by walking.
The Playbook allows him to see the phases of a coordinated plan.
Time-Out! allows him to go off-screen during a fight, reducing enemy
aggression.
He left his **Bad Luck Magnet** trope at home for this storyline, for obvious
reasons.

Camden Tran is the Scholar.

Eureka! helps him find important information within text.

Right Tool for the Job buffs Savvy and Mettle when fighting an enemy with their weakness.

Zippos Are Cheap boosts Savvy for plans that expend a Zippo lighter.

Hide and Seek allows him to outsmart an enemy during a chase instead of outrunning them.

Photographic Memory allows him to display visual information committed to memory on the red wallpaper.

The Immobile Genius allows him to send allies off to enact a plan, giving them a temporary Savvy boost.

Dina Cano is the Outsider.

Guarded Personality resists all insight abilities.

An Outsider's Perspective alerts her to new, out-of-place, or unusual information.

Better Late than Never buffs Mettle and Hustle if she waits until the Finale to assist allies on-screen against the enemy.

A Haunted Past allows her to equip various tickets related to past trauma.

Encouragement from Beyond soothes her when stressed, scared, or in pain and may provide useful information.

Outside Looking In grants her the ability to discern ideal spots to linger and observe events without actively participating in the narrative.

Kimberly Madison is the Eye Candy.

Convenient Backstory allows her to change her backstory to assist with the current task, buffing the relevant stat.

Social Awareness allows her to see the Moxie stat of all enemies and NPCs and get a sense of their relationships to each other.

Get a Room! boosts the odds of important discoveries when exploring with a love interest during the Party.

A Hopeless Plea forces the captor to explicitly deny her release when she asks to be released.

Pregnancy Reveal buffs her Grit when she announces she is pregnant and buffs the father if she is killed.

That's What I Said! allows her plans and ideas to be "stolen" by higher-Savvy allies, with the success of the plan being determined by their Savvy.

Does Anyone Have a Scrunchie? allows her to transfer Moxie to Savvy, Hustle, or Grit by putting her hair up.

She left **Looks Don't Last** at home again.

Riley Lawrence is the Film Buff.

Trope Master grants me the ability to perceive enemy tropes, but at the cost of sacrificing half of my Plot Armor.

With the power of **Cinema Seer**, I enhance the Savvy and Grit of my allies by accurately predicting cinematic and impactful plot elements (but must save it for good predictions).

As an **Oblivious Bystander**, I remain untargeted by enemies while I convincingly act oblivious to their presence.

Escape Artist boosts my Hustle in order to execute plausible escape plans.

Through **Casting Director**, I gain insights into the roles players assume within storylines. Drawing on my upbringing, **Raised by Television** enhances relevant stats when I take larger-than-life or cinematic action inspired by TV or movies, though it often attracts a downturn in fortune soon afterward.

With **My Grandmother Had the Gift . . .** I can equip various tickets related to intuitive or supernatural abilities "inherited" from my grandmother.

I Don't Like It Here . . . provides me with insight into the location of Omens and how to avoid triggering them.

Lastly, **Location Scout** equips me with a list of all primary filming locations within the storyline.

Nancy Cartwright turned around as we approached and began walking through the gate to get into the compound. I found it funny that as she walked, she took the Omen with her, as triggering the Omen required us to get to her with the job flier.

She led us past several figures wearing those big decontamination suits you see in movies and further past a team of doctors examining random NPCs, none of whom had any visible injuries. I heard people grumbling as they lined up to be examined. A baby cried somewhere. I wasn't sure what had happened there.

"Oh, don't worry about that," Nancy assured us as we walked past the medical tent. "KRSL does emergency medical treatment for the city of Carousel. We're happy to be able to help the community that our facility calls home."

"What happened here?" Anna asked.

Nancy turned her head a bit and pressed her lips into a smile. "We can't really talk about it until the people in charge give the go-ahead. Don't want to cause a panic. Plus, it's not like they tell me anything."

She laughed a fake, folksy laugh.

Nancy was a big-city woman. She stuck out in the suburban landscape that was Carousel proper.

"Just follow me right this way," she said, waving a security badge over a black box on the side of the building, which opened the automatic door into the facility.

"This is building security," she said. "I will meet you on the other side after you've been checked out. Security is quite rigorous. Don't be alarmed."

She turned and passed through security, flashing her badge as she went.

Now it was our turn. We still hadn't even triggered the storyline yet.

"All right," Anna said as she walked forward through security. "See you on the other side."

The security line was a maze of curtains and X-ray machines where they checked all of our identities and asked us all sorts of questions. I handed them my driver's license, but I could have handed them anything at this point. I doubt it mattered. Any prop would do.

The staff was very stern. They stood with their backs straight and moved their eyes around the area looking for security breaches. They reminded me of soldiers. Maybe they were ex-military. Whatever they did at this facility must have been important.

I was asked to put all of my metal belongings in a tray. I put my Walkman, sunglasses, and headphones in. The guard at that desk examined them to make sure they were not contraband. I joked, "I have a permit for that," as he was pressing the buttons on my Walkman, but he didn't laugh.

After I had proven that I was not carrying a landmine anywhere on my person, I was allowed through to the other side with my things.

We still hadn't triggered the storyline, though leaving now would be awkward.

As Antoine came out to the other side, I noticed something was missing. He had a confused look on his face.

"They take your bat?" I asked. He had a trope that should have allowed him to bring sports equipment into a storyline as a weapon, but perhaps that was a bridge too far for this storyline. Trope or no trope, bringing a weapon into a secure facility was not going to be believable.

He shook his head in amazement.

"It just disappeared as we walked in," he said, showing his hands. "Just disappeared right out of my hand. I thought I dropped it at first."

He seemed to be doing okay. For now.

"Of course it did," I said.

He laughed.

"Just my luck," he said. For a moment I saw the light in his eyes go out, but it was back soon enough.

"We need this one, Riley," he said. "After this, you think Dina will trust us enough to tell us what she knows?"

Not this again. I was hoping he would drop it. He thought Dina knew something about our plight. Something she wasn't telling us. I wasn't sure that was true. What I knew was that he was getting his hopes up when he really shouldn't.

"We'll see," I said. I hated to be in that situation.

"Come this way please," Nancy said to us.

We did as she asked. As we did, we finally triggered the storyline. The needle on the Plot Cycle switched from Omen to Choice to Party.

Anna, Camden, and Kimberly followed. Dina still hadn't made it through security.

"Congratulations," Nancy said. "You've made it through the interviews. You are now a part of the KRSL family."

I don't remember any job interviews, but I suppose that was not a part of the movie. Easiest job application process I'd ever had. The job flier was no longer in my hand.

"Now it's time for employee orientation!" Nancy said with a distinctively corporate enthusiasm. "I will come to get you individually for a quick meet and greet with your department heads momentarily."

We'd dodged the interview only to get stuck in new employee orientation.

This really was a horror movie.

CHAPTER THIRTY-TWO

SUPERSTITION

As we waited to start our new jobs, I decided to fill everyone in on the roles they had been assigned, thanks to my Casting Director ability. The role descriptions on the red wallpaper were as follows:

Riley (Security Surveillance Specialist): Riley, starting his first shift as a Security Surveillance Specialist, is brother to Anna. His job is to monitor the facility's security cameras, using his vantage point to spot anomalies. As he navigates his new job, he will be able to see most everything happening in the facility, but will he see the truth before it's too late?
Antoine (Security Guard): Antoine, a new hire, steps into his role as one of the facility's elite Security Guards. His strength and size make him a formidable presence, but will he be able to keep everyone safe? As the story unravels, his role as a protector leads him to question who or what he's truly safeguarding.
Camden (Research Scientist): Camden, on his first shift as a Research Scientist, is tasked with studying a mysterious group of people linked to recent disasters. His Scholarly insight is invaluable, but his pursuit of knowledge might uncover more than he bargained for.
Kimberly (Therapist for Test Subjects): Kimberly, cousin to Anna and Riley, begins her first shift providing emotional support and therapy to the test subjects. Her social skills and adaptability make her an effective therapist, but her close interactions with the subjects raise questions about the ethical implications of her employer's work.

> Anna (Test Subject Manager): Anna, Riley's sister, starts her first shift as the Test Subject Manager. Her survival instincts and leadership skills are tested as she manages the bridge between the test subjects and the rest of the facility. However, her new role leads her to question the true purpose of the facility and the nature of the tests being conducted.

Anna, Kimberly, and I were related to each other in this storyline. Well, our characters were. Strange, but nothing unheard of.

"Wait," Anna asked. "Where's Dina?"

Dina still hadn't made it through security. I kept expecting her to waltz out of the maze of curtains and machinery, but she didn't. I wasn't sure where she had gone. She had definitely entered the security check with us. Now she was nowhere to be seen.

Moments later, we were back on-screen as Nancy Cartwright appeared with her fake smile.

"If you will all follow me, I will take you to your meet and greets," she said.

She led us down the hall toward a row of offices where she sent each of us, one at a time. I walked into the office where I was supposed to meet my department head and sat in one of the chairs in front of the desk.

It was a nice office with expensive furniture and wall art. They needed good art at KRSL, as there were no windows in the whole building.

One of the paintings was an abstract depiction of the human brain as you might see it on a brain scan. The colors swirled like fire. Within them, I swore I could see the faintest traces of some shadowy figures dancing in the flames.

I waited for twenty minutes off-screen.

Eventually, the door opened, and I was on-screen.

A man entered. He was a well-groomed scientist in a lab coat. On the red wallpaper, he was called Dr. Truman Mentes. He was an NPC with fifty Plot Armor. Like other NPCs of that level, he had tropes that appeared gray and unreadable on the red wallpaper. I assumed they were enemy tropes.

"Pardon me for my tardiness," he said as he entered. "My name is Doctor Truman Mentes. I am the head of research at this facility."

I stood and shook his hand.

"Riley Lawrence," I said.

He sat behind the desk as I returned to my seat. He carried a manila file folder with my name on it.

"Well, we can assume your interviews went well since you made it this far," he said.

I nodded. I had nailed those nonexistent interviews.

"As you may have guessed, I am not actually your department head. As a surveillance specialist, you do not have a true supervisor. That is how we set up the hierarchy. Your job requires that you work autonomously. Your colleague, Mr. Rowe, is already downstairs. He will show you everything you need to know."

"I can't wait to get started," I said.

"That's wonderful to hear. This is only a meet and greet. If you have any questions, you can ask them. Otherwise, let's get to know each other."

"I do have a question," I said. "What is it, exactly, that we do here?"

"That's a good first question," Dr. Mentes said with a chuckle. "Our interest is in public safety. We monitor individuals we believe may be suffering from latent illnesses or traumas. It really is that simple. We try to keep them healthy. We ensure they are safe to return to the general public."

That certainly wasn't the whole truth, but I couldn't say as much.

"Good to know. Sounds like important work," I said cheerfully.

"It is," he said. "And the work you will be doing helps make it all happen. We cannot protect these people without professionals like yourself. Tell me, did the work schedule intimidate you when you first learned of it? Five days on, five days off would scare away a lot of candidates. Being away from friends and family days at a time can be quite stressful."

Five days? As in, the storyline would last five days?

"No," I said. "I am actually looking forward to it. Plus, my sister and cousin are here with me, so I'm not truly alone."

"That's a good attitude," he said.

He opened the manila folder and began going over my fake resume with me. I had never heard of anything that was on that sheet of paper before, but it could be summarized as this: my character had stared at a lot of security monitors in some very important places.

As he shuffled through the pages, a small white-and-red piece of paper fell out. At first, I thought it was a strange kind of ticket like one Silas might deliver for us. It turned out it wasn't.

It was a lottery ticket.

Dr. Mentes grabbed it off the table.

"You will have to forgive me for my habit. A silly superstition, really," Dr. Mentes said as he tucked the lottery ticket back inside his pocket. "You see, my father once saw that I had purchased a lottery ticket and told me that the first week I didn't buy one would be the week my numbers came up. I have bought a lottery ticket every week since."

He gave me a restrained but pleasant smile.

"That's fine," I said. "I've been known to buy scratch cards myself now and again."

"My father was superstitious that way. I suppose I am too. Those things tend to run in the blood. Tell me, is your family superstitious?"

I thought for a moment. "Yes, I suppose," I said. "They say my grandmother had 'the gift.'"

"Oh? The gift?"

"Yes," I said. "That's what the family says."

Really, it was just what my background card said.

"Would that be your grandmother Holly?" he said, glancing down at the file folder.

My blood froze in my veins as he said it. Holly was the name of my grandmother. The one who, along with my grandfather, had taken me in after my parents died. My *real* grandmother.

I cleared my throat.

"Yes—how did you know . . . ?"

Dr. Mentes again flashed his polite, restrained smile. "We do very thorough background checks here, Mr. Lawrence. It is important work you're doing. We wanted to be sure we were hiring the right candidate. I assure you, all of your coworkers went through the same process."

I nodded slowly.

"Would you say that your grandmother passed the gift down to you?"

I shook my head. "No, no," I said dismissively.

"You can speak candidly here," Dr. Mentes said. "I'm just trying to get to know you."

What was it he wanted me to say?

I tapped the table with both hands. "You know, I am pretty good at guessing the endings of movies. If that's a gift."

My streak lately might not have been perfect, but still. I needed to lay a foundation that I watched a lot of movies so I could talk about it later.

Dr. Mentes chuckled politely. "I am sure that comes in handy."

"Not as much as I would like," I said.

"How about your sister or your cousin?" Dr. Mentes asked. Anna and Kimberly's characters were related to me in this storyline. "Do they have the gift too?"

I shrugged my shoulders. "They always knew when I was making faces at them behind their backs growing up if that counts."

That elicited another polite laugh.

"It isn't every day that we bring in a batch of new hires that are related to each other, but it can hardly be avoided in a small town like Carousel. I imagine that any group of five people from Carousel would likely contain relatives."

Was Carousel a small town? In many ways it seemed large.

"Maybe," I said. "But I assure you, it won't get in the way of our work."

"I do not need your assurance on that matter," Dr. Mentes said. "Now, if you will excuse me, I have to cut this short. I have other matters to attend to. Nancy will help you obtain your credentials and show you to your workstation downstairs."

He stood, shook my hand again, and left.

Soon enough, I had my own badge that would allow me into any of the rooms I was authorized to enter. It also allowed me to operate the elevator.

"I think you are going to like your new workstation," Nancy said. "It's spacious and your bed is right there in your office. Housekeeping should be finished in there now. You'll need to change into your uniform, of course. I recommend wearing a sweater. Your office is quite cold."

We took the elevator to floor 2B, the second floor belowground out of four basement levels.

"Come right this way."

I followed her around a bend to a large metal door that was secured with thick bars and a heavy-duty electronic lock.

The door was open. Inside, a fairly large room with a wall of computer monitors awaited me. There was a chair in front of the monitors. A man, an NPC named Mr. Rowe, sat in it. He was a heavyset fellow with long hair.

"Mr. Rowe," Nancy said. "I have your new colleague here for you."

The man turned around in the chair.

"Great. That means I can go home," he said.

He stood from his chair and came to greet me. He hadn't shaved in weeks from the look of it. We shook hands.

"I'll leave you to it," Nancy said as she turned to go.

Mr. Rowe stared at her as she left.

"Well, let me show you your new home for the next five days," he said. "Linens just got changed in the bunk."

He pointed to a bed tucked away in a corner of the room.

"Follow me," he said.

As I entered the security room, I was immediately struck by the monitors. Specifically, the monitors that contained images of people dressed in white hospital gowns, who appeared to be locked away in padded white cells somewhere in the facility. They looked like they were being contained. They were either very contagious, or they were prisoners.

"Don't mind them," Rowe said. "They're fine."

Yeah, sure.

Mr. Rowe explained the fine details of my job for the next week. I was there to observe and report.

"Remember, if you see anything unusual, anything at all, you write it in the logbook. If you leave the book empty, you'll be out of here in a hot second. It's an easy job, so don't screw it up," Mr. Rowe explained to me. "A lot of newcomers think they can come here and sleep all day and loaf around all night," he said. "No sirree. You keep your eyes on the monitors."

He pulled out a clipboard with a few laminated sheets clipped onto it.

"These are the rounds," he explained. "Security might make rounds in the night. Make sure to unlock doors for them. You do that from this panel. Don't need to during the day, but at night nobody can go anywhere without asking you first."

He then explained to me how the intercoms worked. When someone pressed one of the little white boxes on the walls, a light would flash on my panel, and I would have to press a button to speak to them.

"Periodically check the audio in each room. You can listen to what's being said in a room by flipping the switch next to the monitor. Don't go eavesdropping too much; this is for security surveillance only."

I noticed that there was a little bar next to each monitor that measured how much sound was coming from that area. In the rooms where employees and patients were talking, the little bars danced with each word. Everywhere else they barely moved.

"It worked the same way at my last job," I lied.

He nodded his head. "Good. So you know."

Then he put a hand on my shoulder and said, "Some folks come to this job and the long hours start playing tricks on their minds. They don't last long. Don't be like them. Otherwise, I'll have to take over your shifts until they find a replacement. I really don't want to do that."

"What kind of tricks?" I asked.

"Oh, I don't know. They get stir-crazy, that's all. At night, when you've been staring at the monitors for seven hours straight and everyone else is asleep, you start seeing things that aren't there. Forget I said it."

Nothing to read into there.

"I'll be fine," I said. "Been doing this for years. Don't plan on going stir-crazy now."

"Good man."

With that, Mr. Rowe turned and began packing up his clothes and belongings. "For the mess hall, follow the signs."

"Will do."

Then he left. I was alone in the frigid surveillance room.

I looked back at the monitors and at the eight people—including two children—that were locked away in the facility so that we could monitor them. I wondered how they were going to play into this storyline. It wasn't going to be pretty, that much was certain.

But it wasn't just them that I was worried about.

My Trope Master ability showed me the tropes of enemies when I was physically near them and looking at them, with a few notable exceptions. It also showed me enemy tropes that related to the setting itself even when I wasn't near an enemy. I had seen that at the Astralist's castle and in Benny's cornfield.

Here, staring at the monitors, I saw two terrifying tropes.

A Knock at the Door: This enemy can target characters behind closed doors, turning a symbol of safety into a source of dread. It may be able to lure characters out with deceptive sounds or eerie silence, manipulating their fear and curiosity, or it may be able to simply break or sneak through such barriers. With **A Knock at the Door,** death is just a room away.

Anyone Can Die: This enemy operates under a chilling rule: no character is safe. Whether it's because this film is a rule-breaking reboot or a narrative without a true protagonist, this enemy can target or kill any character without ceremony or hesitation. With **Anyone Can Die**, the only main characters are the ones who survive.

CHAPTER THIRTY-THREE

NIGHT SHIFT

It was noon. I wondered if the five days we were going to spend there were full days or if time would start speeding up once some important scenes were out of the way.

My question was slowly answered. Very slowly.

It was eight hours before my first night shift started. I decided to go find the mess hall.

I got lost almost immediately. It was hard to imagine just how big this floor level was. It must have taken up more square footage than the building on the surface itself. The halls wound around. There were automatic security doors placed at every junction. They were open during the day, but at night they would be closed, turning this place from a maze into a prison.

The front of the level toward the elevator was less restricted, with several different rooms that could be reached without security clearance. I eventually found the mess hall to be one of these.

The mess hall was smaller than I had imagined. NPCs sat at the tables eating prepackaged meals from fancy vending machines that lined a wall. Luckily, the vending machines were connected to our badges and our purchases would be deducted from our salary. I didn't have enough money to pay for food otherwise. Our trip to the pawn shop had cleared me out and the campfire storyline didn't give me much.

I had yet to see my friends since being separated from them upstairs. I decided to wait at the mess hall for a bit in case one of them showed up, but I couldn't wait all day. I had monitors to watch and a pre-shift nap to take.

I was off-screen the whole time. Despite this, NPCs more or less stayed in their roles.

I purchased some meatloaf and mashed potatoes from one of the vending machines that had a revolving shelf filled with prepared meals. Then I sat and ate my lunch. Eventually, I looked up to find Camden making a beeline for my table.

"We keep calling those people patients, but they don't seem sick, and they want to leave," he said, referring to the eight people that were being observed within the facility. "They do not like me at all."

"Maybe it's just your bedside manner, Doc," I said with a nod toward the badge he was wearing on his white lab coat. "Dr. Camden Tran. Didn't think you'd get the degree so quickly, did you?"

"I think I've earned it," he said. "I'm serious. We've got those prisoners so drugged up they don't know what year it is."

"I'm not sure what year it is either. Where are my drugs?" I joked. "Yeah, I've got a view into every cell. If those people are patients, I can't imagine what disease they must have. What kind of doctor are you?"

"Neuroscience."

"A brain doctor?"

"A brain researcher. All I do here is hook them up to machines and monitor some pseudo-scientific measurements."

I thought about that for a moment. "So, do they have . . . good . . . brains?"

"All measurements are within standardized ranges," he said. "That's what the lab guys keep saying. They keep dodging my questions."

He told me about his day so far. We were still at the very beginning of the Party phase. There was still time for discovery.

After a little more back and forth, I decided to go back to my igloo and sleep until my shift.

I tried to sleep. I really did. But I was in a storyline. I wasn't sure I could ever doze off knowing there was something in this place that was going to try to kill me. This week wasn't going to go well.

At two thirty, I decided to get up and watch the monitors. With the security doors open and people walking around, I could likely make sense of the layout of the building more easily than I could at night when everything was shut off from everything else.

I watched, and despite Mr. Rowe's warnings, I listened to anything that looked like it might be useful information.

I found Camden again, on the monitors. He was inside one of the cells with a man in his mid-thirties. The man looked sad and worried. He sat on the edge of his bed.

"Can I at least see my children again?" the man asked. "Our visit got cut short today because a new therapist got introduced. We were promised we'd get an hour today."

Camden shook his head. "I'm not in charge of that. Talk to the relations manager about that."

"She's new too," the man said. "It's not even worth learning people's names around here."

"Just a few more minutes," Camden said as he affixed some kind of diode to the man's head.

The man was slumped over and tired. "We've been here for weeks. Months. I don't know. You haven't even told us what's wrong with us."

Camden didn't respond to that. "Just lay back."

The man slowly leaned back in his bed.

Camden watched a computer monitor on a large cart like the kind teachers would use to wheel televisions from classroom to classroom, except this cart had all manner of electronics built into it. Camden watched as numbers danced on the screen. I couldn't make out what was happening.

After a moment, I saw Anna walking down the hallway with a young man, maybe sixteen or seventeen years old. I switched off the audio from Camden's room and switched on the audio from where Anna was.

"You really think there's something wrong with me?" the young man said. "I feel fine. Just a few sleepless nights is all."

Anna shrugged her shoulders. "The doctors think that you should be monitored. I'm just here to help make sure you are being taken care of."

"Do I have to wear this?" the young man said, holding out the white gown in his hand. "I really don't think that's necessary."

"I can't blame you," she said. "But the sooner you're ready for evaluation, the sooner you'll be out of here."

The kid stared at her for a moment, then nodded. "Okay."

Anna continued to lead him down the hallways, consulting a clipboard in her hand for directions as she went. I followed them along, switching the audio as they moved through the building.

"I see on your chart that you didn't put down an emergency contact," Anna said.

The kid shrugged. "It was just me and my mom. After what happened, it's just me. I'm sorry. They said not to talk about the accident until they said I could . . . Am I in trouble?"

"No, of course not," Anna said. "Here we are."

She presented him with one of the cells. She left him in there for a moment while he changed, then she took his clothes away.

"I'll be back later when I make my rounds," she said.

"Okay," he responded meekly.

He sat on his bed and waited. That made nine patients in total.

Kimberly sat in one of the white cells at a table. Across from her was a young girl who might have been six.

"It's nice to meet you, too, Bethany," Kimberly said. "I was hoping to ask you some questions, and then maybe we could play a little game before you have to go to bed. What do you think?"

"What kind of game?" the little girl asked, looking over at Kimberly's side of the table for a glimpse of whatever game Kimberly might have brought.

"A card game."

"Where's Miss Gloria?"

"Miss Gloria?"

"She used to play games with me too," Bethany said.

"Oh," Kimberly said. "It'll just be you and me."

"Okay," Bethany said in an adorable little voice.

"Do you remember what you were doing when the accident happened?" Kimberly asked.

The little girl shook her head.

"It was a long, long time ago. I don't remember."

"Can you try to remember?"

The little girl was quiet.

"I was with my brother," Bethany said. "He wanted ice cream, but Mommy said we couldn't have ice cream until later." Bethany started to whimper.

Kimberly moved around to the side of the table to attempt to comfort the child.

A voice came over the speaker in the cell, causing high-pitched feedback on my speakers. "Do not touch the subject."

They must have had other people watching the same cameras I was. Maybe the researchers could see the cells with the subjects in them.

Kimberly stopped in her tracks and looked up to where the speaker must have been. She said something under her breath.

She moved back to her seat.

"It's okay," Kimberly said. "We don't have to do the questions. We can just play the game. Do you know how to play Go Fish?"

"Yes," Bethany said.

Kimberly unveiled a pack of cards specifically designed for the game Go Fish, with pictures of different kinds of colorful fish on them instead of the normal suits and ranks.

Kimberly dealt the cards and they started to play.

"Do you have any blue squids?" Kimberly asked.

Bethany shook her head. Go fish.

"Do you have any red sea turtles?" Bethany asked in response.

"Go fish."

"Miss Gloria was better at this," Bethany said.

"I'm sorry," Kimberly said.

They continued playing for thirty minutes or so after that. I eventually tuned out.

I surfed around to other audio feeds. The NPCs were all speaking to each other, but I never once found a conversation worth spying on. I didn't know if that was because my effective Plot Armor was so low that I couldn't discover information as well as the other players or if there simply wasn't any information to obtain yet.

Night crept in slowly. I eventually managed to get some sleep in preparation for my shift. As I awoke, I began doing pre-shift checks for audio and video. Everything checked out. It was busy work. Nothing major.

I noticed something happening in the mess hall. Two NPCs were having an argument with no players around to hear. No players except me.

I switched on the audio.

"You fired Rolf," an NPC said. It was a woman who appeared to be a custodian or something similar. She was hauling around a large trash can and emptying the smaller cans into it. "You expect me to do his job too. I don't have the time."

"We're all working extra shifts, Barb," the other NPC, her manager, said. "We need you to pick up the slack."

"It's too big!" Barb said. "I don't have time to clean it all in one shift."

"You can finish it tomorrow. We need to be out of here by seven thirty. You know the rules."

"If I finish it tomorrow, then I will have to stay late tomorrow too. I will never be finished."

"Let's just go," the second NPC said. "We'll resolve this later. You're going to get us both fired."

Barb dropped the trash can she was emptying on the ground. "Fine."

After some more bickering, they both headed for the elevators together.

It was awfully convenient that everyone on the floor took turns doing important things as if they were coordinating it so that I could spy on them one at a time.

The cameras covered most of floor 2B, but there were things I couldn't see. I wasn't sure which parts weren't covered, but there were places where an NPC could walk off the screen and not reappear until a while later. Dead spots.

My Location Scout ability lined up pretty well with the security cameras, though the trope gave me less information. It mostly just told me where one of Carousel's "cameras" was, not what it covered or anything of the sort. Location Scout told me of several shooting locations that I didn't think were on this floor.

I had yet to see Dina at all. She must have been in one of them.

After the last daytime employee had gone, I was left alone on my watch. I shut the giant door to the security room and locked it.

I stared at the monitors. My friends had all gone to their quarters to sleep. I couldn't see their beds or their bathrooms, obviously; luckily, Carousel didn't put any cameras in the bathrooms.

Most of the job was in the waiting; I considered the two enemy tropes I had seen as I did so. Anyone Can Die meant Anna's Last One Alive trope wouldn't protect her and Plot Armor wouldn't save anyone. I debated over whether Oblivious Bystander would work, seeing as it only protected me temporarily to increase tension. I wasn't sure, but I also didn't think it was worth the risk to try unless I had no other choice.

A Knock at the Door was less clear. The monster wasn't deterred by doors. It wasn't clear why. Could it break them down? Or did it have another way through them, like a security badge?

I waited.

And waited.

Midnight. Finally.

Then two o'clock. The patients slept soundly in their beds for the most part. Only one of them tossed and turned: the new kid.

Three o'clock in the morning. If anything was going to happen, it would happen then, right?

No . . .

It happened at quarter past four.

I was barely able to stay awake as I watched the monitors. I had not seen anything to write in my logbook and was looking for something—anything—to share with my friends, some clue of what it was we faced.

One of the screens showing the back half of the level, where the cells were, looked funny. It wasn't blurry or staticky—it was ever-so-gently warped. Distorted. Like looking at something through an antique window.

There was no visible figure walking through the room. There was no jump in the audio either. It was silent.

I was looking at a hallway with a potted plant, but it was just slightly distorted. I wouldn't even have noticed had I not been looking for something.

Moments later, it was back to normal.

Another monitor became distorted. And then another. One at a time, the monitors would get distorted and then would go back to normal as a monitor nearby would become distorted instead. It was confined to a certain area. I started writing this down furiously in my logbook. How would my character be acting right now? Worried? Would he think it was a hardware malfunction? Yes. That was it.

I wrote down that there was a hardware malfunction. I tracked which cameras appeared to be affected.

I couldn't figure out what was stopping the distortion from continuing its path around the monitors at first. Then I realized—it was the doors. The distortion, or whatever was causing it, could not pass through doors. It was wandering from room to room but only the rooms that were open to each other.

That didn't make any sense. The monster we were after could go through doors; at least, I thought that had been implied. What other reasons could there be for targeting players through them? There was something I was missing.

Eventually, I watched as the distortion stopped in one of the rooms, a conference room of some sort. There was a spike in audio for a split second, then the distortion disappeared.

I watched for the distortion to come back.

I never saw anything else that night.

I wondered if anything saw me.

CHAPTER THIRTY-FOUR

A BUMP IN THE NIGHT

The next day, I watched as the day shift people came back and started their routines all over again. I was tired in a way that I hadn't been in a long time, and yet, I felt like I couldn't sleep. I was the wrong kind of wired. I was afraid to miss anything.

The day began with breakfast for the patients. I didn't know most of their names or code names—that information was above my pay grade—but I did come up with a list based on my own observations: Father, Son, Daughter (Bethany), Teen Boy, Old Guy, Old Lady, the Middle-Aged Woman twins, and Mid-Thirties Woman were our prisoners—or patients.

They were each given so many different colored pills with their breakfasts that I might have thought it was candy if not for the NPC nurses that stayed to watch them swallow every last one.

Old Guy didn't complain about a thing. He seemed genuinely happy to have nurses and other staff serving him and asking him about his day. He also had a large jigsaw puzzle set up on the table in the room that he had nearly finished, along with a dozen more boxes of puzzles on a shelf. The rest of the shelf contained books, and he even had a record player.

Old Lady was not so congenial. When Anna and Kimberly interacted with her, she called them both Jasmine.

"Dammit, Jasmine, I told you I don't want to answer no more questions."

"Jasmine, get me my peach tea. They said if I took the tests, I would get peach tea."

She spent most of her time knitting herself clothes that she would wear to accessorize her white medical gown.

I didn't know how long those two had been there, but they were not new.

Kimberly was doing some sort of therapy exercise with one of the Middle-Aged Woman twins and Mid-Thirties Woman when the topic of why they had been brought in came up.

"I don't know why they blamed me," Middle-Aged said. "That dog terrorized the whole neighborhood . . . It could have been anyone." She stared down at the ground as she said this, her eyes on the verge of tears.

"At least they gave you a reason," Mid-Thirties responded. "I was just grabbed off the str—"

A voice came over the intercom. "Do not allow the patients to relive their trauma. This would be detrimental to their treatment. Follow the instructions as written, please."

Kimberly gave a half-hearted thumbs-up to the camera. She was playing her character as anti-authoritarian, apparently.

She then led the two women in a discussion of their fears and feelings. I decided to tune out. I would have to ask Kimberly if anything interesting happened.

When I first arrived, I assumed that everyone was at the facility because of one recent event. After having eavesdropped a little, I knew that to be untrue; there were multiple events. I didn't know how many.

It took me hours after the night shift to get to sleep, but when I crashed, I crashed hard. I slept until six in the evening. I could have kept going but I woke up hungry, and a quick glance at the screens told me that my friends were in the mess hall.

I fast walked all the way there, eager to tell them about the distortion on the screens from the night before and to find out any important information they might have discovered. The needle of the Plot Cycle was moving so incredibly slowly that I would normally say it was nearly First Blood, but at the rate it was moving we likely had plenty of time.

I quickly walked into the mess hall, and, suddenly, I was on-screen. Unable to tell my friends the news candidly, I decided to solve a different problem.

"I am starving," I said as I passed by them and purchased two meals—a sub sandwich and a rice dish of ambiguous origin—from the vending machines.

When I got back to the table, I saw that Antoine's arm was around Kimberly and they were smiling at me.

"What's up?" I asked.

"I'm pregnant," Kimberly said with a bubbling joy. She was a good actor. I don't think I could announce a fake pregnancy with half that enthusiasm.

"What? No way!" I said with a smile. "So, the family tree grows by one. Congratulations."

Kimberly was my cousin in this storyline. It made sense for me to be excited.

"I hate that I found it out while I was here," Kimberly said. "KRSL is watching us. They probably knew before I did."

"When did you find out?" I asked.

"Just now," Kimberly said. "There are pregnancy tests in the medical center."

Carousel sure did think of everything.

"That makes more sense," I said. "I thought you were going to tell me they sold those in the vending machines too."

We made idle banter and talked about baby names. The whole time, I was thinking about something else entirely.

Kimberly's Grit.

Pregnancy Reveal boosted a player's Grit upon revealing they were pregnant. The logic was that pregnant characters are more sympathetic, and the audience wouldn't want to see them die or get hurt.

What interested me was the degree to which her Grit had been buffed. Six points. Her Grit went up a huge amount from that one trope. That seemed like a lot, though I was not super familiar with the trope yet. Still . . . That must have been excessive.

Was her performance so good that the buff was maxed out? Was her Moxie so high that the buff scaled up to match?

I couldn't really put my suspicions into words, so I dropped the line of thought.

Eventually, we went off-screen.

"I didn't think it was going to end," Kimberly said. "There is something really strange going on here. Like, stranger than the obvious."

The others agreed.

We took turns exchanging information with each other about what we had found.

Kimberly and Anna talked about their conversations with the patients. They had all complained of one thing: insomnia.

"That can't be true," I said. "I watched them all night long. They were sleeping just fine."

"That's what they said," Anna responded. "They were always asking for sleep meds so that they could get some shut-eye."

Strange.

"Maybe the cocktail of drugs they're on has something to do with it," I suggested.

Anna shrugged her shoulders.

"I . . . have some bad news," I continued. I told them about the distortion and the two enemy tropes I had seen, Anyone Can Die and A Knock at the Door.

That was a potent combination in this setting.

I wondered how Anna would take that. She had always been safe in the knowledge that she would survive every storyline.

She got quiet.

"So, whoever is closest to it gets killed?" Camden asked.

"Sounds like it," I said. "Though, it may have other tropes that I couldn't see from a distance."

Camden had his own information to share.

"There is a genetics lab on one of the other floors," he said. "I don't know exactly what they do, but it has something to do with this floor."

"What do geneticists have to do with supposed trauma patients?" Antoine asked.

No one had a good explanation other than that these weren't really trauma patients.

Antoine hadn't found anything yet. He did have one interesting observation, though.

"None of our security procedures are related to the patients. We are not supposed to touch them. All of our training is for dealing with irate employees and outside intruders," he said. "I thought that was odd."

So did I.

Of course, eventually, the conversation turned back to me.

"So, what do you think it is that we're dealing with?" Kimberly asked.

"I'm working on it," I said. "You'll know when I know. I can only use Cinema Seer once or twice if I want it to work well. I don't want to waste it before I know anything for sure."

That wasn't what they wanted to hear.

"Well get on it," Anna said. "Every time I turn a corner here, I feel like I'm in danger."

I felt similarly.

The problem with this story wasn't that I didn't have any idea. It was that I had too many ideas. Ghosts, demons, psychic phenomena—they were all in play still. Not to mention, KRSL could be behind it. Evil corporations have been villainous in many horror movies. Who's to say they weren't the main culprit here? We just didn't know enough.

We finished our food and separated. I had to get to work, as did Antoine, who had the night shift tonight as well. Kimberly, Camden, and Anna had to get to bed.

The events of the previous night repeated again. The same employee who complained about not having enough time to finish her duties had the exact same complaint again. However, she gave up sooner and with slightly more concealed disdain for her supervisor.

All of the day shift employees were off the floor by seven thirty. At eight o'clock my shift began. I went through all the normal checks for audio and video. Everything was working.

Then my watch began.

The first four hours were not exactly riveting. I watched as all the patients settled down to sleep. That night, they all slept soundly. I wondered if they would still complain about insomnia in the morning.

At midnight, Antoine began his first walk around the floor. This place was seriously big. I knew that just from looking at the number of monitors it took to see the entire floor, but I didn't really understand how large it was until Antoine started walking around it. It took him an hour to do a single lap.

Every time he would come to a door, he would buzz me on the intercom and ask for me to open it. I would oblige. Eventually, I just started unlocking the doors as he walked toward them.

When he was about three-quarters of the way done with his tour, he started to slow down. He was walking strangely; he almost looked . . . afraid. I looked around the screen to see if there was something that he was seeing, but there was nothing in the direction that he was looking.

He walked up to a white intercom box and pressed the button.

"Can you talk to me?" he asked. His voice sounded like he was breathing hard. At first, I wondered if the distortion that I had seen the night before had somehow snuck up on him and was having some physiological effect on his body.

But then I realized.

He was just having a hard time walking around alone. The Straggler forest was still taking its toll.

"Yeah, sure," I said. We were risking breaking character if the camera was on, but if he needed someone to talk to, I had no choice but to help him.

"What's the temperature like out there?" I asked.

"It's fine," he answered.

"They have me freezing in here," I said. "I have to wrap myself in a blanket just to sit here."

He didn't respond.

"So, you're coming up on a junction," I said. "If you go left, you'll eventually circle back to the mess hall area. If you go right, you'll find a bunch of conference rooms and eventually get to the patient wing."

Antoine had a map that he carried with him. He checked it and said, "I have to check the patient area."

I flipped the switch that would open up the door on the right. "Go right ahead. The path is clear for a while, but you need to take the next left turn."

Antoine nodded.

He walked along the path. I followed him on the monitors, flipping on the audio switch for each sector as he passed. I continued talking to him. I didn't really have anything to say, but I didn't think it mattered. I thought he just wanted to hear someone's voice, even mine.

As he walked toward the patient wing, it reappeared.

Right in front of one of the patient common areas, the camera distorted.

This was really bad timing. Antoine would be in that area soon. For a moment I considered sending him in that direction just so that he could get a quick glimpse of whatever it was that was causing the camera to malfunction, but of course, that would have been a terrible decision given his current state.

"Antoine," I said, "go ahead and take the next right. I'm opening the door for you."

Antoine stopped and checked his map. "I'm supposed to be going straight here."

I didn't know if he was on-screen. Just in case, I needed to play it in character.

"Go ahead and take the next right. We're having a camera malfunction. I was hoping you could come take a look."

On-screen.

Antoine did as I asked. He turned right and I quickly locked the door behind him.

"Is the camera malfunction still happening?" Antoine asked nervously.

"Just keep going straight," I said.

Elsewhere, the distortion could be seen wandering from monitor to monitor. There was still no sign of what was causing the distortion on the camera. It wasn't exactly following Antoine yet, but it was walking parallel to him.

As he walked, the distortion would move to the nearest door that would connect it to him, but it couldn't go through it. Soon, though, there would be a junction that Antoine would have to cross that the distortion could get to.

"Take a left here," I said to Antoine.

The distortion changed monitors in a way that tracked Antoine's movement. If that thing learned to go through doors, Antoine was a goner.

I continue to guide Antoine one room at a time. I started to whisper into the microphone, worried that it was my very instructions that were drawing the distortion in Antoine's direction.

I had an idea.

I flipped on the audio switch for a camera that was on the opposite side of the floor. If I could lead it away from Antoine, he would be home free.

"Antoine, come over here. Can you hear me? Come over here," I said into the microphone.

The distortion didn't move, not at first.

"That's right, Antoine. Stay right here."

The distortion moved monitors. It was heading through the rooms and hallways that were accessible to it in the direction of my voice.

At first.

With a sudden turn, the distortion started moving across the monitors back in Antoine's direction. It was like it was running.

I flipped the audio back to Antoine. "Keep going straight and take the next right," I said. "Get a move on, will you? Come see me in the surveillance room."

Antoine continued to move in my direction. I opened all the doors that he needed on his path and closed them as he passed through.

The distortion got to the nearest room it could but was stopped again by a door that blockaded it from the rest of the floor. As it got there, the bars on the audio meter spiked. Once. Twice.

It was beating on the door.

Antoine was almost to my room. I quickly moved to my door and started to unlock the manual locks. I looked back over my shoulder and saw the audio meter spiking in the room with the distortion.

As soon as I had my locks undone, I ran back to the monitor and flipped on the speaker. I heard the distortion tapping on the door, slowly getting louder with each thump.

Antoine got to my door. I opened it for him and allowed him inside. I closed the door behind him and locked it.

"What's going on?" he asked.

I showed him the screen where the distortion was.

"I can't see anything. What's wrong with it?" he asked.

"I can't see anything either . . . It was just odd."

"What is that noise?" he asked.

Thump.

Thump.

He didn't know how to react at first. He was still messed up.

"You need to get this equipment checked," Antoine said nervously. "You had me thinking there was a tiger chasing me."

He was trying to stay in character as best he could. It was hard to judge how freaked out his character would be at that point. After all, Antoine knew there was something there to kill us, but his character didn't.

"Sorry," I said. "I just had this weird feeling . . . That's something you need to know about our family if you're going to be a part of it: we act on our instincts."

Antoine nodded. "Yeah, Kimberly said the same thing. Man, you got me freaked out."

He started breathing in and out deeply.

He forced a laugh. "The plumbing is knocking around, and you think I'm in danger."

We both chuckled, though we kept an eye on the monitor.

Luckily, Carousel had mercy on us, and, after a few moments, we were back off-screen.

"It's trying to get out," I said. "It was trying to get . . ." I stopped. I didn't want to freak him out.

"To me?"

I nodded.

"What kind of monster is invisible on camera and can't walk through a closed door?" Antoine asked.

"Sit down," I said. "This is going to take a while. There are so many answers to that question."

We sat and talked about possibilities as we waited for the distortion to go away.

CHAPTER THIRTY-FIVE

ALL IN THE FAMILY

As soon as my shift ended, I fell into bed. I was asleep before my head hit the pillow. I was just exhausted.

My brain hurt like I'd been doing math problems all night. By all rights I should have been up, terrified of what was to come, afraid that First Blood might happen while I was asleep. Despite this, I slept soundly for nine hours. I was too tired to worry.

I awoke to a phone ringing. Up until that point, I had hardly even noticed that there was a phone in the room. It was hanging up next to the shelving unit near the servers. I stumbled out of bed to find it and then stumbled back to bed with it in my hand.

I was on-screen.

"Hello, surveillance room 2B," I said.

"Mr. Lawrence!" the voice on the other side answered. "It's Dr. Mentes. I thought I would call you to find out how you were handling your first shift with KRSL."

I rubbed a hand through my hair and tried to wake my brain up. "Everything is going smoothly," I said.

"Wonderful. I trust you haven't had any incidents beyond—let me see here . . ." I heard him shuffling through some papers. "Some minor camera malfunctions?"

"Nothing to report."

"I am glad to hear it. Remember, if there are any problems with the patients in the night, contact your coworkers for assistance. That's why they're there. The patients' liaison, your sister, is she managing well?"

"Yes. No complaints as far as I know."

I was cold. With the security door closed this place became an icebox. I searched around for my blanket but realized it had fallen on the floor. I leaned over the side of the bed and fished it out. I wrapped it around my body, finally warming up again.

"How is your office? We keep it pretty cold in there, don't we?" Dr. Mentes asked. "We believe it is best. Cold keeps the surveillance specialist awake."

That comment caught me by surprise. Had he just seen me wrap myself in a blanket? Or was it a coincidence? My eyes darted up to the ceiling. There were no visible cameras.

"It's fine," I said.

"Wonderful. Remember, if there is anything wrong at all, be sure to document it in your logbook."

"I will."

"Delightful. Do not hesitate to contact me with any questions."

"Okay," I said.

I hung up the phone.

Off Screen.

I managed to make it to the mess hall to catch Anna and Camden there. I grabbed some food and joined them.

As I placed my food on the table and started to sit down, we went on-screen again. That was inconvenient. I couldn't say much if I had to stay in character.

"This place gives me the creeps at night," I said.

"Can't be too bad," Camden said. "You look like you've been sleeping. I've been up all night worried that my buzzer would go off and I would have to go remotely monitor brain waves."

I was lucky that my bed was in my office.

"It's hard staying awake all night. My rhythm is all off."

"It should be easy for you; it's just like when we were kids," Anna said. "You spent all night watching TV back then too."

I forced a chuckle.

Anna had been my neighbor growing up. What she said about me spending all night watching movies on TV was true. It was likely the thing I got in trouble for the most back then.

"Except now I'm getting paid," I said.

We exchanged idle banter for a bit longer. I focused on eating.

"So, the medical folks have been turning our patients into zombies lately. They can hardly stay awake long enough to complain," Anna said. She looked at Camden. "You know anything about that?"

"They don't tell me anything," he said. "I'm just as qualified as they are and yet they have me doing busy work. It gets frustrating."

We continued our general job complaints for a few minutes after that.

An NPC entered the mess hall. It was the supervisor I had seen arguing with Barb, the custodian who had complained about not having enough time to finish her responsibilities.

"Barb," the supervisor called out. The custodian herself was in the mess hall cleaning a table. "Barb, you better be at that staff meeting. All hands on deck. Eight o'clock. Remember."

"I told you I would," Barb said as she finished wiping off the table. She didn't look too happy about it.

Her supervisor considered saying more, but she looked at the clock on the wall and shook her head as she turned to leave the mess hall.

Finally, we went off-screen.

"Okay," Anna said, "this plot is strange. We constantly go off-screen for conversations that I think are important. I was talking to some patients about the reasons they got thrown in here. Really interesting stuff. A lot of strange accidents. Most of the patients have a long string of strange incidents going back to their birth. Only ten percent of those conversations might have actually been on-screen. If that."

I thought about that for a bit. So, the details of the patients' pasts were being kept sparse.

"Maybe Carousel doesn't want to spoil the reveal to the audience," I said.

Anna shrugged her shoulders.

I took some time to tell them about the previous night's events and my suspicion that my room was under surveillance.

"He said it right after you covered yourself up?" Camden asked. "And this event happened on-screen?"

"The whole thing."

"So, is there a monster or is the company itself the bad guy? They could be messing with the cameras," Anna suggested.

That was one of my theories as well. It would kind of fit. Looking at the enemy tropes, A Knock at the Door could fit evil scientists. They had access to every room, after all, and they could clearly see into every room with the cameras and "target" whoever was there.

"We'll find out soon enough," I said. "First Blood has to be soon. It can't keep dragging out."

"We need to be on the lookout," Anna agreed. "It's going to be tonight for sure."

I then took a moment to consider my words carefully.

"There's something I need to say," I said. "I don't think Antoine is at a hundred percent. He seemed pretty shaken up last night."

Anna and Camden looked at each other.

"He should be better now," Anna said. "He asked Kimberly to help activate his nightmare trope a few hours ago . . . It should help."

That would help, but it wasn't a permanent solution at our low level.

"Okay. Then . . . maybe don't mention I said anything. Not in the storyline at least."

They agreed.

A few minutes later, Kimberly and Antoine came into the mess hall in a hurry.

"Come on," Antoine said. "We found something."

They looked excited.

They led us back through the maze of hallways and intersections toward the part of the floor that was far away from the patient sector and the entrance.

As they led us down a hallway, I immediately noticed that something was wrong.

"I don't recognize this place from the security monitors," I said. I knew that there were some blind spots that weren't picked up, but the idea that there was an entire hallway filled with rooms that I couldn't see was very concerning.

"Hurry," Antoine said. "We wanted to do some last-minute exploration before First Blood. Look what we found. We looked through it, but I think you all need to see it."

I wondered if it was difficult to activate Kimberley's Get a Room trope when your character already has a room in that very building.

He showed us to an office. Most of the things in the room had been cleared out except for a few odds and ends and a box of papers that sat on the desk at the back of the room.

"This looks like my office," Camden said. "It's got the same layout and everything."

He rushed to the box of papers. After staring at meaningless brain scans for days he was probably happy to find actual documents that he could search for clues.

On-screen.

Camden searched through the papers and pulled out a few that his Eureka! ability must have told him were important.

"Check this out," he said. He held out what looked like a family tree chart, but it was slightly different. All of the individuals on the tree were represented with different colored circles and squares. "It's a pedigree diagram."

"What's that for?" Kimberly asked.

Camden looked over the chart for a little bit and then answered, "It's for tracking a genetic trait over generations."

I looked over his shoulder to take a glance at the chart. At the top was a woman whose name was Eloise Mercer. She died in 1903. Every other person on the chart was either descended from her or had married into the family.

"All of our patients are on here," Camden said. "It has both their ID numbers and their real names."

I only knew one of their real names. The little girl. Her name was Bethany. Or Bethany Mercer, apparently.

"They're all related?" Anna asked. "But they don't seem to know each other except for the father and his two kids."

"They're distant relations. Cousins. Second cousins. Different last names but the Mercer bloodline," Camden said, "spread out over five generations. Every other blood relation on this pedigree chart is labeled as being deceased."

No wonder the patients had such limited contact with each other. Eventually, they would get to talking and figure out what they all had in common.

"You said that pedigree charts were for tracking genetic traits," I said. "What genetic trait?"

KRSL tracked down every living member of that family. But why?

Camden shuffled through the papers. He shook his head. "I don't know."

I backed away so that he could keep looking through what remained in the box.

"Whose office was this?" Anna asked.

"Doctor Thornton Thomas," Kimberly said. She pointed to something mounted to the wall.

It was a glass case. At the bottom it had an inscription: "A heartfelt token of gratitude to Dr. Thornton Thomas, whose guidance and expertise touched our lives forever."

Inside the glass case was a signed wooden baseball bat. Antoine's baseball bat.

I couldn't say anything because we were still on-screen, but it was interesting how Carousel had managed to work Antoine's baseball bat into the story. We would probably need it later. The security guards on this floor had batons and pepper spray. This was quite the upgrade.

"You guys," Camden said. "You know how we have a father and two kids as patients out there, right? Well, guess who the mother is."

He waited for a beat.

"Dina Mercer, née Cano. Remember the woman we met on our first day who didn't make it to orientation?"

"Dina?" Anna asked. "I remember her. Her family is in here . . ."

She threw a glance at me. Dina was related to the Mercer line by marriage. She was obviously here to get her kids back. We had thrown around theories about what had happened to Dina. One of those theories was that there was a hard limit to how many players could join this storyline and she had been the odd one out. Apparently, that wasn't the case.

She had to be in the building. All of the filming locations were in the building. We searched the remainder of the office for more clues. We didn't find much.

"You know, this guy only left three weeks ago," Camden said.

"If you ask the patients, it sounds like there's a high turnover rate for employees," Anna said. I had observed the same thing.

"If he quit, why wouldn't he take his bat?" Kimberly asked.

We looked back at the signed souvenir. Was the bat there just as a way to get Antoine's weapon of choice into the storyline? Or was the presence of a sentimental object left inside of his office supposed to be evidence that Dr. Thomas might not have left of his own free will?

Off Screen.

We left the room. We checked every other door in the hallway. They were all locked.

"Be ready for a fight tonight," Anna said. She sounded more nervous than usual. "Something is about to happen."

We all agreed. The needle was slowly moving forward. We didn't have that much longer until First Blood. It looked like I wouldn't be the only person who would be awake all night.

It was nearly eight o'clock. I was back in my office getting ready for the night; my shift would start soon. As I prepared, I ran through the pre-shift checks for audio and video. It was then that I noticed the custodian.

It was Barb, the same woman who had complained about having too much work to get done in her shift both previous nights. She had disobeyed her supervisor and had stayed behind for an extra fifteen minutes. She was emptying trash cans and wiping down surfaces.

She was at the back of the floor, far from the elevator and the patient sector. She kept looking up at the clock on the wall, apparently considering whether or not she could sneak in a few extra minutes to get her day's work done before the doors closed and locked.

I continued doing my checks and then ran to the mess hall to purchase a snack for the night. The needle on the Plot Cycle was close to First Blood. It was going to be an eventful night.

As I went back to my station, I passed by the custodian on her way out. I closed and locked the door to my room and sat back down in front of the monitors.

Whoever was in charge of the medicine for the patients really must have upped their dose of sleep medication because several of them were already in bed. I looked over to the camera that showed the elevator. The custodian was waiting there, tapping her foot. She was cutting it close.

And then I saw it: the distortion.

It was out early that night. It jumped from monitor to monitor faster than I had ever seen it. It was headed straight for the custodian. There were no doors between it and her that I could close remotely.

I fumbled my fingers to the monitor and clicked on the audio.

"Ma'am, can you hear me?" I said loudly.

She looked up at the camera and nodded her head. She didn't appear pleased to hear my voice.

"You have to run right now," I said with as much urgency as possible.

The NPC turned to the camera and said, "I was just finishing up my shift. It's just an extra twenty minutes. I'm leaving, see?"

"Look to your left!" I screamed into the microphone.

She stared up at the camera in confusion and then slowly looked down the hallway to her left.

"Why?" she asked. She didn't appear to be frightened or startled in any way, despite the fact that the distortion was at the end of that hallway. Whatever it was, it wasn't just invisible on camera. She didn't seem to be able to see anything either.

The elevator dinged. The custodian looked at the elevator and then back at the camera.

"I'm leaving, see?" she repeated.

She walked over to the elevator and stepped inside.

The distortion started to move even faster from one monitor to the next. Before the elevator doors closed, it had made it onto the same monitor as the elevator and the woman.

The woman still didn't notice.

The elevator doors closed. The distortion disappeared.

I didn't see it again the rest of the night. A few minutes after the elevator left, the needle on the Plot Cycle hit First Blood.

It didn't move forward to Rebirth like it usually would—not at first.

It stayed there, fixed on First Blood, for thirty-five minutes.

CHAPTER THIRTY-SIX

PLEASE PRESENT YOUR IDENTIFICATION

Ten minutes after First Blood ended, Anna slowly tiptoed out of her living space and into view of the cameras. While her bedroom was not in view of the cameras, the communal space and door that separated her from the maze of hallways were visible. I was keeping watch over all of the monitors with heightened interest, looking for any evidence of what might have happened or what might happen next.

Anna approached the little white box near the door and pressed the button. A little light blinked on the monitor. I turned on the audio.

"Any trouble there, sis?" I asked in my most casual voice.

"Is everything okay?" Anna asked. "Just got a weird feeling. Thought I heard a noise."

I couldn't tell if she was on-screen or not.

"Everything looks okay from up here," I said. "I'll ask around."

"I'll ask Kimberly if she heard anything," Anna said.

She looked up at the camera and then crept over toward Kimberly's room. I switched off the audio in Anna and Kimberly's common area and then switched it on in the one that Antoine and Camden shared.

"Antoine, Camden, just checking in," I said over the loudspeaker.

It didn't take long for them to crawl out of their living quarters and come out to where I could see them. I doubted that they had been sleeping.

"Is everything all right?" Antoine asked.

"Looking good," I answered. "Anna said she heard something. Did you guys?"

They looked at each other and then Camden said, "Didn't hear anything here."

"Me neither," I said. "Just checking around."

"Do you need me to do a patrol?" Antoine asked. He did not seem too eager.

"No, you're good. There's none scheduled for tonight. You can go back to bed," I answered.

And so, I continued my watch, waiting for some evidence of what First Blood might have been or some clue for our characters as to what had just transpired. I had no idea if anything we had just discussed had been on-screen. For me it wasn't. I sat in front of the monitors, waiting and watching for the rest of the night.

I never saw anything move.

There were no distortions.

The longer I saw nothing, the more nervous I became.

As the minutes ticked by, I eagerly watched for the elevator to open. When it did, it would bring a flood of NPCs and, with them, information about what had happened at First Blood. After all, the defining trait of First Blood was how the characters reacted to it.

It was difficult to react when you had no idea what had happened.

7:58 . . .

7:59 . . .

8:00 . . .

And . . . nothing.

The elevator never dinged.

No one walked through the door. There should have been nurses bringing food and medicine. There should have been scientists ready to work with Camden to study the Mercer family.

There wasn't. The elevator never even opened.

I clicked on the audio for Kimberly and Anna's common room.

"Was there something special going on this morning?" I asked.

A few moments later, Anna walked out into the common area. "No," she said. "Not that I remember." She started to walk back to her room but then paused. "Why do you ask?"

"It's time for the day to start and no one has come down," I answered.

"Hmm. Wonder why," Anna said.

"I'll ask around."

I repeated the conversation with Camden moments later. Obviously, I knew that something was wrong, but I was playing it like I had no idea.

"Who didn't show up?" Camden asked.

"No one has come down," I answered.

"That's strange. My supervisor was going to work with me on a special project of some kind this morning."

"I'll call upstairs and see what the holdup is," I said.

I walked across my room to the phone on the wall. I brought the receiver up to my ear and pressed the button that was supposed to send me to the switchboard, where a chipper operator would direct my call to whomever I desired.

Except it didn't.

No one answered.

I thought about what was going on for a moment.

Once again flipping on the audio for Anna's room, I said, "Didn't they have some sort of meeting last night?"

A few moments later, Anna said, "Yes. Company-wide. Except for those on duty."

That was what I thought. The meeting was where the custodian from the night before was supposed to be going when the distortion joined her on the elevator.

"I'm going out to check on things," I said.

"Wait up," Anna said. "I'll get the others. It'll be a minute."

I looked over at the monitors. The Mercers were beginning to wake up.

What were we going to do?

Ten minutes later, Anna, Kimberly, Camden, Antoine, and I were standing next to the elevator. Still, not a single person had come downstairs.

On-screen.

"What's the holdup?" Antoine asked. "I have a debrief with the head of security in half an hour."

"Your guess is as good as mine," I said.

"Can we go up and check on things?" Kimberly asked.

Camden grabbed his badge from his shirt and walked toward the elevator. "I don't even know if we have access."

He held his badge against the small electronic box next to the elevator. Where normally it should flash green, it flashed yellow.

"I guess we don't," Anna said.

"No," I said. "Red is no access. Yellow is an error."

I had managed to learn that in my attempts to travel around the floor on my first day.

"Error?" Camden asked. "What error?"

"Like when a door can't be opened electronically because the manual lock is engaged," I said.

"It's not like someone could manually lock an elevator," Kimberly said. "Right?"

I shrugged my shoulders and pressed my own badge against the device. Yellow again.

"It could just be an old-fashioned error," I said. "Broken elevator."

Antoine tried his badge next. "So, how do we get up now?" he asked. "Is there a stairway in case of a fire?"

I shook my head. "We have a state-of-the-art fire suppression system. I don't know of any stairways. They may not be marked in case one of the . . . *patients* . . . escapes."

Anna turned to the camera on the ceiling. She looked back at us. "You think they're watching?"

"If they are, why haven't they said anything?" Antoine asked.

"I imagine at this point we're the only ones left alive," I said sarcastically. It was time to play the part of the Film Buff.

"Don't say that," Anna said. "You're not helping."

"I was just kidding. But I have seen this movie before," I said. "Now all that's left is for us to get picked off one by one."

"As long as you go first," Kimberly said.

"I just might," I said. "You'll probably make it to the big climax. Being pregnant and all."

"I don't want to talk about this. We are not in a horror movie, much to Riley's disappointment," Anna said. "We need to figure out what's going on."

We discussed what we would do for a while. It wasn't clear what our next step should be. I began worrying that perhaps we had missed something in the Party phase.

"Operating under the assumption that any emergency exits are disguised so that the patients can't escape, we should start looking around for something like that," Camden said.

Everyone agreed. As we did, we all got a temporary double-point buff to our Savvy stats. It was nice to see Camden's new Immobile Genius trope in action.

"What about the patients?" Kimberly asked.

"We can't open their rooms without a nurse badge," Anna said. "Unless Riley can open it from the control room. Or maybe Antoine?"

"I'm not allowed to have anything to do with the patients. I can't even get into their common areas unless they're already open," Antoine said.

"Same here," I said. "You need someone with authorization to open up their individual rooms. And to be honest, I'm not sure we should mess with them right now anyway. We don't have their medicine. We don't have their food."

"Well, we can't just leave them there," Kimberly said.

"Maybe we ought to," I argued back. "If you haven't noticed, they're prisoners here. There might be a reason for that."

"There are children in there!" Kimberly said, and as always, her performance was quite convincing. Of course, it was possible she actually was concerned about the NPC children.

"They're just a liability," Camden said, agreeing with me. "We haven't even been told why they're here. You aren't being logical. Besides, they're safe in their cells."

"Watch how you talk to her," Antoine said. "She's just concerned about other people's well-being. That might be a foreign concept to you."

He started staring down at Camden.

"Enough!" Anna said. "We can't even get them out of their rooms, so there's no point in arguing about it. Right now, we need to save ourselves and work together before we have any chance of helping them."

"Fair enough," Camden said. "Sorry," he said to Kimberly.

"Now, let's go find that exit," Anna said.

As we walked away, all of our Savvy stats received another small boost. Personally, I thought our performance was lackluster, but it was our first intentional on-screen quarrel. We would get better. As I saw it, it wasn't a real fight unless curse words were used. Still, it was enough to activate Anna's Let's Not Fight trope for a quick buff.

Off Screen.

With our standard buffs out of the way, we began our search for a way out.

I went to my room so that I could supervise over the loudspeaker. In the Rebirth phase, the monster could attack at any time—even to lethal effect, assuming that there wasn't something in the script preventing it from doing so. With this storyline, I had no idea.

Kimberly and Antoine more or less made a beeline to go pick up Antoine's bat. I had hoped that by pointing out the potential danger we were in it would be enough justification for him to seek out a weapon better than the baton and pepper spray he had been assigned with his uniform.

Anna and Camden stuck together and went to explore the laboratories and offices where Camden worked. I got the impression that he had seen things over there that were worth looking at now that he had a narrative justification.

I watched the Mercers as they banged on their doors and yelled for attention. I considered sending them a message to calm them down, but I thought better of it. If we decided to help them later, they would never need to know that I was ignoring them. If I spoke to them before we could help them, they might grow frustrated with us if we took too long.

I still wasn't sure how they fit into the narrative. The distortion did appear to emanate from the same part of the level that their cells were in. Whatever this thing was, it was tied to them at the very least.

I watched as Anna and Camden explored the offices that I recognized as belonging to Camden's supervisor. I watched as they walked off of one monitor and didn't reappear on any other. I quickly flipped on the audio for the last room they had been walking in.

"Whoa, you two. Where is it you just went? I don't see you."

I didn't receive an answer for a few moments.

"I think we found something," Camden said. Camden's hunch must have been right.

I quickly alerted Antoine and Kimberly. They came by my office so that we could walk to Anna and Camden together. I didn't want to be walking around alone.

As soon as we walked into the room that Anna and Camden had been in, I saw the area that they must have walked into when they went off camera.

As I entered, I went on-screen.

"My boss was constantly coming back here and telling me that I wasn't allowed to follow him," Camden said. "I figure we should take a look at whatever it is we weren't supposed to see. He comes in here for hours at a time. I was always curious. Now I'm even more curious."

What we weren't supposed to see was . . . another office. Where the first one looked like a real place of work where someone actually spent time—with paper strewn about and signs of life—the second office looked like it was staged and sterile. It almost looked like it wasn't even used.

"You're saying he comes in here?" Antoine asked. "What for?"

It was a valid question. This room did not have the look of a secret hidden location. It was strange that it wasn't on camera. It was stranger still that Camden's boss would need to come in here when there was no evidence that the room had been used. There wasn't even a computer at the desk.

"Can't you hear it?" Camden asked.

We got silent and listened.

Once it got very quiet, I could hear something,

"Is that someone talking?" Kimberly asked.

"No," I said. "Not some*one*."

It was some*thing*.

I had to listen very closely to pick up what was being said.

"Please present your identification. Please present your identification. Please present your identification."

It was a computer voice. The same voice could be heard whenever you stood in a doorway for too long and the system needed you to present your credentials in order to keep the door open.

"Where is that coming from?" I asked.

After a few more moments of silence, Anna moved closer to a bookshelf against one of the walls.

"It's coming from back here," she said, putting her ear up against the wall.

"Maybe there's some type of switch that makes the shelves move out of the way," I said. It looked like we were staring at one of those Scooby-Doo bookcases that would open up if you pulled out the right book. The only problem here was that this shelving unit had no books on it. It didn't have anything on it.

Anna pulled on the bookshelf, and, with a click, it came swinging open like a normal door. No leather-bound book to pull out, no marble bust whose head opens up on a hinge to reveal a button. The secret door opened just by pulling on the shelf. Lame.

"You watch too much TV," Anna said.

As she pulled open the door, the voice got louder. "Please present your identification."

What we saw when we opened the door was a stairway that led upward as well as another that led down. Next to them was an elevator. A private elevator.

"Please present your identification," the voice rang out.

The elevator doors opened, sending us back in shock.

Lying on the floor of the elevator, covered in blood, was Camden's supervisor. I didn't know what could possibly have done it, but he was bleeding from the eyes and the mouth. His torso was mostly intact, though there was a large gash in his chest that exposed some destroyed ribs.

"Please present your identification."

The elevator doors closed.

And then opened.

And then closed.

"I hate being right," I said.

"Please present your identification."

CHAPTER THIRTY-SEVEN

NOTES FROM EXPERIMENT 17

Kimberly screamed.

"Oh my god!" Anna yelled.

I stared at the corpse, looking for some trace of what might have done it. It was the work of something very strong, that much was certain. It didn't really help narrow down my top three theories very much, though out of ghosts, demons, and psychic phenomena, the latter was still in the lead by quite a bit.

But there was more to learn.

Camden slowly walked into the elevator.

"Please present your identification," the voice repeated.

He knelt down over his former supervisor and plucked the ID badge from his chest. He backed out of the elevator and showed it to us.

"This might be able to get us into the patients' rooms," he said. "When it's time for that."

I took a closer look at the body in the elevator. The wounds were clean as if done by a blade, but I couldn't imagine how a blade large enough to do this could be snuck into the facility.

As I turned to leave the elevator, I noticed something quite concerning.

"The elevator only goes up or down one floor," I said. That was strange, even within the world of Carousel. Unless . . . there was something about this building we didn't know yet. "Wait a second. This isn't right."

I saw that the floor above us was labeled "3B." We were on 2B. That seemed backward.

In the other elevator, it looked like 2B was two floors underground, a sub-basement. But this made it look like there were any number of floors between us and the surface.

"We are a lot farther underground than they told us," I said.

The others ducked their heads into the elevator to confirm my findings.

"But why would they lie to us?" Kimberly asked.

Why indeed.

"Where do we go?" Antoine asked.

"Well," Camden said, "I have to think going up is better. We aren't safe here."

"But the thing that did this was up there, wasn't it?" Kimberly asked.

Actually, it wasn't that clear. Had the entity been in the elevator when it brought the body back down to this level?

"It doesn't matter," Camden said. "We can't stay here."

"He's right," I agreed. "Down here we're sitting ducks. At least up there we might find the way out."

And so, it was agreed.

For obvious reasons, we chose the stairs over the elevator. It might have been a mistake. It was clear that floor 3B wasn't right above 2B. There appeared to be a great deal of distance between the two floors.

"This is like a hundred feet," Antoine said. "More than that."

He was right.

After many flights of stairs, we eventually made it to an exit. The stairs stopped. They didn't continue upward at all. The exit was a simple wooden door with the label "3B."

Antoine took the lead, his baseball bat in hand. He gave his baton to Anna and his pepper spray to Kimberly, though I could hardly imagine that helping much.

Antoine tested the door. It didn't even require ID.

The door opened easily.

As it did, a woman's body slumped out to greet us.

Kimberly screamed again. I swear, I thought she might have pepper sprayed the corpse if she hadn't gotten control of herself.

"That was one of the lab techs," Camden said, staring down at the woman's body. She wore a bloodstained lab coat.

Antoine took a few breaths and stepped over the woman's body and into the well-lit room beyond it.

We followed one at a time.

The room inside was another laboratory. This one was far more sophisticated than the ones on 2B.

"Why did they have me lugging that machine around when they had that?" Camden said, looking at a giant series of monitors that showed five of the Mercers' vital statistics, all of which appeared to be updating in real time. Their hearts were racing. Alarms were going off.

His attention was soon stolen away from the monitors. The laboratory, it seemed, was an even more abundant murder scene than we knew.

There were three more bodies strewn about. All of them had been killed with large, clean gashes carved into their bodies. The room smelled of blood.

"What the hell did this?" Antoine asked.

The private elevator doors for this floor were to our left. A door led out and around. Antoine took the lead and slowly crept out of the room and into the hallway.

The longer we walked, the more bodies we found.

"They were running away from something," I said, having noticed the orientation of the bodies.

"The elevator is that way, though," Camden pointed out.

It was true. They were running away from where the main elevator was located.

"We have to risk it," Antoine said.

He moved forward.

We followed him.

As we walked, the differences between this floor and 2B became more obvious. This floor was more populated, for one. Or at least it had been. Bodies littered the ground in every direction. More than that, this floor appeared more well used. There were desks, calendars, snack tables, and all manner of office equipment on this floor that didn't appear on the one below it.

The farther we walked, the more the layout began to diverge.

"There's the elevator," Antoine said.

"Please present your identification," this elevator said. Just like the last one.

The major difference between this one and the last one was that this one had its outer doors ripped open. The elevator car was visible, though it wasn't even with the floor. It appeared as though it had begun to rise when something stopped it. The elevator car was not level either. It had been damaged.

As we walked near it, there was a loud crack and the elevator car snapped loose and fell.

There was a screeching of brakes, but the brakes failed too as the elevator car continued to fall far below 3B. Very far below. Eventually, we heard a crash hundreds of feet down.

"Guess that's what yellow means," I said.

"Look," Kimberly said. She pointed to a large door that was a bigger version of the secure door to my control room downstairs.

The door was open just a little bit. I stepped forward and slowly built up the courage to pull the door open further.

"Oh shit," I said as I pulled open the door and found a severed hand still wedged into the handle on the inside.

"They were trying to get out," Anna said.

She was right. A group had crammed themselves into this room for safety but had found none. The room was a surveillance room like mine, but it also housed a series of desks and computers. It was much larger than my room. It had far more surveillance monitors than mine did too.

I saw a familiar face on the ground. It was Mr. Rowe. He was supposed to be at home on his five days off. What was he doing at work?

"Look," Camden said. He pointed at one of the monitors. It was an image of a stairwell. It wasn't one of the ones we had been in. It showed Dina walking down to one of the lower levels.

None of us commented on it, because at that moment, we heard a cough.

I nearly jumped out of my skin.

The cough had come from the other side of the room behind a large desk. As we slowly moved over there, we saw him.

It was Dr. Truman Mentes.

He was in terrible shape. He made eye contact with me as soon as he saw me. He couldn't speak—his throat had been slashed superficially and his stomach had been gouged open.

"How do we call for help?" I asked.

If he heard me, he didn't show it. Instead, he pointed up toward his computer terminal. I made eye contact with him for a few moments more. Was I supposed to try to help him? To patch his wounds? No. Moments after pointing at the terminal, a gargling sound came from his throat. Soon he stopped moving.

He was dead.

I looked at the terminal. It was a simple computer that apparently ran on a strange, older OS. On the screen was a list of log entries.

"What's that?" Anna asked.

"Audio logs," I said.

I took the mouse and clicked on the first one, then the second, and so on. The logs told us almost everything we wanted to know and more. As the logs played, the camera went on- and off-screen, capturing snippets of the audio before leaving. I could only imagine that there was a flashback or similar. I couldn't know for sure.

"Logs of Dr. Truman Mentes, Project Distortion, Experiment Seventeen. Audio Journal 17.1. Date: June 7, 2006.

"The Mercer-Psychokinetic Entity or, informally, the distortion, so named for its unassuming appearance on recorded video, remains a subject of much intrigue. I seek to prove my hypothesis that the entity is self-determining rather than an extension of the Mercers themselves, or an embodiment of pure id as previously believed. Observations continue to reveal the intriguing nuances of the distortion's manifestation.

"A crucial requirement we've noted is its dependency on an external host, distinct from the Mercer family, to anchor itself, thereby gaining its potent and often destructive properties. It appears that the act of tethering to a host is destructive in nature and the distortion is either unwilling or unable to tether to the Mercers themselves. This could also be the work of some passive immunity bestowed by the Mercers' unconscious gift. Perhaps this could explain why the Mercers are largely unaware of their connection to the entity. Further research is required.

"We've noted some considerable variation in how the distortion manifests depending on the type of individual it tethers to. Without a tether, the distortion is a harmless oddity. It is capable of manipulating the physical world, though it tires when it does so. It seems unable to pass through solid objects, except when in the act of tethering itself. Mostly, the distortion knocks on walls and moves small objects in an unaggressive state. Of course, it has not been so passive of late.

"When the distortion finds an anchor in an average person, it manifests as a formless psychokinetic force. Its actions appear aimless, seemingly guided by nothing more than a sense of capricious chaos and destructive urges. This version has little military use.

"When tethered to an individual of high intellect, the distortion's form remains elusive. Yet its behavior changes dramatically. It evolves from a state of aimless destruction to a more focused and malevolent entity, displaying a disconcerting degree of cunning and purpose in its actions. Granted, we may never know how the entity behaves outside of captivity.

"The most profound transformation occurs when the distortion attaches itself to an individual who possesses latent psychic abilities. Under these circumstances, it is the current hypothesis that the distortion may take on a visible, tangible form—at least to the individual it's tethered to. Despite considerable advancement of modern technology, our cameras are still unable to capture this form.

"Given these observations, the presence of Molly Lawrence's descendants could be crucial in our quest to fully understand the distortion. Genetic analysis does not show any common ancestors between the two clans, an obstacle that had made past experiments less useful. It remains to be seen whether their abilities will allow the distortion to become a more stable, predictable entity, or perhaps even assume a true physical form, thus shedding further light on its relationship with the Mercer family. This is the stated goal of Experiment Seventeen."

"Audio Journal 17.2. Date: June 7, 2006.

"We have successfully sedated the Mercers during waking hours. This should prevent previous incidents from reoccurring. This medical strategy is designed to curb their natural psychic manifestations and enable the entity to become more active during the night when Subject One is awake for his assigned surveillance duty.

"Subject One, a descendant of Molly Lawrence, presents a remarkable potential for psychic ability, according to brain scans, though he appears unaware of this power. Positioned in the surveillance room at the center of floor 2B, we anticipate that his abilities will trigger some level of activity with the distortion during nighttime.

"Subject Two, also a descendant of Molly Lawrence, does not demonstrate the same degree of psychic potential on her brain scans. Despite this, she shares the genetic trait that could still allow for a connection with the distortion. Her role as subject manager puts her in direct interaction with the Mercers, which we hope will facilitate a link with the entity.

"Subject Three, another Molly Lawrence descendant, appears to be a powerful empath, even though she seems unaware of her ability's origin. Her performance in preliminary exams was impressively close to Subject One's results. With her empathic abilities in mind, we've assigned her as a therapist in direct contact with the Mercers. An unexpected factor to consider in our observations is her pregnancy, which she is currently unaware of. It is not known what variables this condition may introduce.

"Subject Four does not exhibit psychic abilities, but his high intelligence could potentially attract the distortion.

"Similarly, Subject Five, though lacking psychic ability, may nevertheless influence the entity through his connection to Subject Three and her empathic abilities. He will have occasional night-shift duties.

"We have managed to track down the final Mercer and add him to our collection. He has been shown through brain scans to be a potent conduit for the distortion. His presence within the group is likely to significantly impact the behavior of the entity.

"All subjects are now under continuous surveillance, with data collection proceeding as expected. This configuration's inaugural night has us optimistic about the prospect of meaningful interaction with the distortion."

"Audio Journal 17.3. Date: June 7, 2006.

"In order to manage the potential risks posed by the distortion, we've implemented a series of precautions. Paramount among these is the design of our research facility, a labyrinthine structure brimming with locked doors and complex passageways. Though the distortion can form a psychic tether with an individual in its proximity despite the existence of physical barriers, it seems unable to transcend solid material unless it is tethering to a host on the other side.

"In several instances, we've witnessed the distortion strain itself to the brink of dissipation in its attempts to bypass solid obstructions. These observations have led us to the conclusion that while the distortion may exhibit signs of self-determination, its ability to interact with the physical world is bound by conventional physical laws, provided it is not connecting to a new host.

"The medicinal regimen we administer to the Mercers is designed not only to suppress their psychic manifestations during the day but also to weaken them during the night. This serves a dual purpose of controlling the distortion's manifestation and preserving the mental and physical well-being of the Mercers.

"Interestingly, we have observed that disorienting the Mercers appears to depower the distortion. This lends credence to our working hypothesis that the distortion, while potentially self-determining, only possesses the knowledge and understanding of the Mercers themselves.

"These discoveries necessitate further investigation and underline the importance of the safety measures we've put in place. As we progress with our study of this enigmatic entity, we must remain vigilant.

"Bethany and Logan Mercer's mother attempted to sneak into the facility again under her maiden name. She appears to have communicated with the test subjects. I can only hope she did not tell them anything that would jeopardize this experiment. We have locked her in a cell on floor 3B. I am not sure what we should do with her. It would be interesting to see how the distortion interacts with the mother of two Mercers, even if she has no Mercer blood herself. I will need to wait for approval from HQ before conducting such experiments."

"Audio Journal 17.4. Date: June 8, 2006—Morning.

"This is Dr. Truman Mentes. Observations from the morning of the eighth: It appears Subject One is showing signs of deep contemplation following his first night in the surveillance room. He hasn't voiced any specific concerns, but his behavior . . . it indicates suspicion. Subject Two remains surprisingly unaffected, professionally carrying out her duties and interacting with the Mercers without any apparent sense of what's transpiring around her."

"Audio Journal 17.5. Date: June 8, 2006—Afternoon.

"Afternoon observations from the eighth: Subject Three's first meeting with Bethany Mercer happened just yesterday. There are already signs of a deepening rapport between them. We'll need to watch this closely. Subject Four has become a thorn in our side, asking probing questions about the Mercers and the tests we are running on them. We underestimated his motivation. We're navigating a delicate balance between transparency and operational security."

"Audio Journal 17.6. Date: June 9, 2006—Morning.

"Morning observations, June ninth: Subject One's second night in the surveillance room seems to have escalated his suspicions. He's quiet, but his behavior, particularly his constant reviewing of last night's footage, suggests an understanding is dawning on him. He may very well be the first subject to witness a fully corporeal manifestation of the distortion. I have waited my entire career for such an event.

"Subject Two remains engrossed in her duties, seemingly oblivious to the growing tension. Her supervisors believe this is a ruse. I am not sure. I will watch her closely. Subject Three has continued developing her relationships with each of the Mercers. Subject Five appears troubled. Perhaps he is plagued by past trauma. This could be a problem for the experiment. I will continue to monitor the situation."

"Audio Journal 17.7. Date: June 9, 2006—Afternoon.

"Subject Three's connection with Bethany Mercer is intensifying faster than expected. After only a few meetings, the strength of this bond . . . it could introduce new variables to our experiment. Meanwhile, Subject Five, our security guard, seems increasingly tense. His vigilance will be paramount going forward. His presence was designed to help keep the other subjects calm. I worry he may be doing the opposite."

"Audio Journal 17.8. Date: June 9, 2006—Evening.

"Subject One is growing more unsettled. He's yet to voice any concerns, but there's a heightened awareness in him. I believe he's become fully aware of the distortion. Reviewing last night's footage, it appears he guided Subject Five away from the distortion. Perhaps he is paranoid. He attempted to play his concerns off. Interesting. Subject Four's frustration has abated, fortunately. I instructed his supervisor to give him more difficult assignments in the laboratory. His distractions have allowed us to maintain the necessary secrecy around our operations. Had the circumstances been different, I might have considered hiring him into KRSL."

"Audio Journal 17.9. Date: June 9, 2006—Evening.

"There's been a breach. The distortion . . . it . . . it has tethered to an employee who stayed too long on 2B. Her access to the elevator should have been denied. Alas, she brought it to us!

"It's moving! Ascended to a floor with . . . with the rest of our staff. The chaos . . . it's indescribable. It is a . . . a whirlwind of horror.

"The entity is killing everyone! The destruction is . . . unimaginable. There's . . . there's so much blood . . . We . . . we sought a psychic weapon of untold destruction. We have succeeded.

"We underestimated it . . . We underestimated its need . . . its anger. Our fail-safes have not been successful. Its weakness to sonic frequencies . . . Was it all a ruse? We thought we could control it, study it . . . Oh god . . . What have we d—"

Subject One.

I was Subject One. We weren't employees. We were the guinea pigs. So much made sense now. My paranoia had been vindicated.

We were rats in a maze.

CHAPTER THIRTY-EIGHT

TOO MANY UNKNOWNS

When I got to the end of the recordings, I started them back over again on a hunch. As I had hoped, we immediately went off-screen when the second play-through began. The audience wouldn't need to hear it again, and we had been on-screen for some time. I needed to process everything we had just learned.

"How are we supposed to escape something like that?" Anna asked.

I had similar questions. The entity latched onto your mind. How were you supposed to outrun something like that?

Worse, could you be oblivious to it?

"We need to watch the tape," I said.

"Tape?" Anna asked.

I pointed to the screens. Many of the monitors for this level depicted the dead. We needed to watch it—to see how they died. We had to learn from them.

I crossed the room over to the control panel for the system. This one was so sophisticated it made mine downstairs look like the security system for a pizza parlor. I had access to everything all over the facility from here.

Even as I first acquainted myself with the new controls, I realized that my time downstairs had prepared me to take point from this new location. I would have to guide my friends out. That was my job here.

On-screen.

"The attack should have happened at around eight o'clock," I said. "That's when the distortion appeared to get on the elevator. If the malfunction I was seeing was actually this manifestation, at least."

I rolled back through the footage to the right timestamp and pressed play.

The footage started with a meeting of sorts being conducted in the middle of the floor. The custodian had not yet arrived with the distortion in the elevator.

Dr. Mentes stood in front of all of them and was speaking. "Experiment Seventeen is running swimmingly. The subjects are none the wiser, and I feel we are set to learn a lot about the distortion. You have all done a remarkable job, and I look forward to viewing the results. Don't forget: constant vigili—"

An alarm started to go off as the distortion emerged from the elevator. Someone must have seen it from the control room.

Barb, the custodian whom the entity had ridden up the elevator with, appeared completely unaware of what was going on, though she was rubbing her eyes with one hand as if nursing a headache.

Having been exposed, the distortion went on the offensive. The attack began as objects began flying around the room. Paper, office equipment, and the like took flight, much to the surprise of those huddled around Dr. Mentes.

"Code six!" one of the security guards called out.

At that moment, the distortion must have switched hosts because the objects silently floating in the air dropped to the ground.

For a moment, nothing happened. Many employees fled. For others, escape was not feasible. They stood their ground with their heads on a swivel looking for movement.

Suddenly, a woman began screaming as she was launched into the air along with a trail of blood.

Everyone started running. Some jammed into the elevator along with a startled Barb. The doors wouldn't close, as there were too many people trying to shove their way inside.

A large group, including Dr. Mentes, made for the control room. Armed personnel closed the door behind them. Those locked outside were soon thrown away from the door.

The distortion moved from monitor to monitor as it chased its quarry. At times, it would reach a dead end and need to double back.

It approached a group holed up in a storeroom. After banging on the door for a few moments, unable to force it open, the distortion "blinked" on the monitor for an instant. Suddenly, it was inside the storeroom.

"It switched hosts," Camden said.

The storeroom was soon massacred.

"There are too many of them," Camden said.

"I only see one," Kimberly said.

"Too many *people*," I said.

"Right," Camden said. "It needs hosts in order to move. There are people all over."

I watched as the manifestation jumped from person to person. When it touched most people, objects in the room would start to fly around. When it tethered to a scientist or other intelligent person, everyone around them would start getting thrown around the room and cut to pieces. Red lines would open up on them as the invisible creature rampaged.

"It isn't killing them right away," Antoine said. "But why?"

He was right. Their wounds were technically fatal. Their legs were breaking, their skin was getting sliced open, and their intestines were exposed, but as time went on a pattern emerged: most people survived their initial attack for some time afterward. They were left to bleed out.

"It's intelligent," Camden said. "It's leaving them alive long enough to be able to tether to them later on."

People lay about in agony, but as the distortion moved from screen to screen, there were always those left breathing, struggling to escape the inevitable. It needed living people to tether to. That was how it managed to move around the entire floor despite being dependent on a host; it left people strewn about to extend its reach.

I flipped the audio off. The sound was terrifying.

As the carnage began winding down, the distortion jumped rapidly around the perimeter of the level, looking for a host to ride out of the building, but none of its victims had made it that far. At first, I thought it had been too greedy, too wrathful—that it had maimed its hosts too soon.

I was wrong.

The victims that fled found themselves unable to access the exits. Even as they banged on doors in order to escape death, they were trapped.

"The doors are locked," Camden said.

I rewound the tape and turned on the audio for the control room we were standing in. After some searching, I found the order.

"Do I initiate lockdown?" Mr. Rowe asked, sitting in front of the control panel.

"Lock it down now!" Dr. Mentes yelled.

The other employees in the control room watched on with resignation as they realized that they would soon die.

"I don't understand," Mr. Rowe said, surprisingly calm moments from his death. "I thought the drugs prevented this. It's never been like . . . this."

"Any number of factors could explain it. I suppose we cannot rule out simple deception," Dr. Mentes said. He was in shock. His answer was almost rote, his logical mind on autopilot. "Perhaps it was biding its time . . . I suppose in the next experiment, we ought to . . ."

You could almost see him realize that there would be no next experiment.

"At least they did the decent thing," Camden said.

"They trapped us down here with it," Kimberly said with a furious glare. "They brought us here so that it could kill us!"

"I'm just saying," Camden replied, "if this thing got out, it could kill a hundred people before it got stuck somewhere without a tether."

Dr. Mentes began recording his message as the distortion decided to enter the room and make quick work of all of them.

As we watched, the distortion jumped from person to person, frantically trying to extend its reach, to move farther.

It tried getting in the elevator with those employees who had attempted to escape, but the elevator was stuck from the lockdown. The elevator was rocked so hard in the attack, a buzzer started going off.

In a last-ditch effort, it tethered to Camden's boss as he entered the private elevator we had just ridden in. It moved downward and, as soon as life left the man's eyes, the distortion vanished for good.

We stood there for a moment just processing the weight of what we had just seen.

"Look," Anna said. She pointed to a monitor far from the others. In it, Dina crouched in a corner, her right wrist handcuffed to a large metal table that she had dragged and tipped over as cover.

"She was far enough away from the others that it couldn't get to her," Camden said.

I fast-forwarded the tape. Eventually, Dina got brave and left the room, table and all. She had to kick the door down, which took her some time. Luckily for her, it wasn't one of the heavy-duty doors like in the important rooms. Then she had to get the table through the doorway and drag it down the hall until she found a dying security guard from whom she could retrieve a handcuff key.

She entered the control room and took Dr. Mentes's badge, but not before listening to the very same recording we had.

At that moment, she was searching floor 2B down below us. If we had waited there, she would have found us.

"We should split up," Kimberly said. "If we're together, we die together."

"True, but splitting up is the one thing you are never supposed to do," I said. "Haven't you ever even seen a movie?"

"Don't start that," Anna said, scolding me.

"Do you at least see that we shouldn't let the Mercers out?" Camden asked. "Now we know for sure."

"We don't know that," Kimberly said. "Leaving them there might make this thing, whatever it is, even angrier."

Truthfully, it didn't matter. If we released them, that would be a mistake. If we didn't, that would also likely be a mistake. We were still in the Rebirth phase and had plenty of movie left. We couldn't get through Second Blood and the Finale if we weren't attacked. The return of the distortion was inevitable.

"There has to be a catch," I said. "If we leave them locked up, I bet that still doesn't solve our problem."

"It seems like a pretty clear solution to me," Camden said. "The distortion has a fixed range within which it can tether. If we stay away from them, it cannot tether to us, and we can find the exit in safety."

"But it's too obvious," I said. "There's something we don't know. Look, I'm not saying we march down there and unlock them. I don't think we should. I'm just saying we shouldn't assume that we can control the situation. That's what got these people killed."

"And your evidence for that conclusion is horror movies?" Anna said.

"Sure," I said. "Also, the Mercers haven't had their medicine, in case you've forgotten—the medicine that weakens the manifestation. We can't pretend to know what that thing is capable of at full power."

"Guys," Antoine said. "Maybe we should talk about this later. Dina, or whatever that woman's name was, she's getting too close to the Mercers."

We turned to look at the monitor. The maze-like structure was hampering her, but Dina was slowly making her way around floor 2B. Without the Mercers' medicine to hinder it, the distortion could appear at any time. Soon, the manifestation would have a host if we didn't act.

I flipped on the audio for the hallway she was walking through.

"Hello," I said into the microphone. "You need to turn around. Take the next left. I will guide you up to the higher floor."

"No," Dina said. "My kids are here. My husband. I have to get to them."

Hadn't she listened to the same recording? Sure, her character might not care, but Dina herself should know the dangers involved.

"That area is dangerous," I said. "If you get near your children, you could be putting all of us in danger."

"I have to," Dina said.

"Your name is Dina, right? We met a few days ago. Please, you have to understand, I can't let you near the Mercers."

"I am a Mercer," Dina said.

Well, in this story she was. By marriage at least.

"Did you not see the carnage up here?" I asked.

"You have to trust me!" Dina screamed. "Please. They need me. I have to save them."

Did she know something we didn't? Had she overheard useful information or was it something else?

"Lock her in the hallway," Camden said. "Here." He leaned over and locked all of the doors in the hallway.

"Not going to work," I said.

Sure enough, as Dina approached the next junction, she waved Dr. Mentes's badge, and the door opened. There was no stopping her. They really needed two-factor authentication in that facility.

After a few moments, we went off-screen.

"What is she doing?" Anna asked.

"She's following her own plotline," I said. "I assume it's scripted."

"If she lets them out, aren't we pretty much dead?" Camden asked.

I couldn't answer. It was possible she was acting foolishly. Of course, it was also possible that she was doing exactly what she should have been.

"Whatever the case," Anna said, "we need to get out of this place. Maybe we can escape before she finishes with her plan."

"We need to plot a course out," Camden said.

"I'll guide you out," I said. "I've had practice with the controls, and I won't hold up in a fight. I'll guide you out, then I'll follow. Once we're clear of the building . . ."

I paused.

I didn't know what would happen.

If we escaped before Second Blood or the Finale, that meant the story would follow us out into Carousel proper. Was that a good thing or bad? Personally, I would like to put fifty miles between myself and the Mercers. I would also like a nap; I hadn't slept. I doubted I would sleep any time soon.

Either way, we needed to figure something out fast. Dina would get to the Mercers soon, and when she did, who knew what would happen?

CHAPTER THIRTY-NINE

CORPORATE RAT RACE

As the truth of our situation was revealed, a lot of things started to make sense: the ease with which we had gotten employment, the requirement for head scans, the questions about my "psychic" grandmother, the strange job descriptions and schedules. We weren't employees at all. We were test subjects. We had so readily assumed that all the weirdness was because we were in Carousel.

Figuring that out was my job, wasn't it? I knew the corporation was hiding something, but I didn't figure out what it was. I thought being spied on was just a clue that the corporation was shady. I knew that they were likely antagonists, but the twist still smacked me in the face.

I would have to do better.

Now I knew that something else was about to drop. In the hours since First Blood, the plot needle had started moving faster, rapidly increasing the pressure on the players. The revelation at Rebirth had come and gone. We were only a handful of scenes from Second Blood.

I needed to think.

Obviously, we needed to escape, but any progress we made would be illusory. It was *too early* to escape. Something else was yet to be revealed. As much as we had learned about the distortion, we still didn't know everything. We didn't even know *what* it was. Somehow, this creature would find a way to assert itself as we tried to escape. I had to be alert.

I pondered all of this as I watched the screens. Dina was almost to the Mercers. She had taken a long route on her own; I wasn't going to help guide her. Antoine, Camden, and Kimberly were currently checking an area of our floor for a hidden exit. Even with the monitors, the exits were hard to find.

On-screen.

"Are you sure there is nothing there?" Anna asked them from beside me. She had stayed behind with me for protection—my protection. Not that either of us could necessarily do anything against the distortion.

"I pulled on all of the furniture," Antoine answered. "There's nothing else to do short of breaking through the drywall."

Anna looked at me.

"Let's save that for later," I said. "The next possible room is three doors farther, room 327. If it's not there, I'm going to have to send you over to the southwest corner to try there."

I flipped the microphone off.

"As soon as we find a way out, trouble is coming our way," I said.

"You're so sure of that?" Anna asked. "You saw it in a movie?"

"I just have a feeling. And yes, anyone who has seen a movie would know there is no way we get out of this without even seeing this . . . thing . . . again."

"Did those movies tell you how to fight it if we do see it?"

I had no answer. If there was a weakness . . . surely we would have seen some hint of it. Unless we missed it. We had already spent an hour at least searching this floor for a pharmacy or wherever it was that they kept the medicine for the patients. That location had eluded us; it was probably on a different floor.

We had discovered sleeping quarters—enough to house all of the supposed day-shift employees. It was all fake. Whoever these scientists were, they lived here and worked here and apparently never left. They devoted their lives to studying the distortion. They devoted this week to studying us.

"I think our best bet is to make sure we don't have to fight it," I answered.

Carousel had given us Antoine's baseball bat, but I was confident that was just because he had brought it and not because it would be an effective weapon. Still, he held it ready to take a swing at anything he came across. I wasn't going to tell him it was useless.

I hoped it wouldn't be useless despite my better judgment.

The plan was to get Antoine, Camden, and Kimberly to the highest floor, and then Anna and I would follow them. There were a lot fewer rooms up there, so we could probably just brute force the search once we got there.

The way we saw it, there were two viable strategies. We either needed to be so spread out that it couldn't hop from one of us to the next, or we needed to be in one group that was so far away from the Mercers that it had no chance of getting to us.

Choosing to be in one big group was literally putting all of our eggs in one basket, but, in the end, we decided that spreading out would be difficult to coordinate and that if we failed, it would be able to leapfrog from one of us to the next all the same.

Antoine was our backup plan. His character wasn't highly intelligent like Camden's, nor did he have latent psychic abilities. Theoretically, on his own he would only have to contend with the weakest version of the distortion. Still, that might be deadly. He was our last resort. If everything went to hell, Antoine would lure the distortion as far away from the rest of us as possible.

"She's there," Anna said, staring at the monitors that covered the Mercers' holding area. I could only hope Dina knew what she was doing.

For whatever reason, she didn't want to tell us why she insisted on saving them. Obviously, her character had motivations, but surely she knew the risks.

Dina had arrived at her destination. She was quick to start unlocking her children and husband. She wrapped each of them in a deep embrace as they cried with joy.

"You heard us!" Bethany Mercer screamed. "I knew you heard us. I knew you would come."

Dina started to cry. It didn't look like she was acting.

"Of course I heard you, baby." She hugged her fake family even tighter.

So that was the information Dina was operating under. Her psychic kids had reached out to her. It was also possible that her Encouragement from Beyond trope was flexible enough to work with kidnapped psychic kids and not just dead kids.

I suppose that was the information that she didn't want to try to explain. When a player arrives in a storyline, NPCs will often point you in the direction you are supposed to go. Sometimes they are subtle, like when everyone was being rude to me in Delta Epsilon Delta, and sometimes they are explicit, like the woman in *The Astralist* literally telling us everything we needed to do.

In this storyline, it looked like Dina had been given her instructions in the form of her psychic kids reaching out to her telepathically or something similar. I could only hope that meant her path would somehow lead to our escape. I couldn't imagine how releasing the Mercers could ever be a good thing.

"Please don't release the rest," I said over the loudspeaker. "There is no telling what might happen. You saw what the consequences were the last time."

Dina didn't respond.

The other Mercers could see from the windows in their doors that Dina had released her family. I could hear them begging to be released. With a glance up at the camera, Dina ignored them, dragging her children and husband out of the cell area and back the way she had come.

It would take a long while for them to get to the floor we were on with the path she was taking. I would have to watch out for her.

"Room 327 is a bust," Camden said.

"All right," I said. "You need to take the corridor to your left. It circles around for a bit. Then you have to go through the employee barracks and out the other side."

"I really hope this one works," Kimberly said. "I feel like we've been walking for miles."

I kept track of the needle on the Plot Cycle. We were really burning through our time limit. The audience might not notice a difference. To them, the Party phase had been chopped up into an easily digestible sequence of events. To us, it had lasted days. Rebirth was only going to last hours at the rate things were going.

I guided Antoine, Camden, and Kimberly as they made their way to the next area that I thought might have a secret elevator or stairway leading upward.

"Why would they design it like this?" Anna asked. "Why hide all of the exits like this?"

My first instinct was to say that it was designed like this so that it would be really hard for us to escape, and they could make a tense movie out of it. But in-universe, there was another reason it was designed this way.

"For this exact scenario," I said. "I think they want it to be really hard to get out of here if you don't know the way. For Mercers, test subjects, whoever."

If that was the case, it was working.

We waited for ten more minutes, and then I saw it.

It wasn't on floor 2B. Somehow, it had appeared on the floor we were on. It had manifested directly above the Mercers' containment area. Just over one hundred feet above, in fact. That was a huge increase; its manifestation range appeared to be much greater than its tethering range.

We had planned on it entering through the stairs somehow. We never expected it to just appear on this floor. This entire facility was designed with that assumption. Without the Mercers' medication suppressing their psychic abilities, the distortion was clearly more dangerous.

It probably didn't help that the remaining Mercers were really upset right at that moment, having been left behind in their cells.

"Look alive," I said into the microphone. "The distortion is seventy feet to your left. I'm going to have to guide you around it. Pick up your pace."

Based on the video from the night before, its tethering range was a dozen or so feet. I needed to get them away from it fast. It could easily have a longer range now that the medication had started wearing off.

I needed them to listen to me very carefully. Unlike the floor below us, 3B had far fewer electronic doors. There were no test subjects or Mercers on that floor, after all. It would be much more difficult to keep the creature away from them.

"I need all of you to run down the first hallway on your right. Antoine, are you up for what we talked about?"

"Yes!" he yelled.

He was ready to make the sacrifice.

"Keep running down the hallway. All of you."

The distortion wasted no time in pursuing my friends. It was hopping from monitor to monitor. Its path was remarkably efficient, as if it somehow knew exactly where they were headed and the fastest way to cut them off.

It was going too fast.

I searched for some path to send Antoine on, to use him as a lure for the distortion so the others would be safe. Antoine was willing. He was the best suited to outrun the entity. He was also likely the one safest from its wrath, because if it tethered to him, it would be in its weakest form.

But I couldn't find a path to make it work.

They were essentially in a big corner. There were no paths I could send Antoine down that would not eventually lead back to the others. If I tried, I might be able to pull it off, but failure would mean losing them all.

"Stick together," I said. "Straight ahead. Run as fast as you can."

They started to sprint.

This wasn't good. Antoine and Kimberly had fairly good Hustle, but Camden's was only at two. He could hide, but I wasn't sure that would work with this enemy.

I switched on one of the speakers nearest to them. I had to speak quickly because soon they would run out of hearing range, and I didn't want them slowing down.

They couldn't afford to slow down.

"Left at the water fountain but then a quick right at the very next hallway. Close the door behind you."

They got to the water fountain and quickly found the door next to it. Antoine opened it and closed it behind them. I quickly reactivated the electronic lock.

"Now you're going to run straight."

The hallway that the distortion was moving along was parallel to the one they were running down. If the distortion caught up to them, I was certain it would be able to pass right through the wall and tether to someone.

"Faster!" Anna screamed into the microphone.

Things weren't looking good. The needle on the Plot Cycle wasn't close enough to Second Blood to make me confident that a death would count for anything. If they died too soon, they would be dying for nothing.

"You have hairpin turns coming up."

After that, they would enter a large room that looked like it might have been a recreational area with a ping-pong table and arcade machines. There was a humongous fish tank in the center that was long and narrow, dividing the space in two. When they got to that room, the fish tank would be all that would be between them and the distortion until they could get down the hallway.

They entered the room.

"Take a right. It's behind you!" I screamed.

There was a loud crash.

The distortion might not have been able to get through a door in its weakened hostless form, but it could make it through a glass fish tank. A flood of water poured out onto the ground as the invisible stalker crashed right through the glass.

"It has . . . footsteps," Anna said under her breath.

It did have something like footsteps. As the distortion trudged through the water, ripples formed in strange, irregular patterns. Dr. Mentes had said that this manifestation had a physical form, even without a host. He was right. There was one large set of footsteps and a bunch of other disturbances in the water I couldn't explain.

"Now run like your life depends on it!" I yelled into the microphone.

They somehow found an even faster speed. Antoine was literally pulling Camden along as Kimberly ran in front.

They were coming up on a T-junction.

"I'm unlocking the door to the junction. You need to take a left and then keep running; it's going to get more complicated from there—a lot of twists and turns—but just go through the open doors."

They got to the junction and made a sharp left.

I didn't lock the door behind them. This thing seemed to understand whether it had an open path. I needed it to think it could follow them.

The distortion was close. I had to hope that it wasn't close enough for a tether. I held my breath as they slowly made their way across the monitors.

As soon as the distortion entered the junction area, I closed all three doors, trapping it inside. The only way it could get through those doors was if it had someone to tether to.

Antoine, Camden, and Kimberly were one room away.

Two rooms away.

Three rooms and a hallway.

Still, I couldn't be sure what range this thing had.

For a few tense minutes, I watched the distortion just to make sure it was really trapped. I could see that there were audio spikes inside the junction where I had locked it in. I flipped on the speaker and heard it faintly knocking against the metal door.

Whatever it was, it wasn't going anywhere.

After ten minutes, the distortion started to blink on the screen and soon it disappeared. As it faded from the screen, I frantically looked at every monitor in the room.

Was it gone, or had it simply manifested elsewhere? It could clearly be summoned at a much farther range than before. I needed to keep my eyes on the monitors. I watched the screens with Antoine, Kimberly, and Camden. There was no distortion.

"It worked?" Anna asked.

"I think so," I answered. "We might actually have a way to keep this thing away from us."

I flipped a switch on the monitor for the room the others were running through and said, "Coast is clear. You can proceed to the southwest corner."

I started figuring out a route for them to take.

Once they got to the level above, it would only be one more floor until I could get them out of the building.

But nothing could be that easy.

A red light began flashing on several of the monitors—those relating to the Mercers' cells.

"HQ OVERRIDE."

The words appeared on the screens of the affected monitors. KRSL was remotely leading the fight to us.

I knew we were due for some bad luck. We couldn't escape before Second Blood or the Finale. That wasn't how these things worked.

"And there it is," I said. "Dammit!"

The Mercers' doors all opened, as did a line of doors leading them to the same staircase we had taken to get up here.

Even with the staff here dead, KRSL would not let us leave. They were watching us still, hoping to see the results of Dr. Mentes's efforts.

We were nearly to Second Blood.

Experiment 17 was still underway.

CHAPTER FORTY

THE DISTORTION MANIFESTS

As soon as Antoine, Kimberly, and Camden got to room 347, Antoine found another stairwell like the one we had used earlier. At least we had that success.

The Mercers had found a staircase too, one that would lead them and the distortion straight to us.

"The Mercers are on their way up," Anna said. "We need to finish here. How do we stop HQ from locking us in the building remotely?"

"In order to sever the remote override, I'm going to have to reboot the system," I said. "That should give us the time we need to get up there with the others and get out."

I was really going out on a limb with that. I had no tropes that guaranteed my planned "reboot" would work. But I did have two things going for me.

First, I had spent plenty of points on Moxie and Savvy for my level—perhaps even more than I should have. They would help me with improvising plot elements and planning. Second, my character was supposed to have a lot of experience as a security surveillance specialist. Carousel decided that, not me. It made sense that my character would know how to undo a remote override.

All I needed was for Carousel to play along. I had never actually done pure improvisation like that before. The veterans did it all the time. I had to hope it would work.

"Do you need me for that?" Anna asked.

I had no idea. I was just going to look for a big switch.

"I need to find the right panel," I said.

Logically, I should be able to reboot it from within this room. I searched behind the servers and the computers until I found it: a prominent switch that said "System Reboot" in small text.

It looked like Carousel was playing along.

"Here goes nothing," I said with a deep breath.

I flipped the switch. All of the lights in the room went off. Some emergency lights came on in a dull red.

"One . . . two . . . three . . . four . . . five," I counted under my breath, hoping that the added wait time would add tension to my actions and make the performance better.

Then I flipped the switch back on.

The lights didn't come back on, but one of the terminals did. I went over to it.

"Begin reboot sequence?" flashed on the screen.

I typed "Y" into the keyboard.

The screen started to dance with letters and numbers as something started to happen behind the scenes.

Then I got a message instructing me on how to finish the reboot. Essentially, I would have to go around to five of the terminals in the room and run through some code. It was busy work. It was Carousel pushing back against my reboot idea.

"I'm going to have to reboot the system sequentially," I said. I looked at Anna. "This is going to take too long. You need to go. Run south until you hit the western corridor and then continue west until you get to the corner. I should have it back online in time to guide you the rest of the way."

"No," Anna said. "That wasn't the plan. We were both supposed to go."

"I'll be right behind you," I said. "Once I get the monitors back online, I can guide you around upstairs to the best places to look for the exit. Then I'll meet you up there."

She didn't believe me.

"I can stay here with you," Anna said. "We can go together. If that thing comes back . . . You don't have to try to be a hero."

"Yes, I do," I said. "Now go. We don't have much time."

She hugged me and then slowly turned and ran away, guided by the red blinking emergency lights.

I quickly set myself to the task of rebooting the system. It wasn't too taxing. In fact, it mostly involved typing a bunch of stuff and answering a bunch of prompts at different terminals around the room. It was a time suck, but if I was going to disable remote override—an enormously helpful feat—I had to *earn* it. There's no free lunch in a horror movie unless you're a zombie.

Eventually, I finished it.

The system came back on, bringing back the lights and security monitors. Luckily, the Mercers had gotten scared when the lights went off and had slowed down their ascent up the stairwell.

I looked at the monitors and found that Anna was most of the way to the southwest corner.

I flipped on the microphone and said, "Keep going; you've got a left up ahead and that should bring you to room 347."

"Is everything all right?" Anna yelled.

"Everything's looking good for now. It should take HQ a while to reestablish the override."

I saw on the monitors that Dina and her family were already up on the same floor as us and were searching around for an exit. I thought about what I should do.

Bringing even three of the Mercers near my friends spelled doom as far as I was concerned, but Dina seemed certain. The question was, did I trust her?

"The exit to the floor above is in room 347," I said over the speaker to the room Dina was in. She had better be right.

Right on time, the distortion reappeared.

It was too close. There were no lockable doors between me and it. The Mercers were much closer than they had been before, and it had manifested less than one hundred yards away from me.

Did I stay and help guide my friends for just a little longer as they looked for the exit, or did I run behind them hoping to survive through a few more scenes?

The needle on the Plot Cycle was almost upon Second Blood.

"Keep going straight, Antoine," I said into the microphone. "There's something that's labeled 'Depot.' Check there. It's near the main elevator shaft, so there might be a stairwell nearby. Anna, take a left and you should intersect with the others in a few minutes."

The distortion was drawing closer. It didn't seem to have locked onto my presence yet, but I could see that it was searching.

I scanned over the monitors looking for some sign, any sign, of an exit so that my friends could get out.

"The northwest corner looks promising," I said. "The way it's built mirrors the setup for the stairwell that was in the laboratories. Check there next."

The distortion was close. Any moment it would cut off my path to rejoin my friends.

Anna met up with the others upstairs. She and Kimberly hugged.

It was too late. My choice had been made. I couldn't run. If I ran, it would likely still catch me, and I wouldn't be able to tell my friends anything about it.

I flipped on all of the switches for the speakers in the areas where my friends were as well as those where Dina and her family were. I turned the knob on the microphone input to increase sensitivity.

I wouldn't have long after the creature arrived. I would need to tell them what it was I saw.

My Moxie jumped up five points. It took me by surprise. What could have caused it? There was only one answer: my Raised by Television trope.

But that created more questions than it did answers. That trope was supposed to assist me in doing something heroic and larger than life. My character putting his life at risk to save his family certainly qualified, but why would I get Moxie?

I needed Mettle!

I needed Grit!

Heck, I would even take Savvy or Hustle.

Why had I been given Moxie of all things? Would Moxie help me . . . distract the creature perhaps?

I felt a heavy weight go over my mind. My Infected status lit up on the red wallpaper.

It was happening. I was a host to the distortion. It was far more powerful than it had been. It was still a couple of rooms away, yet it could tether to me.

I didn't have long.

I started to breathe hard from fear.

Of all things for it to give me, why Moxie? What a stupid trope. Was it giving me Moxie so that Oblivious Bystander would work better? That didn't seem correct. I was literally looking at it on the screen; there was no way I could pretend to be oblivious. I would know exactly when it entered the room. I didn't even know if that trope would work on the distortion, anyway.

Besides, that wasn't my plan.

But what was my plan? To die quickly and painlessly? Or did I intend to fight?

A sudden revelation burst into my mind. Psychic tropes were performative and Moxie-based. Players like Lara put a lot of points in Moxie for that very reason. The distortion was a *psychic* manifestation. My character had *psychic* abilities.

Of course!

I understood.

"I get this feeling . . . I can't explain it . . . I don't think that we can fight this thing with weapons, not with guns or anything like that. That's why the others died. I think we have to fight it with our hearts, our minds," I said aloud over the intercom. My voice had begun to shake, and I could feel tears forming in my eyes from fear. "What was it that Grandma used to say about her gift? That she had Moxie—strength of spirit? She said that was why she was special. I used to think she was just making a joke. I think that's how we can fight it."

One last prediction before I was gone. I theorized that this creature was fought with Moxie, with *psychic* power. The weight on my mind got heavier like my head was in a vise grip.

It was behind me.

"I'll try to hold it off," I said.

"Riley!" Anna and Kimberly screamed over the speakers.

I had to look at it. Otherwise, I would be useless to them. I had to see its tropes.

I turned around.

The room was no longer empty, no longer merely a graveyard of slain KRSL employees. The room was full of people, or should I say, shadows of people. There were at least thirty of them. They were gray in color. They stood spread around the room everywhere I looked.

None of them made eye contact with me or acknowledged me in any way. They looked sad and lost. I didn't recognize most of them, but there were some that shined brighter, that moved faster, that looked livelier. I knew who those few were.

The Mercers.

The very same Mercers that were now exploring floor 3B aimlessly on the security monitors. Somehow, they were in the room with me too, if only in spirit. They looked distracted, completely unaware of what was going on.

The others, the more faded people, were more solemn. They stared off in the distance, not saying a word. I say they stared, but their eyes were dark. I couldn't see where they were looking.

On the red wallpaper, I could see what they were and who they were.

Cosmo Mercer (Shade).
Silvia Mercer (Shade).
Eloise Mercer (Shade).

Eloise . . . The matriarch of the Mercer family. She had died a hundred years earlier.

They were ghosts . . . No . . . less than ghosts. Shades. They were remnants, the final psychic echoes of the deceased Mercers. Even the live Mercers' reflections were called Shades on the red wallpaper.

None of them had any Plot Armor. None of them appeared to be enemies. They were still NPCs.

If these were not classed as enemies, what was it that had gone on a rampage the night before? These ghoulish apparitions were terrifying, but how could they kill anything?

"It's the Mercers," I said aloud. "The Mercers' . . . spirits or something. The living and the dead. They're all here."

I felt the strain on my mind get heavier.

"Wait . . . no. There is something else here too!" I screamed.

It stood in the center of them all, forming out of thin air. Unlike the Mercers, who were made of smoke and shadow, this creature was solid. I could hear scratches on the floor underneath it from its claws. Its large claws. The more I focused on them, the longer and sharper they became.

I looked up at it. I needed to see its face.

It had intelligent black eyes and sharp teeth. It was almost a man at first glance, but it shifted as I looked at it. I couldn't see it properly despite it standing right in front of me. It might have been a demon; its skin was like flowing silk and its form was irregular and changing.

Wherever I looked, the more detail I saw. When I looked at its torso, its body formed into a solid. When I looked at its arms, they became solid too. It was like . . . it was forming as my mind shaped it into existence. It *was* using my mind to corporealize, after all.

A cloak draped down over its arms, but the cloak wasn't fabric. It was an organic flowing darkness.

I could feel its anger, its rage.

"It's some sort of demon . . . a nightmare," I said. But I knew that wasn't correct. That word was the closest thing I could come up with to describe it. The red wallpaper didn't call it a demon.

THE MERCER POLTERGEIST	
Plot Armor: 30	
Tropes	
A KNOCK AT THE DOOR	This enemy can target characters behind closed doors, turning a symbol of safety into a source of dread. It may be able to lure characters out with deceptive sounds or eerie silence, manipulating their fear and curiosity, or it may be able to simply break or sneak through such barriers. With A Knock at the Door, death is just a room away.
ANYONE CAN DIE	This enemy operates under a chilling rule: no character is safe. Whether it's because this film is a rule-breaking reboot or a narrative without a true protagonist, this enemy can target or kill any character without ceremony or hesitation. With Anyone Can Die . . . , the only main characters are the ones who survive.

SHY	This enemy lurks in the shadows, its presence more hinted at than revealed. Leaving subtle signs of its existence, the enemy builds suspense and unease. Its reluctance to emerge may be strategic, logistical, or simply a preference for the shadows. But when it finally steps into the light, the impact is all the more chilling.
PROTECTOR	This enemy is driven by a singular purpose: to safeguard something precious, be it an object, a secret, or a person. The enemy will stop at nothing to ensure its charge remains undisturbed. Its actions blur the line between hero and villain, as it may resort to violence to fulfill its duty. Cross its path uninvited, and you invite danger, for the Protector will shed any amount of blood to keep its charge safe.
JEKYLL AND HYDE	The enemy has multiple forms . . . Watchful: Savvy, Moxie = 2 Disturbance: Savvy, Moxie = 3 Potent: Savvy, Moxie = 5 Corporeal: Savvy, Moxie = 7
EXTERNAL POWER SOURCE	This enemy's strength is not its own but borrowed from an external entity or object. The enemy is formidable, but its power comes with a vulnerability: without its source, it is defenseless. Whether it's a mystical artifact, a cosmic entity, or a technological marvel, severing the connection could mean the enemy's downfall.
SPIRITUAL WARFARE	This enemy exists beyond the realm of the physical and is immune to conventional attacks. The enemy might be challenged by psychic, mental, or spiritual combat depending on the narrative. Its battles are waged not on the mortal plane, but in minds and souls, turning inner strength and resilience into the ultimate weapons. To defeat it, one must engage in a different kind of warfare, where willpower, wisdom, and inner peace are the true armaments.
3 additional tropes not perceptible	

Poltergeists were usually depicted as being ghostly in movies, but sometimes they were manifestations of unconscious psychic energy—just like this one.

"I can feel it. It's linked to my mind," I said. "It wants to protect the Mercers. It thinks we are hurting them." I was yelling so that the microphone could pick it up. "It needs them to exist . . . Without them, it would disappear."

No wonder KRSL brought us in as fake employees. They wanted to ensure the creature would view us as the Mercers' captors.

"I don't mean you any harm," I said. "I can help you and your family leave. You don't have to do this."

It did appear to understand what I had said, but it was not persuaded in the least. An intelligent face stared back at me. All I could see was its rage. The fact that I was wearing a KRSL uniform was probably working against me.

It jumped at me. One swipe of its claw and I would be Dead or Mutilated. I had hardly any Grit to speak of.

But I did have some Hustle.

I jumped out of the way of its claws, barely dodging them. I grabbed a stapler off a desk and threw it at the creature's head. I made contact, but it didn't appear to have done any damage.

That attack used Mettle; I needed an attack that used Moxie . . . What would that look like?

I went with the traditional route. I started to think in my mind, "You aren't real, you aren't real."

That would work in some movies.

It swiped a claw at me. I tried dodging again, but this one grazed my sweater and drew blood from my arm.

It was real.

I needed to figure this out or it would all be useless. I held out my hands and used them to block its large razor-sharp claws from my vision.

"You can't hurt me," I said timidly.

Something was happening. Not much, but something.

"You can't hurt me," I said again more forcefully.

It lunged, and as it did, I noticed that its arms were made of smoke and shadow again just as they had been when it first appeared, before I got a look at them.

I managed to back away. I put my hands back up to help block my view of the creature. Its corporeal form relied on my observation. I had no way of telling if this was working but I thought my efforts might have been weakening the creature.

It swiped another claw at me. They were smaller now, less fully formed, but they were still razor sharp. Its claw collided with my left hand and cleanly sliced off three of my fingers.

I screamed in pain.

It was difficult to think. Fear and the weight of the poltergeist's tether were making me tired. I hadn't slept in twenty hours. I couldn't keep this up forever. *Don't suffer in silence!*

I remembered Lara's warning, her Psychic blessing in the form of four words: don't suffer in silence. I had to tell them what was happening.

"Don't picture it in your mind! Don't look at its claws or teeth!" I yelled. "It needs us to see it to exist!"

I didn't know how its other forms worked, but its corporeal form relied on the power of a psychic person's imagination. I was going to deny it that.

I put my injured hand back up in front of my eyes so that I couldn't view the creature directly, but I could still see the outline of it around my bloody hand.

It struck again. It clawed me in the arm. Its attack was far less forceful, but I only had one Grit. It cut me to the bone. I could no longer use that hand to block it out.

As I blocked out the creature in my mind, I could still see the faded Shades of the Mercer family in the room. They didn't appear to even know what was happening. I realized that this movie was about family: the Mercer family, gifted to create this violent protector; Dina and her husband and children; my character's family, Anna and Kimberly . . .

I finally figured out why Kimberly's Pregnancy Reveal had been so effective . . .

The creature slashed again, opening up my stomach. I was too weak to continue my psychic assaults. Besides, even if I could weaken it, I couldn't kill it . . .

Family.

This movie was about family. Kimberly having a child to pass on her gift fit the themes of the movie. That was why Pregnancy Reveal worked so well. We weren't just fighting to survive. We were fighting so that our family could survive, no different than this poltergeist was fighting for the Mercers.

"Protect Kimberly," I yelled through the pain. "Protect her kid."

The story worked better when you played your role. I hoped that by telling them Kimberly was important, she might just become important. With her extra Grit from Pregnancy Reveal, moving her into a bigger role was to our advantage.

I summoned one last burst of energy and charged the poltergeist. It wasn't that impressive. I had no weapons. I was weak from blood loss and fear. Still, I didn't want to just stand there and do nothing.

I screamed an angry, guttural scream.

As I did, I grabbed at the creature's face with my one good hand and did my best to channel whatever psychic power my character had left into it as I tore at its flesh, its eyes. I didn't know if that would do anything. My thumb dug into solid flesh. It felt like I was hurting it—like I was actually doing damage.

It bit my throat.

Unlike the employees of KRSL, there would be no slowly bleeding to death for me.

I don't remember what happened after that, but as I faded away, I saw the needle on the Plot Cycle turn to Second Blood.

CHAPTER FORTY-ONE

A TICKET TO THE SHOW

Suddenly, I was standing in the control room alone. All around me was still. All around me was silent.

The poltergeist was gone.

The bodies on the floor were gone.

Was the storyline over? Did this mean we had won? I looked at the red wallpaper. No, the storyline wasn't over. In fact, we had just entered the Finale. But how was I alive?

I wasn't.

I thought I might have been a ghost, but then I realized that wasn't right either. The red wallpaper had me listed as Written Off and Dead. As far as I knew, ghosts weren't Written Off. On the contrary, they still had sway in the story. Ghosts were merely Dead. I was both. Must have been really special to achieve that.

But what was I doing there?

My answer came with a familiar voice.

"Congratulations, you've won a ticket!" Silas the Showman said.

As I turned around to see him, I noticed that all the security monitors were frozen. It was like they were paused.

"How am I getting a ticket before the end of the storyline?" I asked. "I'm Dead, right?"

"In Carousel, death isn't always the end. Sometimes it's a well-earned rest," Silas responded, using his canned phrasing. "Other times it's just Carousel's way to say that you talk too much. Hehehe."

I knew the drill. I reached out and pressed his red button. Four tickets popped out: three tropes and one new kind that I hadn't seen before. It was shorter and thinner and had a few scant paragraphs.

Silas recited a poem:

"You can pick one from three, what will it be?

No matter the choice, no room to rejoice.

All three can save your skin or tear it off again.

The question remains, you must choose your pains,

In this game of dread, you can choose well and still be dead."

Of course, Silas ended the macabre poem with one of his signature laughs, "Hehehe."

Pick one from three of what?

I turned over the cards in my hands. The thin one had the words "Start Here!" in big red letters. I took that as a sign.

I focused on the ticket. It was printed black with text that had been printed onto the ticket during its creation by leaving negative space. It featured fill-in-the-blank sections but was otherwise generic.

> You've reached a level where the game starts to get more difficult. Luckily, you are about to get the tools to fight back.
> Having achieved Plot Armor: 21 and having afterward accomplished the requisite feat of [**dying in a storyline**] you have now unlocked your choice of Aspect.
> Choosing an Aspect allows you to decide what type of [**Film Buff**] you wish to be. Good luck!

After I read the ticket, a plaque with lots of writing on it appeared on the red wallpaper.

> As a Film Buff, you have a deep appreciation for the art of cinema. However, the way you engage with films can vary greatly, leading to different paths: the Fanatic, the Critic, and the Filmmaker. Your choice of Aspect will shape your abilities and influence your journey in significant ways.
>
> **Fanatic**: The Fanatic is a superfan, especially of horror movies. Their passion and extensive knowledge of films make them adaptable and formidable in combat. They learn from rewatching films, preparing them for similar situations or enemies. Their approach to film is instinctual, and their vast movie-watching experience equips them with unique, situational meta-abilities. Example tropes that a Fanatic possesses include *Ghoulish Enthusiasm*, which buffs the player when they're perceptibly excited about scary endeavors, *Shared Fandom*, which helps gain info from NPCs by bonding over shared interests, and *Weekend Stage-Fighting Workshop*, which allows them to fake fight, causing enemies to also fake fight temporarily.

Critic: The Critic is an analyst, able to dissect and critique films with precision. They use their analytical skills to understand the underlying mechanics of the storyline and provide valuable insights. Despite their physical fragility, they have strong insight tropes and high Savvy, reflecting their intellectual prowess and deep understanding of film. Their insights can influence the course of the game and unveil new, intriguing story arcs.

A Critic has tropes like *Eye for Intermission*, which gives insight into when breaks from important plot events are coming up, *The Renowned Intellectual*, which assists in getting information from NPCs who admire the player's career, and *A Killer Review*, which allows the player to leave vague reviews about the killer after death that allies can read on the red wallpaper.

Filmmaker: The Filmmaker has a comprehensive understanding of the filmmaking process. They can manipulate the game environment effectively, altering the game's dynamics in subtle but impactful ways. Their abilities are a mixture of meta-insight and meta-rule tropes. They have higher Hustle, reflecting their ability to stay out of the way, stay alive, and remain unseen as they manipulate meta movie elements.

Tropes that a Filmmaker has include *Flashback Revelation*, which allows dead players with **Deathwatch** to echo words they have said on-screen to surviving allies who heard them, *It's Just a Puppet*, where knowledge of movie monster making soothes fear, and *No Stab in the Dark*, which helps ensure that important plot events like death will not occur in low-light locations where the audience cannot see.

Choosing your Aspect is a crucial decision. It not only determines your abilities but also sets you on a unique path. Whether you're a Fanatic, a Critic, or a Filmmaker, your love for cinema will guide you, but your approach to it will define your journey. Choose wisely.

Finally, I got to learn about Aspects. All I knew about Aspects I had learned in passing from the veterans, who had tried to explain them to us but usually their explanations were difficult to follow because we were too low level to even see what the Aspects of our tropes were.

Now I wasn't.

I flipped over the three tropes I was given. I had to choose one. Each was a Film Buff trope, and each was from a different Aspect. Critic, Fanatic, or Filmmaker . . . an interesting choice.

I reviewed the three tropes I had to choose from.

Camped Out on Opening Weekend
Archetype: Film Buff
Aspect: Fanatic
Type: Insight/Buff/Perk
Stat Used: Savvy

As an ardent horror movie buff, you've gone to great lengths for your passion. From taking time off work for premieres and camping outside theaters, to immersing yourself in every detail of your favorite flicks' creation, your dedication is unparalleled. After multiple viewings within the first week of release, you've mastered the nuances of each new horror film. Your love for horror is not just a hobby, it's your way of life.

Deathwatch: the player can observe a storyline after their character's demise. With this trope, Deathwatch allows the player to enter the theater from the red wallpaper and watch the film version of the remainder of the storyline in real time. In addition to this ability, the player may rewatch the film without needing to visit Carousel Family Video.

This ability to rewatch enables the Fanatic to learn and adapt, enhancing their performance. After having rewatched a storyline, they will receive situational buffs when rerunning it. Rewatching storylines will also lead to buffs in new storylines with similar scenarios or enemies to those that have been studied.

This ticket is granted after the first character death following the achievement of Plot Armor: 21. Selecting this ticket aligns you with the Fanatic Aspect. "To a true Fanatic, watching a movie isn't just entertainment, it's preparation."

The Fanatic was tempting. If there was one thing I sorely needed, it was some buffs. It continued the trend of unpredictable buffs that the Film Buff appeared to have plenty of, though. It would be nice to have a melee option.

Press Screening
Archetype: Film Buff
Aspect: Critic
Type: Insight/Perk
Stat Used: Savvy
You perceive films as more than mere entertainment; they are a form of art to you. Your dedication has led you to delve deeply into the theoretical side of cinema, honing your ability to discern and articulate the strengths and weaknesses of a film in a manner that resonates with others.

Deathwatch: the player can observe a storyline after their character's demise. With this trope, Deathwatch allows the player to enter the theater from the red wallpaper and watch the film version of the remainder of the storyline in real time. In addition to this ability, the player may rewatch the film without needing to visit Carousel Family Video.

As a Critic, the player can discern the ratings of characters' performances and choices that influence the rewards after the storyline. After extensive rewatching of storylines in Carousel, the Critic starts to perceive these ratings— between one and five stars—within ongoing storylines that have similar themes and setups. This insight can guide the player to make choices that not only yield better rewards and experience but also unveil new, intriguing story arcs.

This ticket is granted after the first character death post-Plot Armor: 21 achievement. Selecting this ticket aligns you with the Critic Aspect.

"If you are going to review your teammate's performance, remember not to bite their head off. There are plenty of monsters in Carousel that do that already."

Critic seemed like a great option. Being able to know whether we were making good choices would help us improve. From the sound of this one, it might also help with finding new arcs within storylines, possibly even involving Secret Lore.

Director's Monitor
Archetype: Film Buff
Aspect: Filmmaker
Type: Insight/Rule/Perk
Stat Used: Savvy
You're not just a movie fan, you're a creator. You've studied every part of filmmaking, from shot composition to production logistics. Like a director using a video assist monitor to view scenes as they're filmed, you see each film as a moldable work that can be made better.
Deathwatch: the player can observe a storyline after their character's demise. With this trope, Deathwatch allows the player to enter the theater from the red wallpaper and watch the film version of the remainder of the storyline in real time. In addition to this ability, the player may rewatch the film without needing to visit Carousel Family Video.
As a Filmmaker, you step into the director's shoes. The more you rewatch and learn from storylines, the more likely it is that your off-screen plans involving improvisation are to influence the story. With enough experience, you will be

able to help guide storylines from behind the scenes. Beware, improvisation that changes the story too much can cause a clash for creative control, and Carousel is quite the diva.

This ticket is your reward after the first death post-Plot Armor: 21 achievement. Choose this ticket to set your Aspect as a Filmmaker.

"Only in Carousel do the filmmakers themselves have to worry about being killed off."

Improvisation. I had just tried that for the first time, and it had largely been successful. The idea of being able to steer a story, to create plot points out of nothing but logic and effort, was appealing.

Interestingly, they all gave me the same ability: Deathwatch. I had heard that word thrown around at Dyer's Lodge. I knew that Psychics and Wallflowers—as well as some others, I assumed—had Deathwatch, but I thought it was a trope. It was actually an ability, which various tropes could give you, that allowed you to watch the story unfold after you had died or been permanently Written Off.

But which Aspect should I choose?

If it was just me, Fanatic might have been a good choice. Being able to buff myself and actually stand a chance in a fight was something I strongly desired. But that wasn't my role on our team.

My role was to gain insight into the story. Understanding a story and being able to help my teammates get to the end was priority number one. That meant I needed to be a Filmmaker or a Critic. I reread the tropes and the text that had appeared on the red wallpaper.

"Does it matter what I choose?" I asked.

Silas the Showman looked at me blankly. Either he didn't have a response that fit properly, or he wasn't able to speak freely at that moment. Another possibility was that it didn't matter.

As far as I was concerned all three of these tropes were great. They all gave the Deathwatch ability. That was a real prize at that moment. It also explained why I received the tropes upon dying.

I found myself more and more indecisive the more I thought about it.

At the end of the day, Secret Lore was supposed to be really important, and a Critic should be able to help uncover more of it. But something didn't sit right with me about the way we had stumbled upon the concept of Secret Lore. I felt uneasy about the whole thing.

I liked how Filmmaker was good for staying out of sight and surviving long enough to get good insights, which lined up really well with my Oblivious Bystander strategy. Also, the idea of working more improvisation into the game excited me and made me feel optimistic that I could think my way out of overwhelming problems.

I also felt like having too many insight tropes could confuse me and distract from engaging with the story, and Critic was insight heavy.

I thought back to the poem Silas had recited when he'd arrived. Every choice could be the wrong choice. Which wrong choice could I live with?

I took the Fanatic and Critic tickets and slid them into one of the slots on Silas's frontside. I could hear the gears inside spinning as the tickets were sucked into his machinery.

I chose the Filmmaker Aspect. I hoped I hadn't made a mistake.

As the grinding stopped and Silas shut down, I waited for him to disappear, but that wasn't exactly what happened.

Everything disappeared.

I was left staring into inky blackness. All that remained was the red wallpaper. Even that disappeared moments later.

I was sitting in a movie theater, my mind's eye fixed on the screen. I could see four people creeping down a hallway: my friends. The Finale had begun. I was watching them as they attempted to overcome incredible odds.

I would exist there, sitting in that seat, dead in all ways but in my ability to watch what became of us.

All other thoughts faded away as I began my Deathwatch, helpless to intervene, only able to sit by and hope that my friends could make it to The End.

CHAPTER FORTY-TWO

CLIMBING TENSION

It was like I was watching a scene from a movie. The camera angles and lighting were the same. Everything had a slight green tint to it like movies in the early 2000s often did. If it wasn't my friends on the screen, I would have thought I was watching a real horror movie.

They were on the floor directly below ground level. Just one more set of stairs and they would be home free. They stood in front of the elevator doors.

"We need to pry open the elevator and climb up," Camden said. "That's the only way out we know of for sure."

"Are you kidding?" Kimberly asked. "That elevator shaft is hundreds of feet deep."

"Then we don't fall. We have one person go up with a rope, and then the rest of us climb the rope after they've tied it off."

Climbing out? Was that really the best option?

I wasn't sure whether climbing used Hustle or Mettle, but either way, Camden had the least of both stats among my friends.

"One person? You mean me," Antoine said.

"We could break through the ceiling," Kimberly suggested.

"We have no idea how long that would take," Camden said. "There could be concrete between the floors."

If climbing the elevator shaft and digging up through the ceiling were the only options, we really were in trouble.

"We can keep looking," Anna said. "There has to be a way out somewhere around here."

"Look," Camden said. "The underground portion of the facility is far larger than the above ground. I don't just mean square footage. I mean at least half of the width of this floor has no building above it. If we start searching too far out, we could be searching for hours and find nothing."

"We can't just give up," Antoine said. "There have to be other ways out of this facility. Are you telling me that they brought all of this lab equipment and furniture down here on one elevator?"

"No. I'm saying that we could get lost down here, searching for so long that KRSL HQ shows up and we never get to leave."

This brought a hush over the group.

I hoped that this wasn't a real argument. Like many of our on-screen conversations, I hoped it was part of the show, that they were explaining why they were no longer searching for a new way up.

Truthfully, there likely were other escape routes originally. Freight elevators, tunnels, air vents, or any number of ways out. The problem was that discovering an alternative exit needed to be done before the Finale. That was one of the basic rules. Important plot information—the kind that can make success a lot easier—cannot be found after Second Blood. That was one thing the vets had drilled into our heads.

"Frankly, we're lucky they haven't shown up already," Camden said.

"Then we climb?" Anna said.

"We climb," Antoine repeated, eyeing the elevator in front of them.

"It's funny," Kimberly said. "Once KRSL comes down to get us, we'll at least know where the exits are."

The Mercers began picking themselves up off the ground. I hadn't seen why they had fallen, but as they stood, they grasped their heads in pain. Some were more affected than others.

They were injured. But how?

One of the women had a nosebleed. The new addition, the teenager I had seen brought into the facility days before, was throwing up in the corner. He looked pale and sickly.

They were still on floor 3B.

"Paul, Paul, please get up," the oldest Mercer woman said. It was the woman who spent her time knitting. She was wearing several scarves of her own design. "Come on," she said as tears streamed down her face.

She was kneeling over the man that I had referred to as Old Guy. She tried to pull him up into a sitting position, but his body was limp, and his eyes were blank. His face was covered in blood that had apparently come from his left eye socket.

"What's wrong with him?" the woman asked desperately.

"He's dead," one of the middle-aged twins responded. "He didn't make it."

"What just happened to us?" the other twin asked. "Did we get electrocuted or something?"

"My head hurts," the teenage boy said.

"No. No," the old woman said. "We were supposed to escape together."

"I'm sorry, Sherry, but we have to go."

The old woman, Sherry, was beyond listening. She continued to try to rouse life in the body of her slain kin.

"I can't leave him," she said. "He's been my only friend for so long."

The women Mercers all gathered around Sherry and attempted to comfort her.

"If we don't leave now, we may not make it out," one of them said.

They stood and pulled Sherry off of the deceased man's body.

"It isn't fair," she said. "He was so . . . close."

As they pulled her away and began walking down the halls together, the camera panned back to show the body of the old man, Paul. I couldn't think of what might have killed him at first, but then, soon enough, I realized exactly what had done it.

I had.

When I had fought back against the Mercer Poltergeist, they had been the ones to take the damage. Paul took it worse than the others apparently. His left eye was bleeding. That was the same eye I had hit the poltergeist in when I had fought it.

I didn't have long to reflect on that. Soon, the scene changed again.

Dina was walking down the halls of floor 3B with her NPC family. Her husband carried their daughter, and their son walked behind them with a mop handle he had found and was carrying around like it was some sort of bo staff.

Her husband had evidence of a nosebleed too, but none of Dina's family looked as affected as the other Mercers did.

"Room 347 should be ahead," Dina said. "No telling how long it will take to get there with the way this place is designed."

"How did you even make it in here?" her husband asked, massaging his right temple with his free hand.

"Snuck in. Got caught immediately. They locked me up and then I escaped after . . . the attack."

"It was the ghost," her daughter said. "I saw it in my dreams."

"There is no ghost," Dina's husband said. "We don't know what that man was screaming about over the intercom. He was craz—"

He stopped talking as they passed a splatter of blood on the wall. The victim was not nearby. They had likely continued on to find shelter in an attempt to escape the entity.

"There is a ghost," the little boy said as he swung his mop handle around. "Or a demon. The guy said so. He said our last name too."

Her husband wasn't convinced. "Kids, this isn't the time."

Dina stopped. She looked over at her husband like she was going to say something, but then thought better of it.

"What?" he asked.

"What do you think happened here?" Dina asked. "You're so sure of what didn't happen. What do you think did happen?"

"I think the kids have overactive imaginations and whatever it was we heard over the speaker was . . . I don't know. This scares them."

Dina didn't respond. She was not talkative. Not to NPCs, not to players.

The family continued walking down the hall.

Suddenly, the shot shifted to a view of the security monitors. The Mercers wound about aimlessly on a top left monitor. Dina and her family were on a monitor in the middle. My friends were on the top right, visible as the camera panned over.

And then one of the monitors distorted. It was in the center. Right next to Dina and her family. The camera closed in on the screen with Dina just as the distortion moved onto it.

Suddenly, the shot was no longer on the security monitors. Dina was moving forward, investigating the next path they should take.

Her daughter started crying.

Dina fell back onto the ground as her leg was lifted up into the air. An invisible barb had pierced her Achilles tendon, hooking her in one side and out the other.

The entity was in one of its weaker forms, either its Disturbance or Potent form; I wasn't sure. It had tethered onto Dina.

It began dragging her down the hallway as her children screamed on.

Her husband practically dropped their daughter and ran down the hall to catch up. He grabbed onto her and pulled against the force of the entity. Dina screamed out in pain as the psychokinetic barb in her ankle ripped at her flesh. There was a sudden, unsettling sound as the invisible barb was pulled right through her Achilles tendon, freeing her but leaving her Hobbled.

Objects in the room started to shake as the creature's anger grew.

Dina continued to cry out in pain but still beckoned her husband to help her stand on her good leg. They started to run back in the other direction, slowed by her injury.

The objects in the room started to fly at a much harder and faster rate. The creature's frustration grew.

It grabbed onto Dina and flung her against the wall so hard that she was ripped from her husband's arms. Then it flung her against the opposite wall of the hallway.

I had believed that this creature was attacking the staff because they worked for KRSL, the Mercers' captors, but I had credited it with too much. It was a being of pure anger at this point. It was attacking anyone who wasn't part of the Mercer bloodline, including Dina.

As she fell to the ground, the hallway started to shake, the walls themselves unable to resist the raw power of even the weakened form of the poltergeist.

It lifted Dina up into the air. It was about to throw her back down again when Dina's daughter ran forward and embraced her mother's limp arm.

"No!" the little girl screamed. "Don't hurt her!"

The entity suddenly stopped its attack. It dropped Dina, and her husband managed to grab her before she fell to the ground.

The poltergeist hadn't given up yet. It had merely slowed its attack out of a desire not to harm Dina's daughter.

It grabbed onto Dina's injured leg again and began pulling.

"Stop!" the little girl yelled. Her brother joined in with her, yelling at the invisible entity, swinging his mop handle in the air in a desperate hope that he might be able to save his mother.

The entity let go of Dina's leg.

Her family surrounded her, lying on the ground of the hallway, hugging her and protecting her.

"What the hell?" her husband screamed. His character was in full denial, but I didn't think that was his fault.

"I told you, Daddy," the little girl said through tears. "It was the ghost."

"But . . ." He was at a loss for words. As Dina started to regain consciousness, he said, "Dina. Dina, are you okay? What the hell is going on here? Please say something."

Dina opened her eyes.

For some reason, Dina had put off telling her husband what was going on in the facility. I couldn't be sure, but it looked as though Carousel was punishing her for that. Carousel wanted a scene of one of the Mercers having everything explained to them. Dina was probably the only character who could do so. She had listened to the audio recordings the same as us.

Dina sat up and examined her ankle. "We need to talk," she said.

Meanwhile, the other Mercers were still trying to find their way up through the maze that was floor 3B.

"We used to be on this floor a few years ago," Sherry said as she rewrapped her scarves. "Only for a few months."

"Do you remember the way up?" one of the other women asked.

"I'm afraid our captors never showed me the way out," Sherry responded. "I know where the cells were. I know where Dr. Barret's office used to be before his passing. That's it."

They hadn't made much progress as far as I could tell. From this vantage, I couldn't even guess where they were or how far from the exit they were.

"I've been passed around from one facility to another ever since I was mugged.

Well, he tried to mug me," Sherry said solemnly. "Paul had already been here for a decade then."

"Poor guy," one of the middle-aged twins said. "I couldn't imagine being in a place like this for most of my life."

"Neither could I when I was your age," Sherry said. "I still can't fathom it. My life wasted . . . Sometimes I dream of escaping this place, but I never can. I try as hard as possible, but I cannot make it out before I wake up."

"Because the doors won't open?" the teenage boy asked.

Sherry nodded.

"I had the same dream the night I got here," the boy said.

"No need to worry about it now," the youngest woman said. "We'll make it out soon. I have a place on Lake Dyer. We can go there."

They continued walking, looking inside every room and corridor.

"Shh," the teenage boy said. "Can you hear that?"

The Mercers stopped short and listened.

A soft, repetitive banging could be heard.

"It's the pipes," one of the twins said.

"No," the boy said. "My mother said we should listen to knocks. They are there to help us."

"By god, I believe my mother said the same thing," Sherry said. "How many years has it been? It was before we lost our family manor . . ."

"We should follow it," the boy said.

"You're saying that this thing is our fault?" Dina's husband asked.

"I'm saying that the scientist in charge brought you in because you are a Mercer," Dina said.

She was sitting on a countertop. They had found a first aid kit hanging on a wall and her husband was wrapping her injury.

"The monster won't hurt Mercers," Dina explained. "It hurts everyone else."

"But you're a Mercer," her daughter said.

Dina put her hand on the kid's head and said, "I know. But I married in. Apparently, the monster doesn't count that."

"So, we've got to protect you?" her son said, still holding his mop handle staff.

As Dina looked at him, her eyes grew wet with tears, perhaps thinking of her real son. She nodded without saying anything.

"I won't let it hurt you," he said.

"Me neither," her daughter agreed.

Dina looked at her husband. He looked back at her and said, "I don't know what's going on here, but I'll do whatever it takes."

* * *

Antoine finished tying a firehose around his waist. They had pried open the elevator doors and found one of those emergency firehoses rolled up on a red spool.

"I got this. I got this," he said, psyching himself up. He jumped up and down and breathed in and out with several quick breaths.

Antoine would be making the climb. He had his baseball bat handle affixed to the holder that used to house his baton. It hung down behind him, ready to be used at a moment's notice.

"Do you think he'll be able to get the doors upstairs pried open?" Anna asked.

"Oh, I'll get them open," Antoine said.

He approached the open darkness of the elevator shaft and gently moved his hand upward, feeling for something to grab onto on the inside of the shaft. He found it.

In moments, he had lifted his whole body up and began scaling the inside of the shaft. I'm not sure if real elevator shafts were climbable, but it was Camden's plan. Between his high Savvy and how well it fit the narrative, it worked. Antoine was making progress.

"I can see light coming from the doors upstairs," he called down to the others below.

He continued to climb. One hand after the other found purchase and he was really starting to get some distance. Once he could use both his hands and feet to climb, his speed started to increase.

By my estimate, the distance between these floors was about three times what you would normally expect, maybe thirty-six feet. To me, it looked impossible. My fear of heights would have really hurt me with this one.

Antoine continued.

He was making it. I feared for him and the others. Any moment, the poltergeist could arrive and ruin everything.

He climbed.

Only a few more feet and he would be on ground level.

One handhold after another.

He made it. He reached into one of his pockets for a metal implement that looked like it was from inside a filing cabinet and reached over to start prying the doors open.

He stopped dead in his tracks.

There was noise coming from the other side.

I listened closely. Soon, I heard it too . . .

They were voices. I recognized one of them.

It was Nancy Cartwright.

The camera moved through the elevator and suddenly I could see the other side. Nancy, the woman who had greeted us on the way inside the facility, was giving orders to around two dozen or so men outfitted in all manner of military gear.

The men were called KRSL Agents on the red wallpaper. One of them, a man with a red helmet, was called KRSL Commander. They were Plot Armor eighteen and twenty, respectively. Enemies.

I couldn't see their tropes.

It made sense. Trope Master is proximity-based, but I had hoped this would be an exception. I guess it didn't matter. I couldn't tell anyone what I saw even if I knew.

I just wished I could help my friends.

The poltergeist on one side. A room full of killers on the other.

What were they going to do?

CHAPTER FORTY-THREE

A FRESH BREATH OF XEGOST-H SULFIDE

The armed men's faces were covered to the point that you couldn't tell anything about them except that they were lethal.

"I'm not making entry until I know for certain that my men will be safe," their commander said to Nancy Cartwright. "As far as I'm concerned, we could just block the doors and knock this building down. Trap everyone down there, even your pet Mercers."

Nancy glared at the man. "I assure you, that will not be necessary. We are prepared to take drastic action to both protect the scenario and your men. I just hope they are as skilled as I have been told. This isn't the kind of enemy that your firearms will be much help with."

"We know how to handle your little ghost," the commander said.

She waved her hands and two of the heavily armed men carried a large silver canister over to where Nancy and the commander were standing. An open hatch in the wall revealed a strange array of pipes. There were many knobs and handles spread around the pipes, controlling various unknown functions. There was a prominent attachment sticking out of the hatch, a nozzle of some kind.

The men connected the silver canister to the nozzle and fastened it in.

"What even happened here?" the man with the commander asked. "I thought this was a stable scenario."

"It was," Nancy answered. "We have never seen the entity behave this way. Perhaps Mentes botched something. Maybe the Mercers themselves have become immune to the drug regimen that has worked in the past."

As the two armed men finished installing the silver bottle, Nancy leaned over and pulled a yellow handle. As she did, a hissing sound could be heard as whatever was inside that canister started to move into the facility's system.

One of the armed men pulled a few more handles and spun a knob. He held some blueprints in his hands as he worked.

"This will flood all rooms and hallways below," he said. "We should be able to start our descent in thirty minutes."

"For whatever reason," Nancy said, looking down at a red canister on the ground, "the old standby failed to stop the rampage last night. We pumped it into the Mercers' rooms, and it didn't appear to have any effect on the distortion. Yet another question that needs to be answered."

The leader of the armed men watched as some of the dials and gauges started to go crazy in response to the influx of whatever gas was contained in the canister.

"This will stop it?" he asked. "My men will be safe?"

"Oh yes," Nancy answered. "XEGOST-H sulfide will bring anything with cognitive function to its knees. Years ago, we tested it on one of the Mercers, who is no longer with us. It will undoubtedly work. Make sure your men don't breathe it, of course."

"Why didn't you use this stuff originally?" the man asked.

"XEGOST-H sulfide can be lethal with repeated doses," Nancy explained. "The Mercers are very valuable. We wanted to keep them alive and continue the experiment as long as we could. Had that fool not cut off our override, we would never have needed to resort to this extreme measure."

That was a dig against me. I was the fool who had shut off the override. Still, I wasn't certain that it was a bad decision. It was chilling to hear Carousel calling me out in that way. Most of the otherworldly systems in Carousel seemed like a computer program. A player does X, the system does Y. But this remark sounded like banter from a living thing.

Whatever the case, things did not sound good for my friends. Was this Carousel sealing our fate?

The Mercers crept through the halls of the facility in pursuit of the knocking sound.

"Do you think it will lead us out?" one of the twins asked.

"I don't even know what it is," the other twin responded.

They continued following.

"What killed all of those people back there?" the youngest woman asked with a sniffle. "They were torn apart . . . I can't . . ."

"The thing they keep us here to study," the old lady, Sherry, answered. "The monster. I've never seen it, but I have heard them talking about it when they thought I was asleep."

They continued to talk in hushed tones as the camera zoomed out, revealing that the entity was guiding them toward the area just under the gathering of armed security personnel upstairs. Soon, I knew, the entity would be in range to tether to the top floor and butcher the armed guards.

A hissing sound could be heard. There was a shot of one of the air vents on the ceiling. A barely visible gas started to fall down into the hallway.

"I feel funny," the teenage Mercer said.

He grabbed his head. Soon, the other Mercers started to do the same.

"No!" Sherry cried out. "We were almost there!"

She started breathing deeply, hyperventilating.

Above them, ceiling tiles started to crack and fall down to the ground as the entity clawed and pulled its way upward, hoping beyond hope to be able to jump to one of the armed men upstairs. It was no good. It was in its weakest form.

If it had gotten them just a little farther, it might have been able to tether to one of the armed guards upstairs. If it had had more time, perhaps it could have simply manifested upstairs, an act that appeared to have a longer range. Alas, it was unable.

Soon, the Mercers were unconscious, and the evidence of the poltergeist died down too. Whatever that gas was, it put the Mercers out so quickly that they didn't even close their eyes all the way. Their breaths were shallow, and their pupils were dilated.

The scene changed.

I was watching Dina and her family as they slowly made their way through a darkened hallway. I had no idea what floor they were on or how close they were to getting upstairs.

"Wait a second," Dina said.

Her eyes darted directly to the air vent above them. She paused and listened. Then she took a sniff of the air. Her Outsider's Perspective trope had apparently alerted her to something unusual about the air coming from the vent. She was able to put two and two together.

"They're gassing us!" She quickly looked around for some refuge, something they could use to prevent their impending capture.

She saw a small door, the kind that I recognized was used for utility closets and similar in the facility. She threw herself at it, unable to walk there on her own. Catching herself against the wall, she opened up the door. It was a supply closet with cleaning materials inside.

"Quickly, get inside," she said. "Find things to block the doorway and look for any vents."

"What is going on?" Dina's husband asked. "I don't smell anything."

At first, it looked like Dina didn't know how to explain it. "I do. The air changed."

She ushered them forward into the closet. Her children were quick to follow and obey her words. They started looking around the walls of the small closet for ventilation. Her son found a vent pretty quickly.

"Here," Dina said as she reached down and closed the vent. She continued looking around the closet and spied a box of trash bags. "We need to cover all the cracks."

They started opening trash bags and poking them around to insulate the door and under the vent, just to be sure.

The question was, was Dina's Savvy high enough for her plan to work?

Time passed.

A small group of armed security personnel entered the control room on floor 3B. I wasn't sure how they had even gotten down there. That was not shown.

They wore gas masks.

"Tell Cartwright the troublemaker is dead," one of the men said over the radio.

He was looking at my corpse. Freaky.

"She'll be happy to hear that. Can you confirm that Dr. Mentes is deceased?" the head security officer asked.

The squad spread out, looking around the bodies and the room to find one that belonged to Dr. Mentes. It didn't take them long to find it.

"Mentes is down," they said.

"Heard. Reinitiate our connection."

"Yes, sir," one of the men said as he moved to the server and started working on some switches off-screen.

"Do you see the other test subjects or the Mercers on the surveillance screens?" Nancy asked into the radio.

One of the squad members walked over to the monitors and started scanning around for signs of life.

"There are a lot of bodies. It's difficult to tell if any of them are the test subjects. They were dressed as KRSL employees, correct?"

"Affirmative."

That was good news. If they weren't actively looking for my friends, having assumed that they were among the dead, we might just have a fighting chance.

But the question remained, where were my friends? Shouldn't they be passed out near the elevator door that Antoine had entered to climb upward?

The man continued scanning the monitors.

"The Mercers are almost directly below you," he said. "They appear to have succumbed to the gas. One appears to be dead or unconscious on the floor below the others. Three are missing."

The Mercers were probably easier to separate from the dead employees because they were wearing white patient gowns.

The camera panned slowly over the monitors and stopped on the screen that had a view of a closet door. It was the closet Dina and her family were hiding in. Looking closely, I could see the subtle shine of the black plastic trash bags that Dina had used to seal the door.

The man looking at the monitors didn't notice.

"We'll send a recovery unit. Keep looking for the missing Mercers," the commander said. "Do you have eyes on the distortion?"

"No."

"Stay there until the override is reinitiated. Then I want you to get your asses out of there."

"Yes, sir."

"Recovery!" yelled the commander. "The Mercers are unconscious on the floor below us. Recover them. Sedate them for transport."

Another group of five armed men broke off and started making their way through the hallways. I wasn't sure where they were going until they got near the elevator. At first, I thought they somehow weren't aware that the elevator was broken, but as they approached it, they stopped short and turned to what appeared to be a blank wall with nothing but a light switch.

One of the men produced a badge and moved it over the light switch. As he did, a seam appeared, and the wall that had been blank now opened up to a small passage leading to a set of spiral stairs barely large enough for the men to walk down as they turned and twisted.

I wasn't sure how they were supposed to get the Mercers back up if that was the plan.

It dawned on me that when they got to the bottom of those stairs, they would open the secret door and immediately be looking at where my friends had been the last time I had seen them.

The men twisted and turned down the spiral staircase. It seemed like it was going to take forever. When they got to the bottom, they waved a badge over a little white box on the inside of the wall, and the door opened onto the floor.

I could see the elevator doors.

To my surprise, my friends weren't there. The elevator doors were shut instead of being propped open like they had been before. There was no evidence that they had even been there. They had disposed of the red reel that had held the firehose.

I was relieved to see that they were not lying on the ground unconscious.

But where were they?

The recovery unit made quick work of tying up the Mercers and injecting them with yet another sedative. They would then carry them individually back up the small staircase and into the hallway on the ground floor. Despite how valuable the Mercers allegedly were, their bodies were jerked around and stowed away like luggage.

"Who are we missing?" the commander asked.

"Two kids. One of the adults," one of the men on the recovery squad said.

The leader spoke into his radio and asked, "How's that override coming?"

"Nearly there. I'll advise you if we need Cartwright."

"Do you have eyes on the three missing Mercers?"

"Negative."

Nancy Cartwright was standing nearby. "Well, it's not like they could have escaped. They may have found a hiding spot. Will we be able to get footage of where they went?" she asked.

"The system wasn't recording after the reboot," the commander said.

"And how about the mother, the intruder?" Nancy asked. "Has she been found?"

"Not yet. My men have instructions to terminate her as soon as they find her. Same with your test subjects. I hope you can find more."

"Yes, we should be able to when we move to the new facility," she answered.

After she said that, the camera started to move past her until it gave a full view of the elevator. It continued to zoom in until the view moved right through the elevator doors and revealed what was on the other side.

My friends.

They had gotten into the elevator shaft. All of them had made it up to ground level and were hanging from support beams, listening to the conversation outside. The gas did not affect them. They must have been outside of its range. While it had been pumped into the floors below, they had been hiding right next to all of the armed men.

Antoine must have heard their plans to gas the facility.

"Headquarters is going to be very upset that one of the Mercers was killed," the leader of the security forces could be heard saying outside the elevator door.

My friends listened intently. How much had they heard?

I could only hope it would be enough to give them the information they needed to escape.

They were so close and so far away.

The needle on the Plot Cycle told me the Finale was nearly here.

CHAPTER FORTY-FOUR

SEDATION

Kimberly sat on a crossbeam just under the elevator door. She leaned back against the wall. Directly above her, Camden peeked out through a crack between the doors.

"It looks like there is no one near the elevator," Camden said. "They've moved the Mercers somewhere else."

"What about Dina's family?" Anna asked.

"I have no idea," Camden said.

"I hope they haven't found them yet," Kimberly said. "That little girl is so precious. She reminds me of myself at that age. It's strange. It's like I can feel her down there somewhere. She's scared."

I wondered what it was they were planning with that narrative line. They were trying to form a sort of psychic connection between Kimberly and the Mercer girl. If they used it well, there was no telling what they could pull off. I hated not knowing their plans.

"They'll all be fine," Antoine said, reaching out from his position to grab Kimberly's hand. Kimberly held his hand back.

"When I was her age, Grandma told me I was like her. You know, gifted," Kimberly said. "Guess she was telling the truth. All this time, I thought I was just good with people."

Was she trying to use Convenient Backstory to reinforce her psychic background and give her a Moxie boost?

She put her other hand to her stomach. "With Riley gone . . . It's just us left to carry on that part of her," she said to Anna.

Anna closed her eyes and nodded.

"We need to make a move," Camden said. "I'm going to go look for an exit."

"No," Antoine said. "I should go."

"As much as I would like to agree, I think I'll be better at hiding from the guards," Camden said. "You need to stay here and protect them. If I can find an exit or make a distraction, I'll make sure you know about it. When it's time, you need to come ready to run, fight, whatever."

Antoine reluctantly nodded.

He leaned over and, with the combined effort of all four of them, pried the elevator doors open as much as possible.

Antoine needed to stay with the group. Antoine's Playbook trope would alert him automatically when it was time for them to exit the elevator. That would ensure they knew exactly when things would be safe.

Not to mention, I doubted they could get the doors open without Antoine's Mettle.

Camden quickly squeezed through the gap in the silver doors.

"I'll scope things out. I'll take the left hallway toward the front entrance. If you hear gunshots . . . maybe try the other way," Camden said.

The doors closed behind him. He took a deep breath and started creeping down the hallway. With low Hustle and high Savvy, his ability to sneak was not good, but his ability to find a place to hide was great, especially with his Hide and Seek trope.

The question was, could he find a place to hide before he was caught?

He glanced up at the camera on the hallway ceiling. He didn't know if he was being watched. He ran as fast as he could down the hallway while still attempting to stay quiet.

From that vantage, it was difficult to see farther than the reception desk, which blocked much of his view. He started looking for somewhere else where he could get a better look at the front door. Farther down the hall, he could see into a room that appeared to be empty. He took a chance and ran across into the room. Success. He hadn't been spotted.

The room was one of the small offices like the one I had been interviewed in by Dr. Mentes. It held a small amount of furniture—a desk, a cabinet, some chairs, and a couch.

As he stopped to catch his breath, some voices could be heard in the hallway. Camden grew alarmed and scanned over the room for somewhere to hide.

Moments later, the guards entered the room. Camden was nowhere to be seen.

"These missing kids," one of the guards said, "they're small, right? What if they hid in a cabinet somewhere? Do we really need to check every crevice they could have fallen into when that thing—whatever it is—is hunting us? Why not just sit back and wait for them to try to escape?"

"Orders are orders," the other guard said. "Now, where did Mentes keep those extra sedatives?"

"The cabinet."

The man walked across the room toward a large cabinet and jerked open the door. He found rows of shelves stocked neatly with various medical supplies, including a tub filled with small single-use packages, which contained syringes of the sedative. They were the same ones used on the Mercers after they had been captured.

I had worried Camden might have been hiding in the cabinet. To my relief, he wasn't.

"Check the date on those," the other guard said.

"I know the protocol, dammit."

The first guard plopped the syringes on the table and took a seat at the desk. He started to check each of the syringes for the date.

The camera panned down to the space under the desk where your legs were meant to go. That wasn't where Camden was hiding either.

He hadn't hidden under the desk or in the cabinet.

Where was he?

The camera moved down to floor level. I could see the guards' feet and . . . Camden. He was lying face down underneath the couch. He must have tilted it back and let it drop down on top of himself in order to fit under there, as the opening was not big enough for him to get under normally.

I wasn't sure if his Hide and Seek trope was doing the heavy lifting there, or merely his high Savvy. Hide and Seek required a chase scene to work. There was no chase scene. That meant he had one less layer of protection as he hid from view.

"See, I checked the dates," the guard said. "You happy?"

"Let's just get out of here sometime today, huh? Pass those syringes out. We need to be ready."

The guard got up from the desk and took the container of sedatives with him.

Underneath the couch, Camden breathed a sigh of relief. It looked like he had been holding his breath the entire time.

"I apologize, ma'am," one of the guards said as he guided Nancy Cartwright down one of the dark hallways underground. "We need your optical scan and other credentials to reinitiate the HQ override."

"You said you would have it on in a few minutes," she retorted.

"We didn't foresee these circumstances. It looks like the subject blocked us out after he rebooted. We couldn't have anticipated that level of sophistication."

I certainly didn't remember doing that, but I was willing to take credit for it.

Nancy attempted to hide her fear of being two floors underground, trapped with the distortion, by adding extra vitriol to her voice. "Well, I think we should have hired operatives with . . . more . . . skill."

The guard rolled his eyes behind her back.

She was led into the control room and taken to one of the terminals.

"Do you remember your code?" the man sitting at the terminal asked.

"Of course I do," Nancy said. "Let me see the keyboard."

As Nancy was guided through the process of fixing the problem I had caused, the camera floated over to the surveillance monitors. The man that had been posted there was working on one of the terminals. The monitor that had shown Camden sneaking down the hallway and into the office where he had hidden under the couch went unwatched.

The screen fast-forwarded through the scene of the guards checking the date on the syringes while Camden hid under the couch.

After what had been a few minutes in real time, Nancy said, "There, is that all you need?"

"That will do. We should have our override in just a few moments."

"Now take me back upstairs," Nancy said.

Camden tilted the couch back and rolled out into the room as quietly as he could. He peeked out into the hallway. The coast was clear back the way he had come, but in the other direction he could now see fifteen or so guards moving the unconscious Mercers in the direction of the exit. He cursed under his breath.

Just as he was about to cross the hallway to report back to the others, a voice sounded over the intercom.

"Subject Four spotted in room 113."

The message sounded again.

Headquarters was back in control of the surveillance system.

Camden glanced back at the door number next to the room. Room 113.

"Shit," he said aloud.

He appeared to consider running back to the others but thought better of it. He must not have wanted to reveal their location to those watching on from HQ.

He slammed the door, locked it, and started moving furniture in front of it.

A group of five soldiers broke off from those near the exit and ran toward the office he was hiding in.

They began attempting to force the door open.

"Momma?" Bethany Mercer asked from within the small closet where they were hiding.

"Yes?" Dina answered.

"Kimberly needs our help."

"Kimber—" Dina started to say. Her face glistened with sweat. "One of the test subjects?"

"I don't know. She's a nice lady. She's hiding. I think she needs us to find her."

Dina's husband interjected, "How do you—" But stopped and shook his head, dropping the subject. "*We're* hiding, honey. We can't help anyone else right now."

Bethany looked her mother in the eye. "She needs us."

Dina looked at her daughter and then up at the door. They had sealed it very well with trash bags.

As Dina considered what her daughter had told her, the camera panned out to show that the closet the family was hiding in was directly below the control room that Nancy Cartwright was standing in at that very moment.

As Nancy Cartwright moved to leave the control room, one of the guards sitting at a terminal started howling in pain as he grasped his head.

"It's here!" Nancy yelled to the two guards nearest to her. "We need to go!"

She started to run back toward the elevator where the secret stairwell had been, but instead waved her credentials over a light switch and yet another stairwell opened up, this one leading down.

"Why would we go down?" one of the guards asked.

Nancy started to run down the tiny stairwell. As she did, she said, "The remaining Mercers are likely on this floor. The distortion is trying to escape above ground. It has no reason to follow us downward."

When they made it down to the floor below, Nancy opened the hidden door, and they piled out into the hallway.

"We need to go east. There is another stairwell that will take us up to the building across the street from the facility," Nancy said. "Let's get a move—"

Nancy stopped short as she looked down the hallway and saw, to her horror, Dina and her family.

"Shit!" Nancy yelled, realizing her plan was fatally flawed. She was still assuming that the poltergeist couldn't manifest through the floors as had been the case when the Mercers' powers were weakened by their drug regimen.

One of her guards grabbed his head in pain. The poltergeist had tethered to him. Nancy began running down the hall to the east. Her guards followed, abandoning their orders to capture the Mercers out of fear.

"Don't follow me, you idiots!" Nancy screamed as she realized what was happening.

They continued to run, but the camera didn't follow. Screams could be heard in the distance. Then, silence.

"We need to go upstairs now," Dina said as she limped forward toward the stairwell Nancy had just climbed down.

Her husband helped support her weight as she went, their children sticking to their mother in order to protect her should the poltergeist return.

They climbed the stairs.

As they did, the camera zoomed out to show that they were almost directly underneath the very room that Camden was being dragged out of. The higher they climbed the stairs, the closer they became. They had him on his knees in the middle of the room. They had managed to break the door off its hinges and drag the furniture he had stacked up out into the hallway.

Their guns were drawn on him as they awaited orders.

As the shot refocused on him, Camden winced and balled his hands into fists. The poltergeist must have killed Nancy Cartwright and the guards.

It had apparently now remanifested and found a new host: Camden.

He was immediately aware of it.

He looked around the room for a plan, suddenly less worried about the guns. His eyes rested on the white packages sticking out of the guards' pockets—the syringes filled with sedatives the guards had collected earlier.

As he stared at the syringes, two of the guards were forcefully slammed together by an invisible force.

The poltergeist made its presence known.

"Kill the host!" one of the men screamed, aiming his gun around, looking for some clue as to which of them was tethered to the monster.

Before the guard figured out who the host was, an invisible blade cut a deep gash across his chest, slicing through his bulletproof vest and exposing his muscle and bone. He dropped to the ground and started to shake, either from some sort of seizure, fearful shock, or the influence of the psychokinetic phantom.

The poltergeist was powerful with Camden as its host.

The other guards didn't fare any better. They were tossed around the room with ease as they fired their guns into the air, hoping to somehow kill the entity.

The poltergeist worked through the men one at a time, many of whom were trying to escape, inflicting injury after injury. The men would drop to the ground, still screaming from sheer terror and pain. Like in the surveillance video, the distortion wasn't killing anyone. It was keeping them alive as long as it could so it could tether to them.

Camden crawled to one of the downed men and grabbed a handful of syringes from his vest pouch and began injecting each of the screaming men. As he did, they quieted down, their eyes closing.

"What are you doing?" the last uninjured security officer asked as he watched Camden work.

The entity lifted one of the sedated men into the air and started shaking him around.

"Getting rid of potential hosts," Camden answered. He continued to disseminate the sedative. He looked at the last guard. "You need to sedate yourself."

The man was terrified. "Won't it kill us in our sleep?"

The poltergeist shoved the floating guardsman into the ceiling, causing a loud crack.

"Not if we use this stuff," Camden said, turning the package over and reading the label. "Our minds won't be usable for a long while." He inserted the needle into the thick of his bicep and pushed down the plunger. "Not by us. Not by that thing."

His eyes began to droop almost immediately. "They should have hired me . . . for real."

With that, he was unconscious. The man floating in the air dropped to the ground.

His plan had worked.

The guard, having seen the sedative successfully nullify the distortion, grabbed a syringe from his pouch and considered following Camden's warning, but his hands shook.

He winced.

He grabbed his head with his free hand, realizing that he had become host to the poltergeist. As objects around the room started to float and the walls began to shake, he injected the final syringe into his arm. As he did, the shaking stopped.

He fell unconscious.

Nothing in the room moved. The poltergeist had dissipated.

He had taken a lot of the KRSL agents off the board with that move, but there were still a dozen more to go.

They stood between my friends and the exit.

CHAPTER FORTY-FIVE

CURTAINS

The elevator doors opened slowly.

"Something is wrong," Antoine said. "I told you he should have been back by now."

The hallway was empty.

Antoine squeezed his way out and held the doors open for Anna and Kimberly to leave.

"Hush," Antoine said. "Someone is coming."

He brandished his bat and hid near the corner, ready to bash whoever appeared.

As the footsteps got closer, Kimberly held out her hand and grabbed the bat. "Don't."

Antoine wasn't sure, but as the first figure rounded the corner, it was revealed to be Dina's husband.

"Please!" he begged when he saw Antoine's bat. "We have children with us!"

"Miss Kimberly!" Bethany Mercer cried out and ran around the corner to greet Kimberly.

"Oh my god, Bethany!" Kimberly said, taking the little girl in her arms. "You're okay!"

Dina limped around the corner. She was standing on her feet better, likely because of her choice to come to help her allies in the Finale, which buffed her Grit and helped combat her Hobbled status.

There was a silence between them.

Dina's husband was unsure of whether he could trust my friends. After all, they were wearing KRSL uniforms.

After a moment of sizing each other up, Dina asked, "Are we escaping or what?"

Antoine and Dina's husband both nodded.

"I'm guessing there's no exit back the way you came," Antoine said.

"Not that we could see," Dina said.

"Our coworker, Camden, just went around the other direction. He hasn't come back."

"Toward the entrance?"

Antoine nodded.

Dina looked past them in the direction Camden had gone. "I would check it out," she said, "but my right foot is out of commission."

"I'll go," Antoine said. "Be ready to run in the other direction."

He hugged Kimberly and told her that he would be back soon, then turned and followed in the direction that Camden had gone.

It only took a little while for him to find the path of destruction that the poltergeist had left when attacking Camden. One of the guards was thrown out into the hallway along with all the furniture that they had yanked out of the room in order to get to him.

As soon as he saw the guards and the blood, Antoine ran to the room and quickly looked for his friend. Camden and all of the surviving guards lay sleeping on the floor.

Antoine rushed to Camden's side. He would have been able to see on the red wallpaper that Camden was still alive. He was simply unconscious. A needle from the sedative still hung out of his arm.

Antoine pulled it out and looked at it. Between the needle and the unconscious guards, he put together what had just happened.

"Clever."

He picked Camden up and threw him over his right shoulder, easily carrying him. He glanced at the exit. He didn't see any of the guards.

What to do?

Antoine quickly made his way back to the others.

"Oh my god, is he dead?" Dina's husband asked.

"Just knocked out," Antoine said. "I didn't see anyone up by the exit but that doesn't mean they're not there. There are some dead and unconscious guards. We might be able to get some weapons off of them. They had these weird-looking cone-shaped things as well as some handguns."

"Those weapons that they carry are sound based," Dina said. "I learned about them while I was locked up. One of the guards was really talkative. They tried to use them against the invisible thing. It didn't work."

Dr. Mentes had mentioned that. The weapons they had designed to harm the entity had no effect despite previous indications that they ought to.

"I say we take their handguns and make for the exit," Anna said.

With me dead and Camden unconscious, there were no high Savvy players to make a plan. That wasn't to say the others were incapable of making a good plan.

On the contrary, they all had their own strengths when it came to strategizing. But the added security of having a high Savvy player make a plan really made things feel safer. That's what Savvy was for, after all. It helped your plans work better.

"Are you going to lug him around with you?" Dina's husband asked.

Antoine looked offended at the question. "We can't leave him. He helped us."

"Let's just go," Anna said.

She headed off toward the room where Camden had been.

They found three handguns, but only a few rounds of ammo apiece for them. They were lucky to find that much with the way the guards had been blindly firing at the poltergeist. Though each of them was armed, Antoine took the lead. His high Hustle and Mettle was a lethal combo with firearms.

Truthfully, I was concerned. While having the guns might make them feel safe, I worried how Carousel would respond.

As they moved closer to the exit, it almost seemed like they were going to make it, but, of course, that would have been too easy. As soon as they exited the hallway and entered the main lobby, the dozen or so remaining guards emerged from the other hallway to the left, their firearms trained on my friends.

"Go back!" Antoine screamed as a hail of bullets started to pelt the wall behind them.

As he followed them back, he fired a shot at one of the guards, striking him in the face and getting a kill. His next few bullets weren't so well aimed.

As they rounded the corner back the way they had come, Antoine said, "I'm out!"

He had used up all the bullets that his gun had. Kimberly was quick to give hers up, giving Antoine another chance.

Antoine gently placed Camden down against the wall.

"We'll have to come back for him," he said.

"Steven!" Dina yelled.

I didn't know who Steven was. I hadn't seen the first part of the movie.

"Daddy!" Dina's kids screamed.

Dina's husband slumped to the floor. A tranquilizer dart was sticking out of his back. He had strayed too far from the group. One of the gunmen must have been aiming for the Mercers with the goal of putting them to sleep.

"What do we do?" Dina asked.

They couldn't escape, not together. Dina couldn't move quickly on her own. Camden was unconscious. With Dina's husband down, their options narrowed incredibly.

"Kids," Dina said. "Where is the ghost?"

Bethany and her brother looked at each other.

"He's tired," Bethany said sleepily.

As she said that, I realized that really meant Bethany and her brother were tired. Even with a host, the poltergeist still relied on the Mercers to exist. It was down to the two exhausted Mercer children.

Kimberly spoke up. "You know about the distortion?"

Bethany nodded. None of the other Mercers had appeared to understand the presence of the entity as well as Dina's children. Knowledge of such things often faded into adulthood in movies. Psychic kids often had greater knowledge or wisdom than their age might suggest.

More shots were fired.

"We need the ghost," Dina said. "Can you find him?"

Bethany started to cry. "He's hurt."

Even psychokinetic entities needed rest, apparently.

More shots were fired. Antoine fired back, hitting one guard in the neck. He was out of bullets again.

Kimberly got down on her knees with the kids. "What if I helped you?"

Bethany looked at her strangely.

"My family has powers too," Kimberly explained. "I'll help you find the ghost."

"I'm scared," Bethany said.

"He attacked Mom," Dina's son said.

"I know he did," Dina said. "But he will protect you. That's all that matters."

Kimberly grabbed onto the kids' hands. "We'll do it together," she said.

She was going to try to improvise. She had high Moxie and some narrative foundation. Still, I felt this was far more extreme than my improvising a system reboot.

If this didn't work, they would be dead.

If it did work, they might still be dead.

"We can do it," Kimberly said, tears filling her eyes.

Kimberly and the two Mercer children focused their minds. Bethany started to cry even harder.

More shots came over them. Antoine had spent all of the bullets. The guards were getting braver, making their way across the room toward the place where everyone was hiding.

"He's here," Bethany said softly. She pointed to a space ten feet away from them. Right in the line of fire.

Anna looked at the place where Bethany was pointing. Then she looked back at Kimberly.

Then they were gone.

The screen flashed back to the moment of my death. The poltergeist wasn't visible to the camera. All that could be seen was me about to die.

"Protect Kimberly!" I yelled through the pain. "Protect her kid!"

It was a flashback used to show what Anna was thinking.

I knew that because, moments after the poltergeist remanifested in its weakest form, Anna ran across the room in the direction Bethany had pointed. I wasn't expecting her to do that.

As she did, she cried out in pain as a bullet grazed her left thigh. Then she cried out again as an intense headache overcame her, and she trembled as she made contact with the poltergeist.

None of the other bullets seemed to hit her. They were stopping mid-air, bouncing off of some unseen thing.

"Oh my god!" Kimberly screamed as she looked at the poltergeist. Kimberly could see it. So could the Mercer children, if their looks of terror were any indication.

Of course, Anna saw it too.

And it horrified her.

From my vantage on Deathwatch, I couldn't see it. It was invisible on-screen.

The gunmen continued attempting to shoot her. The bullets couldn't get past the poltergeist.

Breaking through the gunfire, a crackle came over the intercom system. "Tell us!" a frantic voice yelled out. "What does the distortion look like?"

Anna took a moment to answer.

The image changed. I didn't see Anna any longer. Nor did I see the armed guards or the exit.

I saw myself. It was another flashback. I was standing in the control room alone, staring at something with a look of abject terror on my face.

It was the scene where I died again.

The poltergeist still wasn't visible to the camera, nor were the spectral Shades of the Mercers.

It was just me, staring at some invisible thing in the center of the room.

"Don't picture it in your mind! Don't look at its claws or teeth!" I yelled. "It needs us to see it to exist!"

My view was back on Anna. Again, Carousel had used a flashback to illustrate what Anna was thinking about.

She held her hands up instinctively, blocking out the creature as I had. She had anger in her eyes as she appeared to contemplate the words I had yelled before my death. She lowered her hands. She wasn't going to block the creature out any longer.

"Tell us what it looks like!" the voice over the intercom screamed. Someone at KRSL was desperate to know more about the distortion.

I could tell she was working things out in her head, watching the creature take form as it drew power from her mind.

"It's . . . enormous!" Anna screamed.

The whites of her eyes turned red as the blood vessels in them broke. A stream of blood started to trickle from her ear.

In the center of the room, a row of security desks started to move across the floor with a deafening screech. Overhead, a hanging light fixture was knocked to the side. Cuts dug into the ground as the invisible creature's claws grew long and sharp.

The poltergeist was getting bigger. Anna wasn't trying to kill it like I had been. She didn't have the Moxie for that anyway. She was making it stronger.

"Kill the host!" the commander of the guards screamed as he ran down the left hallway away from the poltergeist and my friends.

In one fell swoop, three of the guards were cut into ribbons and thrown across the room. The creature easily destroyed the security area that blocked the exit. My friends would have a clear path to leave as soon as the monster was gone.

A KRSL agent came out from behind a desk with a rocket launcher. I didn't know what kind, but it wasn't the kind that was good for killing invisible assailants.

He pulled the trigger. His missile went straight through the area where the poltergeist was and hit a wall behind it, showering some of his fellow agents with debris.

The poltergeist swiftly cut the agent with the empty launcher in half. Adeline did say that rocket launchers were dangerous.

The remaining seven guards turned to follow their commander, sending back shots at the poltergeist and at Anna herself. One brave guard fixed his aim on Anna as the creature attacked again with its claws, skewering two more guards before they could flee.

The guard pulled the trigger.

A spray of red mist burst from the back of Anna's head. She dropped to the ground, dead. My heart nearly stopped when it happened.

The guard that had shot her was shaking, wide-eyed with fear. He turned to the center of the room where the poltergeist had been.

There was stillness.

The guard looked at Kimberly, Antoine, and Dina. It looked like he was about to spray them with bullets when he spotted the two Mercer children. Panic overcame him and he turned to follow his comrades. The camera followed him as he ran through the halls and caught up with the other guards.

"The host was terminated," he said with a quiver.

"Do we go back and apprehend them?" one of the other guards asked, his eyes on the commander.

The commander looked back the way they had come. "Maybe we wait for . . ." He was racking his brain for a reasonable excuse to avoid getting near the Mercers.

Just then, a desk moved across the room and struck one of the guards. The commander assessed his men and saw that one of them was holding his head in pain.

"Kill the host!" he screamed as he shot the afflicted guard in the head.

The desk stopped moving.

Another of his men winced in pain. The commander raised his gun.

"No, please do—" the guard yelled as the commander executed him.

There was silence again.

The remaining three men looked at one another distrustfully.

The commander closed his eyes and raised his left hand to his temple in pain. Horror spread across his face as he realized that he had become the host.

One of his two remaining subordinates motioned to fire at him. They had been instructed to kill the host, after all. But the commander was quicker. He shot the guard in the head first, unwilling to die regardless of whether he was tethered to the creature.

His efforts were in vain.

A red hole appeared in the center of the commander's head as the last remaining guard killed him and was left alone.

The grand irony was revealed as the camera panned around to show that all of the guards had the same sedatives Camden had used to sedate himself and his assailants. They carried them in their vests to use on the remaining Mercers. They didn't seem to realize they could be used to quell the poltergeist.

The large military vehicle that the Mercers had been loaded into was parked right outside the door at the entrance to the building. When Dina limped up to the cabin of the truck, she found the vehicle on with the keys in the ignition.

"Come on!" she screamed.

Antoine carried both Dina's husband and Camden as he made his way toward the exit. The kids were nearly wiped out from exhaustion. That was good. It meant the poltergeist was unlikely to remanifest. Kimberly worked to get them out the door.

Red lights started to blare and the doors to the entrance began closing.

"Shit!" Antoine said. He dropped his cargo and ran to the door.

At first, he tried to hold the doors open with his own strength, but that didn't work well. Then he got an idea.

He took his baseball bat from its improvised holster and held it longways between the closing doors, propping them apart. He and Kimberly then worked quickly to get everyone outside and into the vehicle. They succeeded in doing so before the bat broke under the pressure.

As the credits rolled, they drove away from the facility, having escaped.

The End.

They'd done it! It wasn't perfect, but they had pulled it off. Even in my dark existence, watching the film play out in my mind's eye, I was clapping and cheering.

Red curtains closed, blocking off my mental view of the screen.

Then, for the first time since I had started using Deathwatch, I realized I wasn't alone.

Other people were clapping and cheering too.

I was in a movie theater after all.

As I turned my head to see who was there, all went dark. My true eyes opened. I found myself walking out the door of the facility, resurrected on my feet and wearing my old clothes.

"Congratulations," Silas said. "You've won a ticket!"

I couldn't pay attention to him at that moment.

Who were those people?

CHAPTER FORTY-SIX

WORKERS' COMPENSATION

As I walked out onto the sidewalk where my friends and Silas were, I noticed right away that Kimberly and Anna were having an emotional moment.

"I'm so sorry!" Kimberly said.

"Don't. I said it was okay," Anna responded gently. She had been crying. Her eyes had that empty look that I now associated with dying in a storyline. They continued their conversation with Kimberly continuously apologizing through tears.

As I approached the others, I asked, "What's going on? Are they okay?"

Camden turned to me with a concerned look on his face. "I'm . . . not sure," he said. "I was asleep for the final battle."

Antoine had moved closer to them and was trying to comfort Kimberly, so I looked to Dina for answers. She was watching over the conversation with an intentional detachment.

She took a deep breath.

"The plan was for Kimberly to become the monster's host and then try to control it because of her buffs and stuff. They thought it might work," Dina explained. "She got scared of dying so the other one became the host instead and got shot in the head."

Antoine overheard Dina's explanation. "No. I took us off-screen," he said, attempting to be a gentle diplomat. "We talked it over. It was something we *all* decided."

I understood. Kimberly had always been very afraid of dying in a storyline. Couldn't really blame her. We had to all but promised that we would never put her in the position of dying until she was ready. It was the reason she left her most powerful trope, Looks Don't Last, at home even though it could be very useful.

I didn't care as long as she contributed, which she did. It wasn't like I could complain to anyone. Anna was her best friend and Antoine was her boyfriend. Camden wasn't going to cause a fuss even if it did bother him.

It made more sense that Kimberly was originally the one who was supposed to be the host; she might have been able to control it completely. So much had been set up for that moment. It probably would have worked. Anna rushing in and taking her place wasn't as well set up, even with the flashbacks Carousel used to try to explain it away, but it worked pretty well too.

I wasn't going to get involved just yet, but her decision to back down had undermined a lot of narrative momentum. Eventually, we would have to deal with it.

"Smart thinking with the sedatives," I said.

"Thanks," Camden responded. "I just realized that if the sedative worked to stop the manifestation, it might also work to stop the teth—wait. How do you know about the syringes?"

I smirked and took out my Director's Monitor trope. I told him about Deathwatch and seeing the story from the point of view of the audience. Our conversation even managed to distract the others from their apologies, and I had to repeat it all so they could all hear. I told them about the other people cheering and clapping in the audience.

"And Kimberly," I said, "you did great. I couldn't even tell that something had happened."

I wasn't sure if that did anything to make her feel better, but I had to take a shot.

"So that's how we get Aspects," Camden said. "We have to die?"

"I don't think so. That's how it works for Film Buffs. It's probably different for other Archetypes. Todd said something about it a long time ago, but I didn't really understand it at the time."

"What did the people in the audience look like?" Anna asked. She was tired but trying to sound interested and concerned.

"I couldn't tell," I answered. "I couldn't make myself look that direction in time."

We took some time to discuss who it could be. Dead Film Buffs? Some eldritch audience that we had been enslaved to entertain? Maybe they were just random NPCs. We didn't get too long to talk about it because Silas the Showman was getting impatient.

"I'd say you're really pushing my buttons," Silas said, "but that's exactly what you're not doing! Hehehe."

Antoine walked up to the mechanical fortune teller and slapped his red button. There was a moment of hesitation as his hand got close, but he pushed through it.

He received three tropes, two stat tickets, and a monster card for one of the KRSL agents he had killed. He had gotten his bat back intact, as well as an unloaded handgun that he had pulled off a guard and three syringes of the sedative that he had taken from the guards after finding Camden. He never used them, so that part got cut from the movie. Seven stars for Antoine. He looked incredibly relieved to see it. I could tell he was suffering. I was glad he got a win.

Like a Security Blanket
Type: Buff/Perk
Archetype: Any
Aspect: Any
Stat Used: N/A
Whether in the movies or in real life, holding some means of protection can calm the nerves and make you brave enough to do what needs to be done. When this ticket is equipped, the player's Grit is buffed merely by brandishing a weapon, even if that weapon has little hope of doing any good. The boost to their sense of safety radiates through the player and calms them in scary situations. The more powerful the weapon and the more proficient the player is with it, the more nearby allies will feel the same sense of security. "A knife in the hand is better than two in the chest."

That was an easy buff and a great perk. Easing fear might not be so useful on paper, but as Carousel started to wear on us, every mental health perk we could get was a godsend.

Reload After Cut
Type: Action
Archetype: Any
Aspect: Any
Stat Used: N/A
In a lot of movies, you never see the characters reload their guns during an intense fight. Their guns just never run out of ammo. When this trope is equipped, the player goes off-screen as soon as they start to reload and goes back on-screen shortly after they finish. Requires the guns to be empty when reloading *and* to have more bullets to load. "Off-screen to reload, on-screen to unload."

Arthur had this same trope. I was glad to see it. When Antoine had the ability to bring guns into a storyline, we would have another way to go off-screen. I wasn't sure if it was better than his Time-Out! trope or not.

> Swing Away
> Type: Action
> Archetype: Athlete
> Aspect: Sport
> Stat Used: Moxie
>
> In the heat of a confrontation, a show of force can sometimes be enough to deter an enemy.
> When this trope is equipped, the player's character can swing their weapon, creating a momentary pause in the enemy's attack. This can provide a crucial window of opportunity for the player to strategize or escape. Usually works the first time. Repeated uses succeed based on Moxie and believability in context.
> "Sometimes, the mere threat of violence is enough to keep the monsters at bay."

This seemed like an easy way for some temporary invulnerability. Antoine would have to use it well.

His monster card was the following:

> KRSL Agent
> Killer
>
> Within the depths of the malevolent KRSL Corporation, the ominous KRSL Agent emerges. He is a soulless executioner, trained to kill and obey without question.
> Beware the KRSL Agent, for he is a chilling force without morality or conscience, his actions leaving only devastation in their wake. In the shadows, his presence looms, a harbinger of unrelenting darkness and mechanical laughter, embodying the very essence of KRSL's malevolence.

Kimberly was next. She got one trope and one stat ticket. She only received one star on the red wallpaper, but that was enough for her to level. This was a surprise for me. I thought she did awesome. Apparently, her panicking in the final battle cost her a lot. But with Anna's Shared Experience trope helping her out, she still did okay.

> Carousel Academy Awards
> Type: Buff
> Archetype: Eye Candy
> Aspect: Celebrity
> Stat Used: N/A

The glitz and glamour of awards ceremonies can have a profound impact on an actor's confidence, and this trope captures that essence.

When this trope is equipped, the player's Moxie gets a boost based on their performance in the previous storyline. This reflects the surge of confidence and charisma that comes from the actor's recent notable acting award win. Let's face it, the audience loves an award-winning actor.

Beware: a poor performance can turn this boon into a curse.

"The spotlight's on you, the world's a stage, and every monster's a critic waiting to be impressed."

A basic buff in a good stat for Kimberly. She would have to wait to use it until she got a better performance.

Anna soldiered through her mental fatigue and pushed the button. She got two tropes and two stat tickets. Six stars.

Final Stand-In
Type: Action
Archetype: Final Girl
Aspect: Scream Queen
Stat Used: Moxie

The trope of self-sacrifice is a powerful one in horror movies, often leading to unexpected outcomes.

When activated, the Final Girl can temporarily pass her Last One Alive trope to an established ally during the Finale by performing a self-sacrifice. This must be set up in the Party through foreshadowing. Can only work on the singular character it is set up on. The self-sacrifice cannot be used to prevent nebulous deaths, only those that are imminent. This cannot be used to circumvent trope-guaranteed deaths. If the Final Girl does not die, the effect is reversed. It can only be used if there are no other allies remaining.

"Sometimes, the Final Girl isn't the last one standing."

This was a game changer. We needed to be careful though. It could cause some resentment.

Steal the Spotlight
Type: Buff/Debuff
Archetype: Any
Aspect: Any
Stat Used: Moxie

No matter how important a character may be to the narrative, another one can sometimes steal the scene, or even the whole show, by upstaging them. When equipped, the player can steal an ally's buffs by upstaging them in a climactic moment and stepping in to finish what they started. This can happen in increments or all at once depending on the player's Moxie and actions.
"You stole my thunder!"
"You mean *our* thunder."

Given the fact that Anna had, in fact, taken Kimberly's place in this recent storyline, it made sense that she would receive this. It was ripe for strategizing.

Camden received two tropes and two stat tickets. Six stars.

Peer Review
Type: Insight
Archetype: Scholar equipped with Eureka!
Aspect: Researcher
Stat Used: Savvy

There is no show of raw intelligence greater than to look at a massive report or collection of data and be able to confidently declare that it is wrong. Unfortunately, knowing too much is rarely good for one's health.
When equipped, the player is alerted if scientific, technical, or other documentation they encounter has been altered, faked, or is otherwise incorrect. The higher the Savvy, the more information about the nature of the flaw is received. The player will not automatically know what the truth is, only that something is false.
"Truth is the first casualty of fear, but not on my watch."

Solid but situational.

Fine, I'll Go First
Type: Action
Archetype: Scholar
Aspect: Strategist
Stat Used: Savvy

Convincing others to do something that is scary or uncertain can take a lot of charisma or intimidation. Some characters don't have either. What they might have is the certainty that they are right and the willingness to bet it all on their plans.

> With this trope equipped, the player can substitute their Savvy for Moxie when trying to get other characters to do something for their own safety. All they need to do to activate the trope is to lead by example and be the first to do whatever action they are imploring others to do.
> "Oh sure, copy the smart guy."

That was a great way to get around his low Moxie. Interesting.

Dina received two tropes and two stat tickets. Seven stars for the woman who was alone for most of the movie.

> They Fell Off
> Type: Action
> Archetype: Outsider
> Aspect: Criminal
> Stat Used: Moxie
>
> In movies, almost anything can be used to work the locks on handcuffs in order to unlock them.
> When equipped, the trope allows the player to unlock handcuffs or similar restraints by using small objects to pretend to pick the lock. Only works on-screen.
> "Every lock has a key, and sometimes, it's not what you'd expect."

That made sense. Could be useful.

> Pen Pal
> Type: Perk
> Archetype: Outsider
> Aspect: Stranger
> Stat Used: N/A
>
> The mysterious character whose motives and allegiance are unknown can sometimes be there to help all along.
> When this trope is equipped, it enables the player to leave messages at various locations within the game setting. Allies become aware of these messages when they reach the same location.
> These messages can either be out of character and off-screen or in character and on-screen as part of the narrative. If performed well on-screen, they can carry great narrative weight.
> "What does the note say?"
> "It says the killer is one of us."

At least we would have some way of talking to her about whatever plotline she had been assigned. I felt like this was most useful for very specific scenarios and settings where we wouldn't get many scene breaks.

I received two tropes and one stat ticket as well as a monster ticket. I expected my sacrifice to net me more than that, but I was a higher level than my teammates, technically. Six stars.

Flashback Revelation
Type: Perk
Archetype: Film Buff
Aspect: Filmmaker
Stat Used: Savvy
Sometimes a character's words before death are all they can leave behind to help allies. If only those words are remembered.
When this trope is equipped, a player on Deathwatch can trigger a flashback for an ally to help remind them of advice given before death. It could be anything from an inaudible message heard only by the ally to a complete visual recreation of the original scene that even the audience sees. If the flashback fits the narrative well enough during a climactic moment, it will make the final cut and send allies off-screen temporarily.
The number of flashbacks available depends on Savvy and the quality of dialogue shared between the players. The trope only allows the player to send this information if the ally actually heard the original dialogue. At higher levels, the player can send flashbacks of other characters' words or even images. "The truth was right in front of you. You just need to pay attention."

At least I would have something to do while dead. It could really be useful.

Out Like a Light
Type: Perk
Archetype: Any
Aspect: Any
Stat Used: Moxie
In movies, characters can fall asleep on cue. They can be asleep before their head hits the pillow, or before they even know they are falling asleep.
With this trope equipped, the player will be able to fall asleep on command by lying down and trying, assuming it makes sense within the narrative in some way. Can be counteracted by enemy tropes. "Best sleep well tonight. You'll probably die in the morning."

This was a strong contender for my favorite trope I had ever received.

My monster ticket didn't have a monster on its face or an enemy at all. It had an image of an old man wearing a white gown putting a puzzle together. It was the patient I had accidentally killed when I attacked the poltergeist.

Paul Kimble, grandson of Eloise Mercer
Psychic

Inside the chilling halls of Mercer Manor, a young Paul Kimble would often listen to the captivating tales of the ghostly presence that resided within. Gradually, he came to realize that every place he called home had its own spectral inhabitant. Little did he know that when he thought his home was infested with specters and ghouls, he was actually haunting himself by unconsciously manifesting a protective poltergeist.

In his thirty-fifth year, Paul's life took a tragic turn when the bank where he worked fell prey to a violent robbery. The details remained fragmented in his memory, save for the swift demise of the assailant, which he remembers vividly. From that point forward, his abode shifted to whichever padded cell the mysterious organization known as KRSL commanded him to sleep in. Paul never tried to escape and reenter society, as he never fully trusted the spectral heirloom that he had never been able to control.

That made me feel kind of bad. But all I knew was that I would be testing out my sleeping trope as soon as we got back to the lodge. I had been healed, so my body wasn't tired, but my mind had not rested in days. More than that; I hadn't slept well once.

I actually smiled as we began our trek home.

Or so I thought.

"We're a team. Right, Dina?" Antoine said. "We fight for each other. We trust each other?"

He was on it again. Still trying to find out what her conversation with the psychic had been about.

"Yes," she said coldly.

"The psychic said you were on a quest. I didn't want to be pushy, but there is something going on, right?" he asked.

His hold over his emotions was starting to fade. The trauma of his unspeakable experience was beginning to show through.

Dina didn't answer at first.

"Antoine," Anna said, "I don't think you should be worried about this right now. Let's go back to the lodge."

"We can run that Private Showing with you," Antoine said. "That's what you need, right? A team. We can do it. Please. If you know something, please tell us."

He was still convinced that Dina knew something about our plight that none of us did.

Dina looked like she was thinking it over. "Okay," she said. She looked absolutely terrified for some reason. She was definitely keeping a secret and she was afraid to tell us.

Antoine may have been right.

Dina's ticket had promised her a game of chance. If she won, she got answers. If she lost, we had to play through a storyline.

"Will you tell us whatever it is you're after?" Antoine said. He really wanted her to have answers. It was like he had put himself through that entire storyline, had held himself together, all in the hope that we would gain Dina's trust. He wanted to believe she held the answers.

I did too, but he was in a bad place to be putting so much hope on it.

"I'll tell you what I know if . . . if it turns out it's real," she said.

Anna put her hand on Dina's shoulder and said, "We can go check it out. It doesn't hurt to look. Riley can get us out of there if there's anything dangerous."

That was the easy part.

Berryman's Dive was to the north, a mile or so out of town. In fact, it wasn't too far from Halle Castle. Avoiding Omens felt so much more possible now that I could actually see them before we got to them.

On one of the streets was an open house, where a beautiful colonial home was being sold. We had to literally go around the neighborhood in order not to trigger whatever Omen was involved with that house. I assumed it had something to do with the fact that the door was left wide open.

Eventually, we ended up on a dusty road with not much else around. As we walked down this road, dusk started to fall. It never got any darker or lighter. It was just perpetual dusk. Against the falling darkness, we saw it: Berryman's Dive.

It was just a small country bar out in the middle of nowhere. A few cars were parked outside. It had a large neon sign with its name on it as well as neon signs with the names of a few of Carousel's off-brand beers.

"Are we good to go in?" Anna asked.

I nodded my head. I couldn't see any Omens involved in just entering the establishment.

"I hope you kids brought your fake IDs," Dina joked. She took the lead as we moved closer to the building.

We were of drinking age even if we did recently play high school kids.

I noticed that Camden was hanging back. I turned back to see what was wrong. It was a terrible time to risk ending up in a difficult storyline. I didn't think either of us was in a good mental place to be fighting for our lives again.

"What's up?" I asked.

"Nothing," he said.

"Okay." If he said it was nothing, I wasn't going to press the issue.

"It's just . . . Look at where we are," he said.

I looked around, unsure of what he meant. He pointed his finger along the road that we had traveled and then along another road that intersected it. The bar was in the middle of nowhere at the corner of those two roads.

I figured out what he was trying to point out.

We were at a crossroads.

CHAPTER FORTY-SEVEN

THE WAGER

Berryman's Dive stank of smoke and stale beer. There was an old Southern rock record playing. I didn't recognize the music; in fact, I didn't think it was music that you would find in the real world, and yet, somehow, I still knew that it was way out of date. This place was like stepping back in time.

The furniture was mismatched, and the tables were so old and fogged over with grime that they could probably never be clean. There might have been seating for fifty but there were only ten or so NPCs scattered about.

"Don't talk to the guy scratching his arm," I said. My friends looked over in the direction I was staring.

It was a skinny man with a big coat and a knitted beanie. He sat at the bar near the front of the building, minding his own business. When he scratched his arm, he would pull up his sleeve enough so that you could see large welts that looked like bug bites.

"Don't play number twenty on the jukebox," I said. I had no idea why. I just knew that we did not want to play that song. I saw "This is scaring me" on the red wallpaper. I assumed that was a fairly serious warning.

I continued looking around.

What caught my eye next wasn't an Omen. In fact, I wasn't the only person to notice.

"Look at the bartender," Kimberly said.

He was an older guy. Thick around the middle, unkempt gray hair. He seemed mild-mannered as he cleaned shot glasses behind the bar. He looked at us expectantly, ready to take our orders.

Eugene. NPC. Plot Armor: 90.

That was officially the highest Plot Armor I had seen on anything in Carousel that wasn't an eldritch entity, and it happened to be assigned to some random bartender who didn't even have any tropes that I could see. How strange.

Dina ordered us a round of beers and Eugene got to work supplying them.

For the most part, the bar seemed safe. More Omens might come and go as the day went on, but right then there were only three. The two in the front and the one in the back—the one we had come here to see.

At the back of the bar, a man sat at a table. His dark hair was combed neatly. His face was clean-shaven. He wore a nice suit, the kind you might see on a Southern gentleman walking the streets of Savannah. He was shuffling cards and nursing a whiskey. There were poker chips on the table.

As soon as we walked in, he looked at us and smiled.

"Nice day today, wouldn't you say, Eugene?" he asked.

Eugene nodded and gave out a lackadaisical, "Uh-huh."

"The only thing that could make it better would be a nice game of cards."

"Uh-huh."

They went on talking back and forth like that. They never really said anything of substance. It was obvious to everyone what was going on here.

This was the man we had come to see.

The man playing cards was called Mysterious Gentleman on the red wallpaper.

"What's the trigger?" Dina asked.

I scanned the red wallpaper. Everything that I knew about the Mysterious Gentleman was as follows.

His poster read, "The Mysterious Gentleman in *Antemortem*."

MYSTERIOUS GENTLEMAN	
Plot Armor: 20 (Adjusted from 67 by Private Showing Ticket)	
Tropes	
SOUL READ	This villain has insight into the player's soul. (Moxie)
A DEAL IS A DEAL	This villain will not lie about a promise.
SELF-RESTRAINT	This villain intentionally limits their own power for this storyline.
AMBIGUOUS ALIGNMENT	The villain is morally gray.
BENDER OF TRUTH	The villain will always take advantage, when possible, outside of directly lying.

If he had a higher Plot Armor, he might have had more tropes. These were the basics. Luckily, it appeared that the ticket Dina had been given lowered his level down to twenty.

The red wallpaper told me "Get to the Car!" was the difficulty level.

It also showed me how to trigger the Omen.

"The storyline doesn't trigger unless you lose a wager with him at a game of cards," I said. Carousel must have set him up to be a character that could help you if you beat him in your wager, but if you lost, you would have to play the storyline. That was far fairer than most Omens.

Of course, that assumed that he was beatable.

Kimberly, doing what she could to help, said, "His Moxie is nine. If that matters."

"So just don't make a bet, and we'll be fine," Anna said. "And don't talk to him too much."

Dina thought about that for a moment. She downed her beer. "Here's to getting answers."

She had a look of pure focus on her face, the same one she had worn when she smashed the pumpkin in *The Final Straw II.*

"Buff my Grit," she said.

"Wait," I said.

"You can buff Grit, right?" she asked.

I could. I would have to make a prediction. She must have seen my Cinema Seer trope in action before.

"Buff my Grit," she said again.

She turned back toward the gentleman. Carousel must have been paying attention because as she turned, we were suddenly on-screen.

I had never even noticed whether we could be on-screen for the Omen. In fact, I felt like we had always waited to get into character until after triggering it. Apparently, we could go on-screen at any point in the Plot Cycle.

Dammit.

"Wait," I said.

She teed me up to make a prediction. This was risky on short notice, but if she needed Grit, I had to try. I had a hunch about why she needed it. If I was right, we might be able to avoid this storyline altogether.

I thought for a moment.

"I know that the psychic sent us here, but I think this is dangerous," I said. I tried to look frustrated like I couldn't find the right words. Luckily, that wasn't too far from the truth. "I feel it; I can't explain why. I'm not saying psychics are fake; my grandmother had 'the gift.' Heck, maybe some of it rubbed off on me. Or maybe I've just seen this in a movie before. Either way, that guy is definitely going to try to steal your soul. I bet he's not going to play fair either."

I tried to find a happy medium between my pseudo-psychic background trope and my Film Buff meta-awareness. I would need to practice. I could only hope that such a prediction would be enough.

Dina paused to consider what I had said. "I'll be fine," she said.

I felt I could talk about the psychic, that I could incorporate her into the story. That's what she and the other high-level NPCs were for. Carousel wanted a story. The lack of asthmatic breathing in my ears confirmed that I hadn't broken the rules.

She walked over to the gentleman. We were close enough that we could hear them speaking, but far enough away that we were off-screen.

"Everything will be okay," Antoine said. "Big things will happen for us. We are going to do extraordinary things."

He was desperate for Dina to be a part of the answer.

"What happens if she triggers the Omen?" Kimberly asked.

"She won't," I said. "She's going to win."

I looked over at Antoine. He was tired. All he could do was watch Dina as she got her answers. Then, if the answers were what she wanted, she would clue us in.

Of course, I knew the answer might be that we were doomed, and that Dina was being toyed with.

I tried not to think about it.

She sat down at the gentleman's table and said, "I'd like to make a deal."

The gentleman looked ravenous.

"A deal? I'm just a simple card player. My money wagered against yours. Is that not a good enough deal?"

He smiled a toothy smile.

"I hear you deal in things much more significant than that," she said.

He laughed. "Well, for the right stakes, I have been known to go above and beyond. Normally, there is a bit more conversation, more getting to know each other. What is it you're looking for? The location of treasure? Do you want power? Fame?"

Dina didn't miss a beat. "I want my son back."

The gentleman looked legitimately surprised at first, but then he slipped back into his smile. "Where is he? Do you need a map?"

Dina wasn't amused. "He died."

A tear escaped her eye and rolled down her face. Otherwise, her expression was cold.

The gentleman's eyes lit up with excitement. "Well, you could go find his missing poster and rescue him. Unless you're talking about something else . . . We don't do that sort of thing here." He paused. "Usually."

"But you can."

"That's not just her character talking," Anna said.

"Nope," Camden said.

It wasn't. She had brought up a son before, sort of. In the cave with the Unknowable Host, she had called out to him. I had thought that was just her trope activating.

That must have been what her quest was—to bring back her son.

"We may have to play through this one, so get ready," Anna said.

"She's going to win," Antoine said.

If Dina fumbled, we definitely would. Luckily, the Private Showing ticket had lowered the difficulty to within our range, if only just.

The gentleman grabbed his deck of cards off the table. "I have made all sorts of deals. But bringing a child back to life . . . That may be more involved. Tell you what. I will tell you how to get your son back if you beat me in a game of poker. But if you lose, I get to name my prize."

Dina stared him down. "Alive. Unhurt. No sign he ever got sick. And he lives to old age, happy and free of all this. No tricks."

The gentleman was taken aback. "I would never play a trick. Not when it comes to this. But remember what I said. I will only tell you *how* to get him back. I promise nothing more than that."

Dina thought for a moment. She held out her hand.

He went to shake it but held back. "And I get to name my prize."

"Yes. Now shake my hand," Dina said.

The gentleman reached out and shook her hand. "Oof. So confident. What have I gotten myself into here?" he asked playfully.

He looked up behind the bar toward Eugene, but the NPC wasn't paying any attention. He started divvying up the chips.

"Wait," Dina said. "Why do you get more?"

"House rules, darling."

If I was counting right from where we were standing, he had given himself two hundred chips in various denominations. He had given her 180. If I were to guess, they had each been given ten chips per Plot Armor level.

Dina didn't say anything.

The Mysterious Gentleman began dealing the cards.

Watching them play poker was kind of amusing despite the stakes. I know I should have taken it more seriously, but this game was ludicrous. Every single hand that was dealt was a big hand. Within the first twenty or so, I saw at least three full houses, two straights, and two flushes. This was a movie poker game where every moment was exciting. It wasn't real life.

Chips flew across the table.

I didn't recognize which style of poker this was. Dina seemed to understand just fine. I could see why she was confident.

They were staring each other down, trying to guess what was in the other player's hand.

Everything that the Mysterious Gentleman did seemed to be going off of gut instinct. It probably helped that he could Soul Read, whatever that was.

But here's the thing: he wasn't beating her by that much.

It was back and forth. At first, I thought that this must have been scripted. There was no way that a demonic entity like the Mysterious Gentleman was actually losing at poker. But truthfully, there was *one* way that Dina could win: her Guarded Personality trope.

Up until that point, all it did was prevent me from seeing anything about her on the red wallpaper unless she granted permission, but as they played, I could see the frustration growing on the Mysterious Gentleman's face. He was having a tough time reading her too.

I couldn't see every card played, but I could tell that sparks were flying.

As time wore on, he started to take the lead. I didn't know if he was cheating or if his Soul Read was just too strong, even with her Guarded Personality.

Once the chips started to stack up in front of him, he started getting cocky.

"So," she said. "You said you wanted to pick your prize. Want to tell me what that was?"

"You'll find out soon enough, my dear," he said. "No need to hurry."

"Whatever," she said. "We can raise the stakes next game if you're up for it."

He smiled widely, unable to resist the bait. "I don't think there will be a next game."

Dina remained cold. "And why's that?"

The Mysterious Gentleman was still smiling. "If you really want to know my prize, I'll tell you. I think I'll take your *soul*."

There it was.

My friends all bumped up two Plot Armor. They had been buffed.

When I had warned Dina of the dangers of the Mysterious Gentleman, I had predicted that he would try to steal her soul. It was obvious, but that was the nature of Cinema Seer. Obvious predictions counted too. A prediction he had just confirmed.

My Cinema Seer trope had just buffed her Savvy and Grit. Her Guarded Personality trope was powered by Grit.

Whatever insight he was gleaning from her was now even more difficult to obtain. Dina smiled.

Now the game was fairer. They continued going back and forth. Dina didn't have a runaway victory, but I could see that the gentleman was slowly losing his footing. The cracks in his game were showing.

Within a few dozen hands, he was down to his last few chips.

"You are very difficult to read," he said. "Do you know that?"

"All in," Dina responded.

The gentleman put in his last chips. The cards were shown.

He lost—his three-of-a-kind against her full house.

Just like in the movies.

Suddenly, we were off-screen. Dina hadn't tripped the storyline after all. It turned out that the Mysterious Gentleman *was* beatable.

The gentleman started to laugh. "Well played."

Dina didn't waste any time with pleasantries.

"Tell me how to bring Sean back," she said. "You promised."

The gentleman nodded his head. "A deal is a deal."

The lights in the bar started to flicker. A faint red glow started appearing around the room, but I didn't know what the source was. The Mysterious Gentleman closed his eyes. He kept them closed for a while. His brow furrowed, confused. Still, he continued.

"Strange," he said. "How did your son die?"

Dina cleared her throat. "Cancer."

The Mysterious Gentleman pursed his lips. "I can't find him. You said that he died in Carousel?"

Dina shook her head. "No. It was before I came to Carousel."

The gentleman furrowed his brow again. "Before . . . Carou—"

His eyes shot open. He pressed his hand to his head. It was like he was having a migraine. He started to groan in pain. He threw his body back and forth in his seat.

"The man on the top floor. He watches us through violet lights. He is the one you need. He looks for dark stories. Like yours. Like . . . mine. Your Friends in High Places have set the path. Go!"

He started to look around the room. It was like he had never seen the place before.

"How did I get here?" he asked. A look of sudden realization. "He's done it. That sick man—he's trapped me."

He started to breathe very hard. His face began to change.

His teeth grew sharp and started to get longer. His eyes glowed red. I could even see the faintest of points start to rise from the top of his head.

He became overwhelmed by a panicked rage.

"I have to escape. Where? How do we leave this place?"

Dina backed up from the table. She backed away until she was near where we were.

"Is there no escape? We must go t—"

Bang.

The Mysterious Gentleman dropped to the ground; a large hole had opened up in his forehead.

I looked to my right and saw Eugene, the level-ninety NPC, standing with a shotgun trained on the place where the Mysterious Gentleman had been.

Eugene turned to us. "I had to do it. You saw him. He was . . . some sort of monster."

The man spoke without emotion. He was delivering a line, nothing more. He put the gun back under the bar and went back to polishing glasses.

CHAPTER FORTY-EIGHT

LETTERS FROM CAROUSEL

We ran out of Berryman's Dive like we were being chased.

When we got down the road a mile or so, everyone looked to me to make sure that we didn't trigger any Omens.

I stopped and listened. Had Dina broken a rule? I didn't think so. Everything that had happened on-screen could very well have been something her character said. Still, what we had just seen was not supposed to happen. I didn't need some terrible entity breathing in my ear to know that.

"What the hell was that?" Antoine asked.

"Did that demon . . . just . . ." Camden said, trailing off. He searched for the right words. "Wake up?"

Anna looked at me like I would know.

Someone was saying something about the demon; I couldn't listen to them. I needed silence.

"Quiet!" I said.

I looked behind me. To the left, to the right. I kept expecting to see the Rulekeeper. Did we know too much now? Were we about to be killed?

I tried to calm my breath and listen.

"What's wrong?" Anna said.

I held up a finger to her, gesturing for her to be quiet.

I listened.

Nothing. No loud breathing. No footsteps.

What had just happened?

"We're good," I said. "I think."

They stared at me like I was crazy.

"Just checking for Omens," I said. They didn't seem to believe me but said nothing.

Kimberly shook her head and turned to Dina. "What was all that about you looking for your son? What were you talking about? Is that the secret you're keeping from us?"

Good question.

We all looked expectantly at Dina.

She stared back. "My son died. I came here to try to get him back. It's exactly what you heard."

My friends and I exchanged glances.

"Is this really the place to bring a child?" I asked. "Assuming that the demon gave him back to you."

"That's the reason I came," she said.

I understood missing your kid . . . but Carousel was hardly a step up from the afterlife.

"Wait," Anna said. "Are you saying that you came to the dive bar looking for your son or that you came to Carousel itself looking for him?"

"Oh my god," Antoine said. "I knew it."

Dina was silent for a time. She was contemplating telling us something. We were smart enough to shut up and let her make a decision.

"I don't know what you want me to say," she said, raising her arms into the air. "I did what I had to."

She reached into her jacket pocket and retrieved half a dozen or so letters. Some of them were yellowed and well-worn. They were addressed to her with no return address or postage.

She handed them to us. We found a patch of grass underneath a tree and, over the next half hour, read them.

There were seven letters in total. Some were just duplicates and many of the passages repeated messages from past letters.

Excerpt from letter one:

Dear Dina,

You do not know me, but I have learned the details of your unfortunate situation, and I believe that I can help you. Losing a child is a tragedy I cannot imagine. It has come to my attention that you have recently begun contacting palm readers, mediums, and other occult practitioners in an effort to reconnect with your son.

Look no further. I have a solution you may be interested in: The Game at Carousel.

Despite its name, I assure you that what goes on at Carousel is very real. The horrors that live here are real as well. To revive your son, you will need to play the game and win. Do not worry, the game will teach you its rules. All you need to do is show up and prepare to face true terror. This is a place where death is only temporary, a concept you might find most appealing . . .

It went on to give a very general overview of what the game entailed and then included directions to get to Carousel, the same ones Antoine had been given.

Excerpt from letter two:
As the previous letter went unanswered, I can only assume that you have found your peace. If that isn't the case, I implore you to read further. The way I described Carousel may have disturbed you. I can only imagine what you must be thinking. If I had not come here myself and seen the terrifying magic of this place, I would not believe it either.

Please see past the horror that lives in Carousel. There is strong magic in the sublime. Do not lose this opportunity out of fear.

Letter three was the same as letter two.

Excerpt from letter four:
There is a force that binds us. Your tragedy is connected to the tragedy of every other being, even my own. Many stories find their conclusion at Carousel. Yours is a story within a grander story. Do not hesitate to seek its resolution.

You may fear what I have written. However, if you seek otherworldly intervention, you need to come to another world. I have been moving the pieces into place for you. I will have everything ready when you arrive . . .

Letter five was a rehash of previous letters.

Excerpt from letter six:
I heard that you found religion and lost it all in a short time span. Unfortunately, the answers you were given were not those that you desired. Come to Carousel; here lie the answers you seek if you are brave enough to find them.

The odds are slim. The monstrous beings I have described are ever threatening. Only you can make the choice for yourself. If you take it, you may have an important role in what comes to pass. You may even be able to bring him back, Dina. I have hidden nothing from you because your choice must be an informed one. That is imperative. I am not selling you a miracle. You will have to earn it, and escape will be almost impossible, but I will be Watching Over You . . .

Excerpt from letter seven:
I recently heard that you have been in a dark place. That you considered . . . giving up. Please, if death is something you are willing to try in your quest to see Sean again, why not risk death here? There is a plan. If only the actors involved stick to it, we may all benefit from your arrival, most of all Sean . . . You will need to work in secret as you gather the allies we have arranged for you. Life and death are intertwined. You must already believe that.

Please consider this promise. If you come to Carousel, you will be given everything you need to succeed, to save your son, and to return, all for the better. There are many lives here in need of saving.

All of the letters were signed "A friend at Carousel."

After we had all read the letters, we were in shock.

"Well," Dina said. "Now you know."

I couldn't even think straight. Dina had come here willingly. The letters didn't specifically say what was going on here, but they were very clear that this place was horrific and inescapable. Who would make that choice?

"You knew?" Antoine asked. He was more surprised than he was angry. He started to laugh. He laughed so hard he cried. He fell back onto the grass, a huge weight lifted from his shoulders. "I knew it," he said. Tears streamed down his face. "I just knew you would have answers."

"Yep. Not that it helps us much."

Anna had a very mature reaction. "That's very . . . brave of you . . . coming here to help your son."

"She should have warned us," Camden said. "Why didn't you tell us what we were getting ourselves into? You were right there."

Dina shrugged her shoulders. "I assumed you knew too. Why else would you press that button? Why else would you even be there?"

Camden didn't have a response. He let out a frustrated breath and turned away for a moment.

"You came here thinking that you were going to get your son back? Here? Do you still think that?" he asked. "You were tricked. The same way we were tricked. Carousel said whatever it took to get you here."

Dina narrowed her eyes and said, "Maybe. But if it was all a trick, then why is it still stringing me along? Why did it send me to the demon?"

Camden was stumped. He started to laugh. "It looks like we found the only person in Carousel who wants to be here."

"You wouldn't understand. In the outside world . . . I had no hope."

Camden took a few deep breaths.

"Well, you sure came to an odd place to find hope," he said. Strangely, he looked relieved. He lay back on the grass next to Antoine and looked up at the sky.

"Antoine," Kimberly said softly. She moved down to the grass next to him and rubbed his head affectionately. "We're going to get out."

"It's all just a nightmare," he said with a smile, tears still flowing.

"The first time I have had hope in years was when I was killed and then came back," Dina said. "It was proof to me that this place was real, that death could be defeated."

I thought back to the first day we were here. She had broken one of the rules of *The Final Straw II* on purpose just to test this place. She had gotten beheaded, but she had gotten her answers.

"How long ago did you start getting letters?" Kimberly asked. "Some of them look older."

"Three years ago."

As they talked, I realized that some of the phrases in the letters were familiar. Like the phrase "Watching Over You." That was the title of one of the tropes I had received from Silas when I beat the Grotesque storyline. "There is a plan . . . stick to it," like the Stick to the Plan trope that Anna was borrowing from me. And "A friend at Carousel" sounded a lot like Friends in High Places—the same friend the demon spoke of.

It was all connected. We were here for her.

Anna reached out and put her hand on Dina's arm in a comforting gesture. "It must have been a difficult decision."

Dina's eyes began to tear up. "I just didn't want to go through another Christmas without him. Figured if it wasn't real, all I would waste would be my time. Packed up my van and drove here."

"I can't imagine," Anna said.

"Wait," Camden said. "Did you say you didn't want another Christmas without him?"

Dina nodded. "He loved the lights. We used to drive around the rich neighborhoods and take pictures of them. It's . . . hard . . . to even see them now."

"You're saying you arrived in Carousel . . . right before Christmas?" he clarified.

"Yes . . . Why?"

Camden was onto something. We had arrived at Carousel just after our junior year of college let out for the summer. How was it possible that Dina left for Carousel in the winter and arrived at the same time we did?

Anna sat down cross-legged on the grass. She peered quizzically at Dina. Next to her, Kimberly leaned forward, her hands resting on her knees as she furrowed her brow. Camden stood a little way back, his arms folded across his chest as he listened intently to the conversation.

"It's May. Maybe June now, I can't tell. When did you get here?" Anna asked, her eyes fixed on Dina.

"I got here in early December," Dina replied, one of her eyebrows rising slightly.

"That doesn't make sense," Kimberly interjected. "You got here when we did."

"What year did you get here?" Camden asked, his voice low and curious.

Dina's expression shifted; her curiosity was replaced by concern. "2011. When else?" she said.

My friends and I exchanged glances, our disbelief evident on our faces. Anna shook her head in confusion. "That's not possible," she said, her voice tinged with skepticism.

She was right. It wasn't possible. Not anywhere but in Carousel, at least.

"We got here in 2022."

ABOUT THE AUTHOR

Rob M. Lastrel is the author of the Game at Carousel series, originally released on Royal Road. Fascinated by the eerie and unknown, he writes weird, other-worldly escapism. When he isn't writing, he spends his time hiking and hopes to one day visit every national park in the United States.